C Macpherson

J_2 40p

THE HILL IS MINE

THE HILL IS MINE

BY

MAURICE WALSH

W. & R. CHAMBERS, LTD.
LONDON AND EDINBURGH

Latest Reprint, 1955

Printed in Great Britain
by T. and A. Constable Ltd., Hopetoun Street,
Printers to the University of Edinburgh

DEDICATED

TO

DAISY GUNN

Whose Husband told me
some of this Story

PROLOGUE

THE scene of this chronicle is Scotland of the Highlands, but, for a beginning, a brief sojourn must be made in the saloon bar of the Algonquin Hotel, East Forty-fourth Street, Manhattan Island, between Fifth and Sixth Avenues. The Algonquin is the well-known caravanserai of the Fourth Estate, which, as everyone knows, is fourth because there are only four.

The foyer of the Algonquin, except for the paper and cigar stand, is as sedate and respectable, and as solidly furnished, as an old-fashioned British hotel; and the small bar is secluded somewhat shamefacedly round the corner inside the main entrance. At two o'clock in the morning there were only two customers, both men and both young.

They were transient residents of the hotel, were entire strangers to each other, and each was wondering why two young fellows almost rubbing shoulders in a public bar had to be as formal as two dogs meeting for the first time. A word, a tone, a look might set them talking, and standing drinks to each other—or growling.

One sat at the black-marble counter, his feet intoed round the legs of a tall stool, and his broad hands warming a schooner of the too-cold lager of the States: a short, strongly-built, youthful man in loose tweeds, with dark fierce eyes in a dark, smooth, saturnine face. He was no more than reasonably sober, and was talking casually to the white-jacketed barman.

"No' a bad beer of its kind, Tonio, but caul', cauld."
His accent came from somewhere about the sources of
the Clyde in Scotland. He could speak perfect English
if he wanted to, but was in the habit of using an
occasional word of braid Scots for expressiveness.

"Had it an hour off the ice for you, mister," said
Tonio.

"But still cauld. Never you mind! In three weeks
from now, barrin' accidents on the briny sea, I'll be
sampling real beer in the Glasgow Press Club. Ever
heard of Glasgow, Tony?"

"Oh, sure! England, I guess?"

"Guess again! But you're nearer than you know,
and I'm no' a quarrelsome man—or am I? Yes, sir!
Real beer, but not legal at two o' the morn. I do
admire your licensing laws, boy. That's why I drink
cauld wash to greet the dawn."

"Pussyfoot too strong for you in the old country?"

"No. Grandmothers."

The quiet draw of a Western voice came from behind.

"My grandmother was Scotch."

Contact! The loosing word had been spoken. The
short dark man twisted on the stool. The other
occupant of the bar, lounging in the near-by angle of
a bench-seat, nodded smilingly.

"You're Scotch, are you not?"

The Scot rubbed the back of his head, and a crinkle
came at the corners of his fierce dark eyes.

"You could assume as much on occasion," he said,
"but, going to press, I am not full enough of hard
liquor to be dubbed Scotch. Whisky is Scotch, and
oatcakes are Scotch, and parritch forbye, but bipeds,
even grandmothers, are Scots or Scottish. Just a fad
of ours! Naething in it. Yes, I'm Scotch, and not
always proud of it."

8

The other young man lifted lazily out of his corner and moved across to the counter.

"Excuse me horning in," he said, "but I am some interested in Scotland at the moment."

He was taller than the Scot but, yet, not tall; slenderly, almost wirily built, and in full evening-dress; his lean, long-cheeked face was wind-brown above his white shirt-front; his hair, forcibly slicked down, was a darker brown than his face, and his eyes were so grey that they had no blue in them. His big strong hands were brown too, but, as if used to gaunt-lets, were not as brown as his face; and his legs, while not noticeably bowed, had the straight-toed gait that comes from much saddle-gripping. He smiled gravely.

"Would you mind if I bought a drink for us?" he suggested.

The Scot tapped the black marble with square fingers.

"I am in possession, and I'm no' that prudent in the wee sma' hoors. Put a name to it, grandson of Scotia."

"Thank you. Scotch for mine."

"Scotch is right—and a near-beer, Tony." He looked at the American full and fierce-eyed as was his fashion.

The American pointed a thumb at his own breast-bone and introduced himself. "My name is Wayne—with a y—Steve-Stephen Wayne—sometimes waxy—Bozeman, Montana, land and mines. New York on business—pleasure on the side." He flicked his stiff shirt-front with a thumb-nail. "Excuse the disguise. Been to a show with some boys—night club after, a Peruvian contralto singing folk-songs. Not by a jugful! A Mex yowling with her diaphragm. Didn't like her and came away."

9

"Not misusing her diaphragm that way. Well! Here's mud in your eye, Mr Stephen Wayne."

"Slainje! That how you say it?"

"Slainthe, with your tongue loose." The Scot introduced himself in turn. "My name is Alpin— without the Mac or the aspirate—Kenneth-Kenny Alpin, Glasgow town. I write pieces for *The Herald* bunch of rags—for lucre, but not enough of it to be filthy. Over here taking in your village. At home I'm a Pict of Strathclyde."

"A Pict! Oh, your clan?"

"No, my race. Same like Wallace. You know? The Picts! Erroneously the painted ones of the Romans. In the old tongue we were called Cruitne. Julius Caesar swopped the C and called us Bruitne— Britons—the Isles of Britain—the Pictish Isles. That's us. We beat the Romans too, Tacitus notwithstanding. They had to build Hadrian's Wall to keep us out." His voice went deep. "But, indeed, we were beaten and broken somewhere down the line, for I could not put my finger on a veritable Pict and say, 'You own a bit of Scotland.'"

"I own a bit of Scotland," said Stephen Wayne surprisingly.

But Kenny Alpin was not surprised. His fierce-eyed, smooth face never changed.

"Course you do. And the lord forgi'e me for drink-ing beer in a pub with an American magnate who owns a shooting-box and a grouse-moor and a deer-forest in our Scotland. But don't ask me to love you for it."

"Don't you bite my ear just yet. My blanket-spread doesn't cover all that territory—and I'll sell it to you if you want it. Five hundred down, and a thousand to come—dollars."

Kenny Alpin turned full-faced on him, and his fierce

10

eyes were intent for a moment. Then he shook his head.

"I 'll no' believe it," he said.

Stephen Wayne ran a hand through his sleeked-down hair, and at once that hair rose under his hand into its own natural crisp tousle. That toss of hair changed his appearance astonishingly. This was no business magnate. This was a man who could be gay and dare-devil and tough and dangerous.

"You should not say it right-out that way," he protested with suspicious mildness.

"That's better, and to hell with your disguise." Kenny Alpin nodded his bullet head. "You're not selling a Scottie a gold brick—I 'll no' believe it?"

Stephen Wayne laughed, and tousled his hair some more.

"My selling technique is rotten," he said. "Let me buy two drinks instead. Do you know a territory in Scotland called Banffshire?"

"I 'll stick to beer. I know Banffshire. I have to in my trade. Spent a month there last year with Ruary Farquhar."

"Up in the Highlands, isn't it?"

"It is and it isn't. The County of Banff, half low-land and half highland. Gordons, Grants, Forbes, Fergusons, Farquharsons, Finlays, and MacPhersons. See!" He placed his broad hand thumb-wide on the black marble. "There's Scotland, and there's the Nor'-East thrown abroad like a bat's wing between the Firth o' Moray and the bloody German Ocean. There's Aberdeen and Buchan coming round the out-corner o' my thumb, and here in the angle, where you 'll get lock-jaw if you cut deep, is the Province of Moray, and in between, right there, is the County of Banff looking north to the far Shetlands and all the

Polar Seas. Thirty-forty miles of coast, rocks and sand-dunes and golf-courses, and deep-sea fishermen to beat the world and hell thrown in. And there, right out of salt-water, the county straggles and struggles inland and upland by Spey and Devron waters, south and by west, sixty, seventy, eighty miles into the heart of the Grampian Mountains. From sea-level to four thousand feet, heaving up and falling down; arable land, moorland, mountain land; woods of dark pine and deer-forests without a tree; barley, oats, and neeps; black-faced sheep and black polled cattle; trout and salmon in every pool; partridges, grouse, and ptarmigan; rabbits, white hares, and the wild red deer of the hills; and heather, heather, heather everywhere—not forgetting the peaty reek of guid malt whisky. That's Banff. What's wrong wi' it?"

"Nothing as you say it. Let's get nearer bedrock, if you don't mind. Do you know a town called Knockindu?"

"Knockindhu with your tongue tight round it. I had a drink there—maybe two. If you go up through Banff you have to go through Knockindu. A wee Kirktown of a place, grey and brown, with a clock-tower in the square—two hotels, three pubs, six kirks, and seven distilleries—in the hollow of the hills where the hills begin to throw themselves about. My best friend, though he doesn't know it, comes from near there, Glen Shinnoch. I mean, he knows he comes from there, but he aye spurns friendship from a non-kirkgoer like myself."

"My grandmother came from there, too," said Stephen Wayne.

"I see!" Kenny nodded his head. "I begin to see. Your people owned an estate there?"

"If you call it that. In the documents I hold it is called a croft."

"A croft! That's another kettle o' fish. Sirr! I don't know that I should be seen with you. A mere crofter! Twenty-thirty acres in the hollow and a sheep-run up in the heather! That's a croft."

"Just about. A quarter section or so. It is called the Croft of Balmerion."

"Banffshire is full of crofts. I don't know that one."

"It is two miles south of Knockindu according to the map."

"And you own it?"

"I do. My grandmother used talk by and large of the family lands lost in one of your pleasant obscure cut-throat little wars——"

Kenny Alpin put a silencing hand over his own mouth, and gestured Stephen to proceed.

"But when my grandmother was a girl the Croft of Balmerion was the only thing that remained, and the family had hard hoeing. She came to the States at the age of seventeen; her one brother stayed by the land, married and had a son. That son went to the Great War, got himself a wound, came home, and lived his life out, a lone wolf. He died last year. I am next of kin and the only one. The place is mine to sell, Mr Alpin."

Kenny Alpin put his elbows on the counter, rested his chin in his hands, and looked through the array of bottles with far-seeing eyes.

"The Croft o' Balmerion, twa mile south of Knockindu. That'll be about the mouth o' Glen Shinnoch under the Muckle Kinmaol. That's good country. There's no better country than that country. My certies! Some people have all the luck without

13

knowing it." He straightened up and looked at Stephen, wonder in his eyes. "And you are for selling that place, grandmither's grandson?"

"You can see the papers if you want to."

"I'm no' buyin'. I've my return-ticket, tourist class, and a few dollars again the road. I'm no' buyin', I tell you." He looked directly at Stephen and hinted softly. "One might be needing a few bawbees for current expenses?"

"Chicken-feed! I have a good-enough ranch in Montana, and what in Hades can I do with that family blanket-spread five thousand miles away?"

"Manalive!" protested Kenny warmly. "Don't be irreligious. You can do the world and all with that croft."

"Show me!"

"I'll show you." Kenny Alpin spoke wistfully out of his own desires. "You'd ha'e a cow, and a stirk, a shelt pony, and a puckle sheep on the hill; you'd ha'e a rig o' barley, and twa of oats, and a corner o' neeps, and a long drill o' taties; you'd ha'e a patch o' kitchen garden, kale and such, with a berry bush and a Bramley apple—and blaeberries on all the hills. There would be a covey of partridge in the neeps, and grouse in the heather, and by October the bit birds would be packing in on your corn stooks thick as craws. The laird o' them parts preserves all his policies, and rears his own clutches o' pheasants under clockin'-hens, and it would be a neighbourly thing on your part to scatter a puckle handfu's o' corn round your ain stackyard. There's good trout-fishing in Lettoch Water that runs through Glen Shinnoch, and free at that; and if one o' the laird's salmon rose to a number six hook no one might be watching, and you watching yourself. And far be it from you to line a rifle at one of the laird's stags, but you'd be gey friendly with the head-forester, and he'd tak' you shooting yeld hind in November." He drew a long breath, and irony came into his voice. "And if you were a dam' fool you might take a red-haired woman to wife, and she'd keep a red rooster and a puckle hens to provide you with an egg—or twa—after your mornin's parritch. And there might be weans tumblin' on the floor. And in the long winter nights you'd have time to write the book you had in your mind since you were knee-high to a knuckle-duster. That's all I can give you this instalment, but there's a lot more. Am I getting you where you live, Stephen Wayne?"

"I get your point all right," said Stephen. "You are giving me some pretty fair samples of your own private paradise; but my state is Montana, and it would take me a mighty long session to tell you about it."

"Have it! Have it all! That's the way o' the warld. You despise the few acres that I could be doing fine with; that my friend Ruary Farquhar would give one of his eyes for, and twa fingers."

"Bring your friend along," invited Stephen. "A spare eye and two fingers might come in useful. I can wait."

"You can wait?" Kenny fixed his fierce eyes on Stephen and slapped the counter with a palm. Without turning his head he pointed a finger at the barman. "Fill 'em up, Tony. This is where the talk begins, and if you try to throw us out before 4 a.m., besides not being able, I'll ha'e your boss, Frank Case, before the beak for infringing the rights of a British subject against his will."

"Four is my hour, mister, and out you go," said Tony agreeably. "But you maybe tell me if this

Scotland you talk about such a vera fine place, why too much, many too much Scot-tish men evra-where?"

"Take two chapters to answer that, Mr Alpin," suggested Stephen.

"Where came you out of, Tonio?" questioned Kenny.

"Abruzzio—Gran Paso d'Italia." Tony was proud.

"One hell of a place?"

"Scotland!" cried Tony derisively, flinging his hands to heaven and opening his mouth for speech.

"Wah!" Kenny stopped him with a yell. "Go and explode a brass cap. I saw him first." He turned and pulled a stool close behind Stephen. "Sit ye doon, Mr Stephen Wayne. Tony has answered himself." He shook his black head. "There'll be no word about this the morn. Many a time and oft has my wisdom in the wee sma' hoors scanned like pure balderdash, and my head sair, at high noontide. But where's the harm? Talk I will and you can't stop me, being a gentleman disguised in a boiled shirt. Mind you, I believe every word you say, against reason, though this is a hostelry where fiction assaults you at every turn. Two sober strangers meet in a drink-shop in New York, and one proposes to sell the other a bit of the other's ain Scotland. Furthermore, that bit o' Scotland that ither lad kens, and he kens a man from that place who would give his two eyes to own it——"

"One eye and two fingers," corrected Stephen.

"Ay! and all his ten toes thrown in—or eleven if he had 'em. He'd give you your three hundred pounds too, only he never saw three hundred pounds together in all his days. You were never in your grandmother's Scotland, Stephen Wayne?"

"Hope to take it in some day."

"Och, ay! Off your tall steamer at the Tail o' the Bank, and a motor run through the Trossachs, and a luxury train out of Edinbro to London on the way to Paris. And you think you have taken in Scotland. Like hell you have! If you want to see Scotland you must see it on your own two feet; and while you are on your feet why not stroll up to Knockindu and see your own bit property before you sell it?"

"And what do I do with it meantime?" enquired Stephen dryly.

Kenny Alpin slapped the marble.

"That's the leading question I wanted. Put in a caretaker, with a selling clause. I've got the very man for you."

"Yourself?"

"Not myself. I caretake for no man. Did I mention one Ruary Farquhar?"

"A friend of yours but he doesn't know it?"

"The very man; and Ruary is the very man you want."

"Do I want him?"

"I'm no' deceiving you, Mr Wayne. You know I don't care a damn whether you come to Scotland or not; you know that I have a nefarious motive of my own in urging you not to sell. Correct! Ruary Farquhar is the best friend I have, and I want to give him a chance. He hasn't the money now, but in a year or two—or three—we might raise or steal it. Och!" He gestured a hand disgustedly. "I'm just bletherin'. Let's ha'e another drink and gang to oor beds."

"I like your style, Mr Alpin," said Stephen Wayne. "Suppose you tell me something about your friend Farquhar? I'll take a reasonable interest in your proposition."

"You couldn't say more." He drew in a steadying breath. "All right! I'll tell you about Ruary Farquhar, and then Tony can put us to bed. Ruary Farquhar was born at the top-end of Glen Shinnoch— the Grampian end—half a century ago and ten years added. He was the son of a farmer, and, indeed, he might be inclined to look down on the likes of a man whose grandmother was only a crofter's daughter. As wild a loon as ever stood for a lost cause, and the Farquharsons were in all the lost causes since Charlie was sold for a groat. He was a long, muckle young deevil of a poacher, and in a country with mediaeval game laws and modern lairds, with respect for the same, worse could not be said of any man. He didna care a dom. He began on rabbits with a snare, and soon a pair o' ferrets and a hand-net, and after that a longer net drawn over the coveys in the parks in the dark o' the moon, and went on to grouse in his father's corn stooks in October, and graduated on pheasants with a sawed-off gun in the plantations when the moon was full and the trees bare in November; and beginning by guddling trooties under a bank, he learned how to use an otter-board, a long-handled gaff, a bag net, and a wire noose over a salmon's flukes in still water. And in due time he spent thirty days in Peterhead gaol for daylight poaching. That's the sort he was."

"The sort of man you boost for caretaker?"

"Could you find a man with better training? I'm only at the beginning. Gaol didna cure him. There was no holding him after he came out, and he was never caught again; and at the hinner end he was blamed, and rightly, for taking a stag—a royal hart, mind you —off the laird's forest under the laird's nose. Wae's me! he had gone far on the down road, and there was hell staring him in the face, for, as is well known, hell is the instrument o' the Kirk for the benefit of the landed proprietors.

"So when Ruary's mother died—she was a widow by then—and the lease fell in, the laird's Factor would simply not renew. By that time there was talk going the rounds that Ruary and the laird's son, young Alasdair Finlay, were hand in glove, and spending weeks together on the hill taking toll of the auld man's game. Ruary had to clear out. To Glasgow he went, himself and his young sister Kirsty—the only two left —and he got a job as a stillman in Port Dundas Distillery, for he knew about whisky. Kirsty went to college. That was why Ruary went to town, though he hated crowds. She was a clever sort o' lassie, and might make a schoolma'am of herself, if she did not fall in love. That's the thing she did—fell in love, a tall slip of a lass in her young twenties, and her training not finished. A mad rapscallion of an Irish reporter swept her off her feet and married her out o' hand.

"Ruary said nothing, but he might have ta'en the road to the Highlands only for the coming of the Big War. He joined up in the Scottish Rifles and went through it all without a scratch—a canny auld poacher, he knew how to take cover. He was promoted often, and achieved the full rank of rifleman—four times corporal and four times reduced to the ranks.

"Liam Power, the Irishman who married Kirsty, did not go to the Big War, but he went to a bitter small war in Ireland, and was killed there three months before his only child was born—a daughter. The widow—she loved that Irishman—went queer in the head for a while, and Ruary, home from his own war, took her and her bairn in his two hands and nursed them and minded them, curing one and coaxing the other, and cursing his own fate that held him tied to city streets.

"Ruary never liked servile work, and he got a chance of a small second-hand bookshop at the Glasgow Cross end of Argyle Street—a great reader he was always—and there the three of them are to this day; Ruary, slowly growing old, prisoned by walls; Kirsty in her middle years, young and mad once, and maybe not all sane still; and her daughter, Sheevaun Power, beginning to cut her own swathe. A sonsy bit of femininity Sheevaun. She was well-grounded in what the Scots call education, and has a job in the *Glasgow Herald* Office slinging words on a typewriter, she having ambitions that way. That's how I first met Ruary. I took her home from a Press Association dinner, and, being nicely oiled, bearded him in his den. I bearded him often after that."

Stephen Wayne put a hand on Kenny's arm.

"Reading sign, cowboy, I would say that that girl has red hair."

"You noticed that, did you?" He tapped the counter. "She has red hair. She has an oriflamme of red hair. Come over and see it! She's worth seeing. But we are talking about Ruary Farquhar? Goad! I'm sorry I started this."

"What you start you finish, don't you?"

"I may as well. I'll no' be long. Ruary is the true Highland man. The bens and the glens and the streams are the flesh and blood of him; and, yet, his loyalty to his own kin has made him sacrifice himself without a grunt or a grumble. But once a year, in spring or autumn, he goes off into the country, north and by east, and is lost in the hills for a month. A year ago, against his will, he took me with him. To Banffshire we went. That's how I know Knockindu and Glen Shinnoch.

20

We lived that month, and I will not say how we lived, but we surely lived.

"It is the talk of your croft that put him in my mind. Now that Sheevaun can stand on her own feet, he has in his mind a small place of his own for Kirsty and himself. We talked about it often, and he has been saving up for it. That is all, Mr Wayne."

Kenny Alpin stopped abruptly and beckoned Tony.

"A last one, brither—two Scotch—and we'll go to bed under our own steam. Thank you all for a pleasant evening, and I was glad to hear you talk, Mr Wayne. I'm no' glib, myself. Manalive! If I only had the glib tongue of an Irishman."

The barman hooted, but Stephen Wayne spoke seriously.

"Will you have lunch with me to-morrow, Mr Alpin? They run a nice brand of grub in this joint."

"At your service, sir," Kenny accepted readily. "To-morrow—or is it to-day—we'll be sober—and sensible."

"I am perfectly sober now," protested Stephen.

"Course you are. We both are. Watch me! And good night."

He tossed off his drink, pivoted off the stool, and marched out into the foyer, taking a by-and-large curve towards the lift; a short, strong-shouldered figure, not squat, swaying a little, but light-footed as a cat.

CHAPTER I

STEPHEN WAYNE, used to horses where he was raised, was not much of a foot-slogger. But Kenny Alpin had warned him that if he wanted to see Scotland he must do the seeing on his own two feet; and what Kenny Alpin said went with Stephen. A year ago the two had spent a fairly fast-moving fortnight together in New York, and from the very first early-morning hour an instinctive liking had grown steadily to an easy-going but lasting friendship. That is why Stephen purchased a pair of brown brogues and a rucksack in an expensive, unique, one-sided thoroughfare called Princes Street in Edinburgh. The brogues cost him twelve dollars fifty, and the rucksack three dollars; and the rucksack was worth the money.

He packed the rucksack with a shirt, a sleeping-suit, some socks, handkerchiefs, a toothbrush, and his shaving-tackle; railed his baggage carriage-forward to Knockindu; and set out leisurely to get the feel of Scotland before keeping his appointment with Kenny Alpin at the mouth of Glen Shinnoch in Banffshire.

He did not walk every mile of the two hundred. Not by a long shot, as he would say himself. He took a bus out to the Forth Bridge, and after staring at that colossal double swoop from water-level picked up another bus that set him down at Stirling; and yet another that unloaded him in the heart of the Trossachs. There he loitered about for two or three days, easing his brogues in, and thought the scenery merely pretty compared to his own Yellowstone.

From the Trossachs he slanted off east and by north for Perth and Blairgowrie, through tamed fattish territory of wide vales, easy slopes, and smooth brown hills low on the horizon. He went by bus most of the way. But from Blairgowrie he faced north into the real, honest-to-glory, everlasting hills, set his teeth, and almost made up his mind to foot every yard of the hundred miles by wild Glen Shee, the Devil's Elbow, Braemar of the Gatherings, Royal Balmoral, and the headwaters of the Don.

He set out on a fine August morning. In the first hour a chauffeur and a house male-servant running a baggage-car to a grouse-moor shooting-box on Donside picked him off the grass edging of the road and set him down again that afternoon at a village called Kildrummy within an easy two-day tramp of his destination. They were English serving-men and kindly. They insisted on standing him two drinks and lunch at a wayside inn, hinting that their travelling allowance amply covered such incidental expenses. He had some difficulty in getting them to take the parting drink with him at Kildrummy. To them this lean, brown-faced American was a new type. His oldish Harris-tweed jacket, creaseless flannel slacks, open shirt, and rucksack said plainly that he was a hitch-hiker doing Scotland on the cheap; the Americans they knew went hurriedly from place to place in high-powered English or Italian cars.

To be brief, ten leisurely days out of Edinburgh, Stephen Wayne found himself within an afternoon's walk of the Croft of Balmerion, at the mouth of Glen Shinnoch, where he was to meet Kenny Alpin and Kenny's friend-though-he-didn't-know-it, Ruary

Farquhar. And he had not yet got the feel of Scotland. He was about to. This is where the story begins.

It was early afternoon two days before mid-August, and Stephen was footing it along the lonely winding moorland road that snakes in the hollows of the hills between Devron and Spey. This was not a fat nor a flat nor a tame land, but neither was it a bare nor a bleak land. Rather, it held a serene austerity of its own that depended not at all on sun or sky, wind or weather. On one side of the sandy-brown road, thin-herbaged, grey-green little fields, and patches of corn a fading green, and turnips yellow-green, sloped briefly into folds of heather that rolled up and over into low curves of hills where mountain sheep were scattered like brown stones. In the fold of one hill a pine wood was draped smoothly like a dark-green mantle. Small, strong, grey-stone farmhouses were strung far apart along that side of the road, and around them hung a faint not-unpleasant odour that Stephen recognised, for he had smelled it in his Harris tweed after rain; it was peat and lichen and something else.

On the other side of the road the heather grew from the very posts of the sagging wire fence and swept upwards slowly into breasts of massive stone-ribbed hills that rolled over and heaved up again in rugged grey ramparts that were not yet done soaring; for behind and far away south and west, grey and smoke and blue and purple, towered the veritable clustered masses of the great Grampian Mountains. And the colour washing over all these far-flung hills was a colour that Stephen Wayne had not seen before, for he had never seen heather coming into bloom. It was not the toneless colour of the sage that he knew so well; it was not red or purple or magenta; it was a sort of purplish effusion touched with a smoky blue that lay like a veil on the faces of all the hills; a smooth, soothing wash of colour touched with a strange sombreness. And though the whole pale-blue bowl of the sky was full of sunlight without haze, that queerly satisfying gravity remained, and did not flare in the garishness of the sun.

This was everlasting Scotland. Now and again the black wing of a crow flapped lazily along the breast of a hill; and a small bird—linnet or finch—jerked across the road and said "rweet-cheep" vigorously. That was the only sound. No crow cawed, no dog barked, no grouse crowed from the heather, no human voice came out of house or field. Even the soft flow of warm air that breathed in Stephen's tossed hair was soothing and slumbrous. If he had not felt in such fine form, he would have sought out a shady corner and taken a siesta—like the hills. Once and from far away he thought he heard the sound of gun-fire in the moors. He might have. The grouse season had just begun.

He was at the top-notch of fitness that afternoon. He was getting quite useful at this foot-swinging business, even if he had not walked quite all of the two hundred miles. He looked down at his now-easy brown brogues pacing in the soft dust that was sandy, not floury, and fancied that his gait was not as intoed and his knees not as far apart as they used to be. He threw his chin up, switched his trouser leg with a hazel switch he had cut, and whistled. He was one bad whistler. After a while he filled a pipe and let the smoke drift back about his ears, his mind careless on top but interested deep down.

Here he was in Scotland as he had promised Kenny Alpin; this very evening he would be meeting the great small warrior—and Ruary Farquhar, whom he pictured as old and squat and gnarled and secretive;

and Ruary's sister, Kirsty. Kirsty had a daughter whose name he had forgotten—if he had ever heard it —but she had red hair, and Kenny had hinted an interest in her. Well! red-haired girls usually aroused interest in more than one male breast. She would probably be in Glasgow holding down that job of hers. Good job too! He was not interested in any woman's daughter, though, darn fool that he was, every good-looking girl made his pulse stir—for the time.

He would move circumspectly while here in the North. Americans had a bad reputation for sticking their heads out in foreign places. He would keep his mouth shut and his eyes open, staying quietly in one of the two Knockindu hotels, looking over his Croft of Balmerion, moving round Glen Shinnoch for a week, climbing a hill or two with Kenny Alpin, and then taking a train for Southampton and the S.S. *Washington*, and his own country. But, first, he would dispose of that croft to Ruary Farquhar at a reasonable figure and on reasonable terms. Better have all one's ties in one country, and Montana was his choice. A double allegiance was an impossible ideal. And that was that.

The country was getting wilder. The few cultivated fields had been left behind, and there had not been a farmhouse for the last two miles. The road, no longer fenced, was only a gut winding steeply uphill between stiff craggy braes. Stephen leant to the collar-work and went swinging upwards, turned a corner by a sudden boss of limestone, and found himself on top of the rise. He halted to get his wind and look over the new country before him.

The valley he was in went straight ahead between the folding hills, but, just below, another valley cut strongly across almost at right angles, a valley heavily wooded in larch and spruce, and deep and narrow enough to be called a glen. The swish and gurgle of fast water came to him up the slope, and he saw the roily gleam of it between the fronds of birchen boughs. The birch is the fairy tree. It grows out of penurious soil, and it is as delicate and tough and frail and ever-lasting as life. The small, heart-shaped, multitudinous leaves gleam and shiver golden-green in every blink of sun, and the leaning, banded, silver-brown trunks have a warm gleam of their own in the most sunless of days. Pine or no pine, the birch is the one charactered tree in the Highlands.

The road tip-tilted down the brae and angled suddenly across the stream on top of the high-cocked arch of a grey-stone bridge. Beyond the bridge, at the back of a small bay on the left of the road, tall wrought-iron gates closed a drive that disappeared hurriedly into a wood of filmy-green larch. Some place back in there, Stephen surmised, there would be a shooting-box for a grouse-moor or a deer-forest.

A man leaned against the parapet of the bridge at the top of the high-cock, and looked up at Stephen coming down the brae. At that distance Stephen saw that he was an old man, and at a nearer distance that he was very old. A tall, thin, still-straight, ancient man in shapeless brown-and-white check tweeds patched at knee and elbow, and with a deer-stalker's cap covering his ears. His eyes were a mild and weary blue, and his muttonchop whiskers still showed traces of ginger, carrots, and sand. A black bitch, that looked like a cross between a spaniel and a smooth-haired retriever, slept at his feet, opened one eye as Stephen's foot sounded on the curve of the arch, shut it again, and sighed. Stephen saluted the old man.

"A fine day, grandfather!"

"Eh? I'm no' your grandfaither!" His old voice was startled. "Och ay! A gran' day for the time o' the year."

It was the height of a particularly fine season and the day had to be good; but the Scots are a cautious and deprecatory people.

"This the road to Knockindu?" Stephen enquired.

"Knockindu? The only road in it."

"And Glen Shinnoch?"

The old man straightened up and gestured a knobby old hand with surprising ease.

"Five miles that way to the Kirktoon o' Knockindu, and five mile back that way th' ither side o' Lettoch Water, and you're at the bottom end o' Glen Shinnoch —that airt I'm pointin'."

He was pointing down the cross valley on the line of the private road inside the inhospitable gates.

"There might be a short-cut across that way?" suggested Stephen.

"A' that is the private policies o' Castle Charles." The old man shook his head and scratched under his deer-stalker. "'Tis only half the distance, but na! I darena do it. The gents—a puckle o' them—are in residence for the shootin'."

"Never mind!" Stephen said. "I can make it the long way round."

He leant at the old fellow's side and looked over the low parapet. Thirty feet below, the water ran clear over quartz boulders, but it ran too swiftly for any fish to lie. Downstream the water spread into a pool, and as Stephen looked the surface broke and ringed to a rising trout.

"Fish in that pool!" Stephen remarked.

"Na! There's no' a fush this side o' Lettoch Water. They canna mak' the loup at Falcon Crag. That's a broon trootie you saw."

Stephen learned later that in all the angling North a fish is a salmon and nothing other than a salmon.

The Scots might be called a taciturn breed with exceptions like Kenny Alpin who on occasion would talk the minute-hand off a clock. They are a courteous people too, and hesitate to put the direct inquisitive question to a stranger. But also they have the natural friendly inquisitiveness of the Gael, and a method all their own in satisfying it. The ancient man rumbled in his old throat, and spoke to himself obliquely.

"Glen Shinnoch is a long glen, a gey long bit o' a glen—twal' mile up to the Braes o' the Aon."

"The Croft of Balmerion is my mark," Stephen answered the implied question.

"Ay, indeed! Balmerion! That's where Ruary Farquhar and his sister Kirsty bides this time past." He gave the word Ruary a Gaelic twist that almost made it Ruaraigh.

"You know Ruary Farquhar?"

"Twoscore years and ten I know him."

"An old friend?" suggested Stephen, wondering if that short-cut might not be feasible after all.

"I wouldna say that," said the old man ruminatively. "Na! I wouldna say that at all. I was a man grown with a family a'ready, and he a bit loon. Forbye, I was head-keeper at Castle Charles and him a dom young poacher."

"Fire and water?"

"Just that."

He was a very old man and what the Scots call dottled—in his dotage. Stephen had switched his mind back to the days of his strong manhood, and he forgot his native reticence in the reminiscent garrulousness of the old. He even forgot that Stephen was a stranger.

29

"Ay! a bit loon, Ruary was them days, but I liked him fine, wild an' all as he was. He kent mair about game and fush an' the ways o' them in wood an' water than any man in the country barrin' the young laird Alasdair—him that's auld and done now. The auld laird was bitter against Ruary, an' I hed my duty to do. I caught him barefaced liftin' a salmon out o' the Tomnon pool wi' a snare in the middle o' the noonday, and he got thirty days in Peterhead jail for't. Maybe I shouldna ha'e done it, but there was a young bucher of a under-keeper wi' me at the time—an' the laird was sair hard on Ruary. Ay! Thirty days he got, an' he that young."

"He did not love you for it," said Stephen, suddenly hot thinking of a young lad being gaoled for catching one fish in a Highland glen.

"It was all in the game, and he bare me nae ill-will. It didna cure him nayther. Waur he got, an' cunnin' like a fox, an' he was never trapped again. Ay, but the auld laird was hard! He blamed Ruary for leadin' young Alasdair astray, the twa young deevils in the heather for a week, maybe shootin' a stag out o' season or liftin' a fish off the spawnin' redds. Out o' the glen he was driven at the hinner end, and out of it he was kept for thirty years. He came back for a look once in a while, an' now he's back for guid in a plaicie o' his ain; an' the auld laird is dead, and the young laird is auld and done, no' a bawbee to his name, an' the roof o' Castle Charles over stranger heids. Ay! back Ruary is in spite of all."

"And back for good in spite of hell and high-water," said Stephen, glad that he had been the god-out-of-the-machine that had helped Ruary Farquhar back. "He is too old for poaching now, I suppose?" he half-queried.

30

"I couldna tell you that," said the old man hastily. "He's no' that old, an' my son, the head-keeper now, has twa men steady watchin' him. But they'll no' catch Ruary. No' they! Myself sends him across a wordie o' warnin' when I get the chance."

"Can I take him a word for you?" proposed Stephen, flicking a scrap of loose mortar down into the fast water.

He came back to the present, and glanced at Stephen out of old, washed-out, blue eyes.

"Maybe you'll no' be a kin o' his hame from America?"

He had probably met many American sportsmen in his time, and so was able to peg down Stephen's Western draw somewhere in some millions of square miles.

"No, I never met him," Stephen told him, "but there is a friend of mine staying at the croft."

"Ay! there's a black lowland laddie out o' Glasga bidin' there the best pairt of a week—an' that half-Irish quoine o' Kirsty's. I heard that."

Evidently a variety of the grape-vine telegraph was not unknown in the Highlands, thought Stephen. He straightened up from the parapet, and the old man straightened up with him.

"You're for the road then," he said. "I'll put you a bittie on your way."

His loose old legs made long, knee-bent strides, and there was no need for Stephen to moderate his pace. When they came in front of the tall inhospitable gates, Stephen made to go by on the main road, but the old man laid a hand on his arm.

"This is your road, freen'," he said.

He led Stephen through the gates, locking them behind him.

"I couldna do it," he explained, "only the gents

31

are shootin' the Corryhow Moors at the top-end the day."

He walked with Stephen down a quarter-mile of avenue curving between spindly young larch trees. The sunlight, coming through, barred and dappled the road with light and shade, and a thin lace of old larch-needles deadened their footsteps. Everything was very still and peaceful and almost slumbrous. Once a rabbit hopped leisurely across in front of them, and once a young cock Chinese pheasant, coming to its full plumage, walked chicken-like from one side to the other, and mysteriously disappeared where there was no cover; but the old black bitch trotting at her master's heels took not the least notice. The old keeper no longer made talk, but occasionally muttered half-peevishly at himself. In a quarter of a mile they came to a plain seven-bar gate in a high wire fence.

"The deer-forest bounds," the old man said. "The gents'll be at the stalkin' in three days."

He opened the gate, gestured Stephen through and shut it between them. He cut the air forward with the edge of his hand.

"Keep on the drive till you sight the big house— Castle Charles that'll be—an' don't go any nearer to it. Mind that!"

"I mind it, cowboy."

"Eh! Keeper I was. Keep you left-handed after that, back of the shrubberies, and you'll strike a pony track at the corner of the kitchen-garden wall. Follow that, and in a mile and a bittoch you'll come out high over the Lettoch Water, an' goin' downstream right-hand you'll go up the Falcon Crag and ha'e all the world afore you. The Croft o' Balmerion is straight across the valley on the breist o' the hill under the Muckle Kinmaol, a wee hoosie above a belt of larch—

you canna miss it—the only hoose that side. You'll get at it by a swing-bridge across the Lettoch below Falcon Crag. Fower mile from where you stand this meenit, and you can't put a foot wrong. Awa' you go, laddie!"

Without waiting for a word of thanks he turned and went off in his long, knee-bent strides, his old dog switching in behind him; and Stephen stood looking after him through the bars of the gate. But having gone not more than ten paces he stopped dead, looked at the ground, swung slowly and came back hurriedly, his old eyes glancing warily right and left. The old dog got out from under and sat down disgustedly.

"Hist!" He whispered urgently through the bars. "Tell Ruary—no' from me—that the gents'll be on the Caiplich Moor a' to-morrow, an' that reach o' Lettoch Water'll no' be safe—no' safe at all. The Caiplich—that's it."

He turned and went off, and this time kept going, his dog close behind. Stephen never saw that ancient man again, did not even know his name, but he had a strange feeling that something important had happened, that his feet had been knowingly directed, and that the old man was an unknowing instrument.

Stephen went on down the slow swing of the drive. The valley was opening into a bowl in the hills half filled with the dark-green of pines and rimmed with brown round summits. Another quarter-mile brought him in view of the big house of Castle Charles. It stood up very tall, and narrow for its height, across a wide green lawn clumped with roses and flowering shrubs. It was the usual Scots baronial type of mansion, built when defence was no longer of much importance, with high-stepped gables, pepper-castor turrets, high-set narrow windows, and the stone walls hidden under grey-white rough-casting. An imposing mansion to be hidden there in the waste of hills, even though it did not tone with the gravity of the pines or the quiet certitude of the brown summits.

Two ladies were sitting out on the lawn in canvas chairs under sun-hoods. They sat on the near side of a rose-bed, almost within talking distance of Stephen standing at the side of a thick rhododendron on the edge of the drive. One was white-haired and robed in flowered scarlet; the other was young and dark, in a flimsy dress of faint colours, and, even at that distance, Stephen could see that she was vivid. A rustic table was set between them, and they were having afternoon tea; and Stephen thought that two fashionable ladies drinking tea before a Scots baronial tower under the ancient and lonely hills were out of place. Already he wanted this country to be strong and simple.

There was an opening in the shrubbery beyond the rhododendron, and he edged round quickly to get under cover. But before he could make it a voice hailed him across the grass. He hesitated. Easy enough to dodge into the shrubbery and carry on, but that was not Stephen Wayne's way. After a moment he turned round and walked slowly across towards the ladies.

The lady that had hailed him was oldish and ordinary, stout, grey-haired, kindly-eyed, double-chinned, and she should have not worn flowered scarlet. The moment she opened her mouth he knew that she was a countrywoman of his own—far Mid-West.

The other lady was a vivid dark young aristocrat, but not adolescently young by a good few years. Vivid, described her. Vividness enhanced by the faintly coloured flimsy dress, and her thin black brows and

34

scarlet mouth. A sophisticated modern beauty in a hollow of the timeless hills! The older lady was talking and stirring her tea.

"Got some business in here, young fellow?"

Stephen let his daredevil grey eye flicker a single flicker towards youth and beauty.

"Sorry I haven't, ma'am," he said.

"Are you looking for anyone?"

"Not any more, ma'am," said Stephen mildly.

The oldish lady did not get that, but the young one did. She might have bridled, but, instead, she chuckled. She knew enough of life to take a compliment wherever it came from.

"We do not allow—trespassers—in the grounds," said the oldish lady. She had almost said hobos. "Where are you going?"

"Across into Glen Shinnoch, lady," said Stephen, trying to capture the growling whine of the real hobo. It was ridiculous being ordered off Highland premises by his own countrywoman.

She was a kindly woman. He looked a tough young wastrel to her, but not vicious, and it would be heartless to send him the long road round by Knockindu.

"Ah, well! This far on the road, you may go on. The track is over there."

"I am obliged," said Stephen, finger to brow, and turned to go.

"I'll show you, you young tramp!" said the dark young woman, and with a lazy kick of her long legs was on her feet. Stephen found her walking at his side across the grass. She was nearly as tall as he was, which was not very tall, and her shoulder nearly touched his. There was about her a faint, elusive, pleasant, dark and dangerous perfume, and he moved

35

a foot away from her. She had a cool slow voice of low strong timbre. She said:

"You are American too, of course?"

"Hobo!" said Stephen.

"Hobo? Oh, tramp! Perhaps you are. Have you any particular business in this place? I want no more of your compliments."

This sophisticated young person was not deceived by Stephen's careless appearance. The clear white of his grey eye, the set of his jaw, the carriage of his head, were not trampish, and his brogues were good Scottish brogues.

"You puzzle a fellow too," said Stephen. "What business have you here yourself?"

"You like to be rude. American people own this place, and a young American tough comes slinking out of the shrubbery. What do you want?"

"Slinking like a lynx, prowling like a wolf."

"Foolish of me to ask you. Naturally you will not tell, but you had better be careful."

"You are astonishing people in your hole in the hills," said Stephen equably as he could. "A fellow on the hike crossing the divide, and he gets jumped on by a scarlet woman and a dar—Delilah one."

She laughed frankly.

"We had better be careful too," she said. "Here is the track that will take you over the hill, but you may be back."

They had come round a covering hedge of laurel to where a beaten track skirted round the angle of a high garden wall above which showed a spray of apples still green. The lady faced round and started to walk away slowly.

"Pity I'll not be back," Stephen said. "You might get any secret out of me in about two hours."

She did not look back, but paused.

"Delilah took longer with her poor old Samson," she said. "Go away; you are not profitable."

That was it. He was not profitable for ladies like this one drifting so lazily and easily across smooth lawns. He cursed himself some. She was one complete good-looker, and good-looking women made his pulses stir—for the time.

CHAPTER II

THE track wound steadily uphill through woods of pine; trees of old growth with tall branchless trunks closing the vista within a hundred paces. The ground under the trees was a brown carpet, and even the track was a mat of decayed pine-needles. There was no life in that ancient wood and only one sound; though there was scarcely a drift of air and not a branch moved, a soughing sigh as of a distant sea went over the tree-tops in one unchanging note. There was a sort of faintly eerie cathedral feeling in the dimly luminous columned quiet, and an occasional gleam of sunlight coming through was like a ray laid down on chancel floor through yellow-stained windows.

In less than half an hour he got to the top of the rise, but could not see the country ahead, for the tall pines went on over the brow and showed only glimpses of blue sky. But within ten minutes the trees below him began to thin, and he got flashes of running water far down. That would be Lettoch Water. Shortly after that the track swerved to the right along the edge of a steep brae, and the pines gave way to graceful birches, letting the sun through in golden-green shimmers. Through the tops of the trees Stephen saw the round bald head of a hill miles away, and where the under-foliage thinned he got brief views of a strong wide stream some fifty yards below him.

There or thereabouts he caught a glimpse of something moving on the brink of the water, and twisting his head this way and that made out the figure of a man moving about on a flat slab of rock jutting over a smooth pool. By bending down he found that he could see the man much more clearly. Between the leaning trunks of the birches and under the foliage, close to the ground, there was a clear funnel right down to the water-side. The man was not more than fifty yards below, and the perspective in that narrow tunnel of foliage seemed to concentrate a spotlight on him.

He was a very tall lean man in old heather-mixture tweeds, and his long neck was set forward on his shoulders as he peered warily over the edge of the slab into the smooth water. As Stephen bent over, the long man went on his hands and knees to get a nearer view. Stephen went on his hands and knees too. Still the man could not see all he wanted to see. He lay flat on the rock, his eyes over the rim.

Stephen was going to see this through, so he made himself comfortable. A clump of fern, growing on the lip of the brae at the track-side, was hindering his view, and he shoved his head and shoulders into the heart of it, moved the fronds apart, and lay at ease with an uninterrupted vision. It was rather like a television screen, with the distance miniaturing the man; and at the same time there was a sharpening of outline.

The man lay flat on the slab, feet apart, and Stephen could see the steel-shod heels of a mighty pair of brogues. After a time he took off his cap, showing a mass of grizzled grey hair, and cautiously weaved it close above the surface of the water, thereby cutting off the sun-glimmer and making the pool transparent. The cap steadied over one spot, and the man's whole body, that was still before, seemed to concentrate stillness.

The man drew back slowly and sat upright, and his grizzled head nodded as in affirmation. He sat there resting back on his hands, his long neck leaning forward, his whole attitude one of lazy speculation. He turned his head slowly upstream and down, and Stephen knew that his eyes were going over every rock and bush; then he pivoted round and seemed to be looking directly into Stephen's eyes up the leafy tunnel; but he would need the eyes of a hawk to see a head in that stool of bracken. Stephen could see that he was an oldish man and grizzle-bearded to the cheek-bones.

Satisfied that he was unobserved, the man put aside his leisureliness, and acted smoothly, quickly, definitely. A steel head gleamed in the sun from under a loose jacket, a long handle extended itself miraculously, and Stephen recognised a salmon gaff with a telescope grip.

The poacher was back in his old position, flat on the rock, his chin over the edge, the hook of the gaff taking the water and the handle upright. Slowly the handle slipped under until there was a bare foot above the surface, and there it paused a moment and moved forward inch by inch.

It happened quickly. Stephen saw the upward jerk of one shoulder; and almost in the same instant the man rolled sideways and over on his back. There was a boil and a splash in the pool, and a gleaming, kicking black-and-silver body came explosively out of the water and took a high curving somersault to the flat rock behind the man.

"Got him, by heck!" exclaimed Stephen, and lifted his head.

Something hit solidly between his shoulder-blades, his breast and face were driven forcefully into the bracken stool, and there was a fierce whisper in his ear:

"Got you, you polecat!"

There was a hard knee in the small of Stephen's back, and a leg across his thighs; there were hard knuckles in the back of his neck, and a rude hand grasped a fistful of his hair, holding his head hard down. The brute was as strong as a gorilla, and Stephen, flattened out, could not use the leverage of hand or knee. He could not breathe with his mouth full of fern, and he needed his breath, for he was beginning to boil over. A sharp whistle rang out over his head.

And then he felt himself being shoved over the edge of the brae, and boiled right over. "A hell of an inhospitable country!" was the thought in his mind. "But if I have to go you come with me." He let himself go loose and slung a desperate arm behind him. It clamped at the back of a knee, and never did a tentacle clamp tighter. The gorilla on top roared, fell forward, and two arms went round Stephen's neck. Gravity took charge and the two went downwards in a complicated tangle.

Locked together they went all the way down, but not smoothly or directly. Glancing off birch trunks, rolling, clawing for a purchase, kicking, somersaulting, sliding, and again rolling, gravity took them right down to the path along the river-bank. One moment Stephen found himself staring dizzily at the underside of birch leaves, the next he found his nose in the ground and heard a grunt in his ear. Luckily the man on Stephen's back took most of the bumps, but the grip of one arm never loosed. Luckily also the ground was soft and dampish.

Close to the end Stephen was conscious of every roll and bump, but about that time he must have taken a good hard knock, for the next thing he remembered was his sitting up on the path close to the stream, his hands propping him and trying to hold the world from see-sawing. The big face of rock across the water was swinging gently from side to side. And he was alone. He must have been out for some time.

The cool old poacher who had flicked the salmon over his head and the gorilla who had jumped him had vanished into thin air, but not silently. Downstream from where Stephen sat, the path curved out of sight round a drooping birch, and from there came the sound of hastily receding footsteps. He could not have been out for more than a few seconds.

"The hellion!" cried Stephen, and made to start to his feet.

The world turned completely over, and he sat down again with a thud. It swung back again, and went over the other way.

"Eight—nine—out!" said Stephen, and held his head between his knees with both his hands. He would not move again till the mountains stopped skipping. He heard no footsteps. What he heard was a girl's voice above his head.

"Are you hurt?" A quiet voice, but anxious.

Stephen gave his head a settling shake and looked. There was a young girl there right enough, but she was not alone. She was bending forward and holding the arm of a thin gentleman in a kilt, who stared across the pool at nothing and completely ignored Stephen. Stephen played for time until his head steadied. He looked up at the girl and said:

"Did you do this to me?"

Her eyes opened wide, and they were brown. Her mouth opened a little too, and there was nothing wrong with her mouth either.

"You've had a fall?" she said.

He turned head carefully and looked up through the tunnel under the birches. From the way he felt, that

42

tunnel should have been a devastated landslide, with trees overwhelmed across bare scars of mud and gravel. But the creamy-brown trunks leaned amiably towards each other, the leaves winked and shivered under the ecstasy of light, and not even the bracken clumps showed where two locked bodies had hurtled. As he brought his eyes down again he saw the sun glisten on a few salmon scales close to the bank. That was the only sign to be read.

"I was up there," he said. "I came down—fast— but I had to come down anyway."

"You fell down?"

"Every darn foot."

"How silly!" said this young woman used to hills. "No one should fall all that way. Your nose is bleeding."

"Peeping Tom got his," said Stephen, and scrambled to his feet.

But on his feet he swayed dizzily, and one hip gave him a twinge. A stick with a shepherd's crook grip clattered as it struck the gravel, and a firm small hand grasped above his elbow.

"You are hurt?" There was an anxious kindness in the softly modulated voice.

"Punch drunk—all right in a minute, thank you." He wiped his nose gingerly. It was not broken, nor was there much blood. His nose did not bleed easily. He knew that, for it had been punched frequently before and after he had made the boxing team at Little Rock.

"You have spread the dirt nice and evenly," said the young lady.

She let go his arm, bent quickly, picked up the stick, and thrust the crook of it into his hand.

"See if you can walk?"

43

He propped himself on the stick and kicked one foot tentatively. His hip twinged but there was no grate in the socket. There was an ache in one shoulder too, but the clavicle was intact. One eyebrow felt stiff and his feeling fingers stung it, but there was no broken skin. He took three or four steps forward and back. He could proceed under his own steam all right, but to-morrow he would be stiff as a poker.

"Five rounds in half a minute," he said. "Can do, thank you." He tendered her her crook.

"Keep it for the present. Can we—can I do anything for you?"

"Got knocked off my bearings," said Stephen. "Do I go downstream for the Croft of Balmerion?"

All this time the man in the kilt had not spoken a word or made a single movement. He stood very erect, arm-held by the girl, and looked aloofly over the width of Lettoch Water. But now he spoke as if to himself:

"My young friend, Ruary Farquhar! To-morrow he and I will go to the hill."

His young friend, Ruary Farquhar! Stephen looked at him in some astonishment. He was a tall frail man, but not very old. He wore no head-covering, and his thin white hair was tossed about a sunken-templed brow. His clean-shaven face was lean, indeed emaciated, his cheek-bones standing out above deep hollows and the skin tight over clean-cut jaw. But that upthrown face was dignified, austere, aloof, almost intolerant, and the grey eyes, looking across the water, were half-hooded like an eagle's.

The girl was not astonished, but there was anxiety in the way her arm tightened in the man's.

"We will show you where Balmerion is," she said to Stephen. "Come on, father!"

44

So he was her father. He turned with her at once, and the two linked together walked away from Stephen, downstream. Stephen followed, using the crook to help a slight limp, and falling back to get a fair view of the father and daughter. He was tall and was used to swinging a kilt, for his legs above grey-green hose were brown and hard even if they were woefully lean. The kilt was green and blue, cross-barred red and yellow, and Stephen learned later that it was the tartan of Clann Finlay.

The daughter wore the same tartan, not in a kilt but in a short walking skirt. She was long-legged, and Stephen then thought that her legs were the best of her: clean-ankled above flat-heeled shoes, flowing upwards slimly not swellingly into long thighs that would be well rounded. And he liked the way her darkish, brownish, mousish, well-brushed hair—she was bareheaded too—fluffed out and down the back of her neck. He was not interested in recalling her eyes or her mouth. He was more interested in her father than he was in her. There was something far wrong with that man. His ignoring quietness was unnatural, and his words had no meaning. Who was young Ruary Farquhar, anyway?

She turned her head to see if he was coming.

"You've lost your hat?" she said.

"We save on hats," he said, and caught the flicker of an eyebrow.

The path started to mount, and turned away from the river at the back of black alder trees. It kept on mounting, at last steeply, and Stephen was glad of the shepherd's crook. And then the two ahead halted on a wide platform of rock, and Stephen mounted and stood behind the girl's shoulder. He drew in his breath in sheer surprise, and exclaimed suddenly.

45

For hours he had been closed in by hills and rocks and trees, and now he was standing on a high rock in the sun, and his vision leaped across miles—leaped or soared, that was the feeling. The old keeper was right. He seemed to have the world before him.

"This is Falcon Crag," said the girl.

The crag stood three hundred feet above Lettoch Water, two hundred feet of sheer rock face and one hundred of boulders falling steeply down into the river. And beyond the river an oval valley was scooped out of the hills, and took the eye and the mind soaring. Stephen felt strangely light and detached from earth. He felt that he could throw his arms up and out and take off in a soaring, swooping dive out and down through the empty translucent buoyant air.

That hollow valley might be five miles long by three wide, and it was a small world all by itself. Away to the right, that is northwards, Stephen's eye caught a huddle of grey roofs. A church steeple and a square tower showing a clock face stood up above the low roofs. That would be the Kirktown of Knockindu. To the left, and still northwards, a conical hill stood up from the flank of the valley and was thickly clothed from base to summit in dark green fir. A brown road wound round the shoulder of a hill.

There were many farmhouses and a mansion or two on the far side of the village, but on the near or southern side there were only two houses in the whole width of the valley. But there was an uncountable number of small stone-fenced fields, pasture fields in which black cattle grazed, patches of corn beginning to yellow, squares of turnip and potatoes; and, yet, not a single cottier's house. These little fields, Stephen learned later, belonged to the burgesses of the town.

The Lettoch Water ran fast and strong below Falcon

Crag. A short distance down it was spanned by a flimsy wooden footbridge suspended on wires that looked frail as a spider's staying rope. Still further down on the far side of the water a round low curve of hillock was grown with deciduous trees, and the L-shaped roof of a house showed above the trees on the flat crown. That was one of the two houses southwards of Knockindu. The other house was right across the valley, and as Stephen picked it out the girl said:

"There is the Croft o' Balmerion under the Muckle Kinmaol."

So that was his croft over there all by itself. That side of the valley was closed in by two round-topped bald hills with a fine sweep of saddle-back between. Below the bald crowns a fringe of pine circled the hills like a fringe of hair on a bald man's head. The Gaelic name, Kinmaol, means bald-head. In the saddle-back by the flank of the bigger hill—the Muckle Kinmaol— a small torrent had gouged for itself a miniature ravine that disappeared into a larch grove half-way down the slope. And there, above the corner of the larch belt and back from the little ravine, squatted a small, grey-stone, slated house. A chimney smoked at one end and a skylight in the roof took the westering sun. Three or four small grey-green, stone-fenced fields surrounded the house on both sides of the ravine, and the fringe of pine above fenced them off from the purple-brown wastes of heather.

It was a pleasant sunny place for a small house above a pleasant sunny valley, and Stephen could appreciate Kenny Alpin's desire for a small place like it. Over there a man would dream with the sound of running water in his ears, and wake up to hold by the things that mattered in a tottering world. But not Stephen

47

Wayne! Stephen Wayne came from a country with wider horizons, and all his life had tried to do the things that mattered. After a week or two in this peaceful place he would go back to his own life.

He was roused from his musings by the man's voice speaking remotely, sadly:

"All that! All that!"

The lean man's face was turned sideways showing a ridge of aquiline nose beyond the boss of cheek-bone, his eyes were turned southward, and his left arm thrown out. Stephen looked where he was pointing and saw the real Highland glen in the hollow of its mountains. The peaceful bowl of Knockindu was only a widening at the lower end of Glen Shinnoch. The hill on whose breast he stood and the Muckle Kinmaol across the way, sweeping round towards each other, narrowed the mouth of the main glen. Falcon Crag looked up the first long reach of it. A deep but not narrow glen, and strongly walled. The Lettoch Water ran in the hollow of it, marked by a band of green and clumps of dark alder; heather and schrees and chorries went up on either hand; a narrow brown road was looped from horn to horn; south and west a stark mountain peak towered up from the very floor of the glen, and its rock-crowned conical head was tilted over to look down into the hollow. That was Ben Shinnoch, lord of the glen. Further off on the other side another massive peak reared itself in a double ridge. That was Corryhow. Nearer and beyond, other slopes and contours and hill-tops heaved and gathered and tilted, brown, purple, blue, smoke-grey, to the far horizon where the ghosts of the Grampians were shadowy as a cloud below the pearl-blue of the evening sky.

"All that! All that!" said the kilted man.

His eyes were intolerantly hooded, and his face calm.

48

But it was a fragile calm. It was a calm drawn to the breaking-point over some inner struggle, over some storm of mind, some distortion of time that shut off the present and went groping in the past. There was a surface glisten on his eyes that is never on the eyes of a calm man. The girl took his arm and without looking at Stephen said:

"You cross by the swing-bridge down there. Let us go, father."

He suffered himself to be led off the platform of rock, and the two went down the path that slanted back and curved steeply towards the flying-bridge. Stephen called after:

"Your stick?"

"You may need it," she called back. "Kirsty Power can send it across with the milk."

Stephen did not follow them just yet. He sat down on the rock and waited. The evening sun was warm, and the stone, after the long day in the sun, was almost too warm. He did not swing his feet over the edge, for though he had a good head for height it did not feel good enough just then to poise itself above three hundred feet of dragging emptiness.

There was something wrong with that lean kilted man. He had been too aloof. He either had not been aware of Stephen's presence or he was too impossibly self-important to have noticed. The girl had been considerate even if cold, and had shown traces of inner anxiety. They were evidently aristocrats, and Stephen knew that some of the Highland gentry had the caste dignity of the wiped-out Hapsburgs. To them he might only be an American hiking it with a rucksack, and evidently an American of that type cut no ice in this environment. Already a woman of his own race had resented his trespassing, another woman had been coldly suspicious, some unknown thug had tried to break his neck, a clan chief had ignored him, and a girl had been as cold as charity. Let it ride! An American he was. He would stay his few days, move circumspectly, keep his head well tucked in, and after that if anyone tried to make a sap of him he could not be blamed for the necessary reaction. But good old Kenny Alpin would keep him right—and Ruary Farquhar too. And damn that gorilla!

His thoughts nettled him some, and set his mind on the cold girl. She was not exactly cold in his mind. He could see the swing of her long legs, and the swing of her shapely hips, and the way she carried shoulders below the fluff of fine hair. That was the ordinary male in him, of course. Her face, brown-eyed, wistful-mouthed, he could not quite visualise, but her feline, feminine, smooth way of carrying herself was warm in his mind.

"To hell with them all!" he exclaimed, and scrambled to his feet well away from the lip of the rock.

The man and girl had crossed the flying-bridge and were going down the other side of the water towards the house in the trees on the mound-top. Probably they lived there. A sheltered secluded place above the river and within reach of beauty. Evidently they got their milk from his croft, and evidently she took it for granted that Kirsty Power would know to whom this shepherd's crook belonged. That was the aristocratic training.

He made his way, crook-propped and limping a little, down to the footbridge. The cross-set floor pieces tilted and tipped under his feet, and at the middle he paused to get his balance and have a look at the pool below. The limestone water, flowing smoothly and clear as crystal, showed every rib of the grey-and-white quartz bottom ten feet down. There were trout in the pool too. He saw the flash of them into shelter upstream, and one lazy plump fellow weighing a couple of pounds, soaring half-depth down, let himself slide easily backwards and aside towards the overhang of the bank.

That limpid smooth pool with the slanting sunrays shimmering on the bottom was infinitely inviting. Stephen had not had a bath for three days, and felt clammy and grimy. The thought of cool water sizzling over his hot head was too much for him. The man and girl had disappeared amongst the trees; he had the whole place to himself.

He stumped swayingly off the bridge and went round to the upper side of the straining poles. There he found that the pool was actually a bathing-pool, for a spring-board jutted out from a flat rock a yard above the water. He stripped quickly and stood poised on the matted end of the spring-board. He stripped well, and bigger than he looked with his clothes on, his muscle not massive but long and limber like a boxer's, and the skin of his torso startlingly white below his brown neck. The sun suffused his back with gentle warmth, and a ripple of air caressed his skin delicately. Then he took the plunge out and down, and made the trout wonder if the next county was not a safer place.

The water was cool, but not chillingly so. It came from the high flanks of the mountains, but it had been under the sun all the way down Glen Shinnoch, and the snow chill was out of it. He went down deep, his hand touched a rib of quartz, and he turned over to get the trout's perspective: the refracted light broken short at the surface, the tossing twisted floor of the bridge, the shimmer of green and gold that was the hillside, and one round clear peep-hole where he could see birch leaves quiver. A fish could not see a great deal.

He came to the surface in a slanting drive, lashed across the pool and back again, and trod water to wash his face with one hand, twisting his nose to find it securely anchored, and laving the bump over his left eye. His hip twinged only when he kicked hard. Slowly he drifted with the easy draw of the current, and sat for a while in the gravel at the tail of the pool where the water felt warmer. Then he came back in a breast drive and crawled out on the grey sun-warmed slabs by the spring-board. He rubbed face and hair with a linen handkerchief from his rucksack and let the sun do the rest.

After ten minutes or so he slipped on his clothes, slung his rucksack, and faced across the valley on a narrow motor road between ragged hedges of hawthorn and blackberry briar. The berries that had been green were now red on the way to ripe blue-blackness. Stephen was feeling fine. He hardly needed the crook at all. It was a nice stick of brown hazel with a creamy hand-cut crook and a turned-up nose, and he wondered if that girl would miss it should he sort of forget to return it with the milk. So Ruary Farquhar kept a cow and supplied milk to the neighbours—only one neighbour as far as Stephen could see with the naked eye.

In half a mile he came out on the main tarmac road. The tar was overlaid with bright brown gravel, and the road had a cheerful look. It went one way to Knockindu and over the shoulder of the hills to the sea twenty miles away; the other way it went up Glen Shinnoch and by the upheaved flanks of the Grampians to the Great North Road, at the end of which was London, six hundred miles away.

Stephen followed that south-going road only a short distance, till he came to a rough cart-track turning uphill towards the Croft of Balmerion. He was near the end of the road now.

CHAPTER III

THE sun was swinging west and by north, filling the bowl of valley with golden light, as Stephen went up the track to the croft. He moved slowly, and was beginning to wonder if the inhospitability of the day would persist. Not with Kenny Alpin! Kenny Alpin would do to take along—anywhere. But this Ruary Farquhar, and his sister, and her red-haired daughter —how would they look upon him? The Yankee owner coming to inspect their stewardship? The Scots were a notably reserved people, and would not take a stranger—especially an owner—to their hearts. They would treat him with reserve, hiding their real feelings, whether of gratitude or hostility. He could not help that. He could stand it for a week if they could. He would stay at one of the two hotels in Knockindu, get Kenny to show him the country, get the feel of it if he could, and then make tracks for his own West. And that was that.

He came round the flank of the larch wood and saw the house in front of him up the slope. It was a wide, low, strong building of grey stone with a chimney at each gable-end, one of them smoking. There was a four-paned window at each side of the door, which was wide open, and a skylight in the roof. A house built to endure all storms and be cosy round peat fires in sternest winter. There was a low-paled garden in front showing the gleam of flowers and the tops of berry bushes. At one side was a vegetable patch thick with

54

green stuff, and back of that a short line of iron-roofed steading. A black-and-white sheep-dog slept at one side of the open door.

Stephen had halted and was about to go on when a double, ringing, scrape-and-grate made him turn head to the left. On the slope between the larches and the little torrent grew a belt of tall bracken, and on the edge of this a tall man was sharpening a straight-handled scythe with an easy swinging double stroke. He stood the scythe over shoulder, finished off with a series of swift short strokes on the curving point of the blade, felt the edge with a thumb, slipped the edging-stone into hip pocket, and began swinging into the bracken. His rhythm was perfect: the easy lifting backward swing as his feet slid forward, the smooth sweeping cut with the grating draw to it, and the turning-over flick at the end that left the bracken in an even swathe ready for turning and drying.

Stephen's mouth opened as he looked. The man was fifty yards away, just about the distance that Stephen had seen him earlier that very evening. There could be no doubt about it. The heather-mixture tweed, the long neck, the grizzled mass of hair, the beard high on the cheek—this was the cool quick man that Stephen had seen flick a salmon out of Lettoch Water two hours before. And here he was now with equal efficiency cutting bracken for winter bedding. Sure as shooting this was his caretaker, Ruary Farquhar. Once a poacher always a poacher! Who then was the gorilla that had rolled him down the slope? Light began to break. Gosh! The darn little thug——!

The garden gate clanged and Stephen faced round to it. No! That was not Kenny Alpin. This was a young woman, another young woman, the third young woman of the day. She had banged the gate smartly, and was coming straight down the slope at him, her blue skirts flickering behind her, her head up, and her red bush of hair tossing up and back from her ears. Then and always that back-throw of hair showing her ears gave the impression of a tang of clean air blowing about her head. She was one flaming good-looker, Stephen recognised at once, possibly the best-looker he had ever seen. Her cheek-bones might be too widely prominent and her chin with too much jut, but the subtle quality of beauty was there. Her eyes were the bluest of Irish blue and the angriest, and there was an angry spot of colour high on each cheek-bone.

She was fiercely angry, but also she was nervous. Stephen could see that by the twitch of her eyebrows that were darker than her hair. She came sailing directly at him, and he thought she was going to ram him straight down the slope, but she halted dead within a single pace and thrust her chin at him. She said:

"What do you want?" Her voice had a little lift at the end.

"I want Kenny Alpin," Stephen replied.

"What do you want him for?"

"I want to break his neck."

"You're not able." Her eyes flared. "He's not at home."

"Is he in hospital?"

Her eyebrows flickered again.

"He is on his way to Glasgow. Is that all you want?"

"Grilled salmon for supper."

"You'll not get it. Get out, or I'll set the dog at you."

She turned, took a stride away and hesitated. He saw her shoulders jerk as if a sudden thought had struck her. Her head turned over her shoulder and the anger was dying in her eyes.

56

"Who shall I say called?"

"Wayne," Stephen said. "Steve—Stephen Wayne."

She actually staggered as she came round. Then she pulled herself together, and her hand over her mouth smothered the exclamation she made. Instead of anger there was dismay and astonishment in her eyes.

"Holy Mother o' God!" These were the words her hand smothered, and then Stephen knew that she was half-Irish. She could be none other than the daughter of dead Liam Power, her mother Kirsty Farquhar.

"Stephen Wayne!" she whispered. "Mr Wayne?"

"Steve to you, Miss Chucker-out."

"The owner of the croft?"

"Don't hold it against me."

"But this is dreadful. I—I thought you were a gamekeeper." Her voice went up. "How can I— what can I say——?"

"Forget it," said Stephen. "I see daylight ahead. Is this Alpin coyote far on his flight to Glasgow?"

"He has not started yet," she said faintly but hopefully. This lean brown man was taking it well.

"Fine! Hale him forth and let the pleasant work begin."

"I will." The flare of battle again leaped in her eyes. "We'll break his damn neck in two places—the —the little monument!"

She swung on her heel and let forth an astonishing yell. It was one bawl of a yell with the joy of battle in it.

"Kenny—Kenny Alpin! Kenny, you hound!"

Stephen glanced aside at the tall man cutting bracken. He was not cutting bracken. He stood erect, his arm resting on the pole of the scythe, his bearded face towards them, in an easy, watchful attitude. He was a man who would not interfere in anything until the right moment.

Kenny Alpin must have been watching from a window. The girl's yell brought him tumbling out of doors and half-way down the path, where he halted suddenly to look again. There was no mistaking the short powerful figure and the black head set forward. He came on two more steps—and they were limping steps, Stephen was glad to see—halted again, struck his two hands together, yelled blue murder, and came hirpling furiously towards the gate. Hirpling is a useful Scots word, it so exactly describes a man halt in one leg and in a hurry. Kenny hirpled, and Stephen was happy to see him do it.

The black-and-white sheep-dog, roused rudely from sleep, came round and under his feet, and he fell over it. He yelled again, kicked and missed complicatedly, and the dog was a black-and-white yelp going round the house-corner. Kenny was up. He did not take time to open the gate, but half-vaulted, half-rolled over it; staggered, and came on, mostly hirpling, sometimes plain limping, once or twice hopping on one leg. Stephen and the girl waited for him grimly.

But half a dozen paces away he stopped dead. His mouth began to hang open, and he shut it to swallow with difficulty. He was looking at the bump over Stephen's left eye, at his clothes, at the rucksack peeping round his hip; and as he looked dismay flooded over his face. On his right cheek was a fresh cross of sticking-plaster. He came forward, as if pushed from behind, until he was at the girl's side, and the girl was watching him as a cat watches a mouse. He groaned, dropped his head into his hands, and moved it disconsolately from side to side.

"It couldna be!" he protested lamentably; "it could never be!"

"Couldn't it?" said the red-haired girl in bitter

58

triumph, and struck him a beautiful hand-clenched blow fair between the shoulder-blades.

He jerked forward and tried to cough his heart up; and his hands guarding his ears, he hopped actively round Stephen, who pivoted with him.

"Goad, Stevie!" he implored. "Don't let her murder me."

He caught Stephen by the jacket lapels, and Stephen gripped him in turn.

"Oh, Stephen—Stevie—Steve! Don't say it was you?" He pulled at the lapels. "Don't say it! How could it be you?"

"Look at my stove-in dome!" Stephen was shaking him. "Busted collar-blade, hip out of joint, three ribs floating loose——"

"I'm worse," Kenny shouted. "I'm a dam' sight worse, thank the lord! Spittin' blood, and my kidneys mixed up with my liver. An' look you at that and be happy."

Holding Stephen one-handed, he thrust one leg out sideways, and pulled up a trouser leg to show a shin swathed in bandage.

"Ne'er a scrap o' skin from knee to ankle—grafting it will need, and the devil mend it."

He caught Stephen again and shook him fiercely, contritely. Words poured from him from whom words poured easily.

"How was I to know?" he enquired plaintively. "How the hell was I to know? There I was behind a bush, look-out for the old codger. A hot day and all, and maybe I winked an eye once. And the next thing! A rough-clad keeper-like man with what looked like a game-bag on his back was across there on the edge of the brae, his head hidden in a stool of bracken, and he watchin' the auld lad somersault a fish out of the

Tomnon Pool. Mind you that, Steve darlin'? You had your head hidden and I could only see the back of your poll. How the hell did you get there?"

"Short-cutting over the hill."

"And how was I to know you'd be trespassing on private policies? And what ither could I do than hop you to give the auld fellow time to get away. Mind you, I meant no harm at all. Just to hold you down and give you a trundle over the brae a bittie to give me time to take cover. But the devil in you tangled on me like an eel, and off we went, striking everything once and most things twice. And mind you, doon below and you flat on your face, I didna think to give you a kick in the ribs to hold you. No' me! The nefarious auld sodger was gone, and I rolled round the corner, hoppin' two miles on one leg, my shoe full o' my ain blood, an' my ain blood chokin' me. Ay! but I deserved it. Well I deserved it. Look!" He threw up his black head and extended his flat chin. "There it is! Gie to me! One good jolt to knock my teeth loose, and most o' them loose already. Go on, Stevie! Just one."

Stephen flicked him back-handed on the chin.

"There you are. But wait till I get your back turned."

He shook Stephen almost fiercely, and his face, usually so grave, was such a mixture of feelings—relief, affection, repentance, exaltation—that Stephen had either to embrace him or laugh. He laughed. Laughter took both of them. They held on to each other and laughed and roared and thumped and laughed again.

"Stop it!" ordered a fierce whisper close to them. "Here comes Uncle Ruary."

Kenny stopped, four hooves sliding, and thrust an urgent finger under Stephen's nose.

"Hist! Stevie! my dear freen' Stevie! No' as much as a whisper or he'll run me frae here to Glasga."

"He will," said the red-haired girl, "or I will."

Kenny faced Stephen round.

"Stephen Wayne," he introduced, "this is Sheevaun Power. I'm not ready to marry her yet."

She reached Stephen her hand impulsively, and her cool fingers gripped his firmly.

"It was an awful minute, Mr Wayne," she said. "I—I was simply disgraceful. Won't you please forgive me?"

Stephen held on to her hand.

"Do you know, Miss Power," he said, "coming up the track I was thinking of cold water and ice and things, and you come along and break the ice into a thousand pieces. Do you mind if I feel at home with you two?"

"With me," she said. "Don't have anything to do with the coyote Alpin."

She smiled for the first time, and then Stephen knew that she was, indeed, some girl. It was a quiet smile, and grave and friendly, her mouth gentle, and lights moving in her eyes. Stephen felt his heart stir—for the third time that day.

"There she goes!" cried Kenny savagely. "Startin' to vamp him a'ready. Why, oh why, didn't I root him in the ribs?"

"Uncle Ruary," said Sheevaun Power over Stephen's shoulder, "this is Mr Wayne. You know? Mr Stephen Wayne."

Stephen turned to face Ruary Farquhar. He had pictured Ruary as old and squat and gnarled and secretive, but this man was very tall and lean, and his long neck, the texture of teak, was carried with a forward thrust, not combative but ruminative. He was a grizzled man, hairy to the eyes, and his eyes, small and grey, looked out thoughtfully below a bush of eyebrows whiter than his beard. Those white eyebrows gave him a benevolent look, but he did not look at all old. His wise mild eyes went thoughtfully from Stephen to Kenny and back again.

"I knew he was Mr Wayne," he said in a deep slow voice. "He is very welcome to his own place."

He greeted Stephen with a courteous inclination of the head and a slow lift of a big hand, big-thumbed. He made no movement to shake hands, but when Stephen reached out his he took it firmly. His hand was hard and dry as a countryman's should be.

"We werena expectin' you a day or two, Mr Wayne," he said, "but you are very welcome."

"Why the hell shouldn't he be welcome, you hairy auld atavism?" cried the irrepressible Kenny. "Didn't Sheevaun and myself give him the warmest welcome in the world?"

"Warm is right," agreed Stephen.

The red-haired girl chuckled behind him, and Kenny's hand went to his mouth.

"Keep your flannen mouth shut, Alpin," he warned himself.

Ruary Farquhar moved a thumb sidewards.

"My sister Kirsty is up at the house, Mr Wayne. We could be looking over the place after a cup o' tea."

"Ay! let's up and see Aunt Kirsty," said Kenny.

"She is not your aunt," said Sheevaun.

"She might be nearer if I'm not dam' careful," said Kenny.

"Dinna mind yon pair, Mr Wayne," said Ruary. "They haver even on. Come away up to the house."

They went up the slope together. Stephen heard a scuffle behind and glanced back to see Sheevaun hold-

ing Kenny by both ears and shaking his head back and
forth. He let his head swing easily under her hands,
and in a detached sort of way caught a fistful of her red
hair and let it slip untugged through his fingers;
whereat she thrust him off furiously and turned her
back on him.

Ruary and Stephen went slowly, pausing to look over
the ground and going on again. The sun, turned
orange, was in the notch between the Little Kinmaol
and the conical wooded hill, and all the valley was
strange and beautiful and a little sad in the orange glow.

"I should have minded to thank you for letting me
take care o' this place for you," Ruary said. "It was
gey good of you, Mr Wayne, and I'm no' forgetting it."
He gestured a hand. "It is a good place. All them bit
fields in the drystone walls both sides o' the burnie—
twenty-three acres o' good enough grass——"

"All grass?"

"Ay! Sheep I'm running—crossbreds. Just the a'e
cow for milk and butter. I did well by the lambs this
spring and summer, and wool is rising. I'll pay a
dividend the end o' the year."

A black wide small cow with upstanding horns was
grazing in one of the small fields, but there were no
sheep.

"I'm giving the grass a rest this month," Ruary
explained. "The sheep are up in the heather above
the pine woodie. Good pickings up there about the
head o' the burnie—two hundred acres."

"How do you winter-feed?" enquired the ranchman
who knew something about sheep.

"Ay—ay!" Ruary nodded approvingly. "This is
good grass-land—short and sweet—but gey thin in the
sole for tillage. It might grow a crop o' rye, but rye
tak's the heart out o' land, and I wouldna do the likes

63

by your place. I've a field o' neeps bespoke from a feuar in Knockindu yonder, and I've taken all the laird's hay except what he needs for the pony."

"Who is the laird?" Stephen enquired.

"Alasdair MacFinlay—MacFinlay of Castle Charles."

"The big house over the hill?"

"Ay! But that big house is not his any longer. He lives yon, in Lettoch Lodge." He turned and pointed to the L-shaped house in the clump of trees across the valley.

"A thin man in a kilt?"

"That's him. That crook in your hand I cut and carved for Miss Marian, his daughter."

Stephen was surprised. He lifted the crook and looked at the head of it. It was well carved.

"A short loan," he said. "It goes back with the milk."

"Just that! I noticed you had a bit limp, Mr Wayne." He nodded his head approvingly, for he was a man who approved a certain reticence.

Stephen smiled. Ruary was the perfection of law-abiding crofter, the efficient steward, careful of his employer's talent, the sedate shepherd-like man who knew not that salmon rest head upstream waiting for the spawning urge. Stephen smiled again.

"I got a message for you this afternoon, Mr Farquhar," he said.

The quiet and thoughtful eyes considered him.

"The gents were shooting the Corryhow moors to-day," said Stephen and waited.

"There was shootin' that airt," agreed Ruary.

"To-morrow, they—these mysterious gents—will be shooting the Caiplich—that right? Yes! the Caiplich Moor, and the river will not be safe in that reach—no' safe at all. That's it."

64

"Goad, Ruary!" said Kenny's voice close behind. "He arrived before he started."

Ruary did not flicker an eye.

"The poor dottled auld Erchie!" he said. "He put you the short-cut over the hill?"

"I was put another short-cut as well," said Stephen, and Kenny prodded him in the small of the back.

They entered the garden gate, and the black-and-white sheep-dog came round the corner to smell at Stephen's legs. It seemed satisfied, and moved into the berry bushes out of Kenny's way.

Inside the front door a narrow passage ran right and left, with a door at each end. The passage was made narrower by a steep stair against the wall, and under the stair-head was a third door. The cottage was the usual type in all North-east Scotland—the "But-and-Ben" type. The "But" was the kitchen-living-room, and the "Ben" the parlour-bedroom. The small room between, called the "closet," was also a bedroom. A garret filled the whole cavity of the roof, and in large families was the boys' dormitory.

The pleasant flavour of peat was almost too strong until one got used to it. The door on the right led into the kitchen-living-room, a wide room with a ceiling not more than eight feet from the flagged floor. In this cottage it was used entirely as a living-room, for Stephen's grand-uncle had built a lean-to back-kitchen off it. There was a mat carpet on the flagged floor, and a bright rag-rug before the open hearth, on which a few peats were beginning to flame. It had been a warm August day, but Highland nights begin to sharpen an edge in autumn. The wall was papered in brown, and there were framed pictures, mostly old prints, and one engraving of Robert Burns that had captured the limpid heart-breaking qualities of the poet's eyes.

There was a dresser of delf—brown and willow-blue—and an old bureau topped with a glass-fronted press, full of books. There was a big settee, chintz-covered, by the hearth, and two eared armchairs. At mid-floor was a rectangular table laid for supper, and fully laid, with a fresh white cloth and all the modern implements. There was a brown loaf, and plates of scones, and a platter heaped with curved brown oatcakes. And to Stephen's nose came the fragrance that apprised him of his emptiness. His nose crinkled. There was fish cooking somewhere.

That was a fine friendly room. In a Scots winter with the fire blazing it would be a supremely cosy room.

"Kirsty!" Ruary did not raise his voice.

His sister appeared in the doorway of the back-kitchen. She had washed and dried her hands and was smoothing them one over the other. She came directly, and without pause, and shook Stephen by the hand, her eyes full on him.

"This is Mr Wayne, the proprietor," she said quietly.

"Keekin' through the window, auntie!" cried Kenny. "Aren't we grand! A new cloth on, and fish knives and forks. A high tea—I can smell it."

"Quiet, child!" said Kirsty Power. "You are welcome to your own house, Mr Wayne."

Her voice was Highland, but her English was perfect. Ruary and Kenny and Sheevaun, for the sake of emphasis and even sentiment, often used the Scots word or phrase. Kirsty never did.

She was as tall for a woman as her brother for a man, but whereas her brother was lean she was gaunt; but she was bonily gaunt, not frail; and though not as old by many years, she looked older than her brother. Her white hair drawn tight behind her ears made her look even gaunter, more austere. But the bones of her face were well shaped, and her grey eyes were big and wide-set, and though now hollow-set were still lustrous. She must have been more than good-looking in her youth. Perhaps her eyes were too lustrous. Stephen had never seen eyes like hers except in one given overmuch to religion or to a cause, to some inner or outer fanaticism. Well, she had lost her young Irishman tragically in an Irish rising, and her daughter had been born three months later. Kenny had told him that, and also that she had gone queer in the head for a while. She was not queer now, but the storm might have left some inner wreckage.

"Ruary, tea is ready," she said. "Mr Wayne might like to wash."

Ruary led into the back-kitchen, which was also a pantry and scullery, with stocked shelves, a running-water sink, and a paraffin cooker. He opened a door on the left and showed Stephen into no less than a bathroom.

"Our one bit luxury," he said diffidently. "The women like it. I built it on myself this spring."

"I haven't got the bill yet," Stephen hinted.

"Hoots! the least I could do. I piped the water down from the hill, and got a geyser second-hand fra' the laird when they put in the hot circulation. Guid spring water and you can drink it—or mix it with the drappie. It's fine for the tea, only hard on the kettle because of the lime in it."

They had a high tea, as Kenny promised. A high tea is the one typical Scots meal. Tea, scones, oatcakes, and preserves, but it is the one extra dish that makes it high—rashers and eggs, sausages, finnan haddie, something savoury to use a fork on. Stephen, in ten days, had learned to abjure Scots coffee—the wash they call coffee—and he had not yet got used to tea. Kirsty

Power made good tea, with a kick to it. Her Irishman had taught her that, for Ireland is the tea-drinking nation. The Scots usually make their tea with barely enough strength to get up the spout. Not so Kirsty.

Ruary said the long Scots grace solemnly, and Kirsty placed her hot fragrant high-dish under Stephen's down-bent nose. It was a thick middle steak of grilled salmon—salmon so fresh that the white curd showed between the flakes. He looked across at Sheevaun Power, and her face crinkled.

"Grilled salmon as per order," she said.

The two of them laughed together. She looked at Kenny and laughed the more. Stephen looked at Ruary, the man of law-abiding probity, and laughed with her.

"Weel! weel!" said Ruary equably, and reached for an oatcake. Oatcake and salmon! Why not?

Kenny slapped the table furiously, making cups rattle.

"There they go!" he cried. "What did I tell ye? They ha'e something atween 'em a'ready—something to laugh at atween themselves an' we out in the cauld. Why the hell didn't I root him in the ribs?"

"Take your tea, boy," Kirsty chided him, putting a plate over his shoulder and looking at Stephen. "Kenneth is a nice boy, Mr Wayne, but he thinks to hide his feelings by saying in extravagance what he mostly means."

That was so astonishingly true that Stephen opened his eyes. It was too frank also. Could it be that the small lack of balance in her mind heeled over sometimes into devastating frankness and uncanny awareness? Kenny's dark face flushed.

"Don't you give my secrets away, Aunt Kirsty," he murmured.

"Fill your mouth, you poor mutt," growled Shee-vaun. They had a habit of growling at each other.

"I dinna understand it at all," said Ruary, shaking his head.

"What don't you understand, great hairyness?" enquired Kenny in his folly.

"What time you had a chance to kick Mr Wayne in the ribs—or was it over the left e'e?"

"Goad! I'm afraid to open my mouth."

But it was open, and Sheevaun, at his side, smartly thrust a fragment of scone into the opening. He was about to eject it rudely, but had a second thought and supported it with a smoking forkful of salmon, chewing furiously, and his fierce eyes going about the table. Then he swallowed hurriedly and grinned at Stephen.

"A hell of a gay time we are going to have in the Croft o' Balmerion, Stevie, my son," he said happily.

That brought a thought into Stephen's mind and he looked round the walls of the room.

"Where do you keep your 'phone?" he enquired.

There was no 'phone. There might be one at Castle Charles and half a score in the village.

"I want to engage a room at the hotel," said Stephen.

"This is your own house, Mr Wayne," said Kirsty, "and you will stay in it. There are two beds in the attic, and Kenneth can take the camp one."

"Kenneth'll ha'e to, an' be damn'd to him!" said Kenny.

"Indeed maybe you would be more comfortable in the hotel," said Ruary hesitatingly, "but you'll be welcome——"

"Why the blazes wouldn't he be welcome?" exploded Kenny.

"Mr Wayne will stay," said Kirsty definitely. "You two young men want to be with each other."

69

So it was finally arranged, and one of Stephen's plans went by the board.

After supper the two women washed up in the back-kitchen, and then went up to refix the attic. The men sat round the fire and talked and smoked. Ruary put on some fresh peats, and as the gloom deepened the twisting, licking, whispering tongues of soft peat flame cast a ruddy heartening glow and dancing shadows on walls and ceiling. Stephen Wayne relaxed. He forgot the inhospitabilities of the day. He felt at home. This was like a super-bunkhouse in the West with three friendly men talking about the fire, only the fire was not wood. He could stand a week of this, and he would try and ignore women, even a red-haired one sleeping under the same roof.

When the women returned, the older one said:

"Men like to sit in the dark."

Perhaps she did not like to sit in the dark with her memories, for she, forthwith, lit a paraffin-gas lamp that cast a white glow. The room was still cosy but not so heart-easy as in the glow of the peats.

And after a time Ruary set glasses on the table and brought forth a black bottle of the famous local Glen Lettoch whisky, just for a welcoming drink he said. The men had one, the ladies none, and after some time Stephen found himself stifling a yawn. He had had a long day, with a few knocks thrown in, and he yawned again. Kirsty noticed and ordered him to bed.

But before going to bed, the men, as was the immemorial custom in the Highlands, went out to look at the night.

A fine night in August under a sky of stars, as silent as his own West but not as empty. The bowl of the valley hollowed out below them, not dark, not light, yet with a diffusion of light that trebled depth and distance.

Knockindu, that seemed miles away, was picked out by points of orange light; the conical hill northwards was a strong black peak against the sky where a white glow still lingered; across the valley where a late moon was behind the hills the rounded summits made a dark silhouette and marched southwards, and grew dimmer as they went. Peace was over all that quiet land. No dog barked, no owl hooted, no moor-cock crowed, no breath of air stirred in the pines; no coyote had ever wailed in this land, though not so long ago wolves had howled.

A man, a race would grow attached to this place. It was a land where men might survive. War might shatter Europe and most of Britain, but in secluded places like this life might still go on, and an old culture renew itself and send out offshoots to found a new world as it had done before, when the cities were shattered and decayed, and heresies troubled the remnant of men.

The attic was a long, low-shouldered room with a skylight and an end window. Stephen's white-sheeted bed was at one side of this window, and Kenny's camp-bed away at the far end. Kenny looked from one to the other and shook his head.

"I haven't started to talk yet," he said, "but Kirsty means you to sleep the night. To-morrow night we'll pull 'em cheek by jowl, and I'll be listenin' to you."

Yet Kenny had to talk a little the length of the room, and Stephen did not know when he stopped. Once he heard him swear and thump his pillow, and in no time at all after that he was waked by a cock—not a barn-door cock but a cock-grouse—saying angrily, "Get up! Quick! Be quick!" It was early morning, and he turned over and went to sleep again.

Stephen Wayne was settled in on his own croft.

CHAPTER IV

STEPHEN WAYNE came out into the morning and swallowed mouthfuls of clean air. Presently he would top the air off with a platter of home-ground porridge, creamy milk, two eggs, buttered-toast, marmalade, and strong tea. But the air wasn't bad to start with.

Stephen had already been a week at Balmerion and felt entirely at home. The four people of the croft liked him. He had not thrown his weight about. He did not ask to be shown things, and then compare them, to their detriment, with things he had known. He did not try to be the generous overlord. He was just a plain American man on a visit to the Old Country and quietly enjoying the simple life. And below his quietness and pleasantness his hosts sensed a force that he could draw on to meet an occasion. There was something incalculable about him, and that interested them, something that might break away from the conventions they were used to and go its own debonair, daredevil road.

It had been a pleasant week, without adventures. Kenny and he, thick as thieves, had explored Glen Shinnoch; Sheevaun and he had climbed the big Ben and looked over ten counties; but he had not yet gone poaching with Ruary Farquhar. They had had grouse and rabbits off their own ground, but no more salmon, and not a scrap of venison though the season had opened. Ruary was the God-fearing crofter subservient to the game laws, and Stephen sometimes wondered if he had been the lad driven out of Glen Shinnoch who never hesitated to take toll from the powers that had driven him. Stephen had gone to church with Kirsty on Sunday. She was a Calvinist, but was so loyal to her dead Irishman that his daughter had been brought up a Catholic to the risk of hell's fire.

Another warm day was promised. All that August had been warm and dry, with heavy dews at night and a clear sky all the long day. The whole valley sparkled in the dew this morning; one band of cloud, fine as pearl, circled the conical hill northwards; and a thin veil of mist lay along the course of the Lettoch, with Falcon Crag standing up stark and clear above it. In all the folded breasts of the hills grew woods of pine, and over the shoulder of a hill across the valley a brown road made a curving ribbon. Beyond Knockindu, where the valley widened, a grey old ruin stood on a green mound under a slope of hill rich in bloomed heather: an old Gordon stronghold where Mary Queen of Scots had stayed when she won over the Highlands to the Stuarts for all time.

Kenny Alpin and Sheevaun Power were already out of doors. Sheevaun wore blue slacks and a green pull-over, and her toss of hair on top looked astonishingly red. She was armed with a two-pronged fork, and was scattering piles of bracken to dry in the sun. Kenny, his strong, brown, black-filmed arms bare to the shoulder, was scything ripe bracken with skilful rhythm. They had been neglecting the bracken, and a good pile of it would be required for winter bedding, and later for the lambing. Stephen strolled across to the work-party.

"Glad you came," growled Kenny. "She is abusing me."

The two did spend their time in skirmishing; why,

Stephen was not sure. They gave and took no quarter, and were as frank as daylight. Sometimes they were almost rancorous.

"What are you fighting about on a gay morning?" Stephen wondered.

Kenny cut a couple of furious swathes, and stood the scythe on its point for edging. After a few double sweeps of the stone he stopped and looked up at Stephen.

"I was just wondering if I ought to marry her at all."

"Don't," said Stephen. "I might want to marry her myself—only I'm afraid."

"Of me?"

"Of her."

"That's right. She's a bluidy Tartar."

Sheevaun drove the prongs of the fork into the ground and rested her chin on her hands folded over the grip. Her red hair, the white flame of her warrior face, the blue flame of her eyes, made Stephen's heart queerly hollow for a moment. He was honestly getting afraid of her.

"Well, Stephen!" she said. "Why don't you try making love to me?"

"I'll buy that," Stephen said. "How do I begin?"

She seemed to muse over that, and then moved her jut of chin sideways and back on her hands.

"No, Stephen darling! Americans either make love or they don't. You don't." She looked down at Kenny. "That fellow there, he's no damn'd good."

"At love-making?"

"No. He's no good."

"Sure! Go over a few of his bad points for me. I know only a baker's dozen."

Kenny grunted and began sharpening the scythe. She continued to look at him, her dark eyebrows in a pucker; and Stephen knew that she was more serious than she wanted him to think.

"Look at him! The smooth, lying, secret, smug face of him hiding the years. He's thirty-five if he's a day, and he has been earning good money for years; but at this minute he hasn't a bawbee to bless himself with. He spends his money on drink and books and touchers —worse things maybe. And he talks of marrying—he talks of marrying me—as if he meant it. He will never have a roof to put over any woman's head. That's poor auld Kenny Alpin, last year with a job, now free-lance journalist, hack-writer at the end, with the manuscript of a book in his bottom drawer."

Her voice was smooth and deep, without its usual lift, but Stephen got the impression that she kept it so to avoid being bitter.

"She got out o' bed the wrong side this morning," said Kenny with extraordinary mildness. "I was dam' foolish to start the war. When her temper is up, Stevie, don't you turn your back to her if you want to save your face."

He turned his back to her and cut smoothly into the bank of bracken. But though her hands tightened on the fork handle she only said, "Bah!"

"You rank him too high, Sheevaun," said Stephen. "Even if he had a roof-tree, where would he find a head?"

"The poor mutt! He'll get someone to take pity on him. He's the marrying kind, Kenny."

"That's true for you," agreed Kenny. "When I have a roof-tree I'll astonish the daylights out of you, Sheevaun."

"You will not. My hair will be dirty white then, and grandchildren about my knees."

"I don't care a dam'," said Kenny. "Grandchildren and all—forty o' them—I'll pop you under my roof-tree. Say, Stevie, can you swing a scythe?"

"No—yes! You make it look easy."

"Try it?"

Sheevaun went back to her bracken-tossing, and Stephen tried scything. It was not so easy, he found. The technique is simple enough but demands exactness. The beginner blunts his edge, digs his point, and the grass or bracken slides away from or under his blade.

"The draw in time with the swing as does it," Kenny said. "Wait for the feel of it, this way."

In a quarter-hour Stephen was making the bracken fronds tumble, and was pleased with the pleasant crunch he was making.

"Bracken's easy," said Kenny. "I'll try you out on grass for the coo after breakfast, and you'll rather ate it. See if you can put an edge on without losing a finger."

Stephen was getting warm when Ruary came off the hill, his dog at his heels. He had been up above the pine belt looking over his sheep. He had a fowling-piece under an arm, and a brace of cock-grouse hanging, wings wide, from a hand.

"Them twa has been waukenin' me the last week," he said. "We ha'e too many cocks onyway for our bit ground."

He dropped them at his feet, broke the gun to make sure it was empty, handed it to Sheevaun, and took the fork from her. She went up the rise to the house to give the porridge a last stir, and Kenny, smoking his first cigarette, kept an eye on Stephen.

The gaunt figure of Kirsty Power came round the corner of the larch belt. A small milk-can was swinging emptily at her side. For two mornings now she had taken the milk across to Lettoch Lodge, because the servant-lad over there had been lured away to the seasonal grouse-beating at Castle Charles by the offer of ten shillings a day and grub pile. She came across and spoke to her brother.

"Ruary, Maggie Donald the housekeeper wants to know if you can find a boy to take Sandy's place till he comes back from the beating. You might know someone?"

Ruary shook his head.

"No' a chance, Kirsty. Every lad in Knockindu is out on the moors."

"The lawn is in a state," said Kirsty, "and Miss Marian trying to cut it herself, and that wicked pony of the laird's is kicking the partition into the harness-room."

"Would I do, auntie?" enquired Kenny. "Marian Finlay is a bonny girl."

"She has her looks," said Kirsty, "but they are not blossomed yet." She moved up towards the house, and remembering something else, spoke over her shoulder to no one in particular. "Miss Marian is wondering if that crook you made for her is lying about anywhere?"

Stephen looked at Ruary, who said carelessly:

"It might be. I'll ha'e a look."

Stephen had forgotten about that crook the girl had loaned him a week ago; that showed that she had not stayed in his mind. She was a shapely, good-looking girl even if under some shadow, but at this moment Sheevaun Power was more in his mind than any girl he had ever known. But that was not saying a great deal.

Early that evening Stephen Wayne took the crook and the milk across to Lettoch Lodge. He was not interested in his errand. Part of the way he smoked, and part of the way he whistled, the warm sunlight about him, the dark green woods asleep in the hill folds, and the grave colour of the heather glooming and restful on the brown breasts of the moors.

Lettoch Lodge was built on a big knoll above the river. The top of the knoll might cover an acre trending gently in all directions to a belt of deciduous trees—beech and ash—circling the slope to the base. A narrow motor road wound down the slope, along the river to the flying-bridge, and turned off to join the main road. As Stephen mounted the slope he noted that the beds of bracken under the ashes had not been touched with scythe.

The L-shaped Lodge was single-storied, old, and massively built, the walls of uncut granite blocks, the roof of thick grey slate, and the chimneys short and squat. It had been built in the eighteenth century as a dowager house to Castle Charles, and that explained the bridge and track across the hill to the castle. Some improver had enlarged the original small square windows into tall ones, and these were incongruously framed in brown sandstone. Before the long leg of the L a green lawn, scattered with a few flower-beds, spread to the trees. The grass was good lawn grass but needed cutting badly. A fraction of it had been cut, and a man-power lawn-mower squatted forlornly before a particularly thick patch. Across a cobbled yard from the short-leg of the house was a modern stable, and back of that a walled garden.

Marian Finlay sat on a bench under the one wide cypress tree growing in the middle of the lawn. She sat forward, her hands in her lap, and she looked as forlorn as the lawn-mower. Forlorn was the word—forlorn and captive. Somehow the house itself was forlorn. Squatting there in the still sunlight, surrounded by its belt of trees, it was secluded, secretive, almost gloomy. Marian was the girl's name, and she brought Tennyson's poem to Stephen's mind: "Mariana in the Moated Grange."

> "She only said, ' My life is dreary,
>   He cometh not,' she said;
> She said, ' I am aweary, aweary,
>   I would that I were dead!'"

Who would come? Who would not come? Stephen was coming now, and he would lift some of the gloom or break a bone.

He walked across the thick felt of grass, the milk-pail swinging so that a small trickle came out under the lid. When the girl lifted her eyes he set the crook to the ground and assumed an exaggerated limp. She did not smile. Her face was a little flushed as if she had been running the lawn-mower; that flush of colour, her brown eyes, and her fresh unpainted lips made her attractive.

"I am sorry," she said. "I did not know you needed the crook."

"My excuse was a lame one," he said, and her lips twitched, not quite into a smile. "I am the boy with the milk," he went on. "I hear you are wanting a lad about the place?"

"Does Ruary Farquhar know of one?"

"Would I do?"

He was standing before her, and she coolly looked him up and down. He was in old flannel slacks and canvas shoes, his shirt open at the neck under a rough tweed jacket, and his hair tousled as usual. But her eyes did not go as far as the brown hard-bitten face with the daredevil gleam in the grey eyes. She shook her head but said nothing.

"Samples of work supplied but no references—don't

use 'em out of Sing-Sing. The lawn cut, bracken saved for the pony's bedding—and I'll sure tame that pony——"

"You could do nothing with that pony."

"I would love to try."

"Only my father can go near it."

"Your father is a horseman?"

"No. But the pony will not be ridden by anyone else."

"I'll try him out. No? Right. But you will let me show you a sample of what I can do? Watch this."

This is what he had been leading up to. He had no intention of working at the Lodge, but merely wanted an excuse to give the girl a spell on the lawn.

He laid the crook and pail on the bench and took hold of the lawn-mower. At the first movement it squealed for oil. Also the mouth of it was too wide, and tore and bruised the grass rather than cut it. Stephen ran it up and down by sheer force, and stopped to shake his head at it. The girl said:

"In the Highlands a visitor must take a turn at any work in hand. That will be quite enough, thank you."

Stephen picked up the milk-pail and went round the corner of the house to the working premises. He knocked on the kitchen door, and a cheerful woman's voice called:

"Come ben."

He entered a big flagged kitchen—big enough for a small hotel. There were an old-fashioned range, many old-fashioned cupboards, shining tins giving a cheerful note, a table scrubbed white, and many good old Windsor chairs. And the presiding genius was a stout, white-haired, black-gowned old lady who smiled at him amongst several chins.

"Oh ay!" she said.   "You'll be the Yankee man west at Ruary's."

"The pay is none too good," said Stephen.   "I'm looking for another job."

"Awa', sonnie!   You and that chiel Alpin havena done a stroke of work the hale week."

"Just starting.   Where could I get an oil-can and a wrench?"

"Is it Ruary wants 'em?   Across in the toolshed if they're anywhere."   She came to the door and pointed. "Yon doorie, and dinna open the one right o't or the shelt might kick you heel ower tip.   Come back an' ha'e a crack."

The toolshed had once been a harness-room, and a bridle and an old saddle still hung on the wall.   There was an open set of steps leading to an attic used as a sleeping-place for the servant-lad.   There was a door leading into the stable, and Stephen opened it carefully and peeped in.   Just as well that he was careful.   A beast snorted, hooves rattled on cobbles, and hooves cracked on the partition close to the door.   Stephen shut it hastily.   He got a glimpse of a thick cob of a bay pony not quite as tall as a cow pony.

"I might take a whirl at you one day," Stephen said.

He foraged round and found a bicycle-wrench and a can with some oil in it.   He took them round to the lawn-mower.   The tall girl was leaning on the handle, looking desolately over the strip that had been cut and the back-aching spread still to cut.

"Big as an ocean, ain't it?" said Stephen.

"Hard on the hands too," she said, looking at her palms.

"Spit on 'em!   That helps.   Let's tune the engine up first."

He did not know much about lawn-mowers, but he

81

knew some about machinery, and after examination decided that by loosening a pair of nuts and tightening another pair he could get the sole plate into closer contact with the spiral blades. He applied force and some cursing, and then some oil and more force and more cursing, and a barking of knuckles, to those rusted-in nuts, and finally got a turn out of them.

"If I bust the blame thing," he said, "we'll have an excuse to grow hay."

"An excuse is all I want," she admitted.

"That's queer too. We must have an excuse or perish."

After some nice adjustment he got the sole plate to brush the blades, and tightened it up. Then he poured oil into every hole and crevice and cog, and gave a thrust to the handle. The gallant old machine purred hungrily.

"Stand out from under!" he cried. "Sit you down, Miss Finlay, and relax. Here we go!"

It was a great old machine and repaid the attention. It purred and growled and gulped, and the clean-cut grass curved over in a thick spray. There was no grass-holder. Stephen never let up for a whole hour except to shed his jacket and fold up his shirt-sleeves; the girl sat leaning on her hands and watched him, and after a while she sat back against the cypress trunk and relaxed. At the end of an hour there was left only a narrow straight ribbon twice the width of the cutter. Then Stephen paused, and the girl came across the lawn to him.

"That was splendid of you," she said, and she smiled frankly to him that time.

"Take a turn," he invited, wiping the handle with a tuft.

"Goodness! How did you know my mouth was watering?"

She was no weakling. She had free arm action and a fine drive in her long thighs. She made the machine roar to a finish, and brought it back upside-down on a free wheel. Her delicate nostrils were inflating nicely and her brown eyes glistened.

"This is easy," she said. "Wonder young Sandy never thought of that?"

"Or young Marian Finlay? We should rake that grass, shouldn't we?"

"Please, no! I want something to take—I want something to do." She was going to say, something to take her mind off something. She added quickly, "Would you like some tea?" and glanced hesitatingly towards the front door massively ajar at the head of two granite steps. That was the gentleman's entrance, and Stephen knew what was in her mind.

"Little county snob!" he said to himself. Aloud he said:

"What is your housekeeper's name — Mac— Mac——?"

"Maggie—Mrs Donald."

"She wants to ha'e a crack wi' me," he said, picking up his jacket. He looked back at her over his shoulder. "S'mother day you might smile again for a fellow. You can, all right."

Maggie Donald was scouring the milk-pail at the kitchen sink.

"Sit ye doon, lad," she said. "Did you find them?"

"Didn't you hear the air-plane?"

"Losh me! Whaur?" She waddled towards the back door, her hands dripping. Stephen stopped her.

"That was I—I mean that was me cutting the lawn with a mower like an eagle."

"Eh, man! Did you give Miss Marian a haun'? I'm that pleased. But no' all of it?"

"Between us we did it—every darn blade."

"Guidness! Sandy MacRae wad take the round o' the day to it. You'll need a cuppie o' tay efther that. I've the kettle on."

"Such has been suggested," said Stephen, drawing a Windsor chair well away from the hot range.

Maggie Donald was one natural talker, a gossip of renown, and an expert questioner. Here was a fresh victim, and she proceeded to wring him dry in her own approved fashion. First of all she would sweeten him up by supplying a little innocuous information, and gradually work up to his past life and future intentions. Her handicap was that she liked to hear herself talk, and sometimes gave more information than she wanted to—and got less.

She waddled actively between range and table, and her smooth flexible Doric voice made language easy.

"Och! Puir Miss Marian, young and all, and no young people about her. Avoidin' people she is, puir lassie, and she tryin' to keep the laird out o' the way o' seein' folk." She touched her own solid head. "Nothin' bad, you ken! Juist the memory failin' on him, and he like a child betimes——"

She would have given Stephen the history of the virtues and disasters of the MacFinlay, if an inner door had not opened and Marian Finlay come strolling easily into the kitchen. The girl was a lady and knew that she must not let this young man go away cold-shouldered. Stephen rose to his feet. She noted that too. She gestured him down and moved across to the table.

"I'll have a cup too, Maggie," she said.

"I was takin' a cup through for yourself and the laird, Miss Marian."

"No need. Dad is still asleep."

With a youthful hop she lifted herself on to the table and sat with her legs swinging. Fine clean slim legs from ankle to knee, and her thighs under a thin skirt were finely moulded. A wine-coloured pullover outlined her blossoming woman's figure. She rested on her palms and swung her legs lazily. She was no longer detached or tense. That was only natural. Here in the kitchen of her own house she would be at home. Stephen, if he only knew, was on territory in which no man has an advantage. He was in the one real domain of woman, and these two, like an old female spider and a young one, could suck him dry if they wanted to. The young one looked him over calmly and said:

"You are an American, Mr ——? I didn't get your name."

"Wayne—Stephen Wayne—Steve to his friends."

"Stephen Wayne! That is Irish, isn't it?"

"Might be—or Welsh—thought it was Yorkshire—true-blooded American, in short."

"Holidaying?"

"On the cheap. Sort of a working-hike through Scotland."

"You did your week's work the day, my lad," said Maggie Donald.

"Ain't I getting my tea for it?" said Stephen.

The girl started and flushed, and her legs stopped swinging. That darn heart of his told him that flushing suited her. She was embarrassed, and stammered:

"Should I—ought I to offer——?"

"Forget it," said Stephen hurriedly. "Fathead remark! Don't let us embarrass each other."

"Of course, I knew," she said with relief.

They had tea then. The buttered scones were perfect, but the tea was weak. The only good tea Stephen struck in Scotland was Kirsty Power's. After tea he produced a pack of American cigarettes and offered them to the ladies.

"Awa', sonnie!" said Maggie. "What do you tak' me for? You take one, lassie! I ken fine you smoke a fag or twa in your ain room."

Stephen held a match for her, but the first mouthful of smoke made her cough.

"Not used to our blend," he said. "Throw it in the fire."

She did not, being Scots. She took a soft draw now and then, and blew the smoke expertly in a thin stream. Stephen left the pack on the table.

"You are not a city man?" she hinted, her eyes on and away from his brown face.

"Five thousand miles from here—as far from New York as you are. Headwaters of the Missouri. I ride broncs—hosses. I'll ride your pony."

"You winna," said Maggie Donald. "Mind the lad Forbes, Tomintoul way, Miss Marian?"

"He cost me ten pounds," said Miss Marian sadly.

"He did that, the loon. He wa'd ride the shelt. A'e collar-bone, three ribs, an' a piece out of him whaur he could afford it. Nane'll ride that pony but the laird while I'm about, and I'm tellin' you that, Stephen Wayne."

"Ten pounds is a lot of money. Do I get it if I ride him?"

Marian laughed—a pleasant chuckling laugh.

"Only for hospital expenses," she said. "You'll keep away from our pony."

A door banged somewhere in the house, and Marian Finlay started; and the start took her off the table and moving towards the passage door.

"Dad had a fine long sleep," she said. Her face had again gone serious. Again she was a stranger to

Stephen Wayne. But she remembered to turn from the door.

"Thank you, Mr Wayne," she said. "I'll be able to hold that lawn down now."

Stephen went across to the sink and picked up his pail.

"My evening chores await me," he said.

"Ay so! You'll be stayin' a whilie longer at the croft?" hinted Maggie.

"Long enough to give the lawn another run-over," said Stephen.

He went then. He would not allow Maggie to pump him, and he had no wish to pump Maggie. But, all the same, he had taken Marian Finlay out of her gloom for a brief while. He did not flatter himself. He was not sacrificing himself in the least. She was one nice girl when her face lit in a smile, and that damn'd heart of his knew it.

CHAPTER V

STEPHEN and Ruary went up Glen Shinnoch with a packet of sandwiches—twelve winding miles of glen before it lifts over a brae to splay out into the Moors of A'onside. The Lettoch Water wound its way down the hollow. The strath carried a felt of sound herbage, but was not a quarter grazed except in its lower reaches. The wiry brown seed-heads stood out of the yellowing grass, and a good crop of hay could be cut anywhere. In many places the heather was already encroaching on the grass, and there were traces of rabbit everywhere.

All up the glen there were ruined walls—somewheres in clusters—that had once been walls of human dwellings. Within living memory that glen and scores of glens like it had bred a race not excelled by any race in Europe, a race with a very ancient culture that lived adequately, spiritually and materially. Now that breed was scattered on the face of the earth, with Australia, New Zealand, Canada, the States richer for the scattering; and the domain of the clans was a sheep-run, a rabbit-warren, a grouse-moor, a deer-forest, a preserved recreation ground for wealthy southlanders and foreigners. This glen, where music had been played and stories told, and love made, and claymores drawn, was empty between stern walls and under staring sky. There might be a shepherd with his dogs, a keeper, a ghillie, a forester, but there were no women's voices, and no children. There were scattered sheep and crouching coney, black grouse and hoodie crows, red deer and peregrine falcon—and a golden eagle hanging high in the air over all.

But the water still ran, and the free air blew, and the land waited. Perhaps, when the civilisation that had gathered men into cities and evolved wars for its own destruction had vanished off the earth, the old civilisation might rise again in the glens. Such was the hope of men like Ruary Farquhar and Kenny Alpin.

Ruary Farquhar was getting keen on sheep. He thought he could do well by sheep, and was already negotiating with the Factor of the new owner of Castle Charles for a sheep-run at the top end of the glen fenced off from the deer-forest—actually the land that his forefathers had occupied under clan tenure. Stephen and he walked up there to look over the ground. Stephen could walk like a hillman now, and seldom thought of a horse between his knees. They took a trout-rod and a rifle with them. The trout-fishing— not the salmon—was free in the glen, and Ruary could slaughter all the rabbits he wanted to.

"That's not a rabbit rifle," Stephen said when he saw it.

"You never saw a glen rabbit," hinted Kenny. "They often grow horns."

Kenny was not going with them. He and Sheevaun were off to play golf on the sea links at mouth of Spey.

The rifle was an old sporting one of ·450 calibre, a deer-stalker's weapon with a flat trajectory. But Ruary expressed no intention of going after red deer, not with Castle Charles occupied and stalkers out on the hill.

"We might ha'e our bit o' sport at sittin' rabbits coming hame in the gloamin'," he said casually.

So the two men went up the glen and looked over the old Farquhar lands. The walls of the house wherein Ruary had been born were still standing, but inside was only a mass of rubble and broken slates. There was not even the stale smell of old soot. Ruary pointed out where the old fields had been, and the curved ridges across the pasture where the last corn crop had grown.

"I cut it my ain self with the scythe," he said. "That was sound land then, and you can see the heather coming in on it now."

He spoke without any emotion, and there was no bitterness in his face. A man of firm temper, he would not cry over any spilt milk, but would refill the can in his own way.

Having looked over the wired-in land—sheep and deer do not mix well—they tried a little fishing in the headwaters of the Lettoch, but the water was too low and the sky too clear for any luck. Early in the afternoon they faced down the glen, the long evening before them. The sun was very warm down there in the gut of the hills and they strolled easily, making smoke and some talk, though Ruary was not a talker like Kenny Alpin. They held to the main road for a while. That road did not follow the floor of the valley by the river but looped along the first swell of the ridge from horn to horn of the glen wall, brown loop after brown loop sagging down and lifting up not unlike telegraph wire strung on poles far apart.

Presently Ruary nodded his head forward and said: "There's MacFinlay on his sheltie!"

A horseman riding towards them had come round a horn of the glen half a mile away.

"MacFinlay? Oh! the laird from Lettoch Lodge."

"That's him, but laird is only what you call a courtesy title now. A' this glen and a' the glens and bens ayont yon hill are gone from him—to a country-man of your own, Mr Wayne." He still gave Stephen the mister.

"Sound judge that countryman of mine!" said Stephen.

"That's what the laird wasna—or his fathers before him."

Stephen looking to the rear of the horseman said:

"His daughter Marian doesn't always ride herd on the old madman?"

"He's his own man on horseback," Ruary said, "and he's no madman whatever."

"No?"

"No. All of us go woolgathering with the years."

"Not one Ruary Farquhar."

"Ay then! If you stay on a while you might see me do something dom foolish."

"I hope so," said Stephen, his mind on the daring man who had coolly flicked a salmon over his head in a land thick with watchers.

MacFinlay, riding awkwardly with short stirrups, was not wearing his kilt on horseback. And there was nothing at all strange about him to-day. His eyes were sternly calm in a bony face that was composed, but not composed over strain. Even the pony looked gentle. It was a strong squat beast with a stiff roach, and as it came nearer the walkers it sort of sidled towards them, and Stephen saw by the white-rimmed eye that it had nefarious intentions in its hind-legs. Its rider, knowing it, reined it to the other side of the road.

The laird glanced distantly at Stephen as if he had not seen him before—probably he did not remember— but he greeted Ruary familiarly, and Ruary paused to pass the time of day. Stephen, moving on slowly, heard a few words.

"Are you after one, you old Turk?" He had noted the rifle under Ruary's arm.

"Had you a haunch yet, laird?"

"Could I? Not after selling, Ruary?"

"A body's no' tempted yet," said Ruary.

After a time Ruary overtook Stephen.

"There's certainly nothing wrong with him to-day," Stephen said.

"There's everything wrong with him," said Ruary quietly.

"You ought to know. You began together—how many years ago?"

"Forty—and look at us now! Nothing to our names."

"There's Lettoch Lodge—and the Croft o' Balmerion."

He nodded his head, but said nothing.

"There's your business in Glasgow, of course."

"I can stand that too," he said as a man who had stood it for half a wasted life-time. "But I doot if Kirsty could any more."

"She'll not have to," said Stephen definitely.

"Thank you, Mr Wayne, but auld people dinna matter. 'Tis Sheevaun an' that Kenny that trouble me."

"Yes, Ruary, you are growing old, or you wouldn't be taking youngsters on your back."

"That is so too, but there it is. Kenny is a mad loon —and forthright too. He'll no' be put off by the second-hand."

"By the Croft o' Balmerion?"

"The one thing he might stand by—and I'm in his way. Ach! let us no' be botherin' this fine day. We'll tak' a short-cut across this loop."

The road made a deep detour into a fold of the hill, and they left it and slanted down towards the river. Ruary cast an eye up at the sun.

"We're ower early," he said. "The trout'll be on

the rise when the sun goes behind the Ben. We'll finish the sandwiches and the wee drap in the bottom o' the flask."

At the river-side, where there was a ford and deer tracks splaying in the heather, they ate the last of the sandwiches and diluted the heavy smooth malt whisky with cold water.

"We'll wait for the cool o' the evening," said Ruary. "No—not here. The midges would find us. Back in the heather."

A short distance from the river two big humps stood like islands out of ungrazed pasture-land. They were some fifty yards apart and were thickly grown by old heather. The two men climbed the nearest one and lay down at their ease on top. The heather was so deep that lying between the tussochs the two were invisible even from the hill-tops. Stephen did not attach any significance to that until later on. They talked quietly, or half-dozed, or went into the thoughts of their own.

Ruary had read a good deal but without direction, mostly travel, biography, and rationalist stuff. Stephen, an active man of his hands since leaving college, had scarcely read a serious book, not even a serious book of fiction. Few active men do. He found that Ruary had read very little fiction, but what he had read was, strangely enough, mostly American—stories with the American kick to them, detective stories with slick dialogue, Western stuff well above the pulp class.

"There was a'e chiel always made me homesick," he said. "A lad with a Welsh name, and the Welsh are the homesick kind. About New Mexico he wrote."

"Will James is Montana—you mean Eugene Manlove Rhodes?"

"That's him. He had the sun in his books—sun and mountain and plain and desert, and the colours o'

93

them. And his men were bonny men and trusty—honest by choice, betimes, and not by necessity. Homesick he used make me."

"He was homesick himself, exiled twenty years from his New Mexico. I knew him—a good man to take along, small, virile, and great-hearted."

"Ay so! He was in his books. I haven't seen anything by him these late years?"

"You will not. He rests on top of one of his own mountains."

"Peace to him. Not that it matters where a man rests, only we ha'e them foolish notions. Ay! foolish—foolish."

He went off into ironic speculation of his own, and Stephen left him to it. Stephen was content to lie there in the deep heather and let time go by for a little while. He had seen and flavoured this life in the glen, in a quiet way, and in a few days now he would be leaving with pleasant memories. That was fine. He would remember this land, but he would not be homesick for it. It was a good land asleep in the sun—and asleep in other ways too—and the people he stayed with were salt of the earth.

He turned over on his face, propped himself on his elbows and looked about the glen. Over there was big Ben Shinnoch towering its scarred head atilt in a granite cliff, and with a steep schree of boulders pouring from its throat. And on the other side, near at hand now, massive Corryhow's double shoulders took the sun on grey boulders. And all up and down the glen the great slopes dozed gravely under the grave wash of the heather in bloom.

He turned over on his back again and looked up into the sky, his eyes half-shut. It was immensely high and far away and fragilely blue, and a white cloud soaring miles up was like a small trout suspended half-way down in a deep clear pool. That immensity of sky, swooping far beyond the horizon, dwarfed the up-heaved landscape. The mountains were no longer massive and straining upwards; they were only cowering small crinkles like the crinkles of a stormy sea at mid-ocean. That was how they would look to the golden eagle soaring and sliding high over Corryhow.

He was half-dozing when he was roused by the sound of a rifle-shot from over the hill the other side of the river.

"The stalkers are out on the Caiplich," said Ruary. "That'll be a stag down."

As he finished speaking there came another shot.

"No it isna. That's bad shooting. That's a stag missed—or a stag hit and hurt."

Ruary, his rifle at his side, settled himself down deeply and looked through the heather stems at the sweep of purple and brown hillside lifting smoothly beyond the water. Stephen turned his head aside and looked at him. His calm grizzled face was the face of an ancient heather-god, and his deep-set grey eyes glinted as they moved along the skyline. He was just idly surveying his own ancient hills—or was he? For suddenly a nerve twitched in his cheek and his eyes stilled and steeled on one spot. He spoke, sharply for him:

"Thought so! Lunged!"

Stephen was about to start up for a look when Ruary's great hand pressed on his breast.

"Down and over! This way!"

Stephen turned over, and Ruary moved the heather stems apart for him. Stephen thrust his head through and looked eagerly up at the hillside. It rose from a narrow green carse beyond the water in one bold sweep for some three hundred yards before shelving back into a ridge and lifting into sight again. But Stephen had no need to rake the hillside. He saw at once.

A red stag was coming down the face of the hill. It was a full-grown hart with noble antlers. A big beast. Stephen had stalked and shot deer from Arizona to Canada, and he was astonished at the size and sweep of these antlers. It was bigger than the biggest white-tail, not as tall as the waipiti but much more strongly built, and its antlers were finer than any Stephen had seen. A reddish-brown beast, with a curving neck and a cream underside.

A deer, as Stephen knew, getting away unhurt after being fired over, lights out for safety at top speed and keeps it up for miles. This stag was coming down the hill-face slowly, not bounding or striding or loping, but moving slantwise in a queer rocking trot, its muzzle thrust forward and antlers back on its shoulders. Half-way down it staggered and went forward on its nose, and only its nose saved it from turning a somersault.

"Lunged!" whispered Ruary. "He'll tak' hours to die, puir beast. Hau'd your head still!"

Stephen's head was still, but his mind was active. One would never know what might be in Ruary Farquhar's mind. Had he flattened out at this particular spot on purpose? Why had be brought a ·450 deer-stalking rifle to shoot rabbits with? He would know that the Castle Charles sportsmen—"gents" in local talk—were stalking on the Caiplich, and that stags disturbed on the Caiplich would invariably make for the Sanctuary across the glen on the flanks of Glen Shinnoch. In every deer-forest there is a sanctuary where deer are never disturbed and never shot over. Ruary might be innocent of all intention but the evidence was against him.

When the stag struck the level carse it went on its

knees and nose again, heaved on its feet without resting, and took to the water. There was a knee-deep ford here that the deer used in crossing from one side of the glen to the other. They would swim if they had to, but would take a ford ordinarily. Ruary would know of that ford?

Half-way across, the deer went to its knees again, the water splashing round it, and its nose going under. Its nose stayed under for a while, and when it came up Stephen saw the drip from its muzzle stained a bright red.

"Through the lungs a'right," whispered Ruary.

The stag came to land facing towards them but a little to the right. Stephen was sure that it would make across the level ground between the two heather humps, and was wondering if Ruary would risk a shot to end its misery. It was a risk that Stephen would take. He glanced up the face of the hill. It was empty and glowing softly purple in the sun, and there was no stalker's head over the skyline.

But the wounded stag, instead of keeping to the level, made straight for the knoll to the right of the watchers, and faced boldly at the slope. Against the rise of ground it seemed to gather fresh energy, and went to the top in three or four bounds. There it halted. Propped on four spread slender legs it threw up its noble head and surveyed the glen—for the last time. Then it faced the hill down which it had so painfully come, and looked up at the skyline. It was waiting for the stalker to appear. If no stalker came it would probably lie down to rest, never to rise again. Stephen could see its brilliant, anguished, black-rimmed eye. The stag was on his right, and he lay on Ruary's right.

"Can you take him?" Ruary's whisper was in his ear.

"We should."

"Right! Put him out of pain. I'll keep an eye on the hill. Keep your eye on him and take it slow."

Stephen heard the muffled click of the rifle-bolt, and found the stock below his hand.

"Under a hundred?" he whispered.

"Under eighty. You can see his eye. Twa fingers ahind the shoulder and not too high—dead flat!"

Stephen levered himself over in the heather inch by inch, his eye never leaving the stag, got his left hand out under the stock, and the butt well into his shoulder. The doomed beast never moved, staring nobly up at the skyline. Stephen drew in two slow breaths, looked along the sights at the brown hide a point behind the elbow, and put steady pressure on his trigger finger.

The butt dunted hard into his shoulder, and the explosion went shattering against the walls of the glen.

The stag did not leap and fall to the shot. It gave a jerk against the shock, swayed, sank back on its haunches, fell sideways on the left of the slope and rolled over. It came right to the bottom into deep heather. Stephen saw the pointed small hooves one moment, and then he saw the bare tip of an antler. The tip did not move.

"Keep still as a stane!" whispered Ruary tensely. "You got him?"

"In deep heather this side. I can see the tip of an antler."

"Neat! Just in time!" His hand was on the back of Stephen's knee. "Take care how you look!"

Stephen levered himself back and looked up between two bunches of heather. There were the head and shoulders of a man in a notch of the skyline. He was hurrying, for in a short time his whole figure was outlined. A small puny figure in a notch of the hills

98

against the immensity of the sky, yet Stephen knew that he was a tall man and active. He halted up there on the brink of the dip and seemed to be staring straight down at them. But, then, his head was thrown up and moved about on his shoulders, as if he was looking up and down and across the glen. He could, of course, not pick out men or stag unless he knew where to look and had stalking-glasses.

"One o' they gents," whispered Ruary, "and a quick man to follow a wounded beast. There'll be a ghillie comin' ahint with the glasses. We're in it now, Mr Wayne—for our good deed."

"I'll go along, as far you like," said Stephen.

"Right! I know the lie o' the ground. We'll move when he moves. He'll ha'e to keep his eyes on his feet down the brae."

After one long swinging look over the ground the tall man took to the down slope.

"Wait now!" said Ruary, "and do what you see me do. We'll leave the rifle and take the rod."

He slipped the rifle from Stephen and thrust it out of sight deep into the heather. Then he picked up the trout-rod and slid backwards between the tussochs, his elbows and toes the motive force. Stephen did likewise. Below the head of the slope they were out of sight and rolled quickly to the bottom. There Ruary led across the grass on hands and knees, and in twenty yards dropped into a narrow shallow hollow that had once been the course of a tributary rivulet. It was still damp after a dry summer and grown with clumps of bearded rushes. Never pausing, Ruary, still on hands and knees, proceeded down this old water-course, and Stephen followed. It was a good long crawl and their shoulders and neck muscles ached, for men have been biped too long. Stephen wanted a pause and a change of posture, but Ruary, twice his age, led on quickly and indefatigably.

Presently they heard the chuckle of running water ahead, and Stephen lifted a cautious head to see a line of stunted alders before them. Alders favour damp ground near flowing water, and are often a nuisance to anglers. In amongst the alders they got to their feet and paused briefly, Stephen limbering his shoulders and massaging his upper arms.

"So far, so good!" said Ruary, "but we'll go a bittie yet before filling a pipe."

He strode off down the course of the river. Walking was easy. They were out of sight of anyone upstream now, but Ruary kept on for fully fifteen minutes until another curve of the glen came between. There he stopped over a deep pool below a green bank; but he was not yet done with his precautions. Smoothly and quickly he uncased the trout-rod, set it up, ran the line through the rings, tied on a three-fly cast, and hooked the tail-fly in the bottom ring—one minute's work. He handed the rod to Stephen.

"You are fishin' for trooties," he said, "and you haven't caught any 'cause there was no wind and all sun. You'll get a puckle later. Sit ye doon!"

He sat on the green bank, his feet over the water, blew out and drew in great breaths, and wiped his brow that was a little damp.

"Old I'm gettin'," he said. He cut Irish plug with a sharp blade, and slowly ground it in his hard palms.

Stephen laid his rod along the grass and sat down at his side, and he also leisurely filled a pipe. Ruary, his eyes across the pool, puffed strongly, the match flame pulsing. He spat into the pool, and said casually:

"There was shootin' up the glen a whilie ago."

"I heard some about twenty minutes ago," agreed Stephen.

"Likely one o' the gents after a stag."

"Will he find it?"

"He mightn't, but his ghillie will. He'll know where to look."

"Hell! We could do with one of Kenny's horned rabbits. Will he have a ghillie with him?"

"He has," said Ruary. "There he is across the water. Sanny Grigor—a good stalker, but slow kind."

A hillock of birches stood apart from the main slope across the water, and around the side of this a man was coming—hurriedly for a slow man. He lifted a hand, and halted on the gravel bed on the opposite side of the pool. A big man of full figure, and his face was as red as a beet under sandy hair. Stephen could see the light blue of his eyes staring at him out of that flushed face. He carried a spare rifle under an arm, a telescope in a leather case on one hip, and a cartridge-bag slung over shoulder.

"Ay, ay, Ruary!" He cried the high-pitched Banff-shire greeting across the water.

"Ay, ay, man!" hailed back Ruary.

"Ye didna see ane o' the gents this airt?"

"Gosh, Sanny! I kent you'd lose one. Down a chorrie he'll be, his neck in three halves."

"No' him—the red deevil on his twa feet."

The pool was too wide for easy talk. Sanny tramped down to the tail end, where the water spread out, and walked straight in. He was wearing no rubbers, and the stream ridged up to his thighs. Sanny did not mind. He paused half-way to cup water in his hands and drink. He came up the bank, water squelching in his big hobnailed boots and water dripping from the baggy folds of his breeches.

"Ye didna see him, young Hale o' Castle Charles? No!" He did not give them time to lie. "Dom the luck! A fair bit o' stalking for the first head o' the season, and we had a good one fair in oor pooch over the Tamdhu ridge. A hundred yards downhill, side on, and ten points to him. A guid shot, young Hale, but hasty. I warned him to sight low for the down shot, and he was too low and too far back. He couped the beast ower a' reet, but up it got again and awa', and he missed it clean the second time. Hard hit and it'll run till it drops—an' the young gent'll do the same thing, for he's that kind. Domit, I say!"

"We heard the twa shots, Sanny," Ruary told him, "and after a long time a third one—that way somewhere." He gestured widely up and across the glen. Across the glen the hills folded into a deep side valley. Sanny nodded.

"Ay! The beast was makin' for the Sanctuary in the Baitchoch. It'll be lein' dead ower there, and young Hale waitin' for me. He must ha'e run a mile to the dead meenit. Dom! I'll ha'e to bring the pony all the way round by Knockindu afore the hoodie craws get goin' the morn." He started across the grass, but paused to speak to Ruary over his shoulder. "Tell your young freen' to stick to the trooties, Ruary, and never mind you." He set off at his best pace for the road looping down the valley.

"Will the poor mutt go right up to the Sanctuary?" Stephen asked in a low voice.

"No' him. Sanny knows his work. When he gets to the rise of the road he'll pick up his gent with the glasses. After that they'll put two and two together. There was that third shot, and Sanny for no reason at all puts no trust in me whaur a stag is concerned. He'll know where to look."

102

"Exactly!" Stephen nodded. "That's how we read sign where I come from. We lose out, that's all."

"We don't want another man's stag, Mr Wayne," said Ruary. "We only put the beastie out of pain. If they fail to come on it that's another matter."

"Do you think they will?"

"I couldna say." He smoked solemnly for a while. "No! I couldna say for sure that they'll find it. Depends how far the gent gets from the river when Sanny overtakes him." Again he smoked. "I could do a canny bit o' scoutin' to find out."

"On our stomachs?"

"No, Mr Wayne." Ruary was definite. "Enough harm you've done for a'e day—shootin' a man's stag under his nose. Moreover, in wark like this twa is a hindrance."

Stephen saw the reason in this.

"Right! I'll wait along here, and do some fishing," he said.

"That'll no' do either," Ruary demurred. "The best way will be for you to go on doon by the water, takin' your time. When the sun goes ahint the Kinmaols a bit breeze might spring up, and if it does you'll see a whitey-brown fly coming out of the trees along the water. Your tail-fly matches the same fly, and if you try a cast or twa in the runs we'll ha'e troot for breakfast. Take your time. An' look! When you get to the mouth o' the glen take up a strateegic position off the road and wait for me. It might be a good thing to gang hame together and have the same story to tell Kirsty. She's that particular."

And so it was arranged.

CHAPTER VI

RUARY disappeared among the alders, and Stephen
went down by the long curves of the river, sometimes
among alders, again by ashes and rowans, but mostly
over a felt of old grass. The sun was still above the
western rim, and Ben Shinnoch cast a long black
shadow on the floor of the glen. The eastern side was
in the sunlight now touched with orange, and all the
folds and chorries were filled with a luminous glow.
And when the sun went behind the rim the ridges stood
out more sharply for a while, and gradually bulked to
broader contours; and the valleys that slowly darkened
were weighed down by silence.

As Ruary had promised, a thin breeze eddied for a
little while; a whitey-brown fly came out of the ash
trees, and the trout began to rise. Occasionally a
salmon, its silver red-tinted, came clean into the air,
curved over, smashed the surface resoundingly, and a
wide ring splayed away in steel ripples. Stephen caught
some trout, and grew interested. He was not much of
an angler, but had learned something from Kenny
Alpin in a week. He lost many more than he caught,
but while the rise lasted the trout were greedy, and he
landed a dozen nice ones, some up to a pound in weight,
before the rise went off as suddenly as it had come. A
dozen was more than ample for breakfast, so he took
down the rod, and slanted across the glen to the roadside below the first swell of the Muckle Kinmaol.
From there he could look up Glen Shinnoch and look

down into the bowl of Knockindu. The glen was already deep in shadow, but the wider bowl was still lightsome, and a distant hill-top faintly pink.

Stephen chose his strategic position to wait for Ruary. He crossed the road and went a few yards up the slope to where a grey rock stood out of thin grass and heather. There he slipped off his fishing-bag, sat down against the rock and composed himself to wait as long as necessary. The rock matched the old suit he was wearing, and even in a better light one would have to look twice to see him. He filled a pipe and smoked peacefully. Ruary should be along in a few minutes. No one came for half an hour.

The gloaming was deepening when he heard an iron-shod footstep up the road. Stephen sat up, but when the man appeared out of the gloom he knew at once that he was not Ruary. When he got nearer he knew him for Sanny Grigor the stalker, trudging stolidly, shoulders slack and head down, his rifle under oxter; a very weary stalker now, but holding a pace that he could keep up for ever.

Sanny was alone. No footsteps sounded behind him. What did that mean? Stephen's trained Western mind went to work and chose two alternatives. Sanny had not found his young gent, and that implied that the gent had gone back over the hill before Sanny appeared on the scene; or he had found his gent; and what did that imply? It implied that the gent was still up the glen. Why? To stay by the stag they had found, of course. No use two coming down the glen. Sanny was now on his way to Knockindu, to the nearest 'phone, to ring up Castle Charles for a car. There might be other alternatives, but these two were obvious ones; the others were only speculative. Ruary should be along now at any moment, knowing the game was up.

105

Stephen waited another half-hour, and at the end of that time heard the hooves of a horse on the road. That would be the Lettoch Lodge pony with the laird on top. He was getting home late, and maid Marian would be worrying about him. Wait! There were footsteps too. Was he afoot? No, there were more than one pair of footsteps.

One man was riding the pony, and in the gloom Stephen was not sure if the rider was MacFinlay. He seemed to sit taller in the saddle. It was night now, the three-parts dark of Highland autumn. Two men were at the pony's head, and one of these was a very tall man, and almost certainly Ruary Farquhar. Stephen judged by the forward throw of head, but Ruary made it certain for him. As they went by below, a match scraped and was held cupped to the bowl of a pipe. Grizzled hair and beard, that was Ruary all right. Having lit his pipe, he threw the match forward with the full throw of his arm as if to point out the way. Without a doubt, Ruary, on the watch, had picked out Stephen against the rock and was signalling him on.

Stephen slid down to the roadside, waited till they were a safe distance ahead, and followed after in the silent dust at the side of the road. His two alternatives were wrong. What then? Why were these three men together? One was Ruary, another probably the laird, but who was the third? The stalking gent from Castle Charles—Hale his name? But how was Ruary in that company? Stephen swore. Could it be that Ruary was a captive, or at any rate held for enquiry? Had he been careless in his scouting and found with the dead stag? Stephen was aware that the game laws, especially the laws dealing with the royal sport of deer-stalking, were medievally strict. What would happen to a man of Ruary's reputation caught purloining another man's ten-pointer ? But would a man of Ruary's experience allow himself to be so caught? Absolutely, no. Still, one must not be too sure. Better follow on and see where the road led to. After that——

When the three men came to the track turning up to the croft they held to the main road without pausing, not even saying a word. Stephen did not like that, since it implied prearrangement. For a moment he thought of running up for Kenny Alpin, but decided not to. He might lose the trail and frighten the women, and moreover Kenny would want to attack with horse, foot, and artillery. Time enough to get Kenny when the trail ended and plans had to be made.

The road turning off to Lettoch Lodge was a quarter-mile further on. Into that the three turned, again without pausing. This was better. The Lodge was the only end of this road. That placed Kenny within reach at the croft. If Ruary needed help, Kenny and Stephen between them would, if necessary, employ such mild weapons as thunderbolts and dynamite.

They took the pony right up to the front door. Stephen watched them from the trees on the edge of the lawn. The fanlight showed a light in the hall, and the room to the right was also lighted and the window unblinded. As Stephen looked, the front door opened wide and gave him a glimpse of Marian Finlay, the light from behind shining through her fine hair. The man was off the pony, and the three men were close together on the top step. One man had his hands over the shoulders of the other two. That man was hurt. Was he the laird—or young Hale? And who had hurt him? They went into the hall slowly, and the door closed. Evidently the pony was tied to a bridle-hook by the door.

Stephen waited. He had to wait for Ruary. Meantime he would see what he could see. He moved along the edge of the lawn until he was opposite the lit window—the window of a living- or sitting-room. Stephen saw plenty, but he did not see Ruary Farquhar.

The room was brightly lit by a petrol-gas lamp, and the window opened from floor to ceiling. The laird, himself, was standing up head-bent; Maggie Donald, the housekeeper, was leaning over holding a length of white cloth like a bandage ; Marian Finlay was on her knees; and a young man sat back in a low chair, his left leg, at full stretch, resting on a footstool and naked to above the knee. Furthermore, Marian Finlay was gently massaging the knee between her soft palms. Stephen saw the movement of her hands clearly, for the whiteness of her hands was not as delicately white as the man's bare leg.

The man's profile, under hair that was still sleek and looked dark, struck some memory in Stephen, the kind of memory one has for a face seen for the first time last week or seen often years ago. He moved across the lawn for a closer view. The cypress tree at mid-lawn curved its outer branches not more than thirty feet from the window, and by pulling down the lowermost branch he could see over it and remain three parts hidden.

The girl was still massaging the young man's knee, and he was looking down at her. She looked up at him. Stephen looked at him too. He had a bold, straight-nosed, strong-jawed profile, with a high, bony brow; and his hair was not black but dark-red.

"A small world!" said Stephen. "Budd Hale, his own dam' self!"

Stephen Wayne knew Buddington Hale—Budd for

short. They had been at Little Rock together, Stephen still a freshman and Budd in his senior year. Budd never finished that senior year, but that is another story. Here he was now, son of the owner of Castle Charles, and he was in the sitting-room of the ruined man from whom it had been bought. Stephen Wayne was not pleased to see him there, why he could not tell.

MacFinlay went out of the room, but Stephen did not see him go. He was watching the two young people. Budd was looking down at the girl and talking. Still moving her hands softly she looked up at him and smiled, and the youthful blood mantled her cheeks. Stephen had made her smile with difficulty, but now she was smiling readily, and dropping her woman's eye in a woman's way before the steady eager look of the male. Why not? Her smiling mouth and her colour and the way her hair fluffed, and the flash of her brown eyes downward, all together made no mean weapon. There was something dangerously virginal about her. That would appeal to Buddington Hale. Budd would know. He knew how to look at a girl and talk to her. Damn well he knew, did Budd Hale! Mariana in the moated grange might no longer be lonely, but later on she might weep again. But that was no business of Stephen Wayne's.

Someone tapped the wood of the bough that Stephen held and a low voice said, "Hist!"

"Ruary!"

Ruary's voice was in Stephen's ear.

"Half-hid you are. I saw the glint of your eye from the house corner."

Stephen let the bough drift upwards, and drew back into the shade with Ruary. Side by side they looked at the glow of the window through the branches.

"That's young Hale," Ruary whispered. "Son of the new owner of Castle Charles."

"You're telling me."

"Ay! Am I. He has a sair bad knee, but under the feel o' they bonny hands there'll no be a happier knee in all Scotland. Eh, man! Grand to be young! Did you see yon smile? I didna ken Miss Marian could be that bonny."

Stephen felt that Ruary was ironically probing at him.

"Come away, you old sultan! I thought you were the captive of his bow and spear."

"No' me! I'll meet you at the corner o' the path yonder."

He went across the grass to the pony. Ruary knew about that pony, for he sidled along the wall and got to its head in two jumps; and the pony came away with him docile as an old mule. Stephen met him at the edge of the trees.

"The stable is over there," Stephen pointed out.

"I ken. I'm borrowing the shelt for the night—only the laird doesna know it."

"I see!" Stephen chuckled. "Anything happen up the glen? That stalker came down half an hour before you."

"So he would. I saw you up under that stane. Sanny couldn't pick up his gent with the glass—he couldna—and went up the Baitchoch chorrie to the Sanctuary. From there he'd flank the Ben and get down to the road twa mile back. He'll be thinking young Hale went back ower the Caiplich and hame that way. He'll no' be knowin' yet."

"But what happened?"

"An accident. Wait now! I had no haund in it. The young gent was in a hurry, and him with a gammy knee since his football days. There's lumps o' stanes in the bottom o' that ford, and he twisted a foot on one and out went the knee. Down he went and his rifle into deep water, an' he could only keep his ain head abune to crawl his way out. He couldna put the knee in again without help, so he sat under the bank waitin' for Sanny to come ower the hills; but, as we ken, Sanny took the lower ford. He couldna go in for the rifle either, or he might ha'e signalled Sanny. An hour he waited, and then he pulled himself on one side right up to the road. Well pluckit he is, but he had used up all his swear words by the time I came on him legal and proper. His knee was gey sair by then, but I put it in for him, havin' good thumbs for a bane. Ay! I cleekit it in, an' he fainted right off without a soond. He came to with a cough out o' his ain flask, an' hed gumption enough to invite me to a mouthfu'. I waited a whilie to see if the laird would be riding back—I wasn't so sure if he hadn't turned already—and I was on the point o' makin' tracks myself for Knockindu when the laird rode round the corner. An' that was all. The laird is a good walker."

It is a strange but true fact that it was Stephen Wayne who had given Buddington Hale that lame knee in practice at Little Rock. Hale got his own back three months later by outpointing Stephen in the boxing semi-finals. That was the last time that they had seen each other. Hale left the college a week later—not alone. Stephen remembered that now, and drew his mind away from it.

"That stag is still there?" he asked in a low voice.

"Where you laid him, one tip showin'. Mind you, Mr Wayne, I wouldna touch anither man's stag only for that second bullet-hole. We canna let that be known. That's why I'm borrowin' the pony to bring the carcase down. But first I'll ha'e to go down to Knockindu for the doctor. The lad's knee is swelled bad—in spite o' soothin' fingers—and the knee-cap might be out o' place."

"You're riding down?"

"No dom fear! Not this shelt."

"I'll ride down for that doctor," Stephen said firmly.

"Guid-be-here, man! You darena put a leg across the dom beast."

Stephen was holding the left side of the bridle and he slipped the reins over the pony's head. He felt for the stirrups. A bit short for the Western style but they would do. And then, before Ruary could further protest, he was in the saddle and his knees in the right place.

"God-a-michty!" said Ruary, gripping the bridle hard.

Nothing happened. The pony, head held, was as quiet as an old burro.

"A sulker, are you?" said Stephen. "I'll sulk you!" He leant forward to Ruary. "Listen, Ruary! Go on up to the croft and tell Kenny to meet me on the Glen road. You go to bed, and we'll bring the stag and rifle down. Get out from under! I'm going to kick him in the slats."

"Watch yourself, son!" Ruary stepped quickly away from the pony's head.

Stephen at the same time gave it both heels in the barrel. The pony went from that place. It was no sulker. Stephen was a good horseman, and had ridden some bad horses in his time, broncs much more skilled in bucking than this chunky Scotty. Even on a smooth British saddle the pony could not throw him, though it surely tried. It had no fancy tricks, just plain fore-and-aft bucking, but even after a long day it had abounding energy and bottom. Yes, the bucking was a simple matter, it was the disaster the pony wrought that was calamitous.

It had the hardest mouth that Stephen ever met in a horse, and it took the bit in its teeth and went exactly where it liked. And the place it liked best was that nice smooth lawn that Stephen had cut the previous day. That animal did not miss a square yard of it, and was particularly pleased with the rose and chrysanthemum beds. Moreover it was shod heavily, Scots fashion, on four hooves, and Stephen, busy as he was, could imagine what those iron hooves were doing to that ancient sward. Once or twice the little brute squealed, and the squeal seemed to restore its energy. And the squealing and thudding of hooves were enough to wake a house of the dead. The front door opened and the laird came out hurriedly on the top step.

"Heavens, Ruary!" he cried. "He'll kill you. Are you mad?"

The pony nearly got Stephen that time. He imagined Ruary on top of that earthquake, and laughter loosed his knees.

The sitting-room window went up and he had a glimpse of Marian Finlay's head and shoulders, before the pony took him under the cypress tree. He got his head down in time and the pony's poll bumped his nose. But his nose did not bleed readily. After that the little brute went for the trees in stiff-legged bucks, each buck scoring a yard of turf, and bucketed down the slope to the motor-road. It was mere luck that saved Stephen's head and shoulders from trunk or bough. There it took a fresh hold of the bit and straightened out in a dead run, a short-coupled scuttering run like a terrier's. Half-way to the main road it decided that the game was up, and began to slow down, but Stephen, using his heels, kept it going until it took the turn for the village. There he slowed it to a walk, not a buck left in it.

"Now you know?" Stephen said. "Take it easy! You have a night before you."

There are four short streets in Knockindu and a central square with a clock-tower. The clock face was dimly lit and gave the time as ten-fifty. That meant that the public-houses were shut and most of the people already in bed. A solitary citizen crossing the square courteously directed Stephen to the doctor's house ten doors down the east-going street.

"He's at hame a'reet," he said, "if he's no' in bed."

The doctor's door opened directly on the pavement, and the doctor himself answered Stephen's ring. A short stoutish man with a broad kindly face, he looked from Stephen to the pony standing in the gutter at rein's length.

"Did you ride him down?"

"One gentle hoss, doctor."

"Becod! Has the laird taken a turn?"

"No. Young Hale of Castle Charles bust a knee deer-stalking. He's at Lettoch Lodge——"

At mention of Castle Charles the doctor brightened up. Apart from a good fee there was always the shooting and fishing.

"Young Mr Hale! I'll be at the Lodge in ten minutes. Do his people know?"

"Not yet——"

"I'll 'phone up. They can send the big saloon car across."

He hurried away down the hall, and Stephen hopped on the pony that gave one buck as in duty bound and trotted out of town. The doctor's flivver passed them in some five minutes.

Ruary Farquhar was waiting at the entrance to the

114

croft track. He put a hand on the bridle and a hand on the pony's roach.

"Kenny is up the glen a'ready; you'll overtake him easy. He'll scout before you on the road down. Gosh! I was waitin' here wonderin' if your neck was gone in twa places. You rode him right enough, but you ought to see that bit lawn—even in the dark."

"The laird blames you for that."

"I'll tell him different with the morn's milk."

A pencil of light moved smoothly along the breasts of the Kinmaols and came down towards them: the headlights of a car coming their way from Knockindu. Ruary led the pony a few lengths up the croft track and waited; but when the car reached the Lettoch Lodge road it turned off, and the headlights shone on the wooded breast of the hill across the river.

"The Castle Charles car," Stephen explained. "The doctor 'phoned."

"The auld busybody! Now they'll take the laddie home, an' he'll miss his massagin' the morrow's morn. He'll no be pleased, I tell you."

"He might be back," said Stephen, knowing his Budd Hale.

"He might surely. You know, we do be takin' foolish notions into our heads with the years on us. Here I was waitin' for you and wonderin' how broke was your neck, and at the back o' my mind I was thinkin' that Castle Charles was never without a MacFinlay till a year past; an' here comes the son o' the new owner, his knee, and maybe his heart, under the hands o' the daughter of the auld laird. Man dear! already I was hearin' young voices within the auld walls—an' Mac- Finlay himself restored in body and wit."

Stephen was not sure if Ruary was serious or just pinking at him. He said:

"Go to bed, you darn old matchmaker!"

"I'll stay up to garalloch the beast," said Ruary.

Stephen gave heels to the pony, and the pony, after one ceremonial buck, went up the glen road in a short-coupled canter.

CHAPTER VII

STEPHEN had not many hours' sleep when he was waked by the crow of a cock—not a cock-grouse this time but a barn-door fowl.

"Damn! I can take another hour."

He took two. He rolled out on the bare boards then, and hearing sounds outside thrust a head through the open skylight. He was just in time. Ruary was going down the garden path, milk-pail in hand and a big brown-paper parcel slung over his shoulder. The laird's pony was tied outside the gate, the stirrups crossed on the saddle.

"Belay! You're on my job," called Stephen.

Ruary halted and looked up.

"Do you want it, Mr Wayne?"

"I do not, but I want to look at that lawn, and run. I'll be down in two shakes."

He threw on his clothes, not taking time to shave, but wasting two seconds to turn the blankets down off the sleeping Kenny.

"What the blazes are you after?" Kenny wanted to know.

"A day's work."

"Get to hell out o' here, then." Kenny pulled the clothes up, turned on his other side, and pretended to go to sleep.

Sheevaun was stirring the porridge in the back-kitchen when Stephen went in looking for his shoes. She shook her red head at him.

"Oh, Stephen, Stevie! Am I losing you?"

"Go to the devil, red-head!" growled Stephen.

"Wish you luck all the same, my dear," she said softly.

Ruary was holding the pony outside the garden gate.

"Are you for trying him this morning?" he enquired.

"Knocked all the kinks out of him last night." Stephen hopped on. The pony remained suspiciously quiet.

Ruary slung the brown-paper parcel over Stephen's shoulder.

"Tell Maggie Donald to hang it two or three days," he said, "and she need say nothing about it."

"Won't they know venison on the table?"

"Eaten bread stops a man's mouth—and a woman's sometimes." He handed Stephen the pail, and stepped away from the pony. Stephen gave it a touch of heel and waited for the one buck. He got it.

That pony was a natural bucker, and Stephen should have known that. He might, only he was in a hurry this morning. So was the pony. At the second buck the brown-paper parcel whirled round Stephen's neck; the milk-pail jangled and leaped, and Stephen tried to hold it bottom down. Between venison and pail, his attention was off balance, and the fourth buck, accompanied by a squeal, unshipped him. He went over on his shoulder and rolled. The brown-paper parcel bounced on his head and a hind-hoof kicked it ten feet, but he still held on to the milk-pail, though the lid was gone and the contents soaking into the grass. He scrambled to his feet and rubbed himself down cowboy fashion for breakages. There were none.

The squat house was howling at him. That was Kenny Alpin bellowing laughter, his head and shoulders through the skylight. Sheevaun was at the door,

118

and when she saw that Stephen was unhurt she started to laugh too. Kirsty Power at the door of the byre was not laughing, but her hand covered her mouth. Ruary, his long legs moving with great liveliness, was making a forlorn effort to beat the pony to the gap at the corner of the larches. He just missed a grab at the trailing reins, and the pony just missed with a flying hind-hoof. Then all paused to watch the little brute tearing terrier-like down the lane towards home, the stirrups leaping and urging him on.

Kenny Alpin began to hoot joyously.

"Did the cowboy ride him? The charger returns with an empty saddle. Haste, oh haste! and dry those maiden tears."

Sheevaun had a divot of soft brown peat in her hand, and her marksmanship was good. As Kenny ducked, the divot landed on his crown and his head bumped the frame of the skylight as it disappeared. Head and arm came out again like a Jack-in-the-box, and a right hand flourished one of Stephen's best shoes. But Sheevaun dodged handily into the shelter of the eaves, and Kenny missed the black-and-white sheep-dog by inches.

Ruary came back rubbing his grizzled head, and looked down at the white milk stain on the grass.

"No one weeping that I can hear," he said. "You'll be gey late with the milk this morning." He picked up the pail and hurried off towards the byre.

Stephen was indeed late with the milk, though he trotted most of the way. Passing the lawn he gave one glance, and shielded his eyes with his free hand. Maggie Donald met him at the kitchen door.

"Guidness, sonnie! did Kirsty Power sleep in?"

"The earthquake kept her awake," Stephen said.

"Guid-be-here! What earthquake? I never——"

"Come this way and I'll show you."

She allowed herself to be led wonderingly to the corner of the house where she could see the devastated lawn.

"Some earthquake?" remarked Stephen.

Apparently Maggie knew nothing of the previous night's bronco busting. She skirled.

"Oh, my puir Miss Marian! What'll she say? Them tinklers' donkeys got in again."

"One donkey, anyhow. We'll stick to that."

Stephen unslung his brown-paper parcel and put it in her hand.

"Hang that for two or three days," he told her, "and you are to say nothing about it to anyone."

"Who, me?" Her plump fingers felt the parcel. She knew beyond a doubt, but she said, "Ay so! Ruary kills a bit hoggit this season always. Right guid o' him! Miss Marian has ta'en a scunner at rabbits."

She waddled back to her kitchen, and Stephen, drawing a resolute breath, faced the lawn. It was as bad as he had feared. Two-thirds of it was pitted and scarred with hoof-marks. A family of shotes nosing for ground-nuts could do no worse. Luckily the roses were past their best bloom, and with some forking and pruning might bloom again; and the chrysanthemums, tossed as by a hurricane, had tough stems and might stand staking to show their glories in late autumn. It was the sward that made Stephen groan. There was toil and sweat in that, and the day promised to be hot.

He walked across it feeling with his feet. The felt was resilient and he might manage something with a four-pronged fork and a roller. He stood under the cypress tree and looked at the house. The sitting-room window was raised, and a lace curtain at the side moved softly in a draught of air. There was where Budd Hale had sat last night staring up at Marian Finlay. The window to the right was open at the top and still blinded; so was the next window, and it was open top and bottom. Which was the girl's room? The right-most window answered.

The blind shook and went up with a whirr; the lower sash was raised high and Marian Finlay leaned out into the morning. Her fine hair was fluffed about her ears, and her face was fresh after sound sleeping. She had on a blue dressing-gown, and in the open front Stephen could see a rather high-fitting red bathing-costume. She was on the point of yawning when her eyes took in her lawn. Stephen could hear her teeth click.

"Oh dear!" No, that was not what she said. She said, "Oh damn!"

Her eyes lifted and she stared straight into Stephen's. For what seemed a long time they stared at each other. Then she pulled her dressing-gown close and made a motion to withdraw her head, but not quite all the way. She frowned, all smiles leagues deep. He walked across to the edge of the gravel, one hand up and the other strumming as if he held a guitar.

"Too late for serenade, Mariana?"

"Mariana?" The name struck her.

"You know? Mariana in the moated grange—he cometh not, she said."

The thought of that juvenilely sad poem might have been in her mind sometimes, for she said nothing.

"That tinker's donkey got in again last night?" Stephen said hopefully.

She just sniffed at that.

"You did not even stay on," she said coldly.

"Yes, I did."

"Look at your shoulder and knees!"

There were grass marks plain on one shoulder, and one leg of his flannel slacks was cut across the knee.

"The evidence is against me." He looked down at

his knee and up at her. "If I busted that knee who would massage it for me I wonder?"

Bang! the window shut down.

"Touch! No quarter any more."

In a minute or less the front door opened and Marian Finlay came out and left it ajar behind her. She had a blue rubber cap in her hand and a long towel over an arm; and without a glance in Stephen's direction stepped out across the torn lawn towards the river. Below the hem of her dressing-gown her bare ankles rose shapely out of an old pair of rope-soled sandals.

Stephen began to wonder where that damn pony was? The stable door was shut, but he went across to look inside. The pony was not there. He remembered that at the foot of the slope, near the flying-bridge, there was a small meadow scattered with Ruary Farquhar's hay-cocks, and with a nice sole of aftergrass. The little tartar might have broken in there. Stephen, too, went down the road towards the river. He persuaded himself that he was not following the girl.

The meadow ran down to the river at the other side of the bridge, just beyond the road. It was fenced from the road by hawthorns and briar. Before looking over Stephen glanced towards the bridge. The girl in her red bathing-suit and blue cap was poised on the springboard above the bathing-pool. A shapely figure in red outlined against the green of the birches across the water. Her arms were out and her shoulders back, showing smooth folds, and her shoulders were a lovely ivory touched with amber—paler than pale honey, creamier than cream. Her legs were long and tapered —No! they flowed upwards to rounded thighs—thighs not so much massive as firmly rounded like the thighs of a caryatid. She curved over showing her heels, and the water smacked.

"You took that a bit flat," Stephen said aloud. "If Budd Hale saw you now he would be in to play sleek seal with you. If I had——"

But he had not a bathing-suit nearer than the croft. So he looked over the hedge. The pony was there, still saddled and the reins trailing. It had forced a gap between two bushes, kicked off the top of one of Ruary's hay-cocks, and was now busy trying to crop the juicy second growth. The mouth-bit hampered it, but it was staying by the job.

Stephen, guarding his eyes, forced through the gap in the bushes, and the pony lifted a head and looked at him calmly, as much as to say "Oh! You're back for some more." Then it moved off across the little field, snatching a careless bite as it went, and its feet missing the trailing reins. Stephen followed after, and the pony brought up in a handy corner hind-quarters presented.

"A hell of a tactician!" said Stephen. "I need a rope."

He tried to manœuvre round to the animal's head, but suddenly it backed at him, and pulled the trigger on both hind-hooves. Stephen knew too much about bad horses to get caught that way. He dodged aside, the pony exploded out of the corner, galloped across the meadow and anchored in another corner. It was going to have a good time with this biped, and get a hoof home along the line.

Four times it played that game, and enjoyed it. But the inevitable at last happened. As it whirled out of a corner it put a fore-foot on the reins, stumbled, and had its head jerked down. When its head came up again Stephen had it by one ear and nose. At once the little tartar became as quiet as an old mule, dropping one shoulder nonchalantly.

Stephen got its foot out of the loop, and led it towards

the gap in the hedge. He had already proved that he could ride it, and he had some other work to do.

Marian Finlay was standing outside the gap in the hedge, her dressing-gown folded close about her. There was rather a pleased sparkle in her brown eyes. She had been watching for some time.

"So that was where the poor boy was all night! Look what he has done to Ruary Farquhar's hay-cock!'

"You would be surprised to know where he was last night—after I rode him."

"You rode him on the lawn surely, but what happened after that?"

"I'll show you."

He had had no intention of busting that pony again. All he wanted was to get it stabled and rubbed down before the laird appeared. But this girl nettled him, and she had too high an opinion of the pony's prowess.

"Don't! Please don't!" she cried. "He'll kick you when you're down. Oh dear!"

But Stephen was already in the saddle, and the pony was doing its damnedest to pile him. It was game as a pebble. After a long night, with a three-hundred-pound stag on its withers, it still had abounding energy, and bucked away every atom of the same, but vainly. It could not throw any Western horseman, but it threw down another of Ruary's hay-cocks. With all that energy and a few more tricks to its repertoire that pony would rank in any rodeo company.

As usual, when done bucking, it took a fresh hold on the bit and bolted, making straight for the gap in the hedge. Stephen yelled to the girl, but she had already darted aside. He dodged his head under an arm as they went through, and heard the sound of tearing. Never pausing, the pony tore up the road to the Lodge, clattered into the yard, and made straight for its stable door. The door was open, the kilted laird standing at one side of it, and Stephen was not sure if there was head-room under the low lintel. He was not going to find out. He dropped the reins, gave a thrust with his hands, and let the pony slide from under. That is one difficult trick. He come down sitting, legs thrusting, and turned a somersault backwards away from the flying hooves. In the roll of the somersault he came to his feet and saluted the laird.

"Just bringing the pony in, Mr MacFinlay."

"Yes! yes, of course! I do not think I will ride to-day."

Stephen looked at him. His bony, hollow-templed face was quite calm, but it was not the calmness of yesterday. The calm was a thin skin over strain, and his remote eyes had that strange surface glisten. He walked slowly into the stable and put a hand on the pony's quarters. If Stephen did that he would get kicked over the roof across the yard. The old man was fumbling at the bellyband as Stephen dodged in quickly.

"Let me do that, sir?"

"Thank you."

He moved to the pony's head, and Stephen did the grooming with an old curry-comb and a wisp of straw, the animal remaining as quiet as an old sheep.

It may have been noticed that Stephen Wayne, in this land where the lines of conduct and speech are drawn definitely, had sometimes an unconventional way with him. He said:

"Are you wanting a man about the place, Mr MacFinlay?"

"Are we, sir? Are you not employed here?"

"I am up at Ruary Farquhar's," Stephen said. "I could give you a few hours a day till your regular hand comes back."

"I see. My son Iain——" He stopped suddenly and a shiver went over him. "My daughter Marian deals with these things," he said quickly, and walked out of the stable.

So there was a son, Iain, as well as a daughter, Marian. Where was this son, and why did the father shiver at his name?

Stephen tied up the pony and went out after the laird. Just as well that he moved quickly, for the pony's heels brushed his shoulders in the doorway. Mac-Finlay, walking with decision, was going down the drive towards the river, probably to meet his daughter, if she were still down there? Stephen thought he had better make sure. That man in his present state might wander anywhere, and was without breakfast. Stephen followed on the soft edge of the road outside the bracken.

Marian Finlay was not at the bathing-pool, but her father did not pause to look. He went unhesitatingly across the flying-bridge and up the slope towards Falcon Crag standing up straight and stark above the deep-wooded hollow by the river. High above the rock a peregrine falcon soared out across the hollow, and hung poised, its long pinion tips fluttering. King of the air in this lowland valley, outside the domain of the golden eagle: a bold fierce killer, no eater of carrion flesh.

The track the laird was on was the track over the hill to Castle Charles, his old home. If his mind were slipping backwards that is the place he would go to; and that would never do. Stephen had to take a chance. He hurried up the slope and called the laird's name. He turned round at once.

"Well, sir?"

"Breakfast is ready, Mr MacFinlay."

"Breakfast?"

"Breakfast at Lettoch Lodge, sir."

"Oh yes! Of course, of course! We sometimes have breakfast there."

He walked back and by Stephen, an ancient aristocrat ignoring a menial, but not contemptuously.

Over his shoulder, on the other side of the river, Stephen saw Marian Finlay running. She was wearing white, and her hair fluffed out behind her. She stopped when she saw her father coming, and waited for him at the other side of the bridge. Stephen heard him say:

"Breakfast at the Lodge this morning, Marian. I nearly forgot."

"Yes, dad!" She took his arm, and the two went up the road among the trees. Stephen followed slowly. The laird went in the front door, but she came back and waited for Stephen at the corner.

"Thank you, Stephen Wayne," she said simply.

There was anxiety in her eyes, and her face was too grave for the face of a girl. He had made her laugh yesterday, to-day he could not, but he might lift her mood, with a spice of anger to help.

"Had a nice swim?" he enquired.

"Cold in the mornings—two plunges only."

"I saw you. I was sort of admiring the straight long props under you."

"Oh, indeed?" She showed him the white round her brown eyes.

"Why not? Mind you, if you put on weight you'll be a shade too massive above the knee, but your ankles will never fail you."

"You seem to be a judge of anatomy?" she said coldly.

"Most men can judge a girl's legs," said Stephen.

"I don't think I care for your American outspokenness," she said.

127

She turned on her heels and spurned the gravel smartly. The front door banged after her. He had made her a trifle angry, and that might help. It would not help him much.

He went back to the kitchen. Maggie Donald was not there, but presently she came in from the passage carrying a tray. She was clicking her tongue regretfully.

"Thu! thu! thu! He's ta'en another turn, the puir laird, and him that fine yesterday. A' that comin' an' goin' last night was no' good for him. Puir man!"

"Puir girl!" said Stephen.

"Ay then! Puir Miss Marian!" She nodded at Stephen. "The pail is there on the dresser. Would you like a cuppie o' tay?"

"I sure would. I am going to spend some time investigating the depredations of the tinker's burro."

"Losh! what language is that?"

"The lawn, you know? I am going to invisible mend it this morning—and the divil mend it, as my great-grandfather used to say."

"Oh, the lawn! That's right nice o' you, Stephen Wayne."

"If there was a spoon or two of porridge in that black pot——"

"To be sure! To be sure! No use wastin' time goin' up to the croft. Sit ye doon, lad!"

He sat down to a platter of porridge and a bowl of milk. Maggie sniffed when he sprinkled the surface of the porridge with sugar and poured the milk on top.

"Ye English foreign people are a' the same. Spoilin' the honest flavour o' the meal and makin' sops o't."

"Sugar is a good fuel," said Stephen, busily supping.

"If it's a mornin's work you're for you'll need more

than parritch. They ha'e no lasting qualities in a man's stomach."

Stephen had already noted that the Scots, for some obscure reason, use the plural pronoun in speaking of porridge and soup.

After the porridge he had a brace of fresh eggs, home-made brown bread with butter slightly salt, and tea that had a kick because it had been boiling for ten minutes. Maggie Donald had neither porridge nor eggs. For all her stoutness she ate very little at any time. Now she had boiled tea and a thin slice of brown bread, and she talked more than she ate. After a while Stephen put her a half-question.

"The laird has a son, Iain?"

"Iain!" Her voice leaped high.

"So I gathered from what he said."

"Ay, would you!" Like all the Scots she could put into the quietness of her voice all the weight of drama. "Iain MacFinlay is dead these twenty years."

"Sorry!" said Stephen inadequately.

"He was killed the last year o' the Big War—a tall fair laddie o' eighteen. Miss Marian was only a toddlin' bairnie at the time—fifteen years atween them. Ayeh me! it killed the mother and broke the laird's hert."

Maggie Donald was one grand talker, and she had been bottled up to the explosion point for want of someone to talk to. Now she had Stephen Wayne, his legs under her table, and the Lord ha' mercy on his soul. Moreover, he had supplied an opening. She was a devoted follower of the MacFinlay. She was so devoted that though her own brother, who had lost his wife, badly needed her in his house, she would not leave Lettoch Lodge until she had found and trained her successor.

That morning and other mornings—not all in one

morning—Stephen got the history of the MacFinlay, and of herself, and of the Farquhars, and of Knockindu, and of Glen Shinnoch. He could write a history of the place and have ten libel actions on his hands; for Maggie was a realist as well as a judge of motive and conduct, and her frankness was sometimes Rabelaisian.

The history of Alasdair MacFinlay was the history of many a Highland laird. An indifferently managed estate, divorced from the paternal clan system, could not stand up to the commercial age, poor prices, high taxation, and absentee landlordism. The present laird had heired an already impoverished estate and did nothing to restore it. In the 1914-18 War he was a Major in a Gordon battalion and saw service. His son Iain, a boy of eighteen and a subaltern in the same regiment, never saw the front line. A high-explosive shell into a communication trench, and Second-Lieutenant Iain MacFinlay was not seen again. The news killed his ailing mother, and set a small canker gnawing at the father's mind. High taxation and an accumulation of mortgages finished the estate. It had been sold the previous year to a millionaire country-man of Stephen's, Budd's father, Burton R. Hale, who could afford to run it at a loss as a recreation-ground for three months of the year—salmon in spring, grouse and stag in autumn.

The only portion of the estate that MacFinlay had retained was the dower house of Lettoch Lodge and the few acres around it. He had an income of perhaps three hundred pounds. He could be worse off. A man owning Lettoch Lodge and sixty acres in the bowl of Knockindu at the mouth of Glen Shinnoch, with three hundred British pounds a year besides, was better off than five-sixths of the British people.

MacFinlay's mind had been going for some years.

130

Just a failing of memory at times, people said. But he himself knew his malady and knew the slow cumulative effect. He secluded himself in Lettoch Lodge, and cut himself off from the few county people in the neighbourhood. Sometimes he would be all right for weeks, but even then he avoided the outside world and turned to the solitudes of Glen Shinnoch on his pony. Now the periods of clarity were growing fewer, and shorter, and more irregular; and fear for ever stalked at his side.

Fear also stalked with his daughter Marian. She was devoted to him, and chose to be a prisoner with him. She watched him as a mother-hen watches a duckling. Day or night her vigil did not cease, for she knew that his malady was more than loss of memory. To the outside world his loss of memory was somehow dignified, cloaked in aristocratic calm. But she knew the internal storm that was cloaked in that calm. She had heard him pace his room the long nights through, talking aloud to his son Iain, to his dead wife, to young Ruary Farquhar, to his men, to his hound. She had seen him grow bitter and rail and rage. What she feared was an explosion and all that it might mean; and what she feared most was his being taken from her care to a public institution.

Some of all that Maggie Donald told Stephen that morning. Enough to make him rise to his feet and lower his head when Marian Finlay came into the kitchen. He cursed himself silently for his perverse, teasing, American tongue. After a while he lifted his head and looked at her with fresh interest. She was of good material, tough and uncomplaining; young and virile, vibrating with life in spite of herself, making a man's pulses stir in spite of himself; young and sad, wanting life and denying it for duty's sake. Perhaps

131

after all it was his duty to make life stir in her, to bring laughter to the surface, or even anger—but not love. She would have to learn about love for herself, and there was one man who might teach her, and that man might want watching too. Stephen decided then and there that he himself was not interested in love. He was only interested in her—to help her.

"Mistress Donald," said he, "to beat about the bush, did you ever hear of the Scot that went to Samarkand?"

"If there's such a place," said Mistress Donald, "there would be a Scottie in it."

"He was a man of importance this Scottie, and the panjandrums of that place showed him the sights—the mosques and palaces, and market-places, and fair-grounds, and the river Oxus or something, and all the great mountains on the roof of the world. And the Scot said: 'Guid eneuch! but did ye ever see Princes Street and Holyrood, and Melrose by moonlight, and the Clyde made by hands, and big Ben Nevis, and this and that.' Do you know what happened to the decent man?"

"They made him Prime Meenister?"

"He was not a Scot," said Marian Finlay with spirit. "He was a Yankee, and they buried him at the dawn. You are plagiarising our Robert Louis Stevenson."

"Appertaining to that Scotto-Yankee," said Stephen, "I rise to wonder how it is that you do not make coffee in Scotland?"

"Awa' wi' you! After lunch every day I mak' it," said Maggie.

"I'll show you up sometime, old lady. Meantime, thank you for your fine breakfast, and I am now going to earn it."

Without another word he walked out and across to the harness-room to inspect as odd a collection of poor gardening-tools as he had ever seen. He picked out a four-pronged digging-fork and a spade and adjourned to the ruined lawn.

It is wonderful what can be done with a four-pronged digging-fork and a garden-roller. After all, the original material of the lawn was all there, and he had only to restore it to its proper place. Where the pony's hoof-marks were pitted he drove the fork deep in to one side and worked up the pitted part till it made a hump. When he had a section of the lawn looking like a choppy sea at its worst Marian Finlay came out, had one look, and gasped her dismay.

"Whatever are you doing? Completing the destruction?"

"Looks like the-wrath-to-come, doesn't it? Kenny Alpin told me last week that bairns shouldna see work half-done. Let's complete the experiment."

He ran the garden-roller over the bumps and was himself surprised at the result. There were traces of wounds, indeed, but there was a satisfying smoothness; and with the good growing weather that still could be looked for that lawn might show a new face before the fall.

"It is better," she admitted, "but it need not have happened in the first place."

"An interfering sort o' cuss, ain't he?"

"You are, you know."

"The good Samaritan act fell down on me that time."

"Perhaps you meant well," she said, "but I do not understand you at all."

She walked off round a corner of the house, and Stephen was sure she would not be back. But she was back almost immediately wearing gardening-gloves and wielding a secateurs. She started-in clipping away the broken stems of roses and chrysanthemums, and Stephen freshened up the beds with the spade.

"There's still that job going a-begging," he remarked, "or do I get kicked out on my ear as soon as we have restored the damage done by no hoofs of mine?"

"I wish I had a kick sometimes in those long legs you spoke about." She straightened up and pointed the secateurs at him. Her voice was definite. "You know well that you are not a working-man, Stephen Wayne."

"Nothing else but, Marian Finlay." He held out his big hands for her to see. They were very brown hands, now that he had given up wearing gauntlets.

"They are the hands of a horseman," she said, "and your legs too. Your legs are not long, Mr Wayne, and they are not straight either."

"Who has got a tongue in her head now?"

"I have, and I am going to find out what you mean."

"I wish you would! I don't know myself."

She contemplated him, her brown eyes puckering. She was determined to pin him down if it took her all harvest.

"You are an American, I know."

"Poor but honest—I mean honest-looking."

"Not even honest-looking. If you saw yourself! A rip at your shoulder, a tear at your knee, your hair everyway—and you need shaving. You are disgraceful, and you don't care. I know who you are too. You are the owner of the Croft o' Balmerion."

"Ruary Farquhar did not tell you that?" said Stephen, hiding his surprise.

"I heard him tell dad that he was only caretaker for the time. So you must be the owner."

"Is that a woman's reasoning—or intuition?"

"Neither. You don't know the country, that's all. Everyone in Knockindu knows you are the owner."

134

"And that does not make me the owner."

"But you are. You think because you are the big philanthropic boss at the croft you can play little tin-god at Lettoch Lodge and do what you like."

"I can't," said Stephen heartily. "I can't do what I'd like to do this darn minute."

"What is that? No, don't tell me. I'm too big to smack that way." She threw up her head and laughed at him, pleasant, mocking laughter that crinkled up to her brown eyes.

"You long-legged hoyden!"

"I can touch you. You've a bad temper when you can't have your own way. You can't have a job—and you don't want it, really."

"All right! But what is wrong with a job? I don't know Scotland, and you don't know America. American high-school boys sell papers to pay fees; college boys—undergraduates—wash dishes to make out. Servile work doesn't make a menial. Not with us. I'll do your job if you like, but I'll not be your menial."

"If you were a menial you could have it," she said quietly. "It is because you are not that—that I am afraid of you."

"You needn't be. If I do get that job I will insist on one clause in the agreement."

"What is that?"

"I will not have you making love to me."

She laughed again.

"I bought that one," she said. "And still I would be afraid, you strange American." Suddenly she was serious and turned her eyes on the ground. "I am afraid all the time," she murmured.

Stephen was sobered and queerly touched.

"You know too much about fear, girl," he said.

"Yes, I know fear."

"Bedrock! we have reached it at last. Fear should not walk at a girl's side. That first day I fell on my nose and looked up at you I knew you were afraid. You are afraid now, but you need not be afraid of me, though perhaps I should wish that you might be. You need a man about the house, and I am at a loose end for a few days—that is all."

She slowly took off her gardening-gloves and let them drop with the secateurs to the ground; and then, without looking at Stephen, turned away and went slowly into the house.

"You nearly landed a job that time, Stephen Wayne," he said, "and you don't want it, you dam' fool."

But he was not too sure. Marian Finlay did need a man about the house, and he could fill the bill as well as the next. It was rather pleasant to feel altruistic without feeling a trace romantic. He was nothing else than romantic, only he wasn't aware of it. He did not think of Budd Hale for a moment, but, no doubt, the thought of Budd lay in the unconscious part of him. He knew Budd and did not care so much about him. For one thing Budd had whipped him over six two-minute rounds, and he could not forget that he had very nearly taken Budd in the fifth, even though he was giving away ten pounds and two years seniority when years count.

He worked on the lawn some more, but with little heart in the job now. Getting on for lunch-time he took himself off, for he did not want to embarrass the girl on the question of status—guest or toiler. Neither did he want to face Kenny and Sheevaun just yet. Instead he went down to the bathing-pool, and finding the coast clear stripped and had half a dozen plunges. Even with the sun beating into it all day it had a fine keen tang, and in the morning the tang must have been more than keen. A spunky slip of a girl, that Marian! Well! she would need all her spunk.

After that he went up the flank of the slope and slipped into the harness-room and so into the stable. He knew about that pony now, and got to its head before it could pivot. He took it outside and watered it from a faucet in the yard, led it down to its own paddock at the other side of the slope, slipped the halter off and dodged the flying heels. The pony galloped once round the little field and began a busy cropping.

"Next time I have to catch you, mister, you'll get your first lesson in roping," Stephen promised.

When he got back to the yard, Maggie Donald was standing at the kitchen door.

"Thocht you were lost, sonnie. Your dinner is like a stane. Come awa' ben."

She had kept a big plate of rabbit-pie and potato warm in the oven. She was a culinary master of the rabbit, as are most Scots half-cooks. Something to do with par-boiling and onions and stock and such. That rabbit-pie might have been a good game-pie with chicken flavour.

"You're makin' Miss Marian tearin' mad, young fellow," she said.

"Should I?"

"So long as she wants another skelp at you. I ha'e my eye on you."

She had a saucepan of water on the range, and was fumbling the lid off a canister.

"Coffee?" enquired Stephen. "Let me try it my way this once."

"Only one way I ken, but you're welcome."

He emptied the boiling saucepan into the kettle and

set the saucepan back over the circle in the range. Maggie skirled.

"Guidness! Do you want to scaum my good pannie?"

He held her off with his shoulder and spooned four heaped tablespoons into the hot dry pan, and she wanted to know if he was making a week's supply. The bean had been too long ground and had lost some flavour, so he added two more spoonfuls. He kept it moving until a spiral of smoke came off, and then poured the boiling water slowly until the fragrant brew frothed to the brim. Then he settled it with a dash of cold water, and drew the pan aside.

"That's all!" he said. "Montana camp-fire coffee!"

"Sinfu' extravagance. I'm no' for it in this house, an' the bawbees no' that plenty."

She had a tray ready and took two cups through to the dining-room. Stephen was drinking his when she got back, and he had one ready for her. It was fair enough coffee, but she adulterated it with milk and sugar before tasting.

"Piison!" she said briefly, but she finished her cup.

Stephen was having a second cup when Marian Finlay came through.

"Father is resting," she said, and smiled to Stephen. "I recognise your strong-arm method. Is there another cup, Maggie?"

"Fower—an' the bottom burned out o' the pannie."

Marian had another cup and then half a cup. It was pretty good coffee after all. She sat on the table as before, and swung her legs, sipped her coffee, and smoked her American cigarette. A weight seemed to be lifted off her. Her father was resting, and she had a man about the place. The life in her came to the top, and she was a pretty good-looking maiden, ready to bandy words with any young man handy. Stephen would not rise to her fly. He drank the last of his coffee, wiped some grounds off his tongue, and started to fill a pipe.

"There is a sudden strange quiet in this house," she said.

"In this land in which it is always afternoon—but not for the toiler and moiler," said Stephen, and moved towards the door. He would not start teasing that girl just yet, though she had invited him to.

He went back to the lawn for a while but the sameness of the work irked him. He was no toiler, and wanted a change of employment. He went round to the back and looked into the walled kitchen garden. It had been well planned and once well-cared-for. Now more than half of it was a wilderness of weeds, dandelions, annual nettles, and lamb's-ear. There was a patch of potatoes and a patch of green stuff, clumps of fruitless gooseberry bushes, and currant bushes with over-ripe blue-black clusters. The unpruned apple trees carried small green fruit, but the ragged plum trees were beginning to colour their early Victorias. There was a tomato-house without tomatoes, and a small vinery where the fruit-clusters had not been thinned.

"The lazy young hellion!" said Stephen. He was referring to the boy Sandy.

The profusion of weeds depressed him, and he turned his back on the kitchen garden. In the harness-room he found an old-fashioned scythe with a straight handle, and an edging-board. He essayed to put an edge on the blade, and felt it professionally with his thumb, to find it turned all on one side. He tried again, and got a keen but rough edge, which is fair enough for a scythe. Then he sallied forth to the bed of bracken above the road.

Brackens are easy to cut. They stand up to the

blade and have a satisfactory crunch. Stephen was pleased with the execution, and even experimented with the flick and lift that lays an even swathe. Sometimes he digged his point hard, but the blade was tough and came straight again. After a while he shed his jacket and folded his sleeves, and admired the play of muscle under white skin.

He had driven his tip into an old root and was using language when he heard footsteps on the road below. Marian and her father were going down towards the river. She was holding his arm, and he was looking forward and far away. She looked up at Stephen and shook her head disapprovingly. Stephen leant against a tree to fill a pipe. He realised that he was no man to hold down a steady labouring job, but if there was a multitude of jobs, as round a house and garden, he could carry on by changing from one to the other. That was a good thing about a garden. It was the one natural occupation and offered an all-the-year-round variety. When he got back home he would start a garden. Every American man should cultivate his garden, same as Voltaire. But he knew that he would not start a garden—same as most American men.

The smooth purr of a powerful car came up to him where he was smoking and idly musing. He cocked an ear. Yes, it was a car coming in the Lodge road, curving round at the flying-bridge, and taking the slope smoothly on top. A big grey open touring-car containing only a white-coated, peak-capped chauffeur. It swerved out of sight on to the gravel in front of the house, and Stephen waited. After a time Maggie Donald appeared on the edge of the lawn, and called and beckoned to him.

"A letter for Miss Marian," she said as he came near through the trees. "Did they pass you down?"

"Yes, I'll take it."

She smiled gleefully as she handed him the letter.

"From young Mr Hale o' Castle Charles. There might be an answer."

"Gosh! You're a fast worker."

"A letter o' thanks it will be. A bonny lad, an' he couldna tak' his e'en off Miss Marian, and she plowtherin' awa' at his sair knee. Talkin' for a hale hour they were, an' laughin'."

"There is match-making in your eye, old woman."

"Awa' wi' you! and what for no? See if there's an answer."

Stephen went down to the flying-bridge and looked up and down the river. The two were not in sight, and had probably gone over Falcon Crag. The laird had a habit of going up there to gaze over all the hilly lands and hollow lands that the MacFinlay had once possessed, and that he in his sick mind still possessed.

Stephen went up the steep curving path. He glanced at the letter in his hand. Budd Hale's writing! Strong writing, but some of the letters took odd angles. He was no judge of handwriting, but he had already judged Budd Hale. A quick bold man, and he had a way with women—not subtle, not subtile, just supple. Here now was his first letter to Marian Finlay, possibly the first letter she had ever received from a young man. It would not be the last. Suppose, he tore it in scraps and let them drift with the water; suppose he flicked it out from the top of this Falcon Crag and let it soar and dip across the hollow to be caught in the tree-tops and make a lining for a rook's nest? Would that cramp Budd's style? Not by a jugful!

Some distance along the path from the Crag, the laird and Marian sat on a log. Stephen whistled, and when she turned her head held the letter up for her to see. She came part of the way to meet him.

"From Castle Charles," Stephen said.

She looked at the letter and flushed. When she flushed like that Stephen could not be sure whether she was bonny or beautiful. No, not bonny, but she had qualities of beauty in the bones of her face. As Kirsty Power had said, she had not yet blossomed—but she would. And then?

"There may be an answer," Stephen said. "The shover is waiting."

She turned a shoulder to him as she opened the letter, but he saw that there were four pages.

"Bah!" He was contemptuous. "I don't call that no letter."

She moved a forefinger at him without looking up.

"My first love-letter—the one I wrote—had five pages written on both sides." He pretended to crane his head for a look. "What? No poetry either—not even a sonnet!"

"Damn you, Stephen Wayne! Go and boil your head!" That is what that properly-brought-up Scots aristocrat said.

"I don't write any more love-letters now—too expensive. I'll be up on the Crag."

He ran up to the flat top of Falcon Crag and sat down, his feet dangling over emptiness. The bowl of Knockindu and the Glen of the Shinnoch touched him as ever with the durability of their strength and beauty. That would last for all time, and man could use it if the right mind was in him. He looked across at his own croft. That would last too if a wise man stayed by it to keep the heather in its place. There was a tail of smoke from one chimney of the squat house. That tail would not be absent winter or summer while the house was occupied.

Ruary Farquhar—no mistaking the tall long-striding figure—was coming down the track to the main road. Probably off on a scout of his own; and there might be a cut of salmon to-morrow.

Marian Finlay's voice hailed him from below.

"No answer."

"Cruel, cruel!" He gave her the flat of his hand, and went down the brae to Lettoch Lodge. There was no answer now, but silence would only spur Budd Hale. Damn! Why be hard on the man? She was a worthwhile prize in an honest game. Honest! Why not, if Budd was a free man? She was superior in caste by several layers to the son of an ordinary Yankee magnate; and Ruary Farquhar and Maggie Donald might well dream of a new lady at Castle Charles, and the blood of the MacFinlay renewing itself. No business of his, anyway.

From the edge of the lawn Stephen called across to Maggie. Maggie was still holding the chauffeur captive of her tongue, her hands folded in her apron after the manner of house-gossips everywhere. The chauffeur found it difficult to break free. He opened the door to get in; he had his foot on the running-board, he leant over the door, finally he made the engine roar to drown her voice, and so got away. Maggie waddled across the lawn to Stephen.

"Will it not keep?"

"The castle is full-up like auld times. Besides the folk themselves there's six gents for the shooting—and only a'e lady."

"She is hard-boiled, that one," said Stephen, recalling the dark vivid sophisticated one.

"Young and bonny she is. A flamin' beaute! the driver chap called her. And forbye she's an earl's daughter."

"Sure! We are acquant of an earl's poor daughter —I mean a poor earl's daughter toying with the almighty dollar—man attached."

"Mebbe so! He thinks she is engaged to young Mr Hale."

"And there's the bottom kicked out of your romance."

"Whatna romance?"

"No, it ain't neither! You'll bring your own hoss home by a neck."

"Stop haverin'! Was it a long letter?"

"Long enough. But I hadn't time to read all of it. Not so dusty."

She gave him up as a bad job.

"Awa'! Are you going up by to Ruary's for the milk? The pail is this side."

"S'pose I must face the rending tongue. I'll finish that dam' lawn to-morrow—if I'm let."

"Hist swearing, sonnie! I'll no' hinner."

Going down the road, pail swinging, Stephen heard the crunch of a scythe on the slope above. Ruary Farquhar was laying into the bracken bed with the easy rhythm of the skilled mower. When he saw Stephen, he laid the scythe carefully down, point out of danger, and sat down himself, his back against a tree. He took a black junk of plug, the colour and texture of bog-oak, from his pocket and began slicing it. Stephen went up and sat at his side, but he did not think of smoking for yet awhile.

"Came across for that milk-can," said Ruary.

"Anything else?"

"Nice evenin' for a daunder as well."

"Suppose you give me some advice?"

"Often and often I advised myself and naething came of it."

"I find myself losing my irresponsibility."

"That is the way always," Ruary nodded. "The responsibility aye comes."

"You found that out early. I have responsibility enough in my own place, but here I am on a holiday. I don't want a job, and I guess I can have one."

"What sort of job would that be?" wondered Ruary.

"You think you know, but you don't, quite." Stephen paused to look at him, but he was absorbed in drawing smoke, the match flame pulsing. "You'll know all right, kind mister badger. I met Marian Finlay the first day I arrived."

"I heard you comin'."

"You did. I fell down on my nose and sat up under hers. And even that first day I saw that she was afraid. Her father was with her, but he was also far away in time and space—in time especially. Forty years away, for to-morrow he was going poaching with young Ruary Farquhar."

Ruary's shoulders moved against the trunk but he said nothing. He was letting Stephen explain himself to himself.

"I was only five minutes in their company and I saw the strain on both of them. A week later I returned the crook she had loaned me, and she was trying to cut the lawn with a blunt machine, and ready to weep. I fixed the machine and cut the lawn for her."

"You cut it anither fashion last night. Have you been at it?"

"All day with a fork and a roller."

"That's the way. You saved me a lot o' trouble. I'm interruptin' you?"

"You are. That day on the lawn she was watching the house as if she was in deadly fear of it. She might well be. Her father is mad, Ruary, and at any moment might go like that. Phutt!"

"I ken that."

"A young girl, and the responsibility is too much for her. She needs a man about the house night and day, Ruary. Why should I be that man—or why should I not be? The problem is with you, my wise old father. Get down to it!"

Stephen took his pipe out now and started to fill it. He somehow felt relieved of responsibility. Ruary, smoking thoughtfully, ventured a mild remark:

"She is no' an ugly girl. She has qualities."

"Don't I know it? You are suggesting that this damn'd interfering habit of mine is influenced by these qualities. I'm hanged if I know Ruary, and that's the plain truth."

Ruary leant his head back against the trunk and laughed—quiet laughter with a touch of irony in it.

"Tak' you the job, Mr Wayne. You are the best man for it—at the meenit."

"You have another man in your mind?"

"Only a foolish fancy. You ken?"

"I ken. I don't like that man."

"You'll have your reasons."

"I mightn't have. Budd Hale and I were at the same college——"

"Let me say it," said Ruary. "Isn't it a small world that's in it?"

"He licked me over six rounds."

"Just boxin'." Ruary was contemptuous.

"He got the decision over me and I was sore at the time. Perhaps I'm sore still, but there may be another reason."

"That is what is called a complex," said Ruary. "I mind readin' about they things. But there is more in it than that. Your feelin's are touched—I'm no' sayin' more—and a man has a notion, and a gey foolish notion, that he can protect the weak, sometimes. Very well! Maybe a man, an' no name said, is no' particular—what you call scrupulous—and maybe Marian Finlay is no' sophisticate. What then?"

"And how?"

"Sophistication, Mr Wayne, is the weapon o' the defeated. That girl has a stronger weapon. It might be in her breed or in her caste—an auld tradition o' race. But all the same, there is no harm for you to play guardian angel till the deevil starts temptin' yoursel'. You got a job, I'm thinkin'. There they go now."

The laird and his daughter passed up the road below them. Her eyes glanced at them and passed by. The man held his head up and was armoured in calm— calm brittle as glass. The two men sat on, thinking their own thoughts, not inclined any longer to put words to them. A rustle in the ferns made them turn head to see Marian Finlay coming through the trees behind. Ruary made to scramble to his feet but she was at his side, a hand on his shoulder.

"Doggo, Ruary! I want to talk down to you for once."

She came round to face them, her chin down and her eyes serious, but not too serious. That half-seriousness implied a pleasant quality of character. She pointed a finger at Ruary.

"Was it you sicked Stephen Wayne on me?"

"It was that," said Ruary.

"You wanted some peace and quietness, didn't you?"

"Right enough!" said Ruary. "When Kenny Alpin and Sheevaun, and anither no' named, get goin' you couldn't hear yourself think—no' that you'd want to."

"I asked you to get a boy for me."

"I got him." He gestured his thumb at Stephen.

"Is there a plot between you and your employer?"

"There is that," said Ruary, and came to his feet with the lift of youth. He put his finger on her forearm. "There is a neighbourly plot atween us, my dear. You know how things get known in this place, and we don't want the laird's state to be talked about farther than we can help. There's you here and us over there, and can't we keep it to ourselves in a neighbourly way? I would come myself, only I'm out o' the laird's past an' bad for him. Kenny Alpin would be makin' love to you, and small blame to him—an' Sheevaun might tear someone's hair by the roots. Weel, then? A quiet, douce man we got, no' given to talkin'."

"I noticed that. But, Ruary, it's at night I need someone about the house. I am frightened of the nights, and I cannot keep awake."

"I ken that. Miss Marian, if you maun ken, I have circled the house in the dark twa or three nights in the week this past month. Leave you it to Mr Wayne and myself. Don't you worry about the nights. You need not know unless you want to. There's that garret room above the stable if one of us needs a rest, an' we can keep out of the laird's way. What ither way would you want?"

She stood silently looking up at Ruary, and Ruary clapped his hands.

"Losh, mish! There'll be no milk for the tea."

Stephen picked up the pail.

"I'll come for it," he said, "and talk to Sheevaun a piece."

He had a job. He had two jobs.

CHAPTER VIII

STEPHEN was in the kitchen after tea, smoking and listening to Maggie Donald. Her monologue was like a serial. One could take it up anywhere even if she did mix her instalments. It was mostly about the Mac-Finlays, and it went back and fore over a century; and, in spite of all her apologies, Stephen came to the conclusion that the MacFinlay, laird after laird, had thrown his luck out the window, and brought the family exactly where it deserved to be.

Marian Finlay came in from the sitting-room. She was wearing a green dress and it suited her. Against the white walls the long lissome line of her, not fragile, took the eye. She was not smoking, nor did she perch on the table. She looked very determined and almost stern. She had a closed letter in her hand, and she came straight at Stephen with it.

"Don't you hit a fellow in Maggie Donald's kitchen," he said, starting to his feet.

"If I give this to the postie," she said, "it will not be delivered at Castle Charles until the day after to-morrow."

"What do you expect for three bawbees? I'll take it." He took the letter from her.

"Thank you. Across the bridge and over the hill—there's a path all the way."

"Is there an answer?"

"No answer." She shook her head and was definite.

"There will be."

He knew that this envelope contained an answer to Budd Hale's letter of the afternoon, and that he, the guardian angel (according to Ruary), had to be the bearer of it. He went out quickly, but outside he remembered something and put a head back through the door.

"Just a word with you?"

She came out half-frowning, expecting some more asinine teasing, but he was serious this time.

"Do you lock your father's door at night?"

"I thought of it, but it would not be any use."

"You lock the front and back doors?"

"Yes, Maggie keeps the keys. But if dad wanted to get out he need only step through his own window."

"Thought so. If you are in bed before I get back you can sleep sound. I'll see to it."

"Thanks—Stephen. I am going to bed early to-night."

"Fine! Try a letter under your pillow. I'm off."

In that high latitude the autumn evening is long-drawn-out, and he still had two or three hours of daylight. It was a warm evening, too, and he took his time; pausing on the summit of Falcon Crag to look abroad; peeping down at the river through the larches, and wondering if Ruary was out after a fish; taking the up-slope easily; and at last getting a glimpse of the tall pepper-castored mansion from a corner of the garden wall. When he got along to the edge of the lawn he stopped dead.

Budd Hale was sitting out there not fifty paces away, reclining easily in a wheeled long-chair—one of those East-Indian long-chairs with the footrest drawn out. There was a young woman with him, dark and vivid in a flimsy gown. Stephen remembered that dark vivid beauty, and how she, too, had made his blood move.

Her canvas chair, with sun-hood, was slewed round towards the other, and man and woman were busy making talk interspersed with the laughter that goes with wordy swordplay; and Stephen could gather that the lady was useful at that sort of fence, even against Budd Hale.

Stephen had no intention of delivering Marian Finlay's letter personally. He, somehow, did not want to renew acquaintance with Budd. Stephen's character was sterling enough, and he had no desire to renew an old antagonism. He was not compelled to do so. He slipped back behind the rhododendrons, and circled round towards the rear of the house.

The service premises were in a two-storied modern building attached to the rear of the castle. Stephen knocked at three doors before a servant-maid opened to him. He reached her the letter.

"For your young Mr Hale," he said.

She hesitated and looked at him doubtfully before taking the envelope. He was unshaven, tousle-haired, and rent at knee and shoulder.

"You are dead right, sister," he said. "But that is not a begging letter. Mr Budd Hale will want to get it at once."

He left her looking at the evelope in her hand and went back the way he had come. To get to the path over the hill he had again to approach within fifty paces of the two on the lawn. He stood by the clump of rhododendrons and looked at them. He could hear the woman's cool English voice pitched lower than American voices.

A man in a white front and black tails came across the lawn bearing a shining silver tray, and bowed before his master; Budd Hale took up Marian Finlay's letter, glanced at the lady, who nodded her head, and flicked the letter open. It did not take long to read— it was a brief note—and again he glanced at his companion, who laughed a pleasant but mocking gurgle of laughter. Budd shook a "no-answer" head at the menial, who stalked back across the lawn. It was time for Stephen to go too. He was about to turn when a strong rude hand grasped his shoulder.

"No bluidy tramps allowed in here!" said a voice equally strong and rude. "How the hell did you get in?"

"This spills the beans," said Stephen to himself.

He turned head with some difficulty to see a tall, raw-boned, sandy-bearded man in a badly made suit of brown-and-white-checks.

"On my way over the hill to Knockindu," he said amicably as possible, shifting his shoulder.

"No bluidy fear!" The big fellow gripped harder. "You'll gang oot the road you came. That auld donkey lets every dirty tramp through. Come on! an' in half a meenit you'll be gettin' two roots ahind to help you."

Stephen went. He did not want to start a roughhouse with this head-keeper in sight of Budd Hale; but as soon as they got round a convenient corner—

"Who have you got there, Walker?" Budd Hale's voice came across the lawn. "Bring him along and let's see him!"

The keeper thrust at Stephen; Stephen took the thrust and a bit more, twisted quickly, gripped the wrist of the hand that held him, jerked close in, got a foot behind and drove his free hand into shoulder angle. The keeper went over backwards. If he were a mile high and as strong as Samson he could not withstand that trick trip. Stephen felt his shoulder rip in a new place.

He had the sudden idea of making a run for it, even if he did not run very well. He had one devil of a temper when handled roughly. Dam'd if he'd run! He walked across the lawn towards Budd Hale and the lady. He heard the keeper thumping behind and faced round.

"Keep your paws off, brother!" he warned softly.

The keeper did not intend to, and as he came on Stephen picked a shot in the centre of his short sandy beard. Break his knuckles probably. Pity he was losing his temper. The man was only doing his duty after all. But Stephen had not to hit him.

"Let him alone, Walker!" shouted Budd Hale.

"Just five minutes, Walker," said Stephen. "Meet you round the corner, and nothing barred."

He turned and walked on, and the keeper stayed where he was, within reach if needed.

"Hello, Budd!" Stephen said. "Pleasant welcome?'

"Good lord! Who is it?"

"You don't know me? Fine! You wouldn't be seen dead in my company."

But Budd Hale was not easy to fool. Stephen saw the light of recognition in his eyes.

"Wayne!" he cried. "Stevie Wayne! Little even Stephen Wayne!"

"The beans are spilled all right," said Stephen. "But I wasn't looking you up, Budd. This is not a touch."

Budd Hale straightened in his long-chair, and his leg moved.

"Wow! Dam' that knee! Touch, your granny! Put it there, old son."

They shook hands. Budd Hale was no snob—never had been. When Stephen came to think of it there was not such a great deal wrong with Budd. He was not vicious—just lived too much. His eyes were taking Stephen in.

"Struck a bad patch, Steve?"

"Any tougher and I'll let you know, Budd."

He didn't get Stephen's meaning that time.

"Sure! Glad to help. But what the hell are you doing so far from—Montana, wasn't it?"

"Same to you! Bozeman, Montana. I'm seeing Scotland. On my way across into Glen Shinnoch, and sorry if I'm trespassing."

"All right with me. Hiking?" Budd was no fool. Stephen's dress was pretty awful, but he was no hobo; there wasn't a depraved line on his face, and he remembered those clear daredevil eyes.

"Sort of hoboing my way, Budd," he said. "Seeing Scotland as my grandmother's people saw it—from the ground down."

"If that suits you. You were always a queer cuss. You'll stay for a meal?"

"Sorry!" Stephen looked down at himself. "Another engagement."

"Like hell you have! Don't be silly. They are all up at Carron Bothy for an early morning stalk, and my aunt is laid up with indigestion - heart she calls it. We'll be all alone."

"Not all alone, Budd, for which the Lord be thankit." He turned half an eye towards the dark lady, and a ripple of laughter came from her. "I'd hate to be a third," said Stephen.

"Sorry, Steve!" Budd remembered his manners. "This is Lady Alice Tromes. Steve Wayne and I were at college together, Ally."

Stephen bowed to the lady, and the lady bent her head. She remembered Stephen, but she did not say so.

"I will never believe that this lady is an earl's daughter," said Stephen.

"Careful, you mutt! That is what she is."

"A duke at the very least."

"Neat!" said the lady, and laughed again. "Mine is a courtesy title, Mr Wayne. I work for a living."

"I bet a hat," agreed Stephen.

"I like your friend, Buddy," she said. "He is a dangerous man in disguise."

She was indeed a dark and vivid young English aristocrat, but not too young. Her eyes and her mouth in the clear pallor of her face were astonishing. A dark, flaming beauty was exactly right. And sophisticated. Buddington Hale as a man was just as splendid. A reclining, long, broad-shouldered figure, with well-boned face under dark-red hair. Possibly his forehead had too much bone, and his features might have been too regular but for a slight side-twist to his nose. It was Stephen who had slewed that nose for him in that fifth round where he had so nearly taken him. He couldn't take him now. Stephen hadn't grown an inch after seventeen, and Budd looked all of a light-heavy.

"You will stay to dinner, Mr Wayne?" said the lady. "This Budd Hale tires me."

"Of course he'll stay, and you'll get no chance to make me jealous, Alicia. I'll do the talking."

There was no reason why Stephen should not stay for a meal. Moreover, he wanted to study the relations between these two. He noticed, for the first time—being a male—that she wore a ring on her left hand, but it might not be an engagement ring. He did not know about these things.

A deep-toned gong sounded from the deep-arched doorway of the house. Budd called across to the keeper:

"All clear, Walker! A friend of mine."

"Made an appointment with him round the corner," said Stephen.

"He'll not keep it. Run this contraption across to the door for me, Steve. Darn you, you little thug! It was you started that knee going. College football, Ally—seniors against the ruck. And this nose of mine too."

"Nice friend! It improves you—a little, Buddy—that nose."

"What crocked the knee this time?" enquired Stephen innocently.

"Fell on it following up a wounded stag. Tell you about it at dinner. A mysterious affair, and the stalkers have a theory."

Stephen would take an interest in that theory.

The three had dinner at a long half-acre of dining-table in a huge oak-panelled dining-room inadequately lit by high-set narrow windows. There were also electric candles, softly hooded, reflected deep in the polished mahogany. It was a good dinner. There was fish, but it was not salmon. The salmon were not taking, and the coastal netting season was over. There was no venison either, for the first stag of the season was not in the Castle Charles larder. But there was nothing wrong with that dinner, and there was a bottle of red wine that intrigued even Stephen's amateur palate.

The talk was table-talk for a while, and cast back to college days and men. Then it came round to shooting. Budd was cursing his luck. The whole party of men, including his father, had gone up to Carron Bothy at the top-end of the forest beyond Corryhow after the best head on the ground, a royal hart that had evaded the best stalking for two seasons. Budd himself had once got within a hundred and fifty yards, tried for another fifty to make sure, and lost out. Now, probably, a mere beginner would get it easy as a sitting rabbit. He cursed his luck quite frankly, and when the lady pointed out to Stephen how uncomplimentary that was to her, Budd only laughed.

Budd Hale and Lady Alice Tromes were quite frank with each other, just carelessly friendly; but Stephen sensed some undertone of familiarity, some private understanding that might be intimate. Stephen knew Budd, and Budd gave him the impression that he didn't care a damn, but accepted a certain tie—it might even be the tie of a formal engagement. The lady supplied no information—except by that ringed finger. Much has been made of alliances between impoverished British nobility and American dollars. Most of it is not so. But occasionally an earl's willing daughter is thrown at the head of an agreeable millionaire's son. That sort of unconditional surrender detracts from the charm of even a vivid beauty like Alice Tromes, and it would not appeal to a hunting male like Budd Hale. He might accept it, but it would not cramp his style. He would be just as faithful as he wanted to be, and there was always the chase. He was a hunter all the time, and now he was on another trail. So thought Stephen Wayne.

When the talk got to stalking, Stephen kept it there. It was due to Ruary Farquhar to find out what he could about that stag.

"You didn't say how you bust your knee, Budd?" he put to him.

"The knee is nothing—better in a day or two. The stag is the mystery. I got a good head dead-to-rights on Thamdu, and brought the beast down too, but an inch too far back, thanks to the advice of my stalker, old Sanny Grigor. It went down like a keg of nails and got up again, and I must have missed it clean with

157

a second shot. It made across towards the Sanctuary but was as good as dead on its feet. I followed it over the hill into Glen Shinnoch, but before I got to the top I heard a rifle-shot in the glen. I was looking down into that glen within seconds, and there was no stag and no poacher. There was just nothing—nothing at all. I was standing right on top, a thousand feet up, and the floor of the glen at that point is as bare of cover as the lawn outside. It got me for a bit."

"That was one of those fairy deer, Buddy," said the lady. "Any number of legends about, you know."

"Maybe! But half an hour later, and some distance down, Sanny Grigor came on two men trout-fishing, and one of them was a notorious old poacher—one Ruary Farquhar who runs a place at the mouth of the glen. Sanny insists that Farquhar got the stag, but I don't see how he could. I am dam' grateful to the old boy in any case. I put out my knee crossing the river, and he found me and put it in like one o'clock. Luckily for me, old MacFinlay came along on his pony about then, and I rode down to Lettoch Lodge, his place. Here is the point. Sanny went up the glen this morning to have a look-see. He didn't find the stag, but he found where it was shot, and he found traces of a pony in the same place, and that place was close to— within twenty yards of the ford where I fell down."

"Has this Ruary Farquhar a pony?" enquired Stephen.

"Sanny says not, but he also says that he could borrow the MacFinlay pony; and there is an implication, Highland fashion, that Farquhar, the other man, and old MacFinlay were in the plot. I don't fall for that."

"Who is this MacFinlay?" enquired the lady with interest.

158

"The man who owned this property before dad bought it—over-head in mortgages. He is still called the laird, and lives at Lettoch Lodge across the river. A real old Highland aristocrat in a kilt, and no more mad than I am. His daughter is one nice kid."

"How nice is she, Buddy? You have mentioned her once or twice to-day—and there was a letter."

"She is the goods all right," said Budd easily, and grinned across the table at her. "Knocks you hollow, my dear." Budd knew his technique.

"In that case I'll claim Stephen Wayne," said the lady. She knew her technique too.

After coffee and a kummel, a fifty-cent cigar only half-smoked, Stephen rose to go. The strange wan blue light of the late gloaming was on the window-panes. Budd asked meaningly if he was all right, and being assured of that shook hands and hoped to meet him again some time.

Lady Alice Tromes accompanied Stephen to the door. She picked up a wrap as she went through the hall and flung it over one shoulder.

"Do you mind if I again show you that path over the hill?" she said.

"I'll risk it," said Stephen.

They went across the grey-green, black-dotted lawn side by side. Everything was very still there in the hollow of the hills; the black pine woods seemed to be crouching about the house whispering, "Hush, hush! Sleep ye! We never sleep"; and the smooth black hill-tops under the pallor of the sky were as aloof as death.

She put her left hand quietly in Stephen's arm, and her fingers did not press. A slender cool hand, and he could feel the coolness of it through his sleeve; but the coolness had a tingle too, and he noted that to himself with ironic amusement at his own blood. She was about as tall as he was, and her black hair or herself had that faint dark disturbing perfume; but Stephen told himself that that sort of perfume could be expensive in bottles, much more expensive than his cigar, whose fine perfume could not overlay hers. He looked down at her left hand on his sleeve. There was a ring —pearls and diamonds—on her third finger. Stephen said:

"Don't tell me, Lady Alice, that you are already captive?"

"Captive?" A finger twitched on his sleeve.

"That ring you are wearing?"

"Oh, that?" A small chuckle. "That binds little obligation on one any more." And then she said, "A week or so ago I saw you come in by the shrubberies; this evening I saw you when you first came."

"A handy short-cut over the hill," said Stephen.

"Then you were going, this evening you were coming. I felt you would come again."

"More than I felt."

"You went round towards the rear of the house and you came back again. Don't think up an equivocation! You took that letter to the back door."

That game was up, and denial would be plain foolish.

"When you left the dining-room that time you asked the girl. You are pretty good at reading signs, lady."

"So are you. You and I can get on. You know, I rather like you."

"I'm a blame fool," said Stephen, "but I like you too, and no rather about it. Will you tell Budd?"

"That you like me?"

"Tell him that. About that letter?"

"Don't trust me not to. I don't trust you. Tell me,

are you—how do you put it? Are you laying for him?"

"You implied that before. I might begin to."

"Do you want anything from him?"

"Not even the most precious thing he has."

"I'll not ask you what you mean. What ever did he do to you?"

"He licked me once."

"He could lick you again."

"I may have to give him the chance," said Stephen.

"I could understand that if he had met that Mac-Finlay girl ten days ago. Had he?"

"I hadn't."

"He was there last night, sent a letter this morning—and you brought a reply. Is she such a wonderful girl?"

"Now we are the woman's postscript. I read sign all right, Lady Alice. She is not half as bonny as you are."

"Damn bonnyness!"

"I stand corrected. You are not bonny either."

"That's better."

"A flaming beauty, a man said. That goes. He mixed vividness with fire."

"Are you one of these past-masters too? Nice method you've got, but you'll not get away from that postscript. Tell me about Miss MacFinlay?"

"What do I know about Marian Finlay?"

"Marian Finlay! Nice name! Tromes? Oh, hell! You don't use the Mac?"

"Not in the Highlands, sometimes. Mac means son, I am told."

"I see. Is she a flaming beauty too?"

"She has qualities of beauty, but not yours. She is not vivid—yet. She is cool and young—virginal. She has straight long legs and they flow upwards."

She looked down at her own long easy-striding legs.

"That's right," said Stephen. "If you were a cripple I wouldn't mention legs."

"Past-master, indeed! A cool long-legged young virgin with qualities of beauty. Anything else?"

"Pretty fair, ain't it? She has not blossomed. Her mouth is too grave. She is Mariana waiting in the moated grange. Blast it! You make me talk, woman."

"Woe! Woe! Woe for your young Mariana!" One could almost tell that she had walked the boards.

"Young and not sophisticated," Stephen said, and remembered Ruary's words. "Sophistication is the weapon of the defeated."

"Am I not sophisticated?"

"You are the exception, of course."

"The correct thing to say. You are in love with that girl, Stephen Wayne?"

"Not yet, Alice Tromes. And if I were I would forget it in your company."

She gave his arm a little shake and let it go.

"You frighten me. You are a mystery man. Here is your path. Will you come again?"

"I will not. I would want to take off Budd Hale's hide, and I am not able. You take it off for me?"

"My knife has been blunted, strange man," she said.

They paused in the half-dark under the trees, and she gave him her hand frankly. Under some sudden impulse he bent and touched his lips to it. He felt the pressure of her fingers for an instant, and then she turned and went away across the lawn—not hurriedly. She went in a slow graceful slouch.

Stephen stood in the shadow looking after that lissome figure dimming in the gloaming. She might be a real earl's daughter, and certainly she was a flaming beauty, but she knew how to stoop perfectly. She might be engaged to Budd Hale, and probably was. Budd had been a married man, at least once, but that was a low average in certain classes. If the earl, her father, had thrown her at Budd's head he was doing her a poor service. She should have been allowed to use her own method, and even Budd might have come to eat out of her hand. Why, darn it! She made his own pulses stir. But that was not strange. Any number of good-lookers had made his heart flutter, and went away, or he went away, and the old ticker was ready for some more fluttering.

That dark one was going into the house now. Would she tell Budd that Stephen knew Marian Finlay, and had been her messenger. That would not phase Budd. Budd would only play the game all the more blithely and zestfully. Hell! he could no longer lick Budd, but he might sure try.

CHAPTER IX

AT the first turn of the path where there was a wide opening in the trees, the tall keeper was waiting for Stephen, and Stephen swore under his breath. He could not see himself getting angry enough for a rough-house. But the keeper said quickly:

"'Tis all right, sir! My mistake."

"I apologise too," said Stephen with relief. "There are two beasts you should never touch until you have first spoken—a horse and a man."

"I didn't know you the first time," went on the keeper. "You are the Mr Wayne across at Balmerion with Ruary Farquhar?"

Stephen did not tell him where he was staying now. He realised that Budd Hale would soon hear all about him.

"You were up the glen yesterday with Ruary, Mr Wayne?"

"That's right. We met your stalker—Grigor."

"I wonder would you gi'e Ruary a message from me —Walker, the head-keeper?"

"Certainly."

"Tell him that we know about a certain stag, and that he'll be minding whaur he walks."

"Will he understand?"

"Ay, will he."

"You are just warning me, aren't you?"

"Just that, sir." He gave a bark of laughter. "It'll do no good warnin' Ruary, but I ha'e my duty."

"You should be just so hard on poachers, Mr Walker," hinted Stephen.

"How hard, sir?"

"Hard as you like at the time—not after. They keep you in your jobs—largely."

"That's a fac'," he admitted. "Gosh! but it is, an' it explains how many an auld retired keeper takes to poachin' himself. They're the a'e breed. Guid nicht, sir!"

When Stephen got to the top of Falcon Crag night was down over ben and glen, and all the valleys were filled with silence. There was a light in the croft window across the valley, and Stephen had a small pang of almost nostalgia that he was not under that friendly roof with those four friendly people. It was his own roof if he wanted it. There was no light shining amongst the trees from Lettoch Lodge, and when he got up there there was no glimmer at front or back.

He climbed the steep steps from the harness-room to the garret and struck a match. Right in front of him he saw a small table with a paraffin hand-lamp on it. The bowl had been newly filled with oil and the glass cleaned. He lit it, waited till the glass warmed, and gradually turned it up. And again, as he stood there, he had a touch of nostalgia, but this time for his own West. He was reminded of a certain bunk-house he had stayed in for a season. The odour was just the same: heather, ammonia, horse, and stale smoke. The garret was a low wedge of wooden-lined room with a skylight, and very bare—just a table, chair, truckle-bed, tin pail and wash-basin, and some clean towels on a wall hook. It would do. He was used to doing without things. There were fresh clothes on the truckle-bed, and on top his rucksack and a small portmanteau. Ruary had seen to all that. On the table was a jug of milk and a plate of scones. That was his supper, but he did not need any after that dinner.

Stephen did not intend to stay up all night and prowl about the house. Already he had worked out his method. He took the lamp, and went down to the harness-room. He found a spool of garden marking-cord in a corner. He had already tested it for toughness, and had tied at one end an old iron axle-block weighing several pounds. He took the block upstairs and anchored it to the table-leg. Then he went across the yard, playing out the line, and so around to the front of the house. He hooked the line over the bridle-hook by the front door, and for greater security threaded it through the old-fashioned knocker; led it along the wall across the dining-room window, and, moving cautiously now, came to the laird's bedroom window. The top half was lowered and no sounds came from inside—no pacing of restless footsteps, no mutter in unquiet sleep. He led the line across the lower half of the sash, and moved on to the next window.

This was the girl's room, and the window was open top and bottom. He crouched along below it, and slipped the line over the sill. The line was playing out, and three paces beyond brought him up short. It was just not long enough. A Virginia creeper clothed the wall about there, and it was his intention to stay the line to a twisted stem. He cursed under his breath and put all the strain on the line that he dared, but he still wanted a few inches to make a knot. He would have to go back to the garret and move that axle-block, and, like all men, he hated starting back to the beginning of things, though it would not take him half a minute. Instead, he moved cautiously to Marian

Finlay's window and ran a hand softly over the lower portion of the frame. Many of these old sashes have a nail stuck here and there for no apparent purpose. He found the nail all right, but just as he found it the blind went half-up and the window went up with it.

"Who is that?" That was Marian Finlay's voice, a little startled.

Stephen was crouching, his head above the sill, and the girl's face looked straight into his. Most girls would have screamed.

"Don't you vamp me, Marian Finlay," he whispered.

"Oh! it is you?"

"It is—whoever I am."

"Whatever are you doing?" Her whispering voice was not exactly calm, but she was not afraid.

"Setting a trap-line. Bit of string about you?"

"String?"

"Dash! Of course! This is a much better plan. Take hold o' that. Blast it! It won't bite you."

He put the end of the line in her hesitating fingers.

"That's the trigger of my alarm-clock," he told her, and started to explain. But she understood at once.

"What a brilliant idea, Stephen! Where do I tie it?"

"To the first leg you come to—not your own."

Her dressing-table was aslant at one side of the window, and she was fumbling at the near leg of it. Stephen put his head through.

"No girlish slip-knots," he warned her. "A good tight granny!"

"Teach your granny to suck eggs."

"Gosh! And I thought you were well brought up."

He withdrew his head. She knelt inside the window, her arms resting on the sill. He could see the soft oval of her face against the dark of the room, and the soft shaft of her neck above white-robed shoulders. Soft and tender and warm, and a faint glow about her like the glow of a pearl in faint moonlight—and there was no moonlight. That damned heart of his began to stir again. He whispered quickly:

"If I am needed in the night pull that string—not too hard, or you might break my darn neck down the garret stairs."

He heard her soft snigger.

"Where do you anchor it? To your big toe?"

"Where else? If your father tries to get out he'll wake me up too. You can sleep sound to-night, Mariana."

"I will sleep," she sighed softly.

He was about to turn away, when she put her head out the window.

"You were a long time over the hill," she whispered.

"We want some gossip, do we? Yes, I delivered your letter at the back door like a proper serving-man."

"Not fair to any serving-man. You didn't see——?"

"He was reclining on the lawn. I looked him over. No! I didn't, neither. Too busy admiring a young woman keeping him company."

"Maggie told me about her. She is famous on and off the stage—Lady Alice Tromes."

"Geewhilikins! I knew there was something about her. A flaming beauty! I think that she is more beautiful than you, Maid Marian."

"That would not make her a beauty."

"All the same and nevertheless, Budd Hale will be over to see you to-morrow—or next day, when he can put a foot under him."

"Budd! Budd Hale! Do you know him?"

For some obscure reason he did not want her to know

that he knew Budd. Perhaps he wanted to retain freedom of action in certain eventualities. He said coolly:

"Your letter was addressed, Buddington Hale, Esquire. Bound to be called Budd or Buddy where he was raised. You call him, Tony!"

The window began to close down.

"Good night, Stephen! Thank you, serving-man!"

She felt quite secure in there with Stephen Wayne on guard outside. That was all to the good, but Stephen sardonically wondered whether he should feel complimented or not.

He went back to his garret, closed the door to the last half-inch, and placed the iron block at a nice strain on the edge of the table, so that a small tug would send it clattering against the door and jamb. Then he straightened up and yawned; he had had a longish day and not much sleep the previous night. The portmanteau, packed by Sheevaun, contained a change of suit, clean shirt, socks, pyjamas, dressing-gown, slippers, and glory! a bathing-suit. His shaving-tackle was in the rucksack, and in one corner of it was a flask of whisky. That was good old Kenny. To-morrow he would get in a quart, and Kenny would come over at night for a drink—maybe Ruary too. He was settled in. He had one small drink.

He was asleep within five minutes on a hard chaff mattress. In what looked like another five he was roused by one almighty clatter, and rolled out of bed on to his feet as he had often done before. Bright daylight was struggling through the cobwebbed skylight. The iron block was jammed between door and jamb, and it was jerking like a spent trout out of the water. Stephen threw on his dressing-gown, slipped his feet into his slippers, pulled the weight away with some difficulty, and took the stairs in two hops. The weight came tumbling after.

Maggie Donald, an early riser, was at the open front door, tugging at the line, and a coil of it was around her feet.

"Goad - be - here!" she cried with exasperation. "What is a' this thingumjiggery?"

Stephen released her and took some time to explain. She was not as quick in the uptake as her mistress, and drew a conclusion all her own.

"An' if I was to gang out the back door would you want me to break my dom neck?"

"Impossible!" Stephen said. "You can't break what ain't."

There was no sound yet from within the laird's window; but the window beyond opened, and Marian put out a head of soft tossed hair. She saw what had happened at once, and started to laugh. Stephen dodged past the laird's window.

"Hide that darn key away from her," he said. "Did you sleep?"

"I did until you and Maggie started using language."

She must have slept well, indeed. There was maiden colour in her cheeks, the whites of her brown eyes were as clear as skim milk, and her lips had a new softness. She yawned unashamed and showed a pink tongue behind white teeth.

"What devastating colours you choose!" she said, looking at his fierce dressing-gown. "Why don't you shave sometimes?"

"Slip the line off your leg," he said. "Why don't you button the top button of your own dressing-gown?"

Her fingers leaped and she looked down startled. There was no button undone.

"You dam' cowboy!" she said.

He moved slowly back to the garret, looping the line cowboy fashion. It was barely six o'clock of a fine morning, and the pearly wisps of mist on the hillsides promised another fine day. He was fully awake now, and could not hope to woo another hour's sleep. So he took his rucksack into the kitchen, got some hot water from Maggie, and shaved there. Maggie was stirring the porridge over a new fire, and, housewifely content at having a man about the place, talked to him busily about nothing. She could talk at any time, and Stephen was not a good listener before breakfast. He escaped as soon as he could.

The sun, just topping the eastern summits, was gilding the leaning top of Ben Shinnoch, and a thin haze, faintly blue, lay along the course of the Lettoch. The bathing-pool would have a tang this morning, but the porridge would not be ready for yet half an hour, and he had to do something. The pony was out at grass and would not need grooming. He got into his bathing-togs and ran all the way down to the bridge, slipped off dressing-gown and slippers, and plunged straight in without giving himself time to go goose-fleshy.

He came to the top and yelled loud enough to shake dew off the birchen boughs. There was another head covered with a blue cap in the pool below the bridge. Marian Finlay had been in first. She went away from him, not looking, in a nice side-stroke, her long slender arm making a fine scoop and her wrist at the right angle. He crawled after and circled round.

"Wow-ow! ugh! lamb! How dare you disturb the water which I ain't drinking?"

"The current ran from you to me, please mr wolf." She laughed then, and splashed water at him.

Yes, they were settling down to life—to an everyday sort of life too—for how long Stephen could not say.

He no longer thought of going away—back to Montana —in a day or two. He would go, of course. In a week or two, when that lad came back from the beating; and he would put the lazy young lout through his paces— with a rope-end if necessary. After that he would make a deal with Ruary Farquhar, or Kenny Alpin, and leave this hollow in the hills, probably for ever. Meantime he was justifying his existence in an act for which he wanted no reward. What reward, anyway? None? Yes! No! Damn you, Stevie! At the back of your mind you are doubting your own disinterestedness.

CHAPTER X

STEPHEN lay prone on top of Falcon Crag, smoking lazily. The sun was just down and the gloaming at its slow beginning, but the rock was still warm. All the hills were withdrawn and weary after the long day's sun, and if Stephen listened carefully he could almost hear them sigh. Again was silence about to possess the valleys.

Stephen lifted on his forearms and looked up the river. He could see a long reach of it before it curved out of sight, and then another reach curving again into view beyond. A path went round a birch bluff close above the water, and as Stephen looked a man, back-turned, walked slowly round the bluff and disappeared upstream. He was more than a quarter-mile away, but there was no mistaking who he was. Ruary Farquhar out for an evening stroll, his hands behind his back and his head forward, at peace with all the world, and not a nefarious thought in his mind.

Stephen looked carefully over all the ground. At the other side of the river right into the glen there were scattered trees but no thick cover to hide any movement, and there was no movement. On Stephen's side of the river there were too many trees to see anything. Yet, Stephen was sure that with Ruary Farquhar prowling—no, strolling along the Lettoch—Kenny Alpin would be scouting along some place above him. Fine! Stephen would do some scouting himself. The laird was safe in the house, and he would be back before bedtime.

He dropped down the back of the slope and took the upper fork of the path beyond, and left it, to hold above the stream, where it turned off to Castle Charles. He was now trespassing. But, in fact, he had been trespassing anywhere on the right bank of the Lettoch. There was a notice to that effect at the entrance to the flying-bridge, but Lettoch Lodge ignored it.

He did some careful stalking now, dropping down a slope to a torrent, crossing it by convenient boulders and going carefully amongst bracken and birches. It was not the first time that he had stalked or scouted, and thought he was doing a pretty fair job, not moving forward until he had prospected the ground in front, choosing his next cover, and avoiding dead twigs. Finally he was rewarded by a glimpse of a moving object ahead, manœuvred forward until he was sure that the object was Kenny Alpin, and then set out to stalk him down.

He never once let Kenny out of his sight, and was sure that Kenny never once looked his way. He got within twenty paces when Kenny lay down by a big pine tree, his head out of sight. Now he had him. He looked over the ground between, satisfied himself that there was no rotten stick in the needle mat, and went forward stealthily on the steady flat of his feet, put a hand on the pine trunk, and pivoted round it to fall flat on Kenny's back.

Kenny grunted deeply, but did not explode into action as Stephen anticipated. Kenny's hand came up to Stephen's arm round his neck and patted it. He sniffed at the Harris tweed.

"Fine, Stevie! You got me good and hard."

Stephen gave his black head a soft bump, and rolled over to his side. Kenny turned and rubbed a hand over his own breast-bone.

"You dunted my hause-bane on the knob of a root," he said. "Are you satisfied now, Rain-in-the-Face?"

"You for a scout!"

"Nice bit of work. Saw you just eleventy-two times."

"Like hell you did!"

"First of all I saw you lying out on top of the Crag like a tortoise, smokin' like a young volcano. You got on your elbows and looked up the river, then you got on your knees and looked under your hand at the auld fellow trapesin' along innocent like. After that you tried to see me through the trees, and I put my tongue out at you, and then you came mooching along like a Red Indian. I waited till you crossed the linn, gave you a glimpse, and here we are. A gey guid bit o' work all the same, and I had to know you were on the trail, or I wouldn't know."

"What is Ruary after?"

"I can't never tell you that, but between you and me it might be a bit of a fush—say twenty pounds."

"With a gaff?"

"Not in the dark, as it will be. The river is too well watched for day-work since the netting season finished—not that it's finished for Ruary. He might be thinkin' of drawin' a bit net over a pool later on."

"I'm in on this," said Stephen definitely.

"Goad, man! Ruary'd kill me. He doesn't want his Mr Wayne to ken."

"I don't care. I hope he kills you. I'm in on the salmon too—if any."

"Weel—well! We've an hour yet. Let's ha'e a smoke and a talk to ourselves—not too loud."

They sat against the tree and talked in low voices. Everything was quiet, and the light slowly faded, and the columned pines whispered, "Hush-hush" with the dying sigh of an organ in cathedral gloom. Once they heard a twig crackle on the slope above them, but as Kenny, after lifting an ear, made no remark, Stephen took it for a rabbit, or perhaps a roe deer.

"No' many pools in the river you can draw wi' a net," Kenny said. "Too many humplochs o' rock to tangle on. Ruary marked down two fish in two halves of a gravelly pool this mornin's dawn. We'll go to it when the lights are out."

"But look here! Why did you not wait for dark before prowling about for every watcher to see?"

"You should have asked that question before. You'll see. Say, Stevie, how are you holding that job down?"

Stephen steeled himself for some banter, and then wondered why he should.

"Nothing in it," he said. "The laird was quite sane to-day and went pony-riding. Another week, I guess. The garden is in a bad way, and I hate tackling it."

"I'll be round to-morrow morning," volunteered Kenny. "You might be in gaol."

Kenny did not use his mordant tongue. He was quiet and understanding. He wanted to make things easy for Stephen. After a silence he said:

"Every man has his own problem, and maybe you have found yours. The Lord kens! I ha'e my own. Did you any time gather from a thing I said that I had it in mind to marry Sheevaun?"

"Not any time—every time. And Sheevaun might be fool enough."

"That's the kind o' her. Like the rest o' them, she has an object in life—an' picked on a lame dog. No use sayin' anything to her, an' she tearing mad at me."

"Why?"

"Because I'm not able to say anything one way or another."

"You are a silly old fool, aren't you? A girl like Sheevaun! Why, at this minute I don't think there is a girl in the world like Sheevaun."

"I ken that fine. But what have I to offer her?"

"You have a job."

"Ay, have I! And a guid enough job as jobs go. I can make seven quid a week as a free-lance, and maybe I could keep a wife on that. What way? In a coney's burrow. I could give her a kingdom of three small rooms five flights up without a lift, amongst two million people crowded into a small corner o' braid Scotland. She could talk to the neighbours in the close— and nice neighbours at that—and she could grow green things in a sill-box till the gas an' fog turned 'em yellow —and sew wee things wi' her hands, for, mark you, she's a Catholic, and children she would have. Children amongst the tall houses, and two weeks doon the watter in summer amongst a' the crowd o' captives. The wind would never blow through her red hair except the sooty March gales, and the dark Clyde fog would cloud her eyes. No, sir! All that is no' for Sheevaun Power of the New Alliance. Her father was born under the Comeragh Mountains in Waterford, and her mother up yonder in the glen, and I came out o' the Lowther Hills in the Lowlands—low. Our weans —if any—will breathe clean air and learn living in the twenty thousand square miles o' Scotland that are empty—empty and waiting for the likes o' us. That's it for you now—and it only a dream in the flow o' my Pictish blood."

His voice was deep and vibrant, and touched Stephen deeply.

"That's Kenneth Alpin," he said. "Not even we

Yankees can kill Scotland." He twitched his shoulder against Kenny's. "Sounds like an anti-climax, but there is the Croft o' Balmerion?"

"And no better spot anywhere. But there be Ruary and Kirsty. Hush, sonny!" He chuckled to himself. "Can't I be dreamin' awa' at it? We'd better be moving now."

Stephen was about to rise to his feet, but Kenny held him down by the shoulder.

"Easy! We are now taking steps on our hands and knees. Ruary says you are no' that bad in thin cover."

He crawled off down the slope and Stephen followed. Below the pines was a clump of stunted hazel, and they circled round this and kept going. But Stephen noted that Kenny was now leading downstream instead of up. And he kept on too, over much the same ground that Stephen had followed in tracking him. The night was about down now, but they moved with great caution, taking all the cover that offered, and finally brought up in a bed of bracken below Falcon Crag. Kenny sat down.

"We'll go over the Crag when it's dead dark," he whispered.

"Where the blazes——?"

"Hush! All the time you were stalking me twa keepers were paralleling us up the hill."

"Why not jump us?"

"Wanted to get us red-handed. Moreover, trespass laws are queer in Scotland. They'd have to prove damage, and we were only sitting on our hunkers."

"But where is that pool?"

He chuckled softly at Stephen.

"The pool is the second one—the Grianan Pool— below Lettoch Lodge, and no one would think of poaching it. We were just engaged in drawing the keepers off on a false trail." He again chuckled in

Stephen's ear. "I was calling in for you on the way down."

Ruary knew all the poachers' tricks, and he knew all the keepers' tricks also; and that double knowledge made for safety. Also he realised that an experienced game-watcher could put himself inside the poacher's mind and match strategy with strategy.

Stephen and Kenny went down over the Crag, but did not cross the river by the flying-bridge. They held on down the right bank. Passing the Lodge, on the opposite side, Stephen caught a gleam of light through the trees from the sitting-room window.

They came on Ruary sitting on a loosely filled sack on a bed of gravel facing a wide smooth pool. The sky was cloudless, lit palely by the pale northern stars, and the oiled-steel surface of the pool could just be made out in that faint quarter-light. Above the scuffle of their feet in the gravel there came up from the tail of the pool the remote whisper and whimper of running water. There were no other sounds.

Ruary and Kenny were fumbling at the sack. They drew out a long length of black net and unravelled it full length on the gravel. It might be fifty feet by eight, and meant for fairly shallow water, weighted on one edge with lead and floated on the other with cork along a tough drawing-rope with trailing ends.

The three came together, heads close, for a final word. Ruary was definite.

"Two draws we'll make, and if we're no' lucky we'll wait another night—the risk is ower muckle. Listen now! Mr Wayne, you'll anchor the net on this side. Kenny and me will go over and do the drawing. If you think you hear a sound, give a whistle, and if you are sure, let a yell out of yourself, drop everything, and run as if the de'il was ahint ye. If the alarm comes I'm thinkin' it'll come from the other side, for they'll try to force us the wrong side o' the water. But one never kens for sure. Never mind Kenny an' me; we have our own line o' retreat. If you have to drop everything, make up the hill and keep the upper ground, right over the top if you have to. That's all, an' keep your ears open. Now take haud o' that line, and when I give a tug haul the net across till the first cork is at your toes, an' after that dig your heels in an' wait."

Stephen took the end of the trailing rope, and the other two went across the shallows at the tail of the pool, the net between them. He could just make out the black bulk of their figures on the far bank opposite him. No time was wasted. There was a sharp tug at Stephen's hands, and he began to haul in hand over fist. He could see the net coming across, the water ridging over the first cork. When that cork touched the gravel at his toes he stopped hauling and leant on the rope.

There came a soft splash on the other side. The two were in the water up to their middles, and they did not bother about waders either. There was a gravelly spit across the middle, and they came across, steadily hauling. Stephen felt the strain growing as the net bellied to the slow current, and he could see the line of corks take a deep curve. And then he felt an electric nig-nig at his hands. That was a salmon—at least one—in the belly of the net.

One salmon it was. It did not show itself until the last minute, but kept boring sullenly at the base of the net. Then it was splashing in the shallows, and next instant Ruary was on it. Stephen heard the clump, and the silvery fish was flapping its life out on the gravel at his toes.

"A cock fish—twal' pun'—and a fortnight up. The

one higher up is smaller. Come on! Let's keep movin'."

They saw the other fish from the beginning. It did not take the mesh of the net with nose vainly seeking for freedom. Stephen felt a single nig-nig, and the salmon came clean out of the pool close to the line of corks. It seemed to strike the water right across the line, and Stephen felt the jerk. Again the salmon leaped, and its leap was outside the curve.

"Lost him!" said Stephen, and then his whole body thrilled. For almost on the very splash of the fish he heard a bush crackle behind him, up the bank. He jerked his head round. By heavens! that bush was moving.

Stephen let everything go and swallowed down his heart.

"Look out!" His voice was hoarse and might not carry. "Look out!" This time his voice was shrill.

The river watchers were on them. Some astute one had followed Ruary's strategy home to the brain that had planned it.

After that there was plenty enough clamour. There was a crashing and a scrambling through the bushes, and stentorian savage bellowings. There were many men but no dogs. Dogs cannot be kept quiet on a night stalk. Two men—three men—drove across the tail of the pool in loud splashings. Stephen wasn't sure how many were coming his way. He ducked his head down and ran up under the bank. There was a low bush there not ten yards up the slope. Suddenly it heaved upright and was a man. Growling he leaped straight down at Stephen, and Stephen fell flat as he jumped. His impetus carried him on and a foot trampled between Stephen's shoulder-blades, whereat Stephen heaved and kicked hard, and felt the solid jar. Then

181

half a second's stillness, and a body thudded on the gravel below—and a hurt howl was added to the clamour.

There was the column of a pine dim in front. As Stephen swerved to round it he caught a movement just beyond, checked, put a hand on the trunk, and swerved the other way. A fist brushed his ducked head, and a man's body struck the tree and grunted. Stephen was half a dozen leaps up the hill before the man could turn. He had broken through. Now he had to get away. It struck him at that moment that there had been no shots. An affair like this in the old West, and from the very first shout the guns would be spitting criss-cross through the dark. They might begin to shoot now. They did not. Gun-fights were never Scotch. Claymore and dirk if you like, close in and no quarter, but not gun-fight.

Stephen went up that hill for all he was worth. He must get away. To be caught now would be too ignominious, for it would throw him on the mercy of Budd Hale. The thing to do was to burst himself to get a good start and then try dodging. A good thing, too, that he had lost his awkward horseman's legs. First he slanted steeply up-river and kept that line as long as his wind lasted, sometimes on his feet, sometimes on his knees, now and then clawing over a steep pitch, staggering all the time, bumping a tree, tearing through bushes, falling, rising, but all the time going up and up. He kept on until he had to stop or burst.

He hung on to a low branch, threw his head back, and panted through open mouth. As soon as he could he held his breath and listened. There was hallooing across the river, not from one point but several. The searchers over there were strung out and keeping in touch. That meant that Ruary and Kenny were still free, and were making their get-away as planned. Stephen breathed some more and again listened. There were sounds in the wood below him, and they seemed to be moving towards him and up-river. He took two or three deep breaths and went on, but he changed direction now, going down-river and uphill. He moved steadily, now that he had got a start, and as silently as he could, sliding his feet and fending trunks with his hands. Luckily he had got above the birches and was in a pine wood without undergrowth and with smooth-ridges. He did not fall more than once. And he kept going up—up and up. Ruary had told him to keep the higher ground. That is the best tactic in flight, for a pursuer, getting winded and unsighted, is inclined to sag downhill.

Next time he stopped there was no sound, not even from across the river. That must mean that Ruary and Kenny had won out, or— No! With half a minute's start no one could catch them on their planned line.

Stephen went on slowly now, getting his wind back in case he might need it for another burst. And he still kept slanting upwards, though his tired legs wanted to drift with the slope. In less than ten minutes he came to the edge of the pine wood. Outside it was a sagging wire fence. He saw the posts in time and so avoided rattling the wire. He crawled under the bottom wire and sat down, into dry ragged grass, to work out his bearings.

He was high up and right on the ridge of the hill. It fell away steeply below him into open ground. He looked up at the sky. There was *Ursa Major* wheeling on the pole star, and that was north he was facing. He looked left, and there was the bowl of Knockindu, and there, across the hollow, were the lights of the township within a mile of where he sat.

All he had to do was move carefully down aslant the hill and cross the Lettoch into the safety of the town fields. Some distance down the steep pitch he could make out a dark patch of low bushes. Better slip in amongst them and prospect ahead. He slid down the slope in a sitting posture, but the moment he touched the bushes he recoiled. They were whins and very prickly. He circled round on the outside, and as he got to the lower curve something gave a sick cough close ahead, the cough that an asthmatic man would give in night air. Stephen fell flat on his face, and feet scurried away in front of him. He swallowed his heart in two gulps and sat up to swear under his breath. He should have known that sick cough that sheep give at night. He felt reasonably safe now, for since he had frightened the sheep there was no one else about to have done it. He slanted off downhill more boldly.

He came to the river over open grazing-land in less than twenty minutes. Knockindu was not half a mile away on his right hand. He approached the river cautiously on his hands and knees, slipped over a grass bank on to dry gravel, and lay still listening. Not a sound but the gurgle of running water some distance above. The water looked smooth and deep in front of him, and he crawled up towards the gurgling sound, and looked across a wide spread of shallows to a low bank bare of trees. Over there was safety, and he had to make it.

After some more listening he got to his feet, drew in a long breath, and walked carefully and steadily into the water. At no place did it reach above his knees. He wanted to hurry, but the bottom was stony, and he did not want to make a splash. If his foot turned on a stone he would make splash enough. So he forced himself to move slowly, one foot edging forward over the other, and he had the feeling that he could be plainly seen from the tops of all the hills.

When he got close to the other side he saw above him a short spit of gravel running out at a slant from the bank, and making a shallow miniature backwater. He turned towards the spit and made three or four over-quick strides towards it. The bottom seemed to dip and tilt suddenly, something twisted under a foot, and he fell resoundingly flat. That was only the beginning. The very bottom of the river seemed to explode in his face. A broad fluke slapped him across the mouth, and under his very nose he saw the shining black-steel back of a big fish. He had fallen right on top of a salmon nosing up the shallows. He made a clutch, and his fingers slid off a solid, explosively twisting body.

He had panicked that fish out of its wits. It rushed itself clean out on the point of the gravel spit and kicked itself over into the little backwater. Its back-fin was in the air as it threshed about. Stephen scrambled to his feet, and in two strides was blocking the entrance. The fish, desperate now, came straight at his legs. Stephen never hesitated. He forgot the danger of his present surroundings. They had lost a fish and a net, and here was another fish, and a bigger one. As the salmon charged at his feet, back-fin out of water, he fell right on top of it and felt the water go down his neck like chilled metal.

Stephen and the salmon fought out their battle with abandon and desperation, half in water half in air. He learned the power of a salmon in its own element, even though that element was only a few inches deep. He could not hold it down, but he never let it get out from under. With thighs and knees and elbows and chin he herded it, and his hands pawed for a hold. And then, almost by accident, he found the gills and the game was up. One hand got a purchase, then the other; he scrambled to his knees, to his feet, and the big tail vainly flapped against his legs. He sunk his grip in.

He did not pause to look around. He squattered out of the backwater, heaved himself over the bank, and made straight away from the river towards a low black line beyond a grey-green field. The salmon trailed behind him from one hand, and twice its electric kick jarred his arm to the shoulder.

The black line was a low drystone wall bounding the town feus. He flung the fish on top, rolled over after it, and came down sitting. He slipped his cramped fingers from the gills, the salmon's tail slapped the ground, and its body made a bow. He quieted it with one smart blow of a stone at the back of the head, and then he got to his feet and looked back over the dyke. There was no sound, and nothing moved. He had got out of a close place against odds, and had finally justified himself.

He was sopping wet all over, but he surely was not cold, though his clothes were cold against his skin and water trickled down his neck from his hair. But if he stayed still for a minute or two he would feel cold enough. He was now outside the Castle Charles policies and was safe unless a keeper came on him with a salmon in his possession. He certainly was not going to abandon that salmon. After thought he peeled off his clinging jacket, threaded the salmon's gills with his belt and slung it over his shoulder, the pointed head under his oxter and the tail down his trouser leg. He got his jacket on with some difficulty, and buttoned across. In the dark no one would notice his burden.

Then he faced up the valley and made for home at a

lopsided trot, the water squelching through his toes. There was no mistaking the line he had to take, for far Corryhow was a black wedge against the white glow of a climbing moon. He did not count the scores of fences he had to cross, and the moon was above the peaks before he got into the paddock at the back of the Lodge-mound. Ben Shinnoch and the Kinmaols shone ghostly in the new light, and the hollow of the valley shimmered in a pale radiance.

The back of the house was dark, and he slipped into the harness-room and up the steps into the garret. And there and at last he drew a great breath of relief. But now he found himself in a quandary. He had matches in his pocket but they were uselessly wet. At home he had a little Canadian contraption that held a score of matches in a watertight can. No use wishing he had brought it along! There was another box somewhere about, possibly on the table. He found the table and his hand felt over it carefully so as not to overturn the lamp.

And there, as he groped, he had a strange feeling. His back hairs, wet as they were, actually bristled. He stood dead-still and listened; and gooseflesh ran on his thighs. He was not alone in the room. He caught the sound of a breath drawn softly in the direction of the truckle-bed. Was he in a trap?

After the first shock, a feeling of rebellion flooded over him hotly. This struck him as foul play after a good game had been played fairly. Darn it! He should be safe in his own quarters: This was what an unscrupulous and astute player would do. Ruary and Kenny and himself had been seen on the prowl. They were bound to be the poachers. Ruary and Kenny had escaped, but a final trap was being tried out on him. And he had walked right into it, wet all over, and an incriminating salmon under his oxter. What would Ruary think of such a finish?

Very well! Someone would get smashed in a split-second. He stood very still, fists tight. If there was only one man he would take him apart limb by limb. Two? He would make two know they were in a fight. Why did they not jump him? There was no sound at all now. He moved one foot backwards. He moved the other. If he got time to open the door—and he was a dam' fool to have shut it—he could take the stairs in a leap and play hide-and-seek again—if the front door was not already guarded.

He made the door and found the latch, and as he found it a match scraped and flared. He pulled the door open and leaped. He caught just one glimpse, but he could not stop himself in the air. He actually howled, landed jarringly, struck his shoulder against wood, turned like a cat and went up the steps like a panther.

"Blast you two tinkers!" he roared.

Ruary Farquhar was lighting the lamp temperately. Kenny Alpin was on his back on the truckle-bed, kicking his heels at the ceiling, crowing like an exhausted cock. Stephen went across and pulled him to the floor on his back, and rolled him topside with his foot. The roll took him to his feet, and he caught Stephen's shoulder for support. He was helpless with laughter that he was trying to make silent. But Stephen sensed that the laughter was not all amusement. There was high-strung relief in it. Stephen knew that by the way Kenny's hands patted him.

"By gum! He had to swim for it." His hands moved over Stephen. "Goad, boy! Did they kick your ribs loose? You 're hurt!"

"Hurt, your grandmother!" growled Stephen. "Take your paws off me!"

He wrenched his jacket off and started to struggle with the loop over his shoulder. Kenny shook his head and blinked his eyes.

"Losh mish!" he said softly, and helped the loop over Stephen's head. "Weel! weel! I wouldn't put it past you to rescue our bit of net in the bygoin'."

"You for poachers!" said Stephen, slumping the salmon on the floor and starting to pick scales off his shirt. "Legging it from a coupla boy watchers."

Ruary had turned up the lamp and was looking down at the fish.

"That's no' oor fish," he said. "That's a twenty-pounder. He got it climbin' a bush for red blackberries."

"Damwell 'tain't your fish," said Stephen, "nor half of it neither."

Kenny had his hands on Stephen's shoulder and was whispering in his ear.

"No' for myself, Stevie. The auld fellow! You know? the rheumatics! I couldna find it."

"You were sitting on it. Under the mattress."

Stephen had a bottle of the native malt there. They started to chuckle and laugh and talk, and each had a stiff one with very little water.

"*Slainthe*, Mr Wayne!" toasted Ruary. "How's this Gene Rhodes puts it? You'll do to take along. Let's hear aboot it!"

Before Stephen was done telling there came a sound of knocking on the harness-room door. Ruary and Kenny acted quickly and surely. Kenny had the salmon under the mattress in one heave: Ruary's hand cupped the lamp glass and they were in darkness. A voice whispered:

"Go and swear!"

Stephen went to the door.

"Who is that?"

Whoever it was had opened the harness-room door.

"Is dad up there with you?" Marian Finlay's voice.

Stephen was at her side in two bounds.

"Your father? No, he is not here."

"It will be all right," she assured him. "We often take a walk in the moonlight. I thought he left the house before me. I saw a light in your roof and thought I heard voices."

"Talking to myself in my loneliness. Where will your father be?"

"He is all right, to-night. He sometimes goes up to Falcon Crag to see the glen in moonlight. He may have gone on. I'll overtake him."

She went quickly across the yard. Stephen overtook her. He was in his shirt-sleeves, and the night air licked him with a cold tongue. As they got to the edge of the gravel there came a rustle from the slope below.

"That's dad," said the girl, and moved faster.

The night was almost pitch dark under the full-foliaged trees, and Stephen murmured:

"See you down to the open. Where are you?" He put a hand out and touched her arm.

"Wow! Your hand is cold."

"Warm heart."

"Serving-men have no hearts."

They were half-way down the slope when there came a sudden crashing through the bracken and a black bulk leaped into the road right in their faces.

"Got you this time!" said a man's voice savagely.

Before the man could grapple or Stephen act, the girl screamed and clutched Stephen.

"Oh, my gosh!" That was sheer surprise. "Is that you, Miss Marian?"

She drew a long breath, still holding Stephen.

"What ever do you mean——?"

"Sorry! Sorry, Miss Marian! My mistake! Some dom poachers came this way. Oh lord! I didna mean to frichten yourself—and the laird."

He hesitated before the laird. Stephen did not speak, and he could hardly be recognised in the dark. Without another word the keeper turned and plunged amongst the trees, and they could hear his feet crunching through the bracken across the slope. Probably he, too, was hoping that he had not been recognised.

"One of the keepers," Marian said. "Sanny Grigor —I think."

Stephen did not want to talk of poachers or keepers. He spoke quickly.

"Your father cannot have come down this way. Better make sure he has not left the house."

Anxiety occupied her mind as they hurried back to the front of the house where the door was open showing the lighted hall. She ran lightly across the gravel. She was back in the doorway in a few seconds.

"All right!" she called softly. " Father is in." She hesitated on the step as if about to come across, but Stephen called back:

"Good night! I'll anchor the trap-line outside." He did not want to be questioned just yet.

She shut the door, with rather a bang, and Stephen went back to his garret. He found the lamp relighted and turned low, but Ruary and Kenny were gone. He lifted the mattress and found an honest half of the salmon wrapped in an old newspaper. That was fair and comradely dealing. Ten pounds of salmon was enough for any family. After that he stripped to the skin, rubbed himself with a rough towel until the blood came to the surface, did a little shadow-boxing, put on his sleeping-suit and dressing-gown, and had another small drink. He was feeling fine now, and the night had been a good one, and harmless of grievous bodily hurt to anyone. It would leave no reaction of regret in the morning.

After giving time for Marian to get to her bed he went out with his trap-line, moving as silently as he knew how. He actually crawled under the girl's window and lifted a carefully searching hand over the sill for that nail he had discovered the previous night. As his hand groped it was patted smartly, and he jerked upright on his knees.

"Hell!" he expostulated.

"Hell, yourself!" said Marian Finlay.

She was on her knees inside the sill and leaning on it. She was still fully attired.

"You were poaching," she accused him promptly.

"I am not—not in preserved ground."

"I did hear voices, you know. You were out with Ruary Farquhar, and you've had whisky. I smelt it."

"Whisky and poaching gang together, as Burns said."

Her white hand moved down his shoulder and arm.

"You were in the river too—all of you."

"Your evidence is piling up. Produce the salmon and I'll confess."

"You hadn't time to get a fish, had you?"

"We could do with one," Stephen said. "I am tired of rabbit-pie."

"You'll have it cold to-morrow." Her voice she tried to keep cold too. "The keeper suspected you, and I am suspect too. Nice thing to be living on salmon we no longer own."

To-morrow she would probably have salmon followed by venison for lunch. Would she partake? Stephen was prepared to bet four bits that she would. The thought made him snigger.

"You'll accuse me of shooting a deer next," he said. "You are a harbourer of poachers, and Budd Hale will observe you with a calculating eye."

She took the line from his fingers, and shut the window down to an inch.

"There'll be more about this in the morning," Stephen said, and went to bed.

CHAPTER XI

STEPHEN had a team working in the kitchen garden.
That is, Kenny and he were working, while Sheevaun
Power and Marian Finlay nibbled at over-ripe black-
currants, and sometimes plucked at the more obvious
weeds.

Kenny was a first-class hand at a dutch or draw-hoe.
He had hoed neeps on a Lowland farm in his youth,
and had not lost the nice art of nicking off a weed
without grazing the cheek-by-jowl vegetable. Stephen
did the less precise work amongst the rows, and between them they were beginning to make the garden
look like what a Scots garden should be—and seldom is.

Sheevaun and Marian had met before, but this was
the first time they had come to close quarters. They
got on. Marian was the daughter of generations or
aristocrats, for the Scots county families are amongst
the few aristocrats that are left, and often enough with
all the less admirable qualities of the caste. Marian
was not spoiled yet. She was young, and the strain
under which she was living had broken the crust under
which ancient blood hides its naturalness. Perhaps
Stephen Wayne had helped too. Moreover, Sheevaun
Power was no ordinary wench. She had beauty and
character and virility, and was not class-conscious.
She knew life. Her manner, her talk, her humour, her
attitude, appealed to Marian, who had led a secluded
existence for so long. Sheevaun took the Highland girl
as a girl of about her own age but not her own experi-

ence. She was the slightly condescending one, and Marian was a little shy. Certainly Marian looked subdued by the side of the red-flaming Sheevaun— perhaps not so much subdued as quiet, withdrawn, contrasted, with her soft darkish hair, hazel eyes, and grave lips just touched with eagerness.

In fact, they were four young people together, and were having a pretty good time in their own minds, working or playing at work together in the sun, and with old Mother Nature taking care of their reactions. Stephen could see that Mariana of the glen was beginning to blossom. What she needed was youth around her to make her youth burgeon, something to help break down the walls of the gloomy prison she felt herself to be in.

Yes, they were getting on. Kenny and Stephen were putting their backs into it; the two girls were off in a corner already talking girls' talk. Later on they would have some fun, a swim in the pool, tea on the lawn, and such. And about then—shortly before noon—the door in the garden wall opened and Maggie Donald filled the opening.

"Miss Marian, you 're wanted—visitors I 'm thinking."

Marian went across the garden quickly, pulling off old chamois gloves, and Stephen met her at the door.

"Thought I heard a car," he said. "Keep him out of our garden patch."

There was colour in her cheeks, and a brightish speculation in her eyes. Stephen went back to work, and Sheevaun Power strolled across to him.

"There's one nice girl, Stephen," she said.

"So an admirer thinks," Stephen said.

"Fine! Two admirers at least she should have— and boys! would she not blossom? Are you sure that you still love me, Steve?"

"If you want me to," said Stephen soberly.

"Leave the boy alone, you Irish slattern!" Kenny ordered. He drove his hoe into the soil and looked at Stephen. "The visitor? Young Hale o' Castle Charles?"

"Visitors," corrected Sheevaun.

"Young Hale?" repeated Kenny.

"Probably. He bust a knee——"

"I know. Also I gather you knew him when younger. You don't admire him much, son?"

"What's that got to do with it?"

"Only that you Americans are incurably romantic. Don't you think you are a dam' fool, Stephen?"

"Who is leaving him alone now?" demanded Sheevaun.

"Tell me," Stephen said.

"Ay, will I! If you are in this for the fun of the game watch you don't burn your fingers, and if you are in it as the god-out-of-the-machine you might be sacrificed like one, and if you have a stake on the board play your cards close to your chest or you'll lose more than you want to."

"Three losses and no winnings?"

"What do you want to win?" enquired Sheevaun.

"Dam'd if I know, carrots!"

"And there you are!" cried Kenny. "Young Hale, you tell me, admires your long-legged virgin, and I'll wager that he knows his own mind. I've seen him about. A fine tall chiel to take a girl's eye—no runt like you and me—and an adept in the game. He'll be owning Castle Charles and all the MacFinlay lands later on, and they make a grand makeweight in the romantic scale. And besides, he knows what he wants. You don't."

Sheevaun laughed at the two of them.

"As if it mattered what a man wanted," she derided.

"What does Marian Finlay want? When she makes up her mind some man will think that he has made up his. That's how that game is played, and I should not have told you."

"I suppose you know what you want?" said Kenny sourly.

"I don't want the moon, same as you do, and so I have my chance of getting it."

"The moon?"

"An equally extinct satellite will do as well."

"Ay, faith!" He quoted an old line, "'And I will make her wings of yellow golden sun and her comb of the silver moon.' Let's get a little work done, and to the devil with romance."

Stephen's thoughts were rather forlorn. Montana was the safest place for him. If the huntress in Marian Finlay marked down Budd Hale, that might solve the problem, and an earl's daughter, wearing an engagement ring, must lay another snare as she well knew how. He was rather sorry for that dark vivid woman whose style had been cramped.

Marian Finlay called to him from the garden door, and Stephen went across feeling distant. There was a nice flush on her face, but there was dismay in her eyes.

"They are staying for lunch," she said, and there was dismay in her voice too.

"Who?"

"Old Mr Hale and B— his son, and Lady Alice Tromes."

"Very nice! Now you'll be invited back to dinner."

"It was dad. He takes things for granted. We have nothing in the house but cold rabbit-pie."

"Is that all?"

She snapped at him angrily.

"Damn! Do you think I don't know what is in my own larder?"

"And you want me to make a silk purse out of a sow's ear? I can too—transmute cold rabbit into roast venison."

"You can't, but you can ride the pony down to Knockindu for some cutlets."

"Did you tell Maggie?"

"I am going to."

"Don't trouble," he said hastily. "I'll go in and see what she needs. You'll have your cutlets."

He walked her beyond the kitchen door to where he could hear voices from the lawn.

"Keep them out of the garden," he told her. "Budd Hale makes me jealous."

She gave him a flash of her eyes.

"You are very exasperating, Stephen," she said. "I wish I had a weapon—even jealousy."

She marched off round the house-corner and Stephen sought Maggie Donald in the kitchen. There was a savoury odour about, and it was not rabbit.

"Three extra for lunch, Maggie—the Castle Charles people. What have you?"

Maggie rubbed her hands with satisfaction.

"Eh, man! I'm glad. I'll gi'e them a guid lunch. I was keepin' it a surprise for the laird and Miss Marian."

"What is it?"

"You'll get your share. There'll no' be a better in Castle Charles."

"Right! You just surprise them."

He went back to the garden, but did not tell Kenny and Sheevaun of the surprise lunch that awaited the guests. Kenny would laugh, but Sheevaun might be angry because of the embarrassment to Marian.

The garden gate again opened and the laird came in with another man. Stephen held his breath, but the door shut behind the two. The other man was, of course, Burton Hale, Budd's father. Stephen had never met him. He was a sturdy grizzled man with a strong, not unkindly face and the blue-steel eyes of the American business man. He glanced at the three, who had resumed work amongst the kale, and went on talking.

The laird took no notice at all. He was possessed with a real calm to-day, based on ancient dignity. Possibly he was not at any time completely sane any more. Deep down he was chief of a clan, not the modern courtesy chief who is merely a landed proprietor, but the paternal ancient chief in the clan-system with his obligations more important than his privileges. He would naturally regard the three working in the garden as neighbours or septs taking a turn at any work that was going.

The two men walked about the garden and talked as if alone together. But that is the usual thing. Menials have no ears.

"Poor white thrash!" murmured Stephen.

Hale was congratulating the laird on the nice place he had at Lettoch Lodge, hinting that it had every advantage over Castle Charles for a retired gentleman. He glanced at the three workers and his thought was evident. Old MacFinlay must be comfortably off to employ two men in his garden—to say nothing of that extraordinarily good-looking maid. He must have kept something up his sleeve from the Trustees, who in a business way had been screwed down to the last dollar when the estates were sold. That was only good business, but MacFinlay must have means other than that paltry few hundreds rescued from the mortgages.

Now that they were alone he was again thanking the laird for succouring his son Buddington. Buddington was very appreciative of their kindness, and had pointed out to his father his remissness in not calling long before now. No, it was not remissness, rather a certain hesitation about intruding. There might, one felt, be a certain reserve over change of ownership, and Hale did not want to intrude on privacy unless—well, unless the laird felt that there was no attempt to butt in, as it were. Hale would like to express himself clearly that his acquirement of the mere lands and policies did not deprive MacFinlay of any of his privileges of lairdship. He understood these ancient loyalties, and was, indeed, himself of Scots descent. The MacFinlay was still the MacFinlay.

From that he went on deftly to suggest that, now the ice was broken, as, in the old custom, bread was about to be broken, the relations between the families would grow more friendly—even familiar. And the sooner the better. There were some guests at Castle Charles who would like to make the chief's acquaintance; and he was sure that Miss MacFinlay would enjoy the company of young people. Luckily they would be all at home that evening. Why not come over—just informally—for a meal and a talk? And so on.

The laird was gratified and he was a courteous gentleman. Before he knew how it had happened he found himself appreciatively accepting the invitation for that evening.

"I am deeply gratified," said Hale. "You will permit me to send one of the cars round for you—say at seven."

Stephen heard a good deal of this. No doubt the father had been primed by the son, but he was quite genuine in his desire for friendly relations. After all,

MacFinlay was of the county families, and friendliness with him might mean admission to a snobbishly select society—not so much for himself, who did not care a cent, as for Buddington. A poor earl's daughter off the boards had never appealed to a mid-Western business man.

They drifted out of the garden, and as they drifted out Lady Alice Tromes drifted in.

"Thank the Lord for the sight o' my e'en!" said Kenny fervently. "No' a bone in her long body."

"We're holding a reception this blasted forenoon," said Stephen.

She moved leisurely down the grass path towards them: a dark vivid beauty adorned with all the mostly unsubtle arts of cosmétique, which, as will ever be the case, are the arts of the *demi-monde*.

"I thought I might find a forsaken merman about somewhere," she said, not looking directly at Stephen.

He said:

"This working garden is no place for an adorable hedonist earl's daughter. Do you seek a hoe also?"

He caught Sheevaun's startled glance. This was no way to use even his tongue on a lady that he had not seen before—as far as Sheevaun knew.

"This is Sheevaun Power, Lady Alice Tromes," he introduced. "Kenny Alpin is admiring you with insatiable eyes. Newspaper people—at some useful work."

"Anything I say may be used against me," said the lady.

Sheevaun Power smiled at her.

"I saw Lady Alice in a *Hawk from a Handsaw* at 'The King's,'" she said. "I wrote her up next morning."

"Now we are introduced," said Lady Alice smilingly. "The only person I don't know is one Stephen Wayne." She looked at him, frankly puzzled. "You live in a secret world up here. How does one get in?"

"You'd get thrown out, Lilith, and all of us would be unhappy."

"Do you want to get in, dark lady?" Kenny asked suddenly.

"I don't know. You have freedom in your eyes."

"Gosh!" Kenny smoothed his broad hand down his saturnine face. "She saw that. It is one of the freedoms too. All right, Lady Alice! I've the second sight sometimes, and a'e day you'll be invited in."

There was a silence amongst them, then, and the lady, nodding her head, moved towards the door. Stephen walked with her.

"One orphan turns to another," she said. "I came looking for you. So you are really playing at working-man?"

"Not playing. I eat in the kitchen."

"You are at a disadvantage. Buddy is out there propped on a crutch and devouring your Mariana with what you call insatiable eyes."

"And you to blame, starting off on the wrong gambit."

"I'll play a game with you," she challenged.

"You are. You're making my heart turn over."

"Nonsense! I do not know whether I should tell you, but Buddy, from things he has heard from his men, is wondering if a certain lady is not about as gentle as a sleek panther. And when Buddy begins to wonder, watch out."

"In about half an hour you can add a slithy tiger."

"And then?"

"Belt him back to his allegiance—what?"

"You are not able. I wish you were."

She went away slowly, not swaying her hips.

Stephen went back to his friends, and Sheevaun walked round him.

"Where does he keep it?" she wondered. "His secret life! He has one. You met that lady before, Stevie?"

"Twice. I ate with her, and walked across a lawn arm-in-arm." He told them about it.

"You got on quickly," said Sheevaun. "I don't understand her, Stephen. She is of another layer, and her purposes are obscure—and maybe selfish."

"What else?" growled Kenny. "Leave her alone. She would make a whale of a courtesan if she had that bent."

"She has a ring on her finger," said Sheevaun.

"What difference does that make to a woman?"

"It might make a difference to Marian Finlay," said Sheevaun.

"Ay, faith!" agreed Kenny. "A job on your hands, Stevie! An' you can be a clockin' hen, or a hawk on your own beat. Come awa' hame to oor dinner, red, and leave him to it!"

Stephen stayed on stolidly hoeing. His friends and events were trying to implicate him, and doubtless he had been a romantic donkey to come to Lettoch Lodge at all. Well, he was here now and he would sail on an even keel, or ride the bumps if necessary. He would carry on helping a frightened girl, and if he had to undertake any other task he would do it with his eyes open. He was getting pig-headed.

Maggie Donald put a hot face round the garden door and wanted to know how long more she had to keep his dinner hottering on the stove for him. He followed her to the kitchen, and found her ready to make coffee her own way.

"Don't spoil a good meal, woman!" he said. "Let me."

"Sin' they are foreign people like yourself," she agreed.

After that Maggie and he had lunch—or dinner. Some meal too, well cooked. Salmon, roast venison and rowan jelly, second-early potatoes, fresh peas, apple tart, and black coffee.

"Their eyes bunged out," said Maggie.

"A moderate understatement."

Maggie was pleased with herself. It was grand to see friendly relations opened with Castle Charles. In her plotting old mind she already had her maid Marian queening it at the big house. She hinted as much. She saw the laird ordering things about as of old. She even saw herself re-established as housekeeper, and forgot about her brother's need. Stephen tried to damp her down.

"You had an earl's daughter to lunch too, old woman —the flaming beauty one?"

"Ay, had we! Bonny too, but painted like Jezebel."

"She wears a ring."

"I saw that."

"Who put it there?"

"I'll be findin' that out for certain. Ay, but the young gent couldna keep his eyes awa' from the bonniest girl of all."

"Did his eyes bung?"

Marian did not come into the kitchen, but Stephen gulped his coffee down and made his escape in case of accident. He wanted to give her time to get up either a real temper or a sense of humour. He did not go back to the garden, but, instead, went down to the paddock at the back of the slope where the pony threw up its heels and invited him to come and take it. He refused the invitation and sat himself inside the fence under an old ash tree growing at the side of the stile.

He had a smoke and some confused thought, and after a time he fell asleep, his legs warm in the sun and his head in the shade. He dreamt that the pony was stalking him under bushes and up trees, and finally cornered him to set its yellow teeth in his shoulder. The teeth sank in but did not hurt, and Stephen struggled and yelled strangledly; and waked up.

Marian Finlay took her hand from his shoulder. She was sitting on the bottom step of the stile and leaning towards him.

"What did you bite me for?" he demanded.

"One would never guess your character while you sleep," she said. "But your conscience troubled you at the end."

"Were you looking for me?"

She gestured her hands abandonedly and her voice was despairful.

"I don't know what to do. This is terrible."

"Did you eat?"

"Eat? I had to eat."

"Then you are an accomplice by blood and bone and some attractive-looking tissue."

"Oh, that! That is bad enough. Do you not know? We are going to dinner to Castle Charles to-night—to-night."

Stephen breathed with some relief.

"I heard. It was neatly managed according to instructions."

"You don't understand. My father! He has been fine for two days, and the nights all peace—thank you for that much at any rate! And now! Coming in touch with all the old associations, sitting at the old mahogany table, the old furniture about him, his own trophies of the hill on the wall! And strangers owning the place! How will it affect him?"

He could imagine how it would, once she had put it that way. The thin crust might break, and active madness left a head. And if that happened——

"Why did you let him?" she cried.

"Could I have stopped him?"

"You could. You are good at finding ways. I was learning to put faith in you. Why did you not come for me?"

"I fell down all right," Stephen agreed mildly.

"This time you did." She was unreasonable, and Stephen did not dislike her for it.

"Must he go?"

"He will, and I must. He has accepted. I fear that at the best he is never quite himself, and when he makes up his mind he will not listen to me. He likes Mr Hale, and thinks he has a duty of friendship—or even patronage."

"You may be wrong about association of ideas," Stephen tried to comfort her. "A visit to his old home, to a man he already likes, and who shows him deference, may be the very thing for him. Leave it!" He put a finger on her sleeve. "And if necessary we shall find a way."

"Do you think you can?" she asked hopefully, wishing to be assured.

"Of course we can. I see light already." He changed the subject with temerity. "How did you like your lunch?"

She was glad to change the subject too, and she had not time to get her dander up.

"I did not know where to look," she said. "The

salmon was bad enough but explainable, but when a haunch of roast venison appeared— What can they think of us?"

"They don't own all the deer in Scotland."

"And we own none. It was completely shameless to—to——"

"To shove their own salmon and venison down their necks. Was there calculation in Budd's eye?"

"I was too flustered to look. And look here, Stephen Wayne! Give up hinting. He is engaged to Lady Alice Tromes."

"Did he tell you so?"

"She said enough to let me know."

"She would, but what of it? Woman has no code of honour anyway—short of the altar rails, or a mile beyond. Say, wouldn't that lady knock the sight out of your eye?"

"Have you no code?"

"She made my heart kick sure enough."

"Stop it!" she ordered shortly. "You haven't that sort of heart."

"By gosh!"

"Stop it! Suppose you tell me about that stag. I know about the salmon. Ruary Farquhar is a poacher, and nothing can stop him. We had salmon often in spring but were supposed not to know where they came from. That's my confession, now yours?"

"Just plain curiousness?"

"That's all," she admitted, and crinkled her nose at him.

"Fair enough," said Stephen, and told her. He did his very best to take her mind off her present problem, and he spread himself, letting fancy roam, and not sparing Ruary or Kenny or himself. He had her gurgling in a minute, and in another she was frankly laughing, and then she was helplessly fumbling for a handkerchief. Later on her moral sense would take note of the nefariousness of the affair, but now she was enjoying the relief of an exciting story spiced with humour and devil.

"And all that," Stephen finished, "was to stock the larder in order to make Budd Hale's eyes bung out. In his own mind he is calling you the Poacher Queen, and wondering what hell of a secret life you run. He might do some poaching himself, and why not?"

She rose to her feet and climbed back over the stile. She had sobered quickly.

"I must go to dad now," she said, "but I can do nothing with him in his present mood." She pointed a finger at Stephen. "When I come to think of it, it was you started this, Stephen Wayne?"

"We ain't so dead, are we?"

"But I am not used to life. Indeed, some of it has points. When I wake up in the morning I never know what you may let me in for through the day and— Blow it! One gets to like it—after."

Marian Finlay was learning how to get round a fellow.

CHAPTER XII

STEPHEN went across to the croft for the milk and stayed to tea. Kirsty Power looked him over with her glistened eye.

"The job is not too much for you, Mr Wayne," she said, "but it is leaving its mark on you."

"The cloven hoof!" said Sheevaun.

"Is it true that the laird is having his late dinner at Castle Charles?" Ruary wanted to know.

"It is—the laird and his daughter."

"Let them! It is no business of ours," said Ruary almost sternly.

But he walked back with Stephen to the Lodge, and said little on the way. Stephen could see that he was disturbed. The time was getting on for seven then, and when they mounted to the garret, Ruary went to the skylight, that was fully lifted, and dropped it to two inches. Stephen sat on the bed, smoking, and asked him if he would have a dram.

"We might need one later," he said.

In a short time the purr of a powerful car came up the slope to them, and Ruary peeped from his vantage-point that looked over half of the front gravel.

"That big open tourer!" He started his running commentary. "A lad in livery, and young Hale in a white front under a fawn throw-over. A gran' tall chiel! A stick he has, and not limpin' badly. He'll be on the hill in twa days. Out o' sight now, and I hear voices about the posts o' the door. Ay! the laird is going all richt. Ay man! he's the real auld Highland chief. Black jacket and silver buttons and frills, goat's-hair sporran, dirk an' all. There's nothing wrong with him the night. The lassie is in green, and them green beads. Sheathed in green—like a sword is sheathed, an' just as deadly. Laughin' they are, the twa young ones. Do you no' hear them? The laird into the bucket seat in front. That's it. In with him out o' the way. That's a wrap for her ivory showders—him towerin' over and his arms possessive; an' she glancin' up showin' the gleam in her e'e, and the pearls in her smilin' mou'. Eh, boys! Gran' to be that young! In they are now, an' his preein' nose in her hair as he folds the rug across. Phutt! Them's the wheels spurnin' the gravel. The shover at the helm an' love in the back seat—and to hell wi' the auld laird."

"You have been listening to Mr Ruary Farquhar announcing Budd Hale's victory in the second round," said Stephen.

Ruary came over and sat on the bed at Stephen's side, and Stephen poured him three fingers of whisky. He held it up and looked through the amber sherry of it.

"No business of ours, is it?"

"You've said a mouthful," said Stephen, but ironically. "Stick to it!"

"*Slainthe*!" Ruary took a mouthful of his whisky and savoured it slowly. "Ay! We'll stick to it. The Castle Charles lairds, and this laird among them, saw and helpit the ruin coming, an' this laird saw it arrive. What is it to us that they failed and betrayed? You were up the glen and saw the ruined walls where we were sold and scattered. It is finished now. The glen is finished. The laird is finished; and let the daughter restore the blood if she can, but the name of the MacFinlay will not be known again—nor my name neither. But maybe the MacAlpin, the oldest clan of all, and the New Alliance, will not be betrayed by their loyalties, and the Highlands might live again."

He took another mouthful and nodded his head heavily.

"I'll no' deny it, there's clansman's blood in me, but time for it to turn sour. All these lands—glens and bens and water running—belonged to a way of living that had its own culture, a sort of federal system that the exiles took to exile with them, that, I am told, they copied into the constitution of your federated States—and look who writ your constitution? Let it be. I am a clansman and I ha'e nothing, but while I live I will lift from the clan lands the free wild things that belonged to the clan—an' risk my freedom for it."

He glanced at Stephen, and his face, that had been stern, wrinkled into a small and slightly embarrassed grin.

"And that reminds me," he said, "there's a thing o' mine beyond at the Castle Charles, and to-night it is in my mind to lift it."

"Lift it we will. What is it?"

He finished his drink at a gulp.

"It is that bit of salmon net we lost to them yestere'en."

"Do you know where it is?"

"I know whaur they'd put it. But maybe I should leave it till another time. No' right o' me to run your head in a noose."

"Let us try the noose," said Stephen on his feet. "We are in a humour to-night to lift the lid off hell."

"If you think that," said Ruary yieldingly. "The watchers are all up the glen."

Stephen knew that Ruary was only wanting an excuse to get to the vicinity of Castle Charles. The old clan loyalties were not yet dead in him.

They went over the hill, crossing the river by the

flying-bridge but not going by Falcon Crag. Instead they took the other shoulder of the rise and ploughed up through the undergrowth into the more open pine woods; and down again into covers of laurel and rhododendron at the back of the house. And there Ruary began to move with caution.

"The kennels are round that way," he pointed. "We'll slant off this way with the air."

They came to a low wooden building and skirted its walls. A faint odour of decay came to Stephen's nostrils, and he sniffed.

"The vermin house," Ruary whispered.

The outside of the gable wall was hung with the shrivelled carcases of small vermin: weasels, stoat, magpie, hooded crow, squirrel and hawk—and one red-fox skin.

"Some o' them keepers would like to see my dom hide hung up there," said Ruary. "Watch out now!"

He peered round the end of the house, and when satisfied that the ground was clear moved forward in long noiseless strides towards the back of a long one-storied, raw-stone building behind the service premises. Getting there they slipped along the wall and round the end where a rank bed of tall nettles grew out of old rubble. They got in amongst them, and Ruary stamped round with his big brogues so that they could crouch down against the wall without being stung.

"You'll stay here," he whispered to Stephen. "The store-house is round the corner. It shouldna be locked, for it's in use late and early by the gardeners and others. We'll wait a bit till the light lessens."

The gloaming was already upon them. The tired weight of it was down over the encircling hills, the withdrawn quiet of it amongst the trees. Stephen, turning his head, could see the high-steeped roofs and massive chimneys of the castle outlined against a sky that was still too pale to show a star; but after looking for a time he saw one point of light and then another. They sat on there, sitting on their heels and saying nothing. They were both used to sitting thus, and their thighs did not ache. But they did not sit for long.

"You can see the kitchen door from the corner," Ruary whispered, "but dinna look much. I'll no' be a meenit, but if you hear me comin' knockin' sparks, make that way and keep goin'."

He got to his feet, and leaning a shoulder on the wall took one long roving look round the corner, and disappeared.

Stephen sat there for five minutes and then took a look round that corner. A nettle stung a careless finger, and he put it in his mouth to suck the fire out, but the tender tingle remained. He guessed that Ruary's whole errand was not to recover his poaching-net, and that he was merely searching for it to pass the time. He could see the kitchen premises across a wide cobbled yard, and there was enough light to show him the door where he had delivered Marian's letter. Some of the windows already showed a glow of light, but there was no person abroad; and in the distance he heard a door close and the high faint sound of a woman's voice inside the house. Then he went back to his crouching position and sucked his tingling finger.

He had not to wait another five minutes. A quiet step sounded, not knocking sparks, and Ruary came round the corner. A loosely filled sack was under one long arm. He skirted the outside of the nettles, and beckoned Stephen on. They went quickly across the open to the shrubberies, and Ruary thrust the sack under a fringe of laurel. He straightened up and looked across at the buildings, and Stephen knew that

he was laying down a marking-line. Stephen did likewise, taking two chimneys that would show even in the
dark. When one hides something in the open he very
often hides it from himself also unless he has markers.

"Dom them keepers!" Ruary growled. "They
stuffed the net in holus-bolus and never thought o'
takin' it out to dry."

"Perhaps they tried a draw or two themselves."

"They would, but they didn't need to. We provided the salmon for the night's dinner. Ask Miss
Marian. Come round this way a bit."

They made a half-circle in the security of the
shrubberies until they could see along the front of the
castle itself. The expanse of lawn was empty and turning grey in the waning light. The big touring-car
squatted broadly on the gravel. They could not see the
windows, but there was enough darkness to show a
faint splay of light across the lawn.

"The dining-room is this side the hall door," Ruary
said. Stephen knew that high gloomy room.

"They should be half through dinner now," he said.

"A gey slow way they ha'e o' takin' their food," he
said, and drifted casually across the gravel towards the
corner of the house. Stephen followed and wondered.
Ruary did not sidle along the front wall, but walked
slowly along the grass edging between house and drive.
He stopped by a low green-berried cottoneaster growing
from the base of the wall. Above his head was a lit
window. As has been said, the windows were high-set
and antiquely small. Tall as Ruary was, his head was
a clear foot below the sloping sill set flush with the wall.
The window was closed but not blinded, and from
within came but the faintest murmur of voices. Ruary
looked up meditatively, and rubbed his beard upward
with forefinger and thumb.

"Myself is stiff in the joints," he murmured, "or I might see the laird in there."

"Depends where he sits."

"That's it. If you can see his face tell me how he looks. You told me before."

He bent over and set one shoulder firmly against the wall; one big brown paw came out for a stirrup; Stephen set one foot on it, touched thigh with the other, and, crouching, steadied both feet on the slabs of muscle under shoulder-blades. Carefully he raised his head and looked through the small middle-bottom pane.

Staring from the wan-lit outside he got an impression of a secret and formal rite of luxury. The long, narrow, shining, deeply-reflecting mahogany board was altar-like, lit by shaded candles whose soft glow sparkled on silver and crystal, was richly translucent in wine, and died in the gloom of dark-panelled walls against which silent acolytes moved slowly. White fronts took the light cleanly, a smooth pair of shoulders was svelte and more than alive. His eyes caught a circlet of green beads, and he was looking into Marian Finlay's face.

A clean face and now animated—almost too animated, as if she were trying to hold attention to herself away from something that must not be seen. The light glowing on her sun-warmed skin made it somehow exotic. The poise of her head had a wild aware shyness. Stephen realised, really for the first time, that she was lovely and alluring. That Budd Hale at her side realised the same was evident by his complete absorption. As Stephen looked at her he caught a secretive side-flash of her eyes and followed where they looked. He had no need to seek further. He was looking at MacFinlay at his host's side.

MacFinlay's face was so palely calm that it deceived Stephen for a moment—until he saw his eyes, and then he knew that his affliction was again upon him. He was a man in the company of ghosts, not a ghost in the company of men. He gave Stephen the queer impression that he was the only live man there, and that any moment the light might flare out of him and scatter the shadows about him. Even some of the shadows felt that, Stephen saw by their faces.

Stephen's eyes came back to Marian, and her eyes were looking into his. She was looking at the face in the window with wide startled and beseeching eyes. Her look was so intent that Budd Hale turned his head towards the window and Stephen had just time to dodge below the sill. Ruary's shoulders firmed against the impact of his toes and he came to the ground with a soft thud. He waved his hand urgently before Ruary's face.

"He's gone. He's gone deep down. Something must be done at once."

"That thing is easy done." His hand pressed Stephen's shoulder. "Down behind that bush! Leave this to me! See you how the lassie gets home!"

Stephen, crouching down, looked between the bush and the wall. Ruary stalked straight to the front door and disappeared in the deep arch. Immediately there resounded three hard wallops from the massive knocker, and from somewhere in the house a bell jangled and jangled again. The door opened almost at once, and Ruary's voice was dominantly urgent.

"The laird! The MacFinlay! At once on urgent business. Tell his daughter, Miss Marian, to bring him here at once—to me Ruary Farquhar—at once. Say 'tis urgent. Thank you!"

Footsteps receded hastily. Again there was no long waiting. Marian Finlay would answer that summons as urgently as it had been made. Many footsteps this time and a murmur of voices: Marian's for sure, and Budd Hale's. An electric bulb glowed at the top of the arch outside, and Stephen crouched into his shelter. Next instant Ruary and the laird appeared together on the step and strode together down on the gravel.

"Clan business, MacFinlay," Ruary said strongly. "We are going over the hill." He turned head back to the girl. "Go back and finish your dinner, Miss Marian."

Arm-in-arm the two tall men went across the gravel towards the lawn, and the laird never turned his head. Ruary had done one good quick job of work.

The tall, long-legged girl and the tall man stood out under the electric bulb watching the linked figures growing dim across the lawn towards the path by the garden wall. Then Budd turned to the girl, bent protectingly towards her, and his voice was full of sympathy.

"Please forgive me, Miss Finlay—Marian. All my fault. I wanted to make amends—to see you shining under your old roof. Dash it! in spite of everything I am glad to have you here. Everything is all right. Leave it to me! I'll explain to the others."

His arm went over her shoulder, and Stephen thought she leant a little towards him. Budd Hale knew how to comfort a girl. Before they went in, her glance came along the wall but she could hardly see Stephen behind the bush. The door clanged and the electric bulb went out.

After a while Stephen rose to his feet, walked across the gravel to the darkening lawn, and drifted out on it. Over near the trees by the side of a clump of shrubs he came on two canvas chairs side by side. He sat down in one. It was as good a place to wait as any. He could not be seen from the house, and a prowling keeper might take him for a house-guest. It was a warmish night, and he lay at ease, lapped in the aloof tides of the night, with the faint sleepy sough of the pines like the sough of low water.

He tried to think out who this fellow Stephen Wayne was in time and space. An American with Scots and Irish blood, and some English. The not unusual American Mixture. That did not explain him. In Montana he was known and did not require a label. He moved in his own accustomed sphere among associates who would make allowances or not make allowances for his reactions in any set of circumstances. That was just ordinary living, with problems that might be difficult but not out-of-the-way. In Montana he was an entity. He got that.

Well! He had come here to Scotland on a holiday, and he had to bring that entity with him. And he was not sure that that entity fitted-in in this old custom-ridden land. He had been labelled at once, and pigeon-holed, and was supposed to have no shades of character. That was not exactly so. Ruary Farquhar and Kenny Alpin accepted him as a fellow-human; but Ruary and Kenny were rebels, perhaps revolutionaries, seeking to restore what Scotland had lost, which was the thing that America had found and was now in danger of losing—a sort of individual freedom in unity. Yes, he got Ruary and Kenny where they lived. He even understood the laird, the MacFinlay, weighed down by disaster and shielding himself in immobility; in sane moments building a wall around himself that would hold of sheer inertia when the mind grew tortured. That took character.

But Stephen Wayne did not understand women at all, and so failed to be clear about himself. For he did not know what he wanted ultimately. He had set Marian Finlay apart, created some phantasy about her, sentimentalised some. Darn it! He'd become a mere rival if he did not watch his step. He had done nothing foolish yet. Something unconventional but not foolish; something in the entity of Stephen Wayne. And there was a clue to conduct. Let him retain his own identity in this land with a different culture going decadent. Be Stephen Wayne on his own two feet. Be more Stephen Wayne than ever, not shackled by custom, shocking folk a little, playing his own fair game as the cards lay. And when this small game was played out, he would go back home knowing that he had not been bluffed, or cross-raised, or dealt a hand from the bottom of the pack. So that was all right—if women did not interfere too much in the game. . . .

The electric bulb went on over the arch of the door. Marian was not staying long after dinner. That was white-fronted Budd Hale handing her in to the front seat of his car. And there he was himself, getting into the driver's seat. No chauffeur to-night, and a peaceful ten miles round by the road to Lettoch Lodge. Stephen heard the spurt of the gravel, and the big car slid smoothly along the curve of the drive, the headlights lighting up the clumps of rhododendrons and making the polished leaves a metallic green.

Stephen stirred in his canvas chair. If he hurried he could get to Lettoch Lodge as soon as they did—perhaps before they did, for might not Budd in the good old American way park the car somewhere in the quiet for a little tentative love-making. It would be tentative, for Budd would know how to move with that wild shy one. And there he was again, setting the girl up. She might just be an ordinary sort of girl and not averse to some American love-making on the side. Anyway, he would give them time to get home. He lay back and felt for his pipe, but he did not take it out.

A figure was moving slowly across the grass towards him. He had no need to look close. A woman's figure in a pale dress, something darker about her shoulders. That disturbing dark beauty, Lady Alice Tromes.

He lay still. His figure might be indistinguishable against the green canvas, and she might go drifting about the lawn with her own thoughts. She did not. She came directly, probably knowing that the chairs were there. And still Stephen did not move. She checked for a moment, and he knew that he was seen. And then she came on again and stood over him. She chuckled softly; her voice was just a shade breathless.

"What a pleasant surprise! I should have known that you would be about somewhere."

"Raist yo' feet!" Stephen drawled.

She sank into the chair that was quite close to his, and Stephen wondered if the two chairs were there on purpose, and one of them meant for Budd Hale.

"I claim squatter's right," he said.

"It is yours whatever it is. Have you a cigarette?"

"The tail-end of an American pack."

"I have used them."

Her fingers touched his as she felt for an end, and though they were cool fingers they tingled in that dam' blood of his. He cupped a lighted match under her nose—a sensitive nose and not aristocratically bony—and saw the drowning blackness of her eyes under heavy black lashes, and her red vivid mouth. Her hands were around his; her painted nails looked black, and he could see the red life of her glowing between her fingers. She leaned back in her chair; he heard the indraw of her breath, and the soft whiff of it as she drifted smoke through her nostrils; and then a long comfortable sigh. And the dark dangerous faint perfume was all about him.

"This is nice," she murmured. "I am almost happy."

"The replete tigress! reclining in that chair like a cat poured on the hearthrug before a winter fire."

"I could stay here all night. Shall we—we two poor lost ones?"

"If this chair was mine."

"You can hold it against all comers."

"The comer might be long in coming."

"You would never know." Her chuckle mocked him. He had forgotten to light his cigarette. He did so now and felt her eyes on him.

"You're a nice lean ugly devil, Stephen Wayne."

"I don't feel half devil enough, Lilith."

"Delilah you mean."

"Lilith—night hawk. Eve was short in technique."

"Don't be clever, or you'll spoil the mystery."

"Mystery, your eye!" said Stephen rudely. "What do you take me for?"

"An eccentric American millionaire of course, and my motives are nefarious."

"Do you want me to bait a hook for you?"

"Yes— No! You will not be flirted with, Stephen Wayne."

"You should feel my damn'd heart beat."

"Let it, boy."

She lay still in her chair, and he could see the white of her hands folded over her black wrap on the flat of her stomach.

"No, my dear!" she said. "You and I will not play a game. We are losing the ones we are already playing.

"Sometimes a game is won too easy to stay put."

"You're telling me," she said exactly in his own accent.

"Here is a comer now," said Stephen, "or is he?"

A dim tall figure was strolling across the lawn, strolling, but definitely in their direction. And it could not be Budd Hale, though Budd could be back by now, unless he had been invited in for a drink. The lady said nothing and did not shift from her feline ease. She was leaving the initiative to Stephen, and in his present mood he was ready to accept her silent challenge. He just sat still. The tall man in a dinner-jacket came on until he was almost over them. Then he said in a surprised tone:

"Oh! Excuse me."

"Nice night for a stroll, Chez?" said Lady Alice calmly.

Stephen remained still and silent.

The tall man, Chez—queer name Chez—stood looking down at them, but mostly at Stephen. He would like to bend down and see who this seat-grabber was, so as to know him again. All that Stephen could make out was a black stub of moustache against a long white face. The man was waiting for an introduction, but was too much of a gentleman to ask for one. Still, he was a trier. He said:

"Do you not find it cold sitting, Lady Alice?"

"Cats don't prowl after a meal," she said. "This is lovely."

"I think I'll take a turn," he said. He gave Stephen one last look and stalked off. It was a stalk, though he tried to make it a stroll.

"The perfect English gentleman, Chezzy!" murmured the lady. "What would an American have done?"

"'Get to your feet, polecat!'" quoted Stephen.

"You can remain silent with a vengeance."

"If it's any compliment, I rather like to be silent in your company."

"That is a compliment and a dangerous one."

"In that case I had better boost myself out of that gent's chair."

"The chair is yours. That is Major Eddie Chester—with a wife of his own and two children."

"He might have a dam' bad memory," said Stephen.

"You haven't a wife and two children, Stephen?"

"I believe in children all right, but not so much in wives."

"How improper! I can't be Lilith, for I am fond of brats."

The tall soldier took two turns about the lawn, edged once towards them, teetered on the edge of the gravel, and went hurriedly indoors. He left the door wide-open behind him, and the light over the arch snapped on.

"Damn you, Chezzy!" said Lady Alice.

"A fellow can't be a gentleman all the time," said Stephen.

The light flowed across the lawn. It was dim enough when it reached them, but they could see each other. Her long relaxed figure close to his was surely feline. It was turned a little towards him, and both her hands were under one cheek, her red mouth almost within reach, and that faint perfume about him. As he looked at her her shoulders twitched under the film of wrap and she said:

"It is not exactly a cool night——"

He was aware of the technique. Her shoulder would move again and touch his, and press little by little, and after a while his hand would slip under her shoulder, and her head drift on his shoulder, and he would kiss her painted mouth. And all of it would mean just nothing to her.

He was wrong. She made no move at all. She lay there, turned aside, her hands under cheek, and her dark eyes watching him. He took out his pipe and set it in his teeth, for a pipe in one's teeth is a protective weapon —against one's own inclination. And he cursed himself for the pulse that would quicken despite him.

"Don't you tempt me, Stephen Wayne," she said, and easily as a cat was on her feet.

Stephen was on his feet too, his pipe back in his pocket. She flicked her wrap across the bud of her breasts, and quietly put one arm inside his elbow. They walked slowly across the grass towards the house.

"I am Mariana too," she said, "but when I wait you come. Will you come again?"

"Not again."

"You said that before?"

"And meant it."

"I must wait in vain?"

"For what?"

"I will not tell you. Look! You came out of the woods, and all the dark woods and black hills were watching us. And we failed them. I will go and hide my head."

She looked down at him from the step of the door.

"I could ask you in for a drink, but I want to keep you to myself."

She reached him her hand downwards, and, as before, he touched her fingers with his lips. Her fingers did not tighten, but he felt her other hand softly in the tousle of his hair.

"You are an ugly darling, Stephen," she said. "Damn you!"

The door shut harshly, and the light above it went out, and the dark was darker than it really was; and Stephen Wayne felt strangely lost in it. The entity that was Stephen Wayne was lonely in the dark in a hollow hidden amongst a hundred Scottish hills.

CHAPTER XIII

STEPHEN circled back round the house on the line that Ruary and he had come, until he struck the wooden vermin hut with its faint and ugly odour. There he lined out his two chimney marks as nearly as he could in the dark, and kicked his feet in the fringes of the dark laurels. He felt the sack under the third bush, shouldered it, and worked his way round two angles of the garden wall till he struck the track leading over to Falcon Crag. The going over the untracked shoulder of the hill would be too difficult in the dark, and he had to risk falling in with watchers. He was getting real handy in the night woods now, and could keep his feet on the path even in the darkest patches, following the trend of it by the spacing of the tree-tops, and even jog-trotting in the open places round the beds of bracken. Going down the face of Falcon Crag he met Ruary coming up.

"Thanks be! I thought you were lost."

"I was dam' near lost," said Stephen cryptically. "That net of yours is damp all right."

"We'll give it the sun the morn." He took it from Stephen's shoulder and tucked it under an arm. "I knew you'd be for bringin' it. The sort o' thing you would do. Let's gang to our ain side o' the water. I'd hate to be kernappit, and we that innocent."

They crossed the bridge to the margin of the road, and Stephen suggested that Ruary come up for a last drink.

"Kenny has a bottle," Ruary said. "Moreover, the big car is still up at the house."

"And you match-making outside."

"Ay, was I!"

"How did you get on with the laird?"

"No trouble at all. He came along with me armlinkit, and whispered awa' to himself and to one young Ruary Farquhar. A strange thing, I felt gey queer myself. My hand holdin' him, his trouble came through to me, and time and tide had no meanin'. For ten minutes we were twa mad young fools together. Young again and the hills of Carron Bothy about us, and any dream I ever had I could make it real. An' what is more, I had an itch to make it real. Och! I canna make it clear to you or myself, but it was a gey uncanny feelin' at the time. One o' these days the laird might set out to make a dream real—and there will be trouble. But maybe you'll be wanting to get back to your ain place?"

"I should. Once to-night I felt lost and— Say, how long do the Castle Charles folk stay north?"

"The hinner end o' September mostly."

"I'll stick."

"You will that." He shifted the bag to his shoulder. "I'm for hame. See you the morn!"

Ruary went long-striding down the road and Stephen moved slowly up the slope towards the Lodge. Budd Hale was having a good long visit; but it might be that the laird was causing trouble and he staying on to help the daughter. Stephen moved faster. But half-way up he heard the car start at the front door, and the beam of the headlights slid round and down the foliage of the trees. Stephen moved up into the bracken so as not to be seen, but he underestimated the swing of the curve coming downhill, and before he could cover his eyes and dodge behind a tree he was blinded by the full glare of the headlights. The car went by and Stephen heard the hard scrape of the wheels as the brakes went on. The car came to rest near the foot of the slope, and the headlights were steady on the birch trees across the water. A quiet voice, but insistent, came up the slope.

"Steve! Say, Steve! I saw you, old son."

"Go to blazes," Stephen said, and walked down the hill. He would not turn tail on Budd Hale.

Budd was leaning back in the driving-seat, his two strong-knuckled hands at rest on the wheel. The dash-board light showed his sleek head and strong face, and his white shirt gleamed in the opening of a loose dust-coat. The car purred sleepily and smoothly on eight cylinders. Stephen put his foot on the running-board and his arms on the door.

"Doing some more poaching, Steve?" enquired Budd easily.

"I was, Budd. Poaching your own particular territory—but I don't know how particular."

"Were you at Castle Charles with your team-mate—that old chap, Farquhar?"

"I was quite near you."

Budd leant over and looked into Stephen's face.

"Say, Steve! While we're on poaching, am I by any chance poaching on your territory—and I don't care a cuss how particular?"

"That's how much you would care, Budd. What do you know about my territory?"

"I was just wondering. You have not been very frank, you know. Not frank at all. Those Highland Johnnies of mine run a grape-vine, but they keep their mouths shut except in the way of business. There's Grigor, my stalker, and all he tells me is that the lad who was with Farquhar that day I lost my stag goes by the name of Wayne—a stranger. Many strange Waynes about?"

"Not so many."

"Also the same Wayne was on the river last night."

"And you had a salmon course at dinner?"

"I thank you." He laughed. "I like that old Farquhar and have no inhibitions about poaching. I have about you. You were seen in this vicinity last night."

"And to-night."

"And so I wonder. You know Miss Mac—Miss Finlay?"

"That need not phase you."

"It does—a little. I had salmon and venison for lunch at Lettoch Lodge to-day. Who provided them, I wonder?"

"Didn't you ask Marian Finlay?"

"Marian Finlay? I see. Nice pat way you have. No, I didn't ask her. Haven't got so far yet, but here's hoping. I know you of old, Stevie, and you can be one tough hombre, but that girl puzzles me."

"She interests you also?"

"Interests and puzzles me, yes." He leant back in his seat. "Shy—wild—demure—you know? Respectable——"

"Virginal is the word you want, but you wouldn't know about it."

"I'm learning. And yet she pops my own venison under my nose cool as you like? It was mine, of course."

"You merely don't know our Highlands. We share out the good things and no questions asked."

"That explains nothing. I guess I can get nowhere with you, Stevie."

"All right, Budd! Let us go places. How married are you?"

"Ah! go to hell! No, don't! I see. Playing the Sir Galahad? Let us go. You are thinking of little Suey Grooch the warden's daughter. You had a crush on her, hadn't you, Steve?"

Stephen didn't answer. Susan Grooch had been a pretty, fickle-hearted, pleasure-loving, vain little vixen, and Stephen had fallen for her. Perhaps that was why he was sorry he hadn't taken Budd Hale, for whom she had fallen.

"Never mind!" said Budd Hale. "I did run away with her. She learned quickly, Steve, did Suey. I divorced her by half a length. She has been divorced twice since, making cold cash all the time, and is having a hell of a good time on her own toboggan. Anything else?"

"I haven't heard."

"Oh yes! I tried again. Not even a star, but Hollywood prime. She beat me to it by a short-head. Took too much sleep-dope two years ago. I gave matrimony best after that. That's all."

"A poor show for an early start. Now you are merely engaged to Lady Alice Tromes?"

"So you're on the grape-vine too." Budd Hale stirred. "What about it?"

"Nothing," said Stephen shortly.

"Nothing at all?"

"Only a foolish notion I have that I could lick you."

Budd's game leg stirred impulsively and he said:

"Ouch! Is it a threat, Steve?"

"Not the one you think it is." Stephen laughed. "Gosh, Budd! I should take you now while your foot-work is not so good."

Budd settled back in his seat.

"I licked you just about, didn't I? I think I could take you pretty easily now, Stevie, but I am not trying without cause."

"Cause is never essential nowadays."

"Go to hell, mystery man!" said Budd not unamiably. "I'll play the game as it lays."

The accelerator lifted the purr to a snarl, a clutch moved silently, and the car slid smoothly away almost before Stephen could take his foot off the running-board.

So that was Buddington Hale, and Stephen had to admit to himself that he had assayed out pretty highly as man to man, and that is what counts most when all is said and done. He had not liked the mention of Lady Alice Tromes, but he would go on playing his own game. Stephen was afraid that he had aroused the gambling instinct in him.

Stephen went on up to the Lodge. All the windows were dark, and he decided to go straight to bed. He had some sort of desolate and, at the same time, vindictive feeling somewhere about the diaphragm, and wanted to lie down in the darkness and nurse it. But up in his garret he recognised that he had a duty after all. The laird was deep in one of his attacks, and this, if ever, was a night when he should be watched and guarded. That Stephen could do—and blast his moods! his own moods! He lit his lamp, found his spool of cord, poised his weight, and unravelled his alarm-line across the yard.

He moved as noiselessly as he knew how, listening for any sound. The laird's window was tight shut and blinded, and there was a tortured spirit captive in there. Stephen, his ear at the edge of the sash, could hear footsteps pacing steadily and, once, a low mutter of rebellion. The man had put bars up against himself and wanted to break them. Some night or day he would.

Stephen moved on tiptoe to Marian's window and found the bottom sash lifted full. Marian herself was sitting on a chair close inside. She was still wearing her green dress, but he could not see the green beads against the soft white of her neck. She took the loop of the string from his fingers and whispered:

"He is distressed to-night, poor dad. I thought you would never come."

"We always do come, Mariana-no-longer."

"Hush! Speak lower! I am grateful to you for to-night. It was well done and just in time."

"That was Ruary."

"Both. I saw your face at the window. You and Ruary make a pair—a bad pair often."

"You had our salmon at dinner."

He heard the amused flutter of her breath. She leant out over the sill, and he could see the dark of her eyes.

"You are an American?" she whispered.

"Nothing else but."

"You might tell me something?"

"I might—not."

"Do American men usually try to kiss girls at the earliest opportunity?"

"No trying about it. Forgive me for being so remiss."

He put a hand on her shoulder, but she did not attempt to withdraw.

"No, Stephen!" she whispered.

"Right, old girl! Get to sleep! I'm on the watch."

He brought his palm to her cheek, and her cheek was burning hot. She lifted her hand, which was cold, and softly patted the back of his. And then she drew back quietly and brought the window down to its usual two inches.

Stephen went back to his garret. He was no longer disconsolate or vindictive. He liked that girl, and that girl had just shown that she liked him. He could carry on now.

CHAPTER XIV

STEPHEN went down to Knockindu that afternoon to get some hair sheared at the near-barber's. Kenny Alpin went down to post some of his own and Sheevaun's stuff. They did not go together, but it was not quite by accident they met under the clock-tower in the village square.

It was a clear hot afternoon—there was scarcely a wet day that wonderful autumn—and they adjourned to the billiard-room of one of the two hotels and drank draught Scotch beer, dark heavyish stuff under-hopped and over-isinglassed. They tried billiards, at which Kenny was fairly adept and taught Stephen the British game, had some more beer, and strolled homewards talking busily.

Stephen had parked the milk-pail at the road corner and went up to the croft with Kenny, where, being replete with beer, he refused the offer of afternoon tea. He talked some with Kirsty and Sheevaun, and stayed some minutes till Ruary came off the hill where he had been looking over the sheep. Ruary had a brace of grouse for Lettoch Lodge, and some more talk.

It was well after five o'clock when Stephen finally reached the Lodge. Maggie Donald met him half-way across the gravel, her hands twisting her apron and drama in her eyes.

"What kept you?" she cried. "He's gone! He's awa'!"

"The laird?" Stephen stopped dead.

"Wha' else?"

"And Marian——?"

"She's gone too. Na! No' with him! Lookin' for him."

Stephen dropped the grouse, put the pail on the ground, and laid hands firmly on Maggie's shoulder.

"Now tell me."

"I'm tellin' you."

She told him quite succinctly, as a Highland woman can. When Stephen left the house after lunch the laird was in his own room and Marian was resting in hers next door. She had not slept much for a week, and now she fell asleep and waked in an hour—maybe more. There was no sound from her father's room, and she hoped he was asleep—he had not slept at all for a week and had not recovered from that visit to Castle Charles. She looked in to make sure, and he was not in his room. He was not in the house at all. Nor was he about the grounds; and the pony was still down in its own paddock. After a brief but thorough search Marian made for the river at the run, crossed the bridge and went over Falcon Crag. That was more than two hours ago, and she had not returned. That was all.

"The window was open," said Maggie, "and he must have gone that way. I heard no sound in the kitchen—and I wasna snoozin'."

Stephen's trap-line had not come into use after all.

"He probably crossed the hill to Castle Charles," Stephen said, carelessly as he could.

"She'd ha'e him back ere this," said Maggie. "He was ill-ta'en."

There was no use going across to Castle Charles just now. There was only one obvious thing to do. He left Maggie to take in the milk and the grouse, and ran to the stable, where he picked up the bridle and saddle and a length of rope that he had prepared. Then he ran for the paddock and surprised that pony. The pony had never experienced roping. It kicked up its heels, ran for a corner, pivoted out of it, and was noosed without any difficulty. After that it was like an old mule until Stephen mounted, and then it did its stuff. Before mounting, Stephen had cut a couple of feet off the end of the rope, and that astonished pony had the kinks taken out of it in less than two minutes. In another two it was galloping terrier-like for the Croft of Balmerion, heavy beer joggling in Stephen and making him sickish.

The people at the croft saw his furious coming and knew that something was amiss. They met him at the gap in the dyke by the larch grove.

"He's out and awa'?" Ruary called.

"Hours ago," Stephen called back, checking the pony and slipping off over its shoulder.

"There's Kenny Alpin for you!" cried Sheevaun. She illogically blamed Kenny for keeping Stephen so long from his duty.

Stephen told them what he knew in as few words as possible. And then Ruary asked one important question:

"Did he take the rifle?"

"I didn't know there was one." Stephen opened his eyes.

"A good old weapon, and he kens how to use it. We'll find out." He fingered his grizzled beard thoughtfully. "Three hours—maybe more! Three hours! Miss Marian would have to make sure of the castle, and that'll give him a long start. She'll no' come up on him." He looked round at them. "Did any of ye hear shootin' in the hills the last hour or two?"

Kenny and Stephen looked sheepishly at each other. The only shooting they had heard in a pub-bar was out of their own mouths.

"There was no shooting," said Sheevaun.

"Nor from Castle Charles way either," said her mother, "and it is the thing I would fear."

"I heard nane either," said Ruary, "but I mightna notice if I had. Come awa', you two chaps! We ha'e no time to waste."

He set off down the track in long strides, and without pausing called over his shoulder to the two women:

"We might be gone a time. Dinna worry! I ken where to put finger on him."

Sheevaun looked from Kenny to Stephen with a sea-cold eye.

"You two unspeakable toughs! You'll be sorry you filled yourselves with gallons o' stale beer or the day is done. Get out!"

"Out o' range of your low Irish tongue," cried Kenny, starting off. Stephen, leading the pony, followed hastily. Kenny was cursing himself and Sheevaun.

"How the devil did she know we had a small drop o' beer?"

"She has nose, hasn't she? Were you kissing her?"

"An' lose my ain nose. Gallons, she said, and we had only two tankards apiece."

"Three."

"Four to be exact, and that's no' gallons however you make it."

Stephen flung a hopeless hand round the welter of massive hills.

"How do we hope to track down the laird in all that?"

"Leave it to the auld hound! He knows his quarry."

They overtook Ruary up the slope, and found Maggie

Donald waiting for them outside her kitchen door. She shook her head at Ruary.

"I was hopin' he'd be with you," she said.

"He will be. Is his auld rifle in the house?"

"Ay, is't! It maun be. Miss Marian hid it on him on top o' the clothes-press."

"We'll make sure," said Ruary. "If myself was lookin' for a rifle I'd try the top of a press first thing."

He went into the house with Maggie, and was back in a minute, Maggie behind him, mouth loose. He nodded his head.

"It's awa'. I thought it would be. And the cartridge-bag wi' it."

He put a comforting hand on Maggie's shoulder.

"I'm glad he took the rifle, Maggie. It will lead me straight to him. Miss Marian is on the right track and might be on him by now. We'll bring them both back. You hold the fort and keep the kettle bilin'—and a bit meat in the pot. And listen! Dinna say a word to anyone. Come awa', lads!"

"Wait till I get rid of this beast!" Stephen said.

"No! Bring the shelt. You'll need him."

He started off out of the yard and down the slope, and the two subdued young men followed. He waited for them at the turn to the flying-bridge, and the three gathered about the pony's head. Ruary, like the man he was, had not one word of recrimination in his mouth.

"We ha'e a long road afore us," he said.

"You know where to look?" Stephen wondered.

"I do. The hills back of Carron Bothy."

"Losh!" cried Kenny. "All that way?"

"Ay! the very top-end o' the forest. He'll spend the night in Carron Bothy—if it's empty."

"How can you know?" Stephen wondered.

"Because my mind is inside his. Didn't I walk him

across the hill that night and hear him whisper? Many
the night him and me spent in the Carron when we
were young—and isn't he young again in his own mind
and where else would he go? Mind you! I'll no' say
but I might be wrong, an' we'll take steps accordin'."
He waved his hand before their faces. "Will ye stop
spierin', an' listen to what I'm sayin'. I'll cross over
the hill to Castle Charles and find out where the gents
are on the hill. Some o' them might be on the Carron
beat, but I dinna think so. They stalked it last week an'
missed the muckle hart. From the castle I'll go up the
Don road and in by the slap in the hills. That's for me."

He pointed a finger under Kenny's nose.

"You'll go up the ither side o' the Lettoch to the
Caiplich, and cross over the Tamdhu ridge to the
chorrie in the neck o' Corryhow. You know it?"

"I know it."

"Go right up over the near shoulder and along the
breist, keepin' your eyes open; and if you come on the
laird you'll find your own way o' bringing him hame."

"I'll not find him," said Kenny, "but if I do I will
bring him home."

"Ay! I'm thinkin' you'll no' find him, but we maun
make sure. If he's no' on the Caiplich, work your way
down into the glen and come home yourself. That'll
be well into the morrow's morn, and that's for you."

He turned to Stephen.

"Mr Wayne," he said, "I'm giving you the long
road, but you'll be havin' the shelt part o' the way.
Ride him up to the top o' the glen where the road forks
for the braes o' the A'on, and leave him there his
head for home—he'll find the way. You'll cross the
Lettoch, a small stream by then, and go over the far
showder o' Corryhow making for the rocks on the first
ridge. From there you'll see a heather valley going

away before you south and east—no' a glen, but a wide hollow atween the hills trending that way. Follow that, and in time you'll come to a lochan. It'll be on for dark then and mair's the pity, but you'll find the lochan, sedges the near end and granite sand down the side. Mind you, keep off the gravel; there's peat moss under it, and you'll go to your belly. You have that?"

"I have it," Stephen said, visualising that shoulder of Corryhow and the valley beyond, with the far lochan in wastes of heather.

"You will go on from the lochan, and there is where you would be glad of a bit more daylight, for the ground lifts in humplochs, and it'll no' be easy to pick your road with the deer-tracks leadin' four or five ways. Hold by the east, the left hand, and you'll be in another hollow, and a deeper and a rougher hollow, that is called Glen Briste—the broken glen—and at the end o' that you'll come to a small plantation o' spruce. The bothy of Carron is in the hollow beyond it inside broom banks. I'll be there waitin' for you, and the laird will be with me if he's no' with yourself—or he'll be lying out somewhere, his face to the sky an' no' waitin' for any dawn any more."

"Where is the girl?" Stephen queried.

"She'll be on the hill, for she knows her father, and she knows the hills too. She might no' make Carron, but she'll no' lose herself. Well, I'm off, an' dinna ye blether too long. Luck wi' ye."

The cross-pieces of the bridge clacked under his iron-shod brogues, and the wires hummed as they swayed. The two watched him take the lift of the brae.

"I don't want to meet that girl on the hill," said Kenny gloomily.

"Nor I! I failed her to-day."

239

"I suppose that's my blame."

"You are welcome to any cussed blame you'll take," Stephen said, "and so am I, mister side-kick. Two devils tempting each other! Suppose we go back to our own hells?"

Stephen forked the pony, and Kenny hopped away livelily from the flying hooves. The persistent little brute took half a minute to disillusion itself, and was then scuttering up towards the main road; and Stephen kept it going.

Sheevaun was hurrying down the track from the croft and waving to him. He pulled up and waited for her. She had three hefty paper parcels in her hands.

"Sandwiches," she said. "Ye might be needing them. Where are the others?"

Stephen explained briefly and she nodded her head.

"That's what my mother thinks, but it looks a forlorn hope to me. You'll not be meeting Kenny then?"

"No. I'll take one packet of sandwiches for Ruary and one for myself."

"And you can drink water instead of beer this time. Think of that poor girl wandering the hills alone and you two toughs——"

"Get out from under, nagging wench!"

He pushed her away from the pony, and the pony, giving its ceremonial buck, started up the glen at a hand-gallop. Stephen did not spare it, and had it well lathered before they reached the top-end. It would have time enough to cool down on the road home.

Stephen was getting familiar with this noble glen now; all the tilted head of the high hills, and the contour of the slopes, and the great boulders standing out of the heather where they had crashed and rolled and ridden on glaciers a million years ago, and where they would lie still for yet another million years, terrific force locked in the heart of them. A peaceful, home-like, generous glen meant to breed men and carry the voice of crooning mothers across the hollows. And now it was empty for a little while; but a million years was a long time, and again might a Highland girl sing.

At the top-end of the glen, where the fork of the roads spread wide to make an easy gradient, Stephen dismounted, secured reins and stirrups on top of the saddle, unshackled the bit, and turned the pony's head homewards. The contrary beast did not want to go home. It tried to go over the brae, and Stephen had to chase it with pebbles down the road. But when Stephen was a hundred yards into the heather on his own road the pony turned back for the brae. It was going to have a peep over into the valley of the A'on. Stephen exhorted it to go and lose itself, and went on.

He crossed the young Lettoch dryshod by convenient boulders, and faced up for the mighty boulder-strewn shoulder of Corryhow. It was steep climbing all the way but not difficult, and he held doggedly on in zig-zags till he got to the head of the ridge in a jumble of immense blue-grey rocks. By that time the sun was behind Ben Shinnoch, and in the toneless light all the hills stood up starkly into a pale sky, all the valleys deepened, and the primeval silence settled down as the sure and eternal lord.

He could still look forward to an hour of good light, and he paused to get his wind and prospect the lie of the land before him. There and far below was the valley he had to follow, a wide treeless desolate hollow sweeping and curving out of sight south and east; wide wastes of brown moor, washed over with faint purple, shouldered up into massive brown hills, scarred with chorries, folding over into passes, and shouldering up again far beyond into the smoky blue ramparts of the Grampians. A heart-breaking and heart-broken country.

Stephen Wayne, looking over that tortured landscape, felt a touch of anger at Ruary Farquhar. How could he expect to pick up a lone lost madman in a country like that? All he had done was to put himself and his poacher's cunning in the laird's shoes, saying, "If I were the laird and lost in myself 'tis to the hill I would go." So Ruary would, who had nothing but the hills. But would MacFinlay, once owner of Castle Charles and now again owner in his own mind? More likely that he would be lurking in the woods round his ancestral home and, when night came, taking pot-shots at lighted windows—perhaps, if lucky, winging Budd Hale. And his friends up here in the desolate hills could do nothing.

No use thinking about that now, and no use turning back this late hour. The only thing to do was to keep tryst with the old poacher, and hike back with him to-morrow tails between legs. Stephen laughed at himself and at the seamed hollows of the mountains, and went bucketing down the long slope.

In the bottom of the valley he found a passable pony-track. All these valleys were threaded with such tracks for the deer-stalking. He made good time. Here and there a face of rock sent the track twisting; a heather slope heaved back and up like a sea, snaring huge boulders; schrees of grey-blue stone filled steep folds; and a recent landslide had poured its debris into a hollow where there was a faint tinkle of running water.

The light was now definitely failing, but as yet he had caught no gleam of Ruary's lochan. He went on, and he was no longer angry. His Highland blood began to tell. His horseman's legs were no longer springy but they were finely tough; and over his mind, and deep

242

in, spread an abiding calm. The austerity of this land was not inimical and not friendly, and yet it was of his own spirit. He was hidden in it but was of it. He could go on for ever, and nearly forget why he was there.

The dimness of a northern autumn night was about him when at last he struck the lochan—a few acres of lonely water hidden in a hollow. The dim silver floor of it, still as glass, held a light of its own below the obliterated slopes about it, but as Stephen looked a breath of air whispered out of the heather, and the sheen of it dulled into grey light-edged crinkles; and the beds of sedge moved as if touched at the live roots and said, "Hush-hush!"

The track went up by the left side on a firm bank of dry peat. Below the bank he could see the brownish-white glisten of granite gravel slip into the water, and slide out of sight a yard from the brink. And there he appreciated Ruary's foresight. He felt thirsty and would have stepped down on the apparently firm gravel if Ruary hadn't warned him of its bogginess. At the lower end, where water gurgled deeply in a small outflow, the gravel gave place to a ridge of brown rounded stones, and he went down cautiously and had his drink.

Again there came a whispering over the heather; a breath of air brushed by his ears, the soft lips of the water went lap-lap amongst the stones, and after a time the sedges at the far end hushed for silence. An eerie feeling went over him. He felt that he was no longer alone in that desolation, that someone had passed or was passing him away back in the heather. He turned his head slowly to look. There was nothing and there was no sound. A dim slope flowed upwards, and a sweeping black line curved across the sky with a bright planet star above it.

But that aware eerie feeling remained, for he was a Highland grandmother's grandson. She had told him old tales of lost water among the hills, and water-maidens pale-faced as the moon, sleek-haired as seals, slipping out of the blackness of deep water to lure lost travellers into the depths. He was about to lie over a flat stone and put his mouth to the water, but he had a strange fancy that a long white arm, wet and cold, might fold out around his neck and draw him deep under. He sat back, scooped the water in his hands, his eyes wary, and drank that way. Then he grinned at himself.

He sat back on his heels and took from a side-pocket one of good old Sheevaun's packets of sandwiches. He ate half only, though he was hungry, for he was an old campaigner and the night was before him. And he knew that a good rest after a long hike was better than short rests after short spells. Some of the sandwiches were ham with mustard, and some venison, and these latter were rather dry. So he scooped up another drink of water that had a faint astringency of tannin. Then he lit a cigarette, and held the match up. The flare of it did not flicker in the calm, and was swallowed within a yard in veils of darkness. He hunched his shoulders down under the folds of that darkness, but he was not afraid. When the match went out the darkness, strangely enough, seemed to recede, and the night was only a dim night in autumn.

He smoked for a while looking at a tall rock-face beyond the water. A pebble fell from high up and came down in a sharp loud clatter, and before the silence became more intense than ever a hoarse sigh filled the night. Stephen was startled, but only for a moment. He was an experienced camper in a country even wilder than this, and had heard that husky sigh before. It was the sound a hawk makes at night, and presently it would be followed by a deep husky note. It was.

But as he breathed freely again, another sound came that struck him to the marrow. It came from far away down the valley: a high wail that was at first sharp with fear, and then desolate with desolation, and lengthened out into an angry sadness. His hair raised. He could not place that sound. He had heard stag bell and roar, he had heard hawk and owl and eagle, the howl of a forest wolf, the ululation of a coyote, the scream of a mountain lion. This was none of these. It was too human. It was a *banshee* wail. He had an Irish great-grandfather, that he remembered as a very old hale man, who had told him about the *banshee*, the fairy woman with her wail of doom. But he was a hard-bitten Irishman and held that the origin and explanation of the sound was a vixen-fox calling to her mate. There were plenty foxes in the hills in spite of their deadly enemy the keeper. Only this was not the mating season.

He rose to his feet and threw his cigarette in the water, where it hissed and quenched.

"Get going, Stevie!" He addressed himself. "You'll be seeing things in a minute. Get going, darn you!"

That was good advice. The sooner he got into Glen Briste—the broken glen—the better. Ruary should already be waiting for him in Carron Bothy at the end of it—and the laird? Maybe! He set off, the track a brown line threading the black of the heather, and the going easy.

But in a mile the track lost colour and splayed out into many deep-bitten narrow paths in heavy heather, and he found himself amongst the humplochs—low humps—that Ruary had warned him about. He kept trending to the left and came to another splay of track, and then he found himself going up a slope and stumbling. Should he trend leftwards some more. No! he was on a low skyline and saw a dim and narrow valley opening below him. Glen Briste? Must be.

He went down into it, still stumbling in heavy heather, and once falling despite his care. A broken leg or twisted ankle would never do. He concentrated on his feet.

He went on for a long time—a full hour it looked like —and then he began to wonder. There was no track any more, and this glen was a heathery one, not a rocky broken one as Glen Briste should be. Moreover, instead of trending east it was trending south, as he could see by taking a line on the pole star. But he could not see where he had gone wrong, and Glen Briste must be around the corner. He went on.

In another hour of ploughing and stumbling and occasional falling he was almost certain that he was lost. There was still not a vestige of a track, and the heather slopes swept dimly up on either hand to a smooth skyline. Not a rock anywhere. And now he was trending west instead of east. Well! he would just take one more turn of this blasted hollow and consider the situation. He took it. The hollow swung away dead to the west, and he was brought up by a high wire fence. He was at the boundary of the deer-forest, and he had lost his way good and handsome.

He sat on his heels against an iron post, the old heather to his shoulders, and considered the situation. He was good and lost. No doubt about that. And he was good and weary too. He must have taken the wrong turn amongst those humplochs; and that was two hours back; and he had been trending westwards steadily ever since. Gosh! that meant that Carron Bothy must be miles and miles away over there beyond the hills. He could never tackle strange hills in the dark. The last hour had been bad enough. Rule that out at once! He could turn back? He could—and lose himself in another hollow, after another two sanguinary hours. Or he could walk right out of the picture by keeping on this western valley beyond the wire and coming out somewhere on the Tomintoul road where there were scattered sheep-farms? No, he could not walk out of the picture, not with Ruary waiting for him at Carron Bothy. And when Ruary said he would wait, that is just what he would do, and keep on doing.

Fine! The thing to do was to get to Carron Bothy as soon after dawn as possible. That meant a cold camp, and right in this spot. He dare not make a fire of old heather stems in this ocean of heather after drouthy weeks. He would set all the hills ablaze. Well! he was used to cold camps in colder weather. The night was fine, though a small coldish breeze was beginning to come up the valley. He could get out of the breeze somewhere, maybe, and squat for four or five hours— and even snooze some.

He got to his feet and looked about him. From a little distance down along the fence he heard a faint sound of running water. Good enough! After eating some more dry sandwiches he might need a drink. Wonder how Ruary—and the laird?—were making out wanting that packet of sandwiches. Toasted venison maybe! First he would look for a squatting-place and then eat.

For some time he had been passing an occasional bush of whin or juniper some short distance up the slope. Two or three scattered ones were above him now, and inside the fence. They looked thick enough in the dark to afford a good barrier against the breeze. He would go up and investigate.

The heather thinned as he went, and about the bushes there was only rough grass. One of the bushes looked particularly thick and sheltery, and he bent down and carefully felt for the prickles to see if it were whin or juniper. Juniper is the less prickly of the two. It was juniper.

Something moved under his hand, and there was a high squeal—the squeal of a rabbit or a hare.

In a sudden happening like that one either falls back over oneself or one clutches. Stephen was startled, but in a flash he remembered that a rabbit or a hare might come in useful later when a fire could be lit. He clutched hard—and roused a skirling earthquake. A big body heaved under his hand and he went down sitting but still clutching instinctively. He got to his knees desperately, his hands seeking a firmer hold, and softish but angry claws clawed at him. Strangely enough he remembered a Scots expletive.

"Goad-be-here!"

He was looking close into Marian Finlay's face.

CHAPTER XV

MARIAN FINLAY'S eyes were wide and wild, her mouth was a full circle, and there was nothing wrong with her vocal cords.

"Shut up!" he roared, and shook her: the only thing he could think of saying and doing.

Her eyes blinked and she really saw him for the first time. She gulped down the tail of the last skirl.

"Stephen!" she gasped. "Oh, Stephen! You come again."

She clutched him, no longer with claws, and he lifted her to her feet. But there was no pith in her long legs. She sagged against him tremblingly, completely foredone; he let her sink down sitting behind the bush, and sat down at her side. He had his arm round her shoulders and kept patting it; her head drifted sideways and down half on his shoulder, half on his breast, so that her hair tickled his chin.

"I think I am dying," she whispered.

"Don't be inconsiderate," he said. "I can't hump your long-legged carcase all the way back to Lettoch Lodge."

She turned her head up and looked closely at him.

"Why, yes! You are really Stephen—tongue and all."

Suddenly she threw her head back and laughed. It was not nice laughter and it kept on too long. His patting changed to pretty fair thumps between the shoulder-blades. Then he shook her until she gurgled and her teeth rattled. She caught hold of his arm and gripped tightly; and drew in a long breath.

"I am all right now, Stephen," she said sanely. "Thank God! I am safe now!"

"Safe as a house," said Stephen, "if we had one. Ain't you far from home?"

"My father—don't you know?"

"I know."

"Oh, Stephen! I am so sorry." Her hand tightened. "You could not go away for an hour but I must fail you."

Here was a fresh aspect of this girl, and no mean one. He would not change it for the world—not yet. Better keep her talking until she found her balance.

"How did you get this far?"

"I walked—and then walked. Dad was not about the castle or in the lower glen, so I thought he would be on the hill. I came by the back of Tamdhu, but there was no sign of him, and I went on and on. I could not turn back. Ridge after ridge drew me on, and after a time I was afraid I was lost."

"And then you were good and lost."

"I was. And back there a big stag startled me and I screamed, and grew angry at myself, and simply bellowed that stag over the skyline."

"I heard you. You bellowed right hearty."

"And then I got to the wire, and knew I could never make the bothy at Carron to-night. So I hid under a bush, and after a while heard something trampling in the heather, and I could not see what it was against the dark hollow. I covered my head, but the thing came up and fumbled about with its nose and pawed me. I thought I would die."

"Pause there!" said Stephen. "You are not talking about me by any chance?"

"Like a great snuffling beast." She leant out and felt over the ground.

"Vixen yourself!" said Stephen. "What have you lost?"

"My heart. It jumped clean out of my mouth."

"You'll do to take along," Stephen said. "So you were making for Carron Bothy?"

"Dad is there if anywhere. Do you know where it is?"

"Fine that," Stephen said confidently. "Over the hill there, but a goodish bit. Your father is there with Ruary Farquhar."

He made it good and strong while he was at it. If she had the same notion as Ruary she might as well have her confidence confirmed. She had had a hard day, and she had a hard night before her, and the removal of anxiety for the time being was a grand help.

"Oh, Ruary! Good old Ruary! Ruary would know. Is dad all right?"

"Right as rain!" Stephen said heartily. "Righter than you are. How hungry are you?"

"Stephen! Please don't! I've been chewing grass stems."

"You know that trick? Try your teeth in that."

He had the half-packet of sandwiches open on her lap and one in her hand.

"Oh! You dar—ling!" She split the word in two with a snap of her teeth. "Um—um! Venison! I'm glad you're a poacher."

"Try this one next."

She bit alternately at the two.

"Ham! Yes, ham! That's better. Why are you not eating?"

"It was a big parcel. This is your bare half. I ate my half back at the lochan."

He was hungry, but he said nothing about the other

packet of sandwiches. Pity he hadn't taken Kenny's one too.

"How did you know I was on the hill?" she enquired, her mouth not empty.

"Ruary knew."

"But how ever did you find me?"

She was assuming that Stephen had been to Carron Bothy and had come out looking for her. Stephen would let her assume that for the present.

"You took the only wrong turn there was and missed Glen Briste. I took that turn too. You were stopped by the fence. So was I. You sat under a bush and I chose the same bush, nosing you like that big beast. Quite simple!"

She wolfed down that half-packet of sandwiches like one o'clock. No wonder! A fit girl out in the hills for ten hours would be ready to bite rod-iron.

"There's water down there," she said as he crumpled the paper into a ball and thrust it into a pocket. That paper might come in useful if they wanted a flare.

They went down cautiously, feeling forward with their feet. The ground about the spring was soft but not boggy, and they found a tiny runnel between two bunches of rushes. She cupped water in her hands and drank. The water was cold and she shivered.

"Don't drink any more now," Stephen said. "We shall be cold enough. I want to tell you that we cannot make Carron Bothy to-night."

"I knew that," she said quietly. "I could not face that valley again in the dark."

"I would not like to. The bothy is over that hill and over another, and we could not hope to make it to-night."

She looked round at the silent dim slopes closing them in, and drew an even breath.

"I can stand this if you can," she said. "The night is not cold."

Nor yet was it a warm night. The sky was hazing over and a light breeze was drifting up the valley. A southerly breeze, but it had come over the Grampians and brought a little more than coolness with it. They went back to the juniper and sat close together in the lee of it. Stephen had some American cigarettes left, and they smoked one apiece; and she rested her shoulder against his with a complete confidence that was, perhaps, touching but not entirely flattering.

"What can your serving-man do for you now?" he enquired, watching the red end of her cigarette glow and dim.

"Tell me how long it is to dawn? I haven't a watch."

"Nor I. Say five hours."

"Wow! That is a long time. Did you ever read Charles St John? No! You must. He wrote wonderfully of sport and wild life in the Highlands—oh, nearly a hundred years ago."

"Some sport yet—and this is wild life, isn't it?"

"This would be nothing in his day. He tells how the wild poachers of Ross used bed down in the open heather as late as October. There might be five of them, and, first, they'd cut a big pile of heather with their sgians—their black-hafted knives, you know—and then four of them would lay down under their plaids, leaving a space for the fifth in the middle, and the fifth would thatch them with the heather, from the heels up, stems in and tops out, and then slip backward into his own place. Sometimes they would be a mound of snow in the morning but cosy as—as anything."

"As five bugs in a rug. We haven't a plaid, have we?"

"I've my tartan skirt."

"I'll lend you a jacket."

253

"With a thin American shirt below it. We'll have to thole as we are."

They were silent then. He was considering this girl and her poacher's bed. She had had a terrific afternoon and evening, worse than his. His own thighs were aching, and there was a numb feeling below his knees from ploughing in deep heather. He would be stiff as a post the first hour in the morning. She had not yet had time to stiffen up, but as the chill of the night got into her she would probably take cramp and, as like as not, be unable to move at all in the morning. It was up to him. He was captain, and it was his plain duty to take his team out in good order and on its feet, so that it could look back in retrospect—and bore listeners. He spoke suddenly:

"Thanks for telling me! You called me a poacher and I am going to try that poacher's bed."

After a longish pause she said in a low voice:

"Very well! Perhaps I shouldn't——" she stopped.

"Here is another cigarette for you. I have a pretty useful sgian, including a corkscrew and cap-lifter."

The thick long heather was just below them. He went down and despoiled it. The stems were tough and took some cutting, and after a trial he found it easier to tear them out by the roots. He gathered a double armful and went back to the juniper.

"Choose your lair," he ordered her briefly.

There was a thick mat of old dry grass by the side of the bush and he heard her fumble in it.

"I was a girl-guide in my time," she explained. "Oh! it seems a hundred years ago. I am making a hollow for my hip. There!"

She lay down and reached a long arm to pull her walking-skirt as far as it would go down her long shanks.

"Do you itch anywhere?"

"No-o! Wait." Her hand was busy at the back of her knee.

"Give it a good one while you're at it."

And then he thatched her in from the feet up in the approved fashion. It took four armfuls to finish the job thoroughly. When he got to her neck he folded his handkerchief over cheek and chin to keep the stems from scratching. She said with hidden timidity:

"But you have left no place for yourself?"

"What do you take me for?" he enquired sternly.

After a distinct pause she said:

"I don't mind, Stephen."

"I am very particular."

"Yes, I have noticed that—in some things," she said, and chuckled softly.

He finished the job and patted it over like a workman. She was hidden in a dark mound nearly as big as the juniper bush, and he could just make out the white of her forehead below one end. He sat down near that end.

"This is fine," she murmured.

"You'll warm up in about five hours."

"I'm warming up now. What about yourself?"

"I'll make out. I've been using cold camps all my life."

"Will Ruary and dad wait for us at the bothy?"

"I arranged that with Ruary."

"They will be all right there. Dad, and Ruary too, know where a spare key is hidden. We used keep emergency rations in all the bothies. I suppose they still do. Potted meats, and oatcakes in sealed tins, and minerals."

Stephen was glad to hear that. He had use for Ruary's packet of sandwiches. Only he was not sure if Ruary and the laird were at the bothy, but there was no use worrying about that.

The girl was completely confident and, now, cheerful. The hills and the desolation did not cow her. They were her very own hills. She came of generations that familiarly called this welter of mountains "the hill"— going to the hill, out on the hill, "the hunter home from the hill." They were all hunters. In fact, all men everywhere were hunters. And even in these modern days the hills were drawing men from the cities who could afford to pay through the nose for the satisfaction of a primeval instinct.

Feeling that fine confidence there inside her thatch, weariness flooded over her overwhelmingly. They talked for a little while longer, and then Stephen heard a breath drawn deeply and exhaled in a long slow sigh. He got to his feet and started to move away softly.

"Good night, Stephen!" she murmured.

"Mind your prayers," he said, "but a shout will do as well if you need me."

"Um—um!" she murbled, and if that was a prayer it went with him.

He looked up at the sky. It had dimmed in patches of haze, but there were no masses of cloud. He knew where north was, but he made sure by picking out the pole star in the dim field of the sky. Yes, his north was right, but he had to hold it there till morning; for in the morning-light the contour of this country might look very different, and with an overcast sky he might not be too sure of his orientation. There and then he made sure of it. He took a line from the bush where the girl was bedded and strode north twenty paces to another. That bush was slightly off line, but near enough. He thrust the crumple of paper from his pocket into the prickles of it—it was a whin—and went round to the lee and squatted down.

He filled a pipe and smoked, and looked at the contour of the hills against the autumn brightness of the sky in the north-east. Away up there somewhere was wide-shouldered Corryhow, but the nearer hills hid it. They had come a long way and had a long way to go. The girl back there had a complete trust in him and in his ability to get her out. Not so many days ago she had no trust in him or his Western outspokenness, but he had changed that. Don't be feeling proud, Steve! What you are doing is the only thing to be done. Get this girl, who trusts you, out on her own two feet as far as Carron Bothy, as far as Lettoch Lodge if necessary; and get her out so that later on she can recall the tough time with pleasure, saying, "It was tough all right, Stephen, but I didn't let you down. You said I would do to take along."

He put away his pipe and lay on his back, working one shoulder under the breast of the whin until the prickles warned him. Then he lay still, staring up at the faint stars. Many a night, and five thousand miles away, he had lain and looked up at these stars through a clearer air; generally his camp was warmer, but sometimes it was colder. He could stand this now. He could keep on standing it. He could keep on standing it if it grew colder . . . colder . . . colder . . .

It was colder. He had been asleep, and waked up to find a chill breeze blowing in his face. The breeze had been south and by west earlier in the night, and now it had swung west and by north. That north shift was a sign of more fine weather to come, but the north had put its own keenness in the breeze.

He scrambled stiffly to his feet, and felt the cold in his bones. Even his lips were stiff. This would not do. He took a stride out into the grass, side-stepped quickly, hooked him with right and left, hooked him again, thrust him off with a stiff left, and whipped the right across to the jaw.

"Like that, Budd? Bit stiff yet, but wait till I get going."

He went in under his guard head down, both hands pounding the ribs, and dropped to his knees. "Haymaker! Didn't see it in time." He took a short count and was up again, both hands swinging like windmills. In two minutes he counted, "nine–ten–out," held his own hand up to the stars, and panted. He was just shadow-boxing to warm himself. He did too.

He thought of his baby under the heather. Would her coverlet hold secure in this change of breeze? Better see! He moved across quietly, slipped on the edge of a tough clump and went down flat. An ankle nearly went that time. He crawled the rest of the way. She was asleep, but had turned over from the breeze, and one hand was outside the cover. The heather at her back had come unthatched.

"Careless little so-and-so!" he said under his breath.

He tried to build the fronds up over her arm. In doing so he touched the back of her hand and found it cold—too cold. On his knees he bent over her and peered close at her side-face. He could see the black line of lashes and one delicately firm cheek, and could hear her breath slow and long with a small flutter at the end that told she was not as cosy as that bug. He touched her cheek with the back of his fingers, and her cheek was cold too. He had to get some warmth into her.

He fumbled the heather at her back, lay down full-length on his side between her and the breeze, and gradually drew closer; and like a child in sleep she nestled into the warmth and went leagues deep into sleep. . . .

He waked in the earliest streak of grey dawn stiff with the cold. The breeze had died away and the chill was out of the air but stayed in his bones. The mound of heather in front looked shrunken, and he lifted carefully on an elbow to look. The girl was not there at all. He turned head but could see no sign of her. He put a hand under the heather mound and found the nest still warm, so that she could not have been long out of it. He lay down again and considered.

She must have waked up not so long ago to find him close at her back. That would startle her. All her shyness would be startled in the stark dawn light with no kindly darkness to shelter in. Her first reaction would be to draw herself out of her nest. What would her next reaction be? If he removed himself now, the knowledge would be shared in both their minds, and she would be embarrassed. He wondered what the woman in her would do. It was up to her.

He heard her feet swishing in the grass, held his head turned down, shut his eyes, and let his breath flow easily. Her feet stopped at his side, and he knew that she was looking down at his cold ear. And she would be feeling the cold too after getting out of her cosy nest. Would she wake him up and tell him it was dawn? At that point he very nearly started, for he felt her fingers brushing his cheek, and her fingers were warmer than his cold skin. And he heard her soft whisper:

"Poor boy! He kept me warm."

Gosh! Poor boy! Her feet came round his head and he opened his lower eye and saw her ankles above a heather-scratched, scuffled pair of brown brogues. She was fumbling at the heather, and before he knew she was cautiously working her way back into her nest.

This was exactly right. Since she assumed that he was asleep and so did not know that she had left her bed she was putting it up to him. Nice work, Miss Long-Legs.

He felt her body gradually nestling back to its old position, and had a small urge to slip a hand softly round her waist. He did not. Instead he lay still and breathed easily, until her breath, which had been held, began to flow easily too. Then he stirred naturally, yawned, rolled over on to his feet and slouched off towards his own bush without looking back. He did not know whether she was asleep or not.

He did some more shadow-boxing and lay down on his side. Grey dawn, without the dawn wind, was about him, and in the cold even light all the purple-brown hills were withdrawn and brooding. Here and there wisps of mist lay quiet on broad breasts. These were all round-topped hills, heathery hills without faults or chorries, more of the grouse-moor than the deer-forest. And why deer-forest, he wondered? When is a forest not a forest? When it is a deer-forest. This deer-forest covered fifty thousand acres, and outside the surroundings of Castle Charles there wasn't a tree to a hundred acres. An old Scots custom, he supposed, dating from away back to when there were real forests.

They would have to take the trailless trail soon. But if that girl were sleeping he would let her have a last snooze—say an hour— No! half an hour. They must make Carron Bothy at the earliest possible time and by the shortest road. Half an hour! He turned over on his back and looked up at the fragile sky. Little tails of pearly mist floated here and there against the face of it, and he knew they were going to have another warm day.

He did not need to give her that extra half-hour. In a few minutes he heard her feet coming on the grass, and again he shammed sleep. She did not come close, and in a little while her feet drifted away towards the runlet of water in the hollow. In a few more minutes he heard them coming back and stopping close to him. He opened his eyes and looked up directly into hers.

"Sleepy-head!" she called him.

He yawned frankly and rolled to his feet.

"Gosh!" he exclaimed, "I don't think I moved more than once."

She had splashed water on her face, and with one hand was busily massaging each cheek in turn with his handkerchief. The other hand was picking bits of heather out of her hair. That darkly-fair hair of her fluffed about her head, and one moist tendril lay on the white of her brow. She brought the young-blood to her cheeks, and her eyes were as clear as the dawn. She was even cheerful, and Stephen envied her, for he was inclined to be down-in-the-mouth and disillusioned in the dawn.

"How did you make out?" he enquired.

"A bug wasn't in it—or an earwig. But I had a strange dream. I dreamt I was cold in the night and a big ugly grizzly bear came on its hind-legs, but not to eat me up. It had a hot-water-bottle in its mouth, and a down quilt in one arm and a bolster in the other; and it put the bottle to my feet, and covered me with the quilt and pressed the bolster close to my back. A lovely old ugly bear!"

"Some grizzly!" said Stephen. "A real Kodiak would have kissed you—and bitten your head off."

She looked at him with frank and innocent eyes, and he tried to copy her look. She knew and he knew who that bear was, but she thought that he did not know that she knew. Was that right? As long as she knew that he did not know that she knew she could gaze at him innocent-eyed. Women were all the same.

"Are we ready for the road?" he enquired.

She kicked one foot and then the other.

"Bit stiff!" she said. "Not more than another ten hours in me."

She did not expect a quarter of that time, and neither did he; and that was a good thing, for actually ten hard hours were awaiting them and saying nothing.

She looked all round her at the smooth contours of the hills and at the sky above the round summits. The sun was still below the lifted horizon, and she looked for the glow of it in the wrong place.

"I am lost," she said. She pointed down the valley through the wires. "I know I am wrong, but I would call that east."

"East! You've swung the compass right round." He showed her his marking-line between the bushes. "That's north, and Carron Bothy is eastwards over that hill."

She shook her head helplessly.

"Lost! and in my own hills. I'll just have to follow where you lead."

"Right. We can go back two hours, and make a long leg up Glen Briste, say another two hours; or we can take a short-cut over the hill, up and down, and save two hours."

"Two hours nearer bully beef and oatcakes. Let us break new ground. It cannot be worse than the valley."

"Are you hungry?"

"No-o!" She put a hand on her flat stomach. "Empty but not hungry. I don't want to eat somehow."

"To the road, then!"

They faced the hill.

CHAPTER XVI

THEY made the real top of the hill in good time. There were three ridges that looked like the top, but the real top gave them a wide view. She was better on the hill than he was, taking it in long easy zigzags, placing sole and heel flat to ease the leg muscles, and having the hill-man's trick of foot-swing in deep heather. He found it mighty hard going to keep near her, and she led him twenty yards to the top of the hill; and laughed back at him. But they did not see Carron Bothy from the top of that hill.

All they saw was a long slope going down before them to a wide hollow covered with reddish-brown grass, and a long slope beyond going upwards to a round summit like the one they stood on. The hollow ran right and left and curved out of sight, and the whole landscape was as empty as on creation day.

The sun was over the summits now, and they could see immensely far over that tortured territory. There northwards was Corryhow with one small bank of cloud faintly pink above its peak, and across all the south bulked the blue and grey Grampians, bands of pearly mist still atwist from gorge to gorge.

"Now I see where I am," said the girl. "The bothy will be over there. We can make it."

Over there was over the hill across the hollow. She set off down the slope in front of him. Half-way down, over a shelf, they struck a rough patch: tilted slabs of blue stone, miniature chorries, and the gouged-out dry channels of winter torrents. At one place a trickle of water sleeked down over green moss and tinkled from the points of a hart's-tongue fern. This was the place Stephen was looking for. He tried the water in his palm and found it cold and pure.

"Are you hungry yet?" he asked her.

She turned her back to him, and shrugged her shoulders as much as to say, "Why mention it, blast you?" She cupped both hands under the trickle and drank. When she turned again, Stephen was holding the open packet of sandwiches under her nose.

"The bread is gone dry: it was too long in the wizard's top-hat."

Her hazel eyes softened and glistened, and she put her hands under his.

"I take it all back, Stephen," she said. "I'm a brute. Do you know what?"

"It ain't so."

"You'll do to take along. Isn't that it?"

"Don't flatter yourself with vain hopes. You get only half."

"And I beginning to think that I wasn't going to enjoy the day—much."

They ate shoulder to shoulder, squatting, and took their time like old hikers, talking of this and that.

"You can thank Sheevaun Power for these sandwiches," Stephen said.

"That lovely red-haired girl! Are you in love with her, Stephen?"

"I don't know. She makes my heart go pit-a-pat, but so do you and—one other."

"I am flattered to be in the company. Who is the other? Oh yes! I know." She laughed. "I don't think you ever fall in love, Stephen—not really."

"Tell me about it so I'll know."

"You are not even the flirting kind—or—or——"

"Or what?"

"I'd make love to you."

"Didn't I warn you about that? But you can thank the Lord all Americans are not like me."

A small flush came to her face.

"I know what you mean. I don't understand it. I think no man should kiss a girl unless he really knows her—has time to like her."

"In that case I am due a kiss or ten."

"I wouldn't mind one of your kisses, Stephen."

He put his hand over hers and felt the shy startle.

"I will remember that on a suitable occasion, you dam' little flirt," he said. "The hills are watching now."

He had one cigarette left and he gave her that. He filled a pipe for himself. And then, both smoking, they went down the slope in the best of form, crossed through the thick untracked grass, and tackled the long, long rise beyond. The sun was getting warm, and that long rise took the early resilience out of them. From the foot it looked one even slope, but there were a good few ridges to disappoint them, and they had to rest frequently. The girl was not leading Stephen any longer, and they made the summit shoulder to shoulder. He was not now envying her capabilities on a hill, but rather thankful that she had long strong legs under her.

They made the top, and again there was no bothy in sight or any trace of a spruce grove to mark it. There was a steep hillside below them this time, and a glen-like hollow, and a steep rugged hillside beyond; but there was no least trace of a clump of trees or a bothy beyond it.

"Short-cuts don't seem to pay," Stephen said. "They never did."

"But we must be near there," Marian said. "You know where the bothy is?"

She still assumed that he had been at the bothy the previous evening.

He swung an arm east and north.

"I wasn't this way yesterday. More hills than I bargained for between."

"We must make it," she said doggedly. "Stephen, I must make it on my own two feet."

"I've been envying the length of your legs the last two hours. We'll make it under our own steam."

All the way down the hillside was one woeful, thigh-wearying, neck-breaking holdback. But they made it, legs and necks intact. Stephen had worn all the silk off his good condition, and was carrying on on his reserve, but he knew from experience that having once got down to that reserve he could, without thinking further about it, carry on for the required number of hours or days. He did not know about the girl. She was supremely fit —she had to be fit to have stood up to yesterday—and she was resolutely plucky; but she was only a girl, and he did not like the white that was beginning to show about her nostrils. One good long rest was what she needed.

For the first time since yesterday they found a track. It wound in the bottom of the valley and went away out of sight on either hand.

"The stalkers come this way at any rate," she said.

They sat down to rest at the side of the track, and she leant a tired friendly shoulder against his.

"Let's consider a mite," Stephen said. "We knew that the bothy was east from where we started, and we have come east."

"East as ever was, and then some."

"No mimicking! But that bothy might be a bit

north—or south of east. North if anything! In that case we may have passed the bothy out of sight in the last valley, or it might be out of sight in this one."

"Or the next!"

"No! If it is out of sight from the top up there we have definitely come too far. If we go up to that top and see nothing, then we will have to come down here again and prospect this valley—northwards I think, for, at the worst, it is on our way out."

She saw that at once.

"You mean——"

"I mean that it would be foolish for two of us to go up if two of us have to come down again. You will stay here and rest. If I see the bothy I will come down to that point where you can see me and wave you up. That's plain Jane and no nonsense."

She looked up at the steep hillside and smiled bravely at it.

"Yes," she agreed. "I would hate to tackle that hill straight off, but I can do it, Stephen."

"After a rest you will." He got to his feet and pranced a step or two out of bravado. "Lie on your back and spread your limbs abroad. That's the way to rest. Give me an hour."

He took two. He was weary all the time, but he was no more weary at the end than at the beginning. He had got down to bed-rock, and it was rock. Like a boxer over-trained he felt stale but could go on for ever. He made the top.

He looked northwards and saw nothing. He groaned. The terrain beyond no longer ran in ridges. It was a rugged and tumbled territory of bluffs and peaks and draws, chorried and shattered and beetling: first-class stalking-ground but full of difficulties. The bothy might be hidden away in any hollow. But no! Turning his eyes hopelessly to the south he saw in the distance a clump of dark-green trees below the mouth of a fold. They were stunted spruce, for beyond and over them he could make out the stone chimney and gable-end of a small house. Slantwise over the breast of the far fold a grey road wound down into the hollow where the house nestled.

That must be Carron Bothy, though he had not known about a road leading to it. They had held too far north, instead of too far south as he had calculated, but the bothy was within reach if he could get the girl over this hill.

He turned to look into the valley, but he could not see the bottom of it for the intervening ridges. He went down over two shelves before he picked her out at the side of the track. She was lying down, and did not answer the waving of his jacket over his head.

"Asleep? Of course."

He tried yelling, but it was a far carry and he could not yodel at all. She never stirred. He went down two more tilts and tried again. And then she sat up and waved back at him. He was mighty glad, for he had been afraid that she had collapsed. He signalled her up, and she tackled the hill at once, climbing steadily, if slowly, conserving all her energy like a good one. He went down to meet her. She was very repentant and there were tears in her eyes.

"Oh, Stephen!" she panted. "To bring you all this way down. I was asleep. I just hate myself for being a drag on you."

"Fine!" said Stephen, and put a supporting hand round her shoulder. "Let me tell you the truth for once: any other girl but yourself would have gladly sat down and died five hours ago. Take a rest now."

He told her what he had seen, and she reassured him.

"That is Carron Bothy all right. The road you saw is the private one going out to the main Don highway. They bring cars right in to the bothy from that side."

As they sat there the sound of a distant rifle-shot came over the hill from the direction of the bothy. A second shot followed almost immediately, and then two more in quick succession.

"Into the brown of them," said Stephen. "How is it that we have seen no deer all day? I suppose they keep to difficult country during the season."

But the girl was looking at him wide-eyed.

"Stephen!" she said. "The stalkers are up——"

He patted her shoulder.

"Do not cross any rivers until you come to them. We'll investigate that shooting."

But he was more disturbed than he cared to admit to himself. If the stalkers were up, where was Ruary—and the laird? Better not think too much about it. Ruary would find a way out. The laird had a rifle, and Ruary might be doing a stalk on his own—but not firing four shots. Would it be a signal to himself? It might. And if the stalkers were up that would mean a car to give this girl a lift home. As for himself—Better investigate, son!

Three hours later they were down on reasonably level country and within a mile of the bothy. Marian by that time had not much to come and go on, but a fine foolish pride would not allow her to accept any help. For the last mile Stephen kept ahead of her just to draw her on, moving slowly and evenly, as indeed suited his own weary legs. The going was over stony ground with patches of thin heather and thinner grass. Flat slabs of rock, a bare couple of inches out of the ground, were everywhere, and these he edged round instead of striding over.

Within a short distance of the spruce belt he glanced over his shoulder. Marian was sitting on the ground a hundred yards away, propped on her hands. He went back to her, and was glad to see that her legs were straight in front, not twisted under her. She threw back her head and laughed for and at him, and patted a flat slab at her side.

"Just a last rest, Stephen. I was too ambitious and tried a short-cut. This was too far up in the air for me, and I fell down the first mile. I'll try it again if I have to crawl."

He got his hands under her arms and she came to her feet. She rested against him for a moment; and then shoulder to shoulder they stamped over the stone, and marched arm-in-arm towards the trees. She was going on her own two feet, but his arm stayed her erring steps. They came to the back of the belt.

"We'll go through the trees and take a look-see."

The belt of stunted spruce was long, but not more than forty yards through, and it was surrounded by an easily-surmounted earth-mound grown with scattered broom from which hung brown seed-pods. It was used as a shelter and feeding-ground for deer in a hard winter. They crawled on hands and knees over the mound between two broom bushes and in amongst the close-set, spindly trees. There was no undergrowth, and the ground was a trampled mat of spruce-needles. Across the length of it there was a wide, shallow drainage ditch, the bottom of it now bone-dry and choked with matted grass and needles. Stephen slipped down into it, and Marian slipped in at his side and kept on slipping until she sat at ease, her head and shoulders against the bank. She sighed deeply and her eyes closed. This was as good a place as any to rest in before scouting, and Stephen sank down at her side. A shaft of sunlight came down slantwise through the tops of the trees and showed a glint of red in her hair. There was a spot of colour high on each cheek, and the pallor round her mouth was more marked.

"We are here," Stephen said, "and it was one dam' fine piece of work, Marian Finlay, my dear."

It was too. That girl since early morning—and it was now evening—had climbed over three tall hills and ploughed through unnumbered acres of heather. She smiled but did not open her eyes.

"Find things out for me, O tireless one!" she whispered.

He needed a rest just then about as much as she did, but he had to find out how things lay as soon as possible. He scrambled out of the ditch, went across to the earth-mound not twenty yards away, and crawled to the top under the shelter of a bush of broom. But from there he could not see any of the bothy except the top of its one chimney. It was in a small hollow beyond a low broom-grown ridge. But he was not interested in the bothy just at that moment. He saw something else that did not surprise him, having heard those rifle-shots earlier in the day.

Budd Hale's big open touring-car was parked just in front of him on the near side of the ridge. There was no one near it, but away to the right two pack-saddled Highland ponies were tethered on a patch of thin grass: sturdy beasts, under fourteen hands, capable of packing a three-hundred-pound stag over ten miles of mountain track. So the stalkers were out on the hill, Budd Hale amongst them, his knee again sound. Where then were Ruary—and the laird? Not in the bothy? He would have to find that out, but it would have to wait. There was something else he must try first, for the girl's sake.

271

He had a good look round to make sure there was no one in sight, and then rolled down the front of the mound and made a crouching run for the car. He was in luck. There was a luncheon-basket on the back seat —a huge basket and well filled. It contained several labelled packets of sandwiches, half a dozen bottles of beer, a flat box of cream cheese, a carton of biscuits, some bottles of soda-water, and a flask of brandy with a silver bottom cup. He picked two packets of beef sandwiches—Scotch beef makes about the best sandwich— two bottles of beer, a bottle of soda-water, and the brandy-flask. His conscience remained as dormant as a tortoise in winter. Then he bolted back to the wood with his spoil.

Marian was asleep, her head fallen wearily aside against the bank. The colour was out of her cheeks and there was a black shade under her eyes, and in about a minute she would be leagues deep. He hated to rouse her but he had to. He took her hand and squeezed, and that brought her up before she got too far down. She opened her eyes sleepily, smiled at him, and was inclined to go off again.

"Wait! Drink this first. Down with it!"

He had the silver cup under her nose. It contained a fairish peg of brandy hidden in soda-water. He grasped a handful of her hair at the back, tilted her head back, and actually poured the drink down her throat. She gasped, spluttered, blew through her mouth, blinked water out of her eyes, and came alive.

"Damn! What have you done to me?"

"You'll know in a minute."

Stephen did not have any brandy. He would like to, but he needed the little pith left in his legs, and he knew that alcohol on an empty stomach would not help. That girl there could not now get out from under even if that grizzly bear was coming at the jump. Her brain was clear but her legs pithless.

"Sandwiches!" he said. "Borrowed some from Budd Hale."

That brought her fully alive. She sat up.

"Budd Hale! Is he here?"

"His car is. He don't know he loaned me this provender—not yet. On the stalk probably. Remember that shooting we heard?"

"But——"

"But me no buttons on an empty tummy. Eat hearty! You're drunk on his brandy already. We'll talk after."

"Thieves!" she said. "What'll he think?"

"He'll be glad to tell you any time."

Hunger was again alive, and she bit cleanly.

"Baby beef!" she said. "I don't mind being a thief."

They polished off the two packets. Stephen drank the beer and she finished the soda-water. And everything would have been just splendid but for the thought that was in both their minds.

"If Mr Hale is stalking——?" she began.

"—Where is your father? I don't know. I lied to you last night."

She nodded.

"I know. You were not here at the bothy yesterday."

"Gosh! When did you find out?"

"Suspected last night—knew to-day."

"You would. I lost myself good and hard, same as yourself. You and Ruary were so sure that your father was making for Carron that I took the line of least resistance for the sake of a night's peace. I might have known better. Well! Where do we go from here?"

"Wait! Let me get this clear." She looked at him consideringly and a little eagerly, the grape-spirit stirring in her head. "You did not lie when you said that Ruary came to the bothy last evening?"

"He set out to come, same time as I did, by a different road."

"Then he got here. Ruary doesn't lose himself on these hills. And if he thought dad came here, dad did. Ruary would know. And if he found my father here they might stay in the bothy all night, but you may be sure that Ruary would not allow himself or his friend to be caught in the bothy by any stalker. They would have moved out in time."

The weak spot in that chain was her assuming that her father had come to Carron, but Stephen did not point it out. He said:

"Where are they now?"

"On the hill somewhere, or back home."

"Back home for choice. That's it, by gosh! Ruary took your father straight home in the morning, and he is now probably on his way back to pick us up." He put a sudden hand on her shoulder. "That means that you are riding home in Budd Hale's car."

"Wait!" She shook her head. "How are we supposed to get here?"

"Leave me out of it. You got lost yesterday, didn't you? Make it to-day. A long walk on the moors, a wrong turn, you kept on and on, and then you heard shooting and came towards it, found yourself on the track to the bothy, and hung about hoping to get a lift back. Budd Hale might give you a lift; you ask him."

"But you?"

"I must remain a free agent. Ruary is sure to come up for me, and I must stay. If necessary, I can break into the bothy for the night amongst the bully-beef and oatcakes. Now I am going to have a closer look at that bothy to make sure. And then I'll hole up. Give me ten minutes, but don't go to sleep. After that, slip out to the car and hold down a seat till the stalkers come in."

They were on their feet together, and she caught his hand partly to steady herself but mostly on an impulse of friendliness.

"Stephen!" Her eyes were friendly, and he patted her hand before letting it go.

"Hold up! I'll take that proffered kiss when the game is played out."

He turned from her, booted the empty bottles and loose papers deep amongst the spruce-needles and long grass, and put the flask in his pocket. He chuckled.

"If Budd investigates his luncheon-basket I leave it to you to explain how you wolfed two packets of sandwiches, two bottles of beer, a bottle of soda-water, and a flask of brandy. Nothing at all!"

He left her there half-chuckling and ready to weep. He crawled up the mound, had a good look, and made a down-head run for the low ridge hiding the bothy. At that point the ridge was grown with broom and the seed-pods rustled dryly as he went up through them. He got his head up by the root of a bush and prospected the ground before him. He saw all there was to be seen.

CHAPTER XVII

THE bothy was a squat single-storied stone building with an iron roof. He was looking at the front of it from a rather acute angle, and saw the closed door and two windows at a slant. The lower sash of the window beyond the door was raised a couple of inches. With the grass growing up to the walls and door the house had a sad and forsaken look, a house used to emptiness. The ridge he was on made a seven-eighths ring round the house at a distance from it of not more than fifty yards. It looked like an artificial bank and probably was. There was an open shed at the back in which there was still a small mound of old hay. The deer could come down there in winter for shelter and food.

Stephen looked at that partly-lifted window and considered. That was a habit of his or, rather, it was a Western habit. He read sign. He put himself in the other man's place. He put himself in Ruary's place. Ruary had been in that house with or without the laird, and he had had to clear out before the stalkers. He trusted Stephen to turn up ultimately, and he would leave a sign for him. Somewhere about the door, probably inside that lifted window, perhaps a careless scrap of paper with a pebble on it scrawled with one word, say, "Home" or "Lodge" or "Croft" or just "Wait." Right! Stephen would go across and take a peep through that lifted slit of window.

He was on the very point of crawling out of his shelter when a head appeared over the bank a quarter-way round from him, just about facing the house beyond the opening in the ridge. It was lifted cautiously, and a hand was lifted above it; and the hand displayed for the empty house to see one of those quart-size, ancient, wicker-covered hunting-flasks, with a pewter drinking-cup covering the lower half.

The head was lifted higher, and the head belonged to Budd Hale.

Stephen had a fancy for a moment that Budd had seen him and was inviting him over for a drink. But no! it was the house he was inviting, and the house remained dumb. Head and arm remained still for quite a while, as if giving time for the house or someone in it to see. Then his shoulders slowly appeared and the flask went higher above his sleek bare head. Again he waited and beckoned the house with the flask. When half his body was above the bank he lifted up his voice:

"Come on out and have one on me. The game is up."

So there was someone—at least one—in the bothy. Ruary Farquhar? Ruary Farquhar would never be trapped in it alone, but with the laird he might be—if the laird had turned obstreperous. Stephen crouched under his bush and watched with all his eyes.

Budd Hale was acting foolhardily if anyone inside there had a rifle and was in a biting humour. But the house gave no sign. Another head under an old deerstalker appeared at Budd's hip, but that canny head came no higher. It belonged to Sanny Grigor, Budd's stalker. The barrel of a rifle showed by Sanny's head.

Budd went on bravoing. He removed the pewter cup from the flask and poured out a stiff drink. He stood the flask carefully on top of the bank close to his side, lifted the cup invitingly and beckoned with his free hand. Then he set the cup to his lips. The house gave him, "*Slainthe*."

A rifle cracked; the flask on top of the bank leaped in the air and fell flat; whisky splashed over Budd Hale as the cup fell from his hand; and Budd himself dropped behind the bank like a Jack-in-the-box. But he was up again like one, and he was in one tearing rage. He had the rifle in his hand, flung it to his shoulder, and fired point-blank at the bothy window. The crack of the rifle and the ping of splintered glass were on each other's heels. Next instant Budd was down under cover, and silence resumed its sway. The house looked empty as ever.

Stephen knew only one man who could have replied to Budd Hale with such complete adequateness. The salt of the humour and the clearness of the warning belonged only to one man. Ruary Farquhar! Stephen Wayne would eat his hat if Ruary Farquhar had not pulled off that biting joke.

Stephen lay under his bush, and again put on his considering cap. Darn it! things were being put up to him. He would assume that Ruary was in there with an unmanageable laird. But why had not Ruary come out and explained the laird's condition? Budd would understand, remembering that dinner at Castle Charles, and be only too glad to make allowances. For some real reason Ruary could not do that. Ruary was bent, to the extent of rifle-fire, on the pursuit of another course—to remain unidentified. Then it was up to Stephen to help.

As usual, he put himself in the other man's place. He himself was holding that bothy and he wanted to get away without being recognised. Of course! He was only waiting for the dark. In the dark he could get away even if the laird were with him, for Budd Hale and Sanny Grigor could not guard a ring of some three hundred yards against a man used to night work. And that was that.

Then there was Budd Hale and Sanny Grigor. They were no fools. They could put two and two together—especially Sanny. They would know; and they still had three hours of daylight to work in. The obvious thing to do was get in more help before dark. Sanny could hold the house with an occasional rifle-shot, and Budd could slip the car out to Castle Charles and be back with a posse in two hours—or in less. Budd, as Stephen knew, would hate not to be able to handle this thing himself, but he would hate worse to let the poachers win out. Any minute now he might decide to go for help. And that was that.

Finally there was Stephen himself. What could he do? The thing he had to try to do was obvious. He must try to prevent help coming before dark. He must no longer consider Marian Finlay's needs as paramount. He must only consider his friend Ruary Farquhar—and her father if he was there. And he had no time to waste. And that was that.

He slipped backwards through the broom, ran across to the car and lifted the bonnet. It was an American car though it had a right-hand drive, and he knew something about American cars. His job did not take him two minutes, but he was very nearly caught at it. He heard voices coming round the curve, dropped the bonnet silently, and ran crouching for the end of the belt, keeping the car between him and the people coming. He dodged round the corner, threw himself flat and peeped out again. No, he had not been seen. Budd and Sanny were just coming round the tail of the car and were not looking in his direction.

He went round to the back of the belt and climbed in

at about the place of their first entrance, slipped through the spindly trees, and dropped into the drain. The girl was not there. He looked up and down. She was not in the drain at all and his heart went hollow. But she was not far away. Lifting his head, he saw her long legs projecting from under the broom bush on top of the mound. Evidently she had been roused by the shots and had crawled across to investigate. She might have seen him at the car, and now she was watching Budd Hale. She was safe enough there if someone did not come into the wood. Or would she take her cue now and make known her presence?

But someone did come into the wood, and it was Budd Hale. Stephen saw the girl drop her head, slide back as if about to make a bid for the drain, and then flatten out. Immediately Stephen dropped on his knees and lifted a cautious eye over the edge.

Budd Hale stood on top of the mound and looked round him, a fine stalwart figure in stalking-tweeds. Perhaps he had heard the rustle of the broom, for his eyes turned that way. Anyway, he was bound to look down rather than up. The safest place to hide is above the ordinary line of vision. Budd saw the prostrate figure in the first second. Stephen knew that by the check and start. He walked quietly round the bush and stood looking down at Marian.

That girl kept her head, and she went on keeping it. She was not going to let anyone down. Now she played possum. She seemed to be sound asleep, her body nicely relaxed and her head turned over on an arm.

Budd was down on his knees now. He was leaning over her, one hand on the ground beyond, and Stephen could see his face between two spruce trunks. He was smiling, but it was not the smile on the face of the tiger.

An honest sort of male smile, something of hunger in it, and pity, and—well, possession. She was there asleep between his arms, and he took only what was a man's due. He bent down and kissed her softly at the corner of the mouth. She stirred and turned her head up, gave a little startled squeak, and tried to start up and out between his arms. Budd Hale could not help himself. She was lifted into his arms, her face to his. Stephen saw the way she drew her face forcibly below his chin and the wild-bird flutter of her body.

He had one knee over the edge of the drain when Budd Hale remembered to be a gentleman. A good job for Stephen too; in his then condition Budd could have pushed him over with one hand. Budd had released her and, holding both her hands, was apologising sincerely and soothingly.

"I am sorry. Please forgive me—Marian! I—I couldn't help myself, you looked so lovely. It's all right, my dear! Just a stolen kiss!"

She was trying faintly to free her hands. He let one hand go, and she swayed away from him, her legs sagging. Immediately he stayed her with a hand round her shoulder.

"Don't do that, Mr Hale," she said distinctly. "Please leave me alone."

There was a tree close behind, and she put a supporting hand on it. He still retained the other in both his.

"Don't make me ashamed," she said.

"Please—please!" He patted her hand. "I just couldn't help it. But not again. I—I was just taken off my feet. It is all right now, my dear."

She let him keep her hand. Budd knew where to get off, and this wild shy one was no slouch either.

"How in the world——?" He stopped. He could not help linking that bothy held against him with this girl found asleep in the wood. Perhaps Marian read his thought, for she said quickly:

"I lost myself—in my own hills too—I—I mean the hills I thought I knew."

Her voice was quick, fluttery, anxious, as it should be. She was not acting, but the intent to deceive was not entirely absent.

"My poor darling," said Budd Hale.

"I was on the hills, took the wrong turning and missed the glen. I kept going on and on, and then— oh! hours ago—I heard shooting and came this way. I saw your car and knew you were stalking, so I came into the wood and waited, hoping you could give me a lift. Could you, please?"

"Don't be silly."

"I was terribly tired and fell asleep. Was there more shooting—or did I dream it?"

"Tired! You must be about dead—and—famished——"

"Oh!" Her voice was startled. "I must confess. I was hungry and stole two whole packets of your sandwiches—and some soda-water. I couldn't look a sandwich in the eye."

She was hoping for the best about the beer and brandy. Stephen admired her. He couldn't fix on a straight lie all down the explanation.

Budd was playful and prompt.

"Little thief! You've done more stealing than you think." He drew her hand, "Come on, my dear! I'll drive you straight home."

You will, like hell! was Stephen's thought. Then he had another. When he kissed her that time had he smelled brandy. No, not with whisky down his own stalking-tweeds.

They went out over the mound together, his arm

helping her. He was protectingly gentle, and she needed help. She did not look back, but she swung her free hand out and behind and moved her fingers up and down. She was playing the game as well as she knew, and was probably enjoying it. Stephen had the wood to himself.

His curiosity got the better of him in about ten minutes. For most of these he had been hearing the metallic purr of a self-starter. He crept up to the thickest broom bush on the bank, carefully wormed himself under it, and took a peek. Marian was in the front seat, Sanny Grigor was disgustedly staring at the radiator, Budd Hale's head was lost in the bowels of the machine under the bonnet.

Half an hour later, Budd was still trying to start that car. His coat was off, and his hands and powerful fore-arms nicely greased. He just did hate to be beaten, did Budd. He was strong, he was concentrated, he was angry; he would take that blasted car to pieces and make her go. He didn't. He even removed the distributor cap, but did not look closely enough. As an amateur he did not know enough. If he knew that the car had been tampered with he might have known. Marian might know, but though she was losing a lift she said nothing. She sat, her hands folded, her face calm, and had sense enough to offer no suggestions to an irate male.

The battery began to run down when he finally gave in. His temper was gone too, but he restrained himself finely. He wiped his hands in a yellow cloth and spoke loudly and cheerfully:

"I'm afraid it's got me down, Miss Finlay. But we've got the ponies."

"But—" she hesitated. "Would they not send a car up for you?"

"They do not expect me back to-night. We were to do an early morning stalk for the big fellow."

"Don't you still run a private 'phone to all the bothies?"

That was a smart one, Marian, and the answer might be informative, for she was not yet aware that the bothy was held. The 'phone was there all right, but Budd would not admit that some real tough hombres were denying him his own bothy.

"Out of order," he said briefly. "The ignition or something in this darn thing is gone phutt. Do you think you could manage a pony, my dear?"

"Certainly—if you think that is the only way."

"Don't see any other. We'll pad the pack and fix a stirrup." He was really cheerful again, and probably anticipating a nice, pleasant, leisurely, shoulder-to-shoulder, ride home with this astonishingly nice and puzzling girl.

"Mind if I make a few arrangements with Grigor?" he said.

He led the old deer-stalker aside and spoke in a low voice so that the girl would not hear; but he had led him right under Stephen's bush for Stephen's benefit.

"No go, Sanny!" he said. "We could never get back before dark now. Do you want to stay by it?"

Sanny did not want to stay, not by a barrel full.

"Nae use me alone!" he said. "Thim dom Cabrach poachers'd blaw my brains out in the dark."

"Very well! We'll leave it for another day."

But Sanny hated all poachers professionally, and particularly hated to give them best on his own ground.

"Look you, Mr Hale!" he said, "my mind has been plowtherin' about at this. Them fellows—there's two anyway, maybe four—ha'e a stag in there, or they'd never get themselves trappit that way."

"By heck! You're right. Miss Finlay heard shooting earlier in the day—before we were up. Hope it ain't our big fellow."

"It might well be," said Sanny gloomily. "The Cabrach deevils were after him last season a week before the ruttin'. This is what I'm thinkin'. They'll want to get the stag out and that'll hinner 'em, an' if we hurried we might nab one or two o' them, an' teach the buckhers a lesson they'll no' forget for years."

"How do we hurry?"

"You'll ha'e to tak' the pony-track out to the Don road, but I could make the short-cut by the slap in the hills and save a guid hour—or mair. The Major is at the castle, an' we could fill the twa big cars and meet you on the road."

"But dash it! I want to be in this, and I must see Miss Finlay home."

"I thocht o' that, sir," said Sanny, hesitatingly diffident. "What do you say to me askin' Lady Alice to bring her two-seater to pick Miss Marian up?"

"Yes—yes—that could be done—but——" He made up his mind like the prompt man he was. "By the Lord! We'll do it. That's bright, Sanny. How long will it take?"

"I was calculatin' three hours to be back here, and it no more than half-dark. We'll save the stag anyway."

"Come on! You get going right away. I'll fix the ponies."

Twenty minutes later Marian Finlay and Budd Hale rode away from Carron Bothy. Stephen watched them go from the other side of the wood. Side by side they went up over the brown slope on the narrow grey road. She was sitting high on the padded saddle, and his head was level with hers. His long legs wagged below the pony's barrel, for he had no stirrups. At the head of the slope she lagged a pace behind, lifted a hand and moved it back and fore behind her head. That was her farewell, and Stephen suddenly felt a great loneliness. She had been one good companion, and was playing the game out to the end.

CHAPTER XVIII

HE did not give them more than five minutes to get away, for he could not afford any more. Then he went across to the car, lifted the cap of the ignition distributor and removed a scrap of cigarette packet from between the points; and hoped that there was still some juice left in the battery.

He walked round the ridge to the front of the house, paused, rubbed his tousled hair, and grinned at himself. He certainly was going to take a risk if Ruary was not in that bothy. "Thim dom Cabrach poachers" might be losing their sense of humour. But he had to find out. He faced the ridge and never paused till he stood right on top: His foot struck Budd Hale's flask, and the shattered glass rattled inside the wicker-work. He was a much better mark than that flask, with the low sun shining full on him. His midriff squirmed. The door in the shadow remained obdurately shut; the partly-lifted sash never moved; the top pane stared at him out of a starred bullet-hole eye; and there was no movement inside. The strain made him boil over, and he yelled with all his might:

"Does your dam' dog bite?"

And then the door opened and Ruary Farquhar came out, bending his long neck under the low lintel. They met half-way across the ragged grass, and were quite casual.

"Sorry I woke you up," said Stephen.

"I expected you a bittie later," said Ruary. "You were hurryin'?"

"Some. Got lost following fat-head instructions, and made a cold camp over yonder."

"See anything of Miss Marian?"

"She's just gone home with Budd Hale."

"I didna hear the car start."

"Budd couldn't start it. He and Marian went pony-back, and Sanny the short-cut. They'll be back with a posse in three hours."

"A posse? Oh, ay! Three hours! As good as a week. Come awa' in!"

"Wait, Ruary! Marian Finlay doesn't know the bothy was in the hands of a dom poacher. She thinks that you and her father were in it last night but got away before the stalkers came. She is keeping her trap shut."

"Ay, will she!" He flicked a thumb towards the bothy. "I couldn't get away. No one need know you spent the night in the heather—all your lane. Come awa'!"

In that brief dialogue they had made everything clear to each other.

The door opened directly into the larger of the two rooms the bothy contained. The biggest stag that Stephen had ever seen lay slanted across the concrete floor, a rifle propped against it. But Stephen had no time to admire that royal hart just then, for his eyes went to Alasdair MacFinlay sitting on a bench by the empty fireside.

The laird was wearing his kilt, but above the kilt he was completely naked. He was very lean, but he had a fine bony, hairy barrel of a torso. Blood was trickling from a bullet-gash above the right nipple. It was a cross-gash, not much more than a graze, and the old

hunter was letting it bleed freely.   But what Stephen
was pleased to see was that the man had recovered his
sanity.   The glisten was gone from his eyes, and was
replaced by a troubled calm.   Stephen liked the calm,
but misunderstood the trouble in it.   The laird, for a
man of his caste, had done in his madness the unforgive-
able act of poaching a stag on the lands he had sold, and
was in grievous danger of being caught and disgraced.
Stephen could not appreciate that.

The grand stag lay with its delicate nose stretched out
and touching the foot of the man that had killed it; and
its mighty antlers stood up as high as his shoulders.   A
royal hart, and there were not a dozen alive in all
Scotland.   A complete crime to destroy the splendid
beast, but such is the royal sport.

The laird's lean aristocratic head bent towards
Stephen.

"I am grieved, Mr Wayne, that you find me like this.
A most unfortunate affair."

He had seen Stephen about the Lodge, though he had
scarcely ever spoken to him.

"The affair is finishing all right, Mr MacFinlay,"
Stephen said.

"My daughter—does she know?"

"Miss Marian is safe at home, laird," Ruary said
with confidence.   "She only knows that you are on the
hill with me."

"The scandal would be too much for her," said her
father.

Stephen restrained his smile.   Marian Finlay, as
Stephen knew her, would not scandalise worth a cuss.

The laird, though calm and sane, was terribly spent,
and Stephen could see that Ruary was apprehensive of
the long road before them.   A drop of brandy might
cheer them up, and Stephen still had Budd's flask with

him. He did not tell the laird that the brandy had been lifted, and the laird was glad of a stiff neat drink. So was Ruary, who coughed in the proper manner.

"There was mair than enough to eat," he said, "but that stone beer had no muckle taste. Weel! let's be getting ready for the road."

He knew the internal economy of the hut and had found a roll of emergency bandages. He started binding up the laird's wound.

"Gi'e it a good wash night an' mornin'," he said, "and in a week it'll be mended. No one need know."

"No one but you two gentlemen," the laird said. "The wound is only a scratch."

Stephen put Ruary a question.

"Is the motor-road by Knockindu the only road to the Lodge?"

"No roads for us," growled Ruary. "The hill-track we take."

"There is the road on the south half-circle, Tomintoul way," the laird answered, "but it is ten miles longer."

"Ten miles is nothing in a car," Stephen said.

Ruary lifted his head and looked at him.

"If the sky fell you'd catch a lark," he said.

"One hour to Lettoch and one back, and Buddington Hale would find his car in the same place. I think I could drive a car at a pinch."

Ruary's fingers stilled for a moment.

"Maybe you think you can start one?"

"I'm agreeable for to try," Stephen said mildly, "If you would only get a move on."

"I'm sayin' nothin'," said Ruary, "only all day I had a friend o' mine as an ace-card up my sleeve. Get your shirt on, MacFinlay. No time to waste."

He did not use the laird's surname with familiarity. The chief of the clan was plain MacFinlay.

The laird got his shirt and jacket on, Ruary picked up the rifle. Stephen paused over the stag.

"It's the laird's stag," said Ruary, regret in his voice.

"No—no—no!" cried the laird. "It is Mr Hale's stag. We simply could not touch it. Dear me! Dear me!"

He had partaken of poached venison only last week, but there it was. Stephen had a sudden antic notion.

"We'll leave it at the roadside for him," he said, and winked at Ruary.

"If you have fun in your mind," agreed Ruary. "'Tis as well to leave no evidence we can help inside the bothy."

The laird did not protest further, and the two with some difficulty carried the carcase down through the opening in the ridge and deposited it on the side of the bank.

"Budd will be some astonished," Stephen said, "when he sees that stag where I'll put it."

"I see what's in your mind," Ruary said. "Let's see how a car is started."

Stephen slipped into the driver's seat not at all sure of himself. He had driven many cars in his time. He had even driven that make of car, but with a left-hand drive. What did trouble him was the run-down condition of the battery. He should have tried the car before arousing hope in two tired men. Holding his breath, he put his foot on the accelerator. The battery had some juice left, and the high metallic syncopation of the self-starter was quite satisfactory. But nothing else happened.

"Oh! Hell!" said Stephen, and tried again. Nothing doing.

Ruary leant over the door and pointed at the instrument-board.

"Shouldn't there be a red bit o' light thereabouts? Something about ignitin'?"

"Just trying the battery," said Stephen with dignity. "Now I'll switch on."

The eight cylinders answered to the first touch. Never was there such a fine deep growl of a purr that shrieked happily to the whip of the accelerator.

"Take your seats, gentlemen," invited Stephen.

They made the turn to Lettoch Lodge in an hour over one of the most picturesque roads in the North; an awesome road in places, twisting up on the flanks of the Grampians, hanging over sheer valleys, falling down twistingly into the bottom of rocky glens. But Stephen had no time to admire any of the marvellous views. He kept his eye on the road and drove carefully, and as fast as he dared. Ruary sat in front with him, remembered not to talk to the driver, and directed all the turns with a great right hand. They came into Glen Shinnoch at the top-end, and not until then did Stephen draw easy breath.

"Hope that pony got home," he remarked.

"Uh-uh!" said Ruary. "Take this loop easy!"

"And old Kenny too," said Stephen.

"Uh-uh!" said Ruary. "You'll put us over the bank."

"Don't mind if I do," said Stephen.

To save time and avoid being seen from across the river, Stephen swung the car round at the entrance to the Lodge road, and his passengers got out.

"Maybe I should go back with you?" suggested Ruary, his hand on the open door.

"No!" said Stephen. "You talked too much on the way down. Moreover, you and Mr MacFinlay have a story to prepare."

"That wouldna take long."

"Do you want to come?"

"I do. 'Tis a twisty road, and you lose your way that easy."

"Listen! We took all the right-hand turns coming down—every last one. I'll take all the left-hand ones going back, and the last one is the turn to the bothy. That right?"

"Right enough. A gey lonely road an'——"

"Don't be sentimental."

"Dom't! Haven't I every right?"

"You haven't. One head is enough in any noose. Moreover, I intend camping out to-night—maybe in the bothy. Go back to your bed-roll!"

Ruary grumbled some more, but he knew that Stephen had reason on his side.

He did the road back in another hour, maybe a few minutes longer, for he had to put the lights on at the end and go slower. The headlights showed the stag lying on the bank as he had left it, and Stephen recalled how he had once left a buck lying out for two hours, and what a feast the coyotes had. But, no doubt, the foxes would find the stag too if it were left out all night.

He manœuvred the bonnet of the car as near the bank as he could get it, turned off the lights and sat in the half-darkness. At once the great silence settled down over him and everything became remote and strange. It seemed not hours but days since he had been in this place before, and there was no reason in the world for hurry. No reason at all. No reason much in anything. He could sit back in this tub-seat and rest, and go to sleep—and he could go to sleep in one half-minute—and what could Budd Hale do to hurt him where he lived? Ah yes! It was not what Budd Hale could do, it was what he would refrain to do and feel magnanimous. Queer how he was up against Budd, and Budd hadn't done a mean thing to him. He wouldn't take favours from Budd.

He bestirred himself with some difficulty and got stiffly out of the car. Gosh! he was stiff, and there was a long road before him. Budd Hale would give him a lift if he asked for it. He grinned at the thought.

He rolled the carcase of the stag on to the mudguard of the front wheel. That was easy enough, but to get it where he wanted it on the bonnet was the very devil. By dragging and levering and pushing and shouldering and some cussing he did it at last. Like most men, he had a touch of nausea in handling a dead beast. The carcase was stiff, but once he got it on top the stiffness was useful. He got the hind-legs clamped at either side of the bonnet close to the windscreen, and the slender fore-legs over the front of the radiator. The varnish might suffer some, but that could not be helped. The stag's muzzle was resting on a mascot of a winged victory, and the great antlers sloped high and back. And that was all. Just a foolish joke, for it would give Budd Hale furious reason to think.

He switched on the power again and worked the car round so that it faced the incoming road.

"Take a look at that, Budd!" he said.

He switched off all the lights and got out. He stood there head down, fingering his lower lip, and considered if they had slipped up anywhere. No! Marian was safe at home now; Ruary and the laird were at home too; he had only to make his getaway and the trail would be stone-cold. Wait! There was the bothy, and Ruary had said that no evidence should be left inside. There was some blood—man's and stag's—but not traceable. But they had left in a hurry, and it was possible that some little thing might be overlooked. Then he remembered Budd Hale's brandy-flask. It was empty, and he slipped it into a front pocket in the door of the car. Yes, he would just take a good look over that room, and then borrow the last of Budd Hale's beer. Budd would not mind a little thing like that.

He was half-way across the grass to the door when a pencil of light swung across the moors beyond the spruce belt, steadied, and swung again in his direction. A car coming in on the private road. There was no time now to inspect the bothy. He knew that road over the slope could be seen above the trees, and he had to get under cover before the headlights picked him up. The spruce belt was on his line and he could get out the other side and make for the fold in the moors.

The headlights were now in a hollow, and he had ample time to get back and climb into the wood. In there the night was almost black. He bumped one spindly tree and then another. Spruce-needles sprinkled on his shoulders and one down his neck, and as he felt for it inside his open collar he walked into the open drain and fell forward. The mat of grass was thick, and he hurt nothing but his temper. He rolled over and sat up, and stayed sitting.

There was no hurry. No hurry at all! The wood had a cosiness and warmth of its own, this couch was as comfortable as a spring-mattress; and after four or five hours' rest he could face the road with renewed vigour. Also there was the natural curiosity of the human kind, and he would just love to see how Budd and his posse took the situation. He would just hang on.

He heard the purr of the cars now and saw the head-lights flash over the tree-tops. Better stick to your drain, Steve! But then he could see nothing. Without waiting for another self-protest he bumped his way back

295

to his favourite broom bush. There wasn't a chance in a hundred that they would search the wood with torches. He had only to lie still under his bush and watch a free show.

He could see the long grey bulk of Budd's car across from him under the ridge, and the dark bulk of the stag riding the bonnet. He had not long to wait. The brilliant headlights of a car came round the top of the belt; a second car followed on its tail; and the lights were already shining on the stag's frontlet.

That leading car behaved as if frightened in its iron bowels. It checked, almost stopped, and then crept forward timorously. It halted dead in front of Budd's car, but no one got out just yet. That stag facing them must have looked an extraordinary sight. Crouching there on the bonnet, its nose forward, its majestic antlers towering, its blind eyes glaring in the light, it would make most men pause. But not for long. A bark of laughter came from the leading car, and a man tumbled out. In about a split half-minute there was a press round that stag, and laughter rang. There was almost a crowd—nine or ten—the guests in force and three or four keepers, and all armed either with rifles or shot-guns.

Amidst the laughter Stephen gathered that they were already beginning to chaff Budd; and Budd was trying to bear up. Stephen watched him. His dark-red, sleek head was moving about under the light, and he was plainly puzzled. He stepped away and looked at the position of the car. He saw at once that it had been moved—pushed or under its own power? He could find out. Another man found out first; a tall man that Stephen recognised by his stub of moustache against a long horse-face as Major Chester. He was standing at the radiator and suddenly shouted:

"Damme! The bloody thing is hot."

He moved towards the car door, but Budd was there first and, pushing him forcibly away, slipped into the driving-seat.

Next instant the eight cylinders went with a muted roar; and the roar was drowned by a gale of laughter. When the gale thinned, the engine had been cut off.

"Forgot to switch on, old man?" someone said. "One does, you know."

Budd waited till the laughter died and said coolly:

"No! I don't remember switching on, but I remember switching off—twice."

He switched on the light on the dash and sat very still, looking at the metres. Then he nodded his head, and got out of the car. He said nothing. Sanny Grigor's voice was lifted up.

"Goad, Mr Hale! 'Tis the muckle stag himself."

"I see that."

"The dom robbers got the car fixed."

"And then, Sanny?"

"They was for packing the stag out on top, an' heard us comin'. They'll no' be far awa'."

"Let's try the bothy," a voice called.

"Too bright to be such silly blighters," said Major Chester, "but we'll make sure. Spread out, chaps."

In another five minutes there was no sound other than a slight rustling here and there. They had surrounded the bothy and were crawling up on it. It was time for Stephen to go too. Sanny was one wise old bird and would almost certainly suggest searching the spruce belt; and if they had electric torches—that would be just too bad.

CHAPTER XIX

STEPHEN was on the point of crawling off through the wood when a light flashed on the tree-tops and the sound of another car came to his ears. A third car was coming at a really dangerous speed—a small two-seater coupé; it rounded the corner of the wood like a pony turning after a steer. It came so fast that Stephen thought it must butt the tail of the second car, but it stopped dead with a protesting jar just in time. Whoever drove it was surely in a hurry, for the car had barely bucked to a halt before a dark head—a woman's head—was thrust through the open door, away from the wheel. It stayed there as if listening, and then a soft whistle came across the dark.

Stephen without an instant's hesitation replied with a whistle on the same note, for he realised that that soft whistle was meant for someone hidden—and he was hidden.

The headlights went out, but the roof-light inside went on for about two seconds and went off again. The woman was Lady Alice Tromes.

Stephen's heart went up to his neck. He did not give himself time to think. He simply took a chance. Or something deep-down in him knew he was not taking a chance. He tumbled down the outside of the bank and walked quickly towards her. He had reached the open door when a voice spoke from the break in the ridge surrounding the bothy:

"That you, Alice?" And then quickly, "Who is that?"

Stephen's instinct was to bound for the shelter of the wood, but, before he could move, a hand caught at the side of his jacket and a tense whisper said:

"Get in, damn you!" The hand jerked, and Stephen sat on the edge of the seat. He pivoted his legs in, and found a cool bare hand clamped on his wrist.

"Got you captive, Samson! Here comes the Philistine."

"The call is with you, Delilah—never," said Stephen.

Budd Hale, striding fast, was at the open door. He could not see very well into the half-darkness inside the car. He thrust head and arm in, and Stephen, thinking he was going to be ignominiously dragged out, clenched his right hand hard. But Budd's hand fumbled somewhere behind his head and the roof-light went on.

"Well! if it ain't little Stevie Wayne!" he said derisively.

Before Stephen might reply, and he was not going to, Lady Alice Tromes spoke casually.

"Stephen Wayne and I thought we'd like to see the fun, Buddy. You know how he hangs about that very nice cage with its lovely singing-bird."

"You hurried?"

"Touching sixty all the way. Didn't want to miss anything. Did you get them?"

"No-o," said Budd slowly. "But I dam' near did."

He looked down at Stephen, stepped back for a better perspective, and kept on looking. Budd could read sign too, and Stephen showed him a few. His tousled hair was seeded with heather and broom and spruce, his old suit crumpled, his face unshaven and not too clean; and his brogues, which he could not now pull back out of sight, were grey and scuffled.

"All the way up for a bit of fun, Steve?"

"And a nice escort too, Buddy," said the lady.

Budd Hale frowned. He was thinking of Marian Finlay. It suddenly dawned on him that when he had found her asleep Stephen Wayne might not be as far away as Lettoch Lodge—perhaps no further away than the bothy. Had that girl, so shy and proper, been making use of him? He bent down to Stephen:

"We meet everywhere, Stevie. I just wonder what game you think you are playing?"

Stephen brought his hand up to his breast and looked down at it. It was the unmistakable gesture of an old poker-player playing a hand close to his chest. Budd recognised it.

"With the roof off!" he said, and leant across to the lady. "You've been playing games all your life, Alicia, but no woman can play poker. Get out of this while the going is good."

"You don't know any game I play, you poor fool," she said coldly. "Take your hand off my car!"

The accelerator made the engine roar, and Budd, banging the door, had to jump for it. She went as near getting him as tuppence. The handy little car whirled, grating the back bumper of the big car in front, and went off on the jump; it took the wood corner on two wheels, and roared up over the brae. Then Lady Alice changed gears and came to a comfortable pace.

"You can be dumb as a fish when you like, Stephen Wayne," she said.

"Your game as it lay, Lady Alice."

"Sorry I showed temper. I have one."

"So has a good steel," said Stephen quietly.

She chuckled, but there was a touch of unbelief in the chuckle.

"We don't mean that, do we?"

"I do. But sometimes I don't know what I do mean in your company."

"Yes, you little tough, we are bad company for each other."

"You had better company on the road up. Gosh! I haven't the manners of a pup."

"Not fair to the pup—that right?"

"On the nose. Here I am out of a snarl and riding home with a lovely lady—and not a word of thanks."

"This is my fun. Shut up!"

"Wait! You didn't know I was up here?"

"A good guess."

"Choked it out of poor Marian Finlay?"

"So you even know that I relieved Budd of his precious burden. A nice girl, Stephen—and just developing. I warn you that she'll rule her house and her man."

"Same as the rest of you."

"I only play games. She didn't give you away, but I talked to her. She was lost on the way to Carron Bothy; and there were poachers in the bothy, as I knew. She had often been at Carron Bothy, but she was lost this time. Queer! Where was the little thug, Wayne, who was never far away? I did not ask her directly, for the young should not be invited to lie."

"She is not so much younger than Lady Alice Tromes."

"No, but how much older is Alice Tromes? I guessed that you were trapped and that she had somehow drawn Budd off to give you a chance. So I dropped her on the main road above the Lodge, turned tail, and scooted back to capture you myself."

"You don't read the sign so well," said Stephen, "but you got there."

"You men flatter yourselves," she said. "We two weak women took a hand in your silly game and made it come our way. Hope the others escaped? I'm only a two-seater."

"There are no others."

"Of course not, though you run in threes. I mean that. You would not be in this car if the others were still about the bothy. Here is the main road."

"Take the right-hand turn round by Glen Shinnoch," half-suggested Stephen.

"I don't know that road."

"All right-hand turns, and Budd won't run us down; and I'll have your bad company ten miles longer."

Without another word she swung into the right-hand road and drove on at a sedate speed—not more than thirty. She laughed softly and ruefully.

"You have a technique all your own, Stephen, and one would never guess it. I am inclined to back you against Buddy, with Marian Finlay for prize. Perhaps you've won already."

Stephen stirred irritably.

"Leave Marian Finlay out of it," he said almost angrily. "Dammit, woman! in your company there is no other woman in the world. I don't know who you are, Lilith or Eve, Delilah or a plain earl's daughter, but I am playing no games—not even with you. You are the player, and I am sorry if the cards are staked against you."

"Gawd help all poor women!" prayed Alice Tromes.

Stephen slumped gloomily down in his seat, and they drove on silently. The quiet purr of the car and the easy motion began to get him, and he found himself stifling a yawn. She glanced aside at him.

"One authentic hobo this time," she said. "How long have you been on your feet?"

"For ever, it looks like."

"Poor boy! Never mind your manners. I don't want to have my nose bitten off a second time. All right-hand turns? Sleep if you want to."

"I don't want to sleep."

"Shut up then!"

She did not want to go on talking, and Stephen liked that about her. She was disturbing, and she was restful too. He found himself drifting and sagging. His shoulder touched hers, and came away, and touched hers again, and her shoulder yielded and then firmed against his. He was lazily contrasting Marian Finlay's shoulder that had rested against his last night. That was a different shoulder, a friendly shoulder. This was an electric shoulder and sent sleepy tingles through him. And a friendly shoulder too. There was something tickling his brow, and he moved his head and found a support. . . . There was a deer running in the heather and he was ploughing along behind it. . . . The heather flowed in waves to the horizon and he was lost in the middle of it, and he sank down and the waves flowed over him for evermore. . . . And the heather had a faint, dark, pleasant perfume that made him sadder than he ever had been in all his life, for there was something that he had lost and could not remember what it was. . . .

He did not wake till the car stopped, and then he waked slowly. His head was resting on Alice Trome's shoulder. He let it rest there, and got again that faint dark perfume that was never heather. Her right hand came across to his tousled hair and tugged sharply.

"You are not asleep now. I heard you wake. We are here."

Stephen sat up. The black bulge of the Lodge mound was above them, and the river sang over there. They were on the level near the flying-bridge. He stretched himself stiffly, and put a hand on her shoulder, and her shoulder that had not drawn away from his head drew away from his hand.

"I can say nothing, kind lady," he began, keeping his voice in control.

"Get out!" She spoke almost harshly. "Get up there and see that your white virgin is safe for the night."

He got out without a word, and she reached him her hand but held it firmly from his lips.

"Good-bye! I shall not see you again," she said. "I am going south next week."

"You are going away?" He held her hand firmly.

"I am. Try and remember me not unkindly."

"There's your hand for you." He put it inside the car. "I will remember you, but not kindly; and every time I remember you I will curse the dam', blasted, foolish, no-good, hellish life you have to lead. Go away, woman!"

"I will not curse life," she said. "I will curse Stephen Wayne."

She banged the door herself, and the car swung and went away angrily roaring.

"Damn you, and the things we can do to each other!" he said savagely.

He went draggingly up the slope. The front of the house was dark, but there was a light behind the blind of the kitchen window. He had no desire to go in to talk with Maggie Donald, though hunger was gnawing at him. He was not so much weary as stiff and chilled; and he felt a strange depression on him. But that was natural enough. He had been under strain for a long time, and after strain comes a relaxed greyness. What he needed was a stiff drink and a long sleep.

He went up to the garret and lit his small lamp. The place looked dim and homely, and the truckle-bed invited him to come along and forget this queer sense of loss or want that was troubling him. He poured himself four fingers of whisky, found a packet of British cigarettes, sat on the bed, took a deep gulp, and waited to feel the first stir of stimulation, that first small lift of the mind that is proud to observe dispassionately the futility of most things. Gosh! he was hungry, but it was a physical hunger and nothing spiritual about it. But he could forget hunger in sleep. He would just put on his old slippers and quietly run his trap-line across, and come back to bed. There might be no need for an alarm-line to-night, but after yesterday—was it only yesterday?—he would watch every break. The girl would be leagues deep in sleep by now, and he would not wake her. He tossed off the last of his whisky, bent to his shoe-laces, and stopped himself in time from topping on his head. Not drunk, just pithless!

A soft insistent tapping came up from the door of the harness-room.

"My conscience is clear," he said, fumbling his way to the door. "Who the——?"

"I saw your light. Come on down!" That was Marian Finlay.

"Anything wrong?" he asked quickly.

"Everything fine. Come and eat."

"Still in the game, ole girl. Fine!" His tongue was inclined to slur on him.

He went down to her, his hand helping along the wall. She took his arm and led him across the yard; and he went like a lamb, his feet not too certain. Alcohol on an empty stomach is one bad actor.

"Poor boy! You must have run all the way."

He had been called "poor boy" several times lately. Queer how slips of girls will mother pretty hard-boiled fellows on occasions.

"You've had a drink." She shook his arm.

"One. Remember how that brandy made you cock-eyed?"

She chuckled at that.

"I've a lot to tell you. Father is home. He and Ruary were home before me. And he is all right."

"Most effort is wasted anyhow," Stephen said.

He was beginning to cheer up, whether it was the whisky or the girl. She was a fine friendly girl, and he felt the friendliness flow from her. A natural, nice sort of girl, with no more wiles than she needed in her trade.

The kitchen was bright and cheerful and secure after the austere and eternal hills, and Marian no longer looked like a hoyden on the tramp. She did not even look tired. She had had a hot bath and was in dressing-gown and slippers; and her colour was fresh and delicate and warm, and her hair was a soft nimbus about her head. She could not have tramped the hills for twenty hours!

One end of the table was laid, and there was cold grouse and scones, and a great pot of hot coffee his style.

"I sent Maggie to bed," she told him. "She did not sleep at all last night."

"In what silken boudoir slept thou?"

"Very nearly in——" She stopped in time and blushed. "There was a great snuffling bear——"

"Dam' fool beast!" said Stephen.

He ate most of that grouse. She had a pick off a wing to keep him company. And thereafter they drank coffee and smoked cigarettes and talked. They were like a young couple home from a night-hunt and raiding the pantry. She did most of the talking, Stephen directing it to try and learn how much she suspected.

Her father had come home with Ruary just about sunset, and long before she herself had got home. She had not seen Ruary, and she had naturally refrained from questioning her father, who was very tired and in bed. She would get it all from Ruary in the morning.

("Like hell you will!" said Stephen to himself.) Maggie Donald knew nothing except that they were on the hill somewhere. But she still thought that they had been as far as Carron and got away in good time. She looked at Stephen.

"There were poachers in the bothy, Stephen. I heard the shooting, and the cars went back loaded."

"Of course there were poachers," he said boldly. "I stuck around till I got a look at them to make sure. Two dom savage-lookin' fellows out of the hills. They made off in good time, shortly after you left. They had a scout on the outside too. I was sorry to see you go pony-back. Pity about the car."

This was ticklish ground, for he was not sure if she had been watching under the broom while he was tampering with the car. She said quite innocently:

"It was queer about the car. Perhaps that outside scout got at it."

You could never tell. She might mean exactly what she said, or she might be just pinking at him. She could outplay him, and he left the subject.

"Had a nice ride down?" he enquired.

"Your Budd Hale was—he couldn't be nicer. He only brought me part of the way. Lady Alice Tromes drove me home. Stephen, that woman suspects that you were up there."

"How could she?"

"She kept working the talk round, and wondering how one got lost, and why was I alone, and so on."

"No! She only suspected you of running down Budd, and that is exactly what you did. She's jealous, and no wonder."

She yawned in his face, not quite a sincere yawn.

"All right!" he said. "The house adjourns. You go to bed and I'll run up my trap-line."

"Dad will sleep sound to-night."

"We'll take no risks. But for my running-out on you yesterday all this would not have happened. Yes, old girl, take any blame you like, but I was dead in the wrong. Off we go."

She was at her open window when he ran the line up, and her fingers patted his as she took the line.

"None of that!" he warned her. "I'm one real grizzly."

She was busy at the table leg, and he called a soft good-night.

"Wait! Just a second, Stephen." Her face came close to his. "I am not thanking you, but you saved——"

"Go say your prayers!"

"Whisper, Stephen!" She put her two cool hands, one on each side of his face, and kissed him honestly on the mouth. Then she shoved him off so firmly that he sat down hard on the gravel. And the window shut full with a clack, and the blind shrilled down.

He sat on the gravel and looked up at the blinded window.

"That's how a bad habit begins," he said, and went to bed.

CHAPTER XX

THE bracken was nicely dried, and Ruary and Stephen were engaged in building a storage stack amongst the trees back of the lawn.

"Not much of a harvest crop?" Stephen remarked.

"There's the hay as well, but you're right," Ruary agreed. "The laird is no' makin' muckle use of his sixty acres o' sound land. I am often thinkin' that this place run kind of co-operative with your croft and out-run would be what is called an economic holding."

"Why not speak to the laird?"

"I would if he was—sound in the mind."

"He is completely sound this last week, and talks to me now like a fellow-biped. That crisis at Carron pulled him out on the right side."

"Whatever about his mind, he looks gey sick in body," said Ruary gloomily. "Do you know if he's dressin' that bit wound?"

"You'd better ask him. He's coming across."

The laird came across the lawn and in amongst the trees towards them. He certainly looked frailer than when Stephen had first seen him on Lettoch side. Then he was emaciated, but now one felt that there was no flesh at all under the skin drawn tightly over the bones of cheek and jaw. But that surface glisten was no longer on his eyes; there was only calmness and weariness—weariness of it all.

He greeted the two workers pleasantly, and sat on a high old log resting against a beech trunk. He leant shoulders and head on the smooth bark, sighed wearily, and shut his eyes for a moment. Ruary looked at Stephen, shook his head, and leaning forward on the handle of his fork spoke to the weary man:

"That bit wound, MacFinlay? Is it troublin' you?"

"It does not matter." He moved his hand back and fore. "There is something else that troubles me more, and I want you to see it as I do. I came across to talk to you, Ruary."

Stephen started to move away amongst the trees, but the laird called to him in a strong voice—his voice had never weakened.

"Don't go, Mr Wayne. I want you to hear this."

Stephen came a little nearer and set his back to a tree, the rake grip under his midriff. Ruary leant forward towards the laird, and the laird looked up at him.

"You do not own Balmerion, Ruary? You have no tenant rights?"

"Caretaker meantime, laird."

"I know." He smiled. "In fact, I gather that Mr Wayne is the owner. You and he have been helping Marian to look after me. I can understand that in you, old clansman, but—" He smiled again and moved a hand. "I suppose young people will have reasons of their own—and whisper to each other at night. You were a good team, you two—adequate and debonair—recalling our youth, Ruary, only you do not grow old. But let that be. You do not want to return to Glasgow?"

"I can thole it if I have to," said Ruary quietly. "Kirsty would not stand it that well."

"No, Kirsty would not. Kirsty wants to milk her coo, and feed her hens—and wonder why they're no' laying so well. And her daughter will marry. My daughter will marry too, Ruary, but the name is lost.

Castle Charles and Glen Shinnoch, Corryhow and Carron Beat will not know MacFinlay any more. We men who were chiefs and fathers failed, Ruary; failed ourselves and failed our clan, and the glens are empty. It is a terrible thing to be done and old, and know that I am one of a long line that failed, that I helped the failure, that even my son Iain, if he had lived, could not restore what had been broken. Let it be so. The MacFinlay is finished."

"The MacFinlay never turned tail," said Ruary. "Mind that, MacFinlay!"

"Small good it did us or you to hold by our *Carn na cuimhne*—our cairn of remembrance. But let that be too. It is my daughter Marian I want to talk to you about, Ruary. When the Trustees sold the estate all that came to me was this lodge and the few acres about it, and some securities yielding an income of three hundred pounds. That is secure and unencumbered, and it is all that Marian will have—when I am gone."

Stephen saw Ruary's mouth twitch below his beard. If he had sixty good acres and a strong house, to say nothing of an annual income of three hundred, he would not swop them for a select corner of paradise.

"I want Lettoch Lodge secured and guarded for her," MacFinlay went on. "That is why I am telling you this, Ruary. Maggie Donald is old and her brother needs her. You are the only man I can turn to, the only man I would turn to, my friend. Will you and Kirsty come to the Lodge to live—Mr Wayne will not object, I am sure?"

"I will not object, Mr MacFinlay," Stephen said quietly.

Ruary was about to speak, but the laird stopped him.

"Wait, Ruary! Marian may marry and go away,

but I want her to have this place in the glen that was ours; I want her to have this place to come back to, to know that it is always here as a secure resting-place—as a refuge if she needs one. I know her, and it is what she would want herself, and I want you to look after it for her. I will secure you with a lease of the land and reserved quarters. Will you, old friend?"

"Before I answer you, MacFinlay," said Ruary firmly, "I would remind you that I am a failure too. If I was not what I was I might still be in Glen Shinnoch under my own roof-tree."

"If you were not what you were, if you had the servile mind, if you were not the last of the clansmen—" MacFinlay rose to his feet. "It is because you are what you are that I ask you. I have not been very clear, Ruary. It is not this place of Lettoch I want you to look after. As my brother clansman I want you to be guardian of my daughter Marian."

Their hands met and held. Ruary spoke quietly:

"I will do by Marian Finlay what I would do by my own daughter."

"I know, Ruary. I knew so well, that my solicitor is coming up this evening with all the documents to sign. We will sign them and make a finish."

"But, laird, what's the hurry? You are not an old man yet?"

"There is one last thing I have to tell you, Ruary." MacFinlay smiled again, and put his hand up to his right breast. "I am dying."

Ruary straightened up and drove his fork prongs deep into the ground.

"Not your wound, MacFinlay? You minded it?"

"I minded it. I am not committing suicide, old friend. I did not think of that road when in madness I was terribly aware of my own state. I dressed the wound—only a scratch—night and morning, but I cannot renew my blood. I feel it here in the armpit, and I feel the clouds gathering, gathering. I am saner now than ever I was, but to-morrow I shall be mad for the last time."

He went away then, pacing smoothly across the lawn, his shoulders back and his head upright. On the doorstep he faced round and looked up at his own serene high hills, saying a farewell for the last time. Then he went into his house, and never came out again on his own two feet.

"Should we get the doctor?" Stephen enquired.

"Maybe we should, and maybe we'll ha'e to." He considered deeply. "When a man thinks he's dyin' he might get a bit time to think maybe he won't, and a doctor canna help much one way or another. Miss Marian will let us know when the doctor is needed, but we need be sayin' nothing to her."

It was next afternoon that Marian came running to find Stephen in the garden, distress in her eyes.

"My father!" she cried. "He has taken ill. He is wandering again. Oh, Stephen! He is really ill——"

"All right, Marian! I'll have the doctor here in twenty minutes."

She ran back to the house, and Stephen ran to the stable for his rope, damning the pony. It hadn't been ridden for a week and would jolt him for five minutes when he was in no humour for jolting. But as he came from the stable on the jump he heard the now familiar purr of Budd Hale's big car coming up the slope. Budd had been over four times in the last week, and Marian and he were on at least friendly terms. They had gone for a couple of drives together and come back in good spirits and with shared laughter. The girl was learning her woman's business. She knew how to take Budd now, and Budd did not know at all how to take her; and that was good for his immortal soul.

Stephen ran across the yard calling to him, and he stopped the car abruptly and wiped the quick frown off his face. "Gosh! he don't like a hair on my carcase," was Stephen's thought. He was wrong. Budd did not dislike him, but did not understand his position in the house or with the girl. He was afraid of Stephen, not physically afraid, but just afraid in the bottom of his heart.

"Well, Steve?"

"Look here, Budd! MacFinlay is very ill. I have to get the doctor, and that dam' pony——"

"MacFinlay ill! The doctor? Sure! Leave it to me, son."

The car swept round on the gravel and swooped down the slope. Budd was prompt as ever and would love to do something for Marian, something that would kind of get him into the clique that he felt he was being kept out of.

Alasdair MacFinlay took three days to die, and he died at sunset on the third day.

Stephen and Ruary did not get much rest in these three days. The sick man was out of his head all the time, and often had to be kept in bed by force. The district nurse could simply not handle him, and the doctor was puzzled. "Septicaemia at its worst," he said. "But that sore! How did he get it?"

Marian couldn't tell him.

"That's not an ulcer," he said again. "That is a gash. Did he have a fall?"

"He might, surely," Ruary said, "and say nothing about."

The doctor had to accept that. Marian did. Her father might easily have gashed himself on a rock.

The last afternoon the dying man was at his worst, and Ruary and Stephen could not leave the room for an instant. But in the last hour he quieted down and fell into a deep coma-like sleep. Marian whispered hopefully, "The crisis may be over." It nearly was.

He awaked quietly, and the flame of delirium was quenched in his eyes. He looked at Marian and smiled, and his hand stirred on the coverlet. She took and caressed it, the light of hope in her eyes. He turned his head to Ruary at the other side and whispered:

"Lift me up, brother."

Almost of his own volition he sat up. It had been a warm clear day, and the window was open. The sun going down lit all the hills across the river into a golden orange, and the black pines glistened slumbrously on the slopes.

"My own hills," he whispered.

He looked across the smooth lawn whereon the house cast a deep shadow to where the beeches were full of light in contrast to the paler green of the ashes, and a great light lit in his own eyes. His voice was strong.

"There's Iain coming up the hill. Give him a hail! Oh, Iain lad! I'll be with you."

The light slowly went out in his eyes, but his face remained content. Ruary let his head drift gently to the pillow. He drew three long breaths.

"He is with him," Ruary said deeply.

Marian fell on her knees, her face pressed against the relaxed hand that she still held. Stephen did not even put a quiet hand on her shoulder. She wanted to be alone with her dead.

MacFinlay, the last of Castle Charles, was dead, and nothing better could have happened him.

CHAPTER XXI

THE funeral was three days past. It had been the biggest funeral in living memory. All Knockindu and all the county people and the Hales of Castle Charles were there to see the last laird to his last lairdship. And now life was beginning to resume its everyday course.

Ruary and Kirsty were being established in the Lodge, but not yet staying overnight. Stephen was back at the croft with Kenny and Sheevaun, who in a disgruntled fashion were preparing to go back to town. Maggie Donald, knowing that she must go, was loath to go, and stayed on with the excuse that she must show Kirsty the run of the house.

It was afternoon, and Stephen was sitting on the old log among the trees beyond the lawn, and he did not know what he should do. He had nothing to do now. He was empty of all impulse to do anything, but he knew that would not last. And he was troubled in his mind, for there was an object in life at the back of his mind and he was not in the least sure whether it was the object he wanted. All he wanted was an incentive to set him moving one way or another.

Tall Kirsty Power came across the lawn, milk-can in hand, taking a short-cut down the slope. She saw Stephen and came across to him; and he got to his feet and reached for the can.

"I'll go for the milk, auntie, and boost Sheevaun to the milkin'."

"No, boy. I want to talk to Sheevaun. She's too hard on poor Kenny."

"Gosh! Can't we do anything about it, Kirsty?"

"Can you do anything about yourself, boy?" She looked at him out of her brilliant eyes. "You are troubled."

"You tell me, auntie?"

"Are you going back to your own country?"

"I sure am, come hell or high water."

"Hush! Your heart is touched, but it is a strange thing that I do not know how or where. You like Marian Finlay?"

"And then some."

"Is some enough? Is that your trouble? Listen, boy! To-day or to-morrow that girl will be wanting sympathy, and go looking for it. The first man that gives her that will be taken straight into her heart. That is all I can help."

She turned and went away down amongst the trees, and Stephen considered what she had told him. Marian Finlay had been prostrated with grief. He had never imagined that her grief could be so intense, but he should have. She had taken care of her father for so long, and so mothered him, that she could not easily get over this awful emptiness in her life and her heart. But she would get over it. Yes, he could follow Kirsty's intuition with reason. The girl was young and full of life, and she had not seen much of life. Life and eagerness would stir in her soon, and sympathy and understanding would just get her where she lived. Well! He could give her that sympathy, couldn't he? He supposed he could. And so could . . .

A stick crackled in the wood below him and he looked that way.

"Think of the devil!" he said aloud.

Budd Hale was coming up through the trees but had not yet noticed Stephen sitting still on the log. Budd had not seen Marian Finlay for a week—she had refused to see anyone—and was in a perplexed and angry temper. He felt that there was a conspiracy against him, and wondered whom to blame besides Stephen Wayne. He just hated to be played with, especially when he wanted to play no more.

Almost at the same time that Stephen saw Budd without being seen, his side-vision caught another movement amongst the trees, and he looked that way. Kenny Alpin was coming up the slope, a brace of grouse hanging wings-wide from one hand. Kenny had been keeping the house in game for the past week, and if the game was not off the croft-moor it was because the game had gone over the boundary and Kenny was not so particular about boundary-lines.

Kenny saw Stephen sitting on the log and came straight across, but he did not see Budd. Budd caught the movement and swung that way. He had not seen Kenny before. All he saw now was a small tough-looking guy carrying a brace of grouse, and he jumped to the conclusion that the grouse had been poached off the Castle Charles moors. Here at last was the chance of a show-down, and he was in the humour for one. He strode straight across at Kenny, who brought up dead and faced him. Budd did not halt until he was towering right over the small man.

"Got you!" he said. "The third of the poaching squad. Think up a good excuse while you have time."

Kenny looked down at the grouse in his hand and then looked up at Budd. His fierce black eyes glinted in his fierce dark face.

"A dam' queer thing!" he said. "Accused in the wrong for the first time in my life."

"Get out of it, will you? You fellows think you can do what you blasted well like with the present owners of Castle Charles. This is one time you can't. I've got you where I want you."

He lifted a hand and Kenny started back.

"Mister Long-Fellow," he said quickly, "don't you put a hand on me. Some of me is fragile."

"I wouldn't mind smashing some of it."

"Suppose we remember where we are?" suggested Kenny with unusual mildness.

Budd pulled himself together. He did remember where he was. He took a good look at Kenny.

"You're too small to swipe," he said, "but I've got you taped for keeps. Drop those birds and get out!"

Kenny again looked down at the grouse. He too was minding where he was and kept a fine hold on himself, but the eyes he turned up at Budd had a fire behind them. His voice was reasonable and inviting.

"You are Hale of Castle Charles. I am Kenneth Alpin of the Croft o' Balmerion. Come you up there this evening and see where you've got me. Leave it at that."

"For the present. Drop those grouse!"

"Don't be a dam' fool!" said Kenny warmly. "You don't own everything you see."

Kenny turned and took a stride in Stephen's direction. Only one stride, for before he could take a second his shoulder was gripped and he whirled or was whirled round. There and then he dropped the grouse. But the fragile thing in Kenny had broken, and the only fragile thing in him was his temper.

Stephen started to his feet, but before he could get there, Kenny had grappled the big man like a compact bull-dog tangling on a mastiff. It was the speediest progress to intimate contact between two strangers that Stephen had ever seen.

The two fell as if their feet had been snatched from under them. Who did the felling Stephen did not know, for they fell side by side and rolled. Budd was on top at the end of the roll, but they rolled again and there was Kenny. That roll took them over the lip of the slope and they went on rolling. Stephen recalled how Kenny and himself had rolled down the birch brae that first day, and now he went after them in bounds, hoping to save a neck—Kenny's neck.

Kenny was a small man, even if he was a packet of giant powder and with some galvanic force in him not related to muscle. But Budd was big, and big in the right places, a trained athlete and a good boxer. That is, he used to be a trained athlete and still looked perfectly fit. He was probably forty pounds the heavier of the two, and what chance had Kenny in a close grapple?

So Stephen hurried, and grew angry as he hurried. By the Lord! Kenny and he would now proceed to make this big fellow see reason, and use any method necessary, even to the removal of some of his gadgets.

Just as well that he hurried. But not for Kenny Alpin's sake. They had brought up against a tree halfway down the slope, and Budd Hale's legs were kicking, like the legs of a rabbit snared by the neck. Budd was on his back. Kenny had a thigh across his midriff, a knee holding down an arm, a hand clamping a hand, and the other hand throttling a neck with a complete and hearty intent towards strangulation. The packet of giant powder had exploded. The helpless flapping of Budd's long legs was ludicrous.

Stephen made sure in about five seconds that Budd would be minus a windpipe in another five. He put an arm over Kenny's shoulder and round his neck, and

tugged. The moment he felt Stephen's arm Kenny let go all holds and allowed himself to be lifted to his feet. He turned his head over Stephen's arm and grinned at him.

"You dam' Pict!" said Stephen. "Couldn't you choose a man your own size?"

"Thanks, Steve! Sorry I let go of myself. Don't tell Sheevaun. Will I give him one root in the slats?"

Stephen swung him away and up the slope.

"Take the grouse round to Maggie." He bent to Kenny's ear. "Let me talk to Budd Hale for a minute."

"You big brute! What has he done to you?"

He slipped from Stephen's hold and ran lightly up the slope.

Budd had made no attempt to rise and resume. He was sitting up against the tree, fully employed in getting oxygen back into his blood; twisting his head up and back, and pulling at his crumpled collar. He had very nearly panicked. And no wonder! He had felt helpless lying there under that dynamic force that only a few men possess; and his windpipe was not cast-iron. That was panic dying out of his eyes and giving way to anger. Stephen sat on his heels in front of him and waited.

"That was a Pict, Budd," he said. "You know? The buckeroos that belted the black and blond legions."

"Blast him and you! If I got him at arm's length——"

"You couldn't keep him there. I've tried. Why don't you thank me?"

"Go to——!"

"Ssh! Don't be angry. You got stung, and I came along and saved your windpipe. You were one dam' fool to begin with, for them there grouse were not poached. They came off the Croft o' Balmerion, and I own it."

"You think you own the whole dam' place."

"All right! I'm a dam' fool too."

Budd Hale did not rise to his feet and take himself off. He was not hurt at all, and his wind was back, but he just sat there and contemplated Stephen. Things were still rankling in him, and now was as good a time as any to find out how things lay.

"Look here, Steve Wayne!" he blurted out. "Isn't it about time you and I had a show-down?"

"If I had anything to show, Budd."

"You've hidden things a-plenty. All you people seem to be making use of me."

"What people?"

He gestured a hand widely.

"I'm not baulking at anyone. Three of you seem to be using this place as a hideout for poaching, and you do not seem to be unwelcome."

"You've got it all wrong, Budd——"

"Have I? Suppose you take a look at my hand, and tell me where it's busted? Listen, Stevie! You and that long fellow finished my stag in Glen Shinnoch, and that's not guessing. Some nights later, three of you were alarmed netting the river, but you got a fish it seems. That same night you were seen in the vicinity of this lodge—and you were not alone. Next day I had salmon and venison for lunch right here. Might I not deduce that the venison was my own—right under my nose, and no one turned a hair?"

"It looks mighty bad as you put it——"

"I am not finished yet, son. You lacked frankness. You brought me a letter one evening at Castle Charles and you were not one bit frank; and I noticed that wherever Miss Finlay was you were not far away, and she knew it. She was at Carron Bothy, whether lost or not, and you were there too; and you were

there all the time, whatever Alice Tromes said—
blast her!"

"Woh, Budd! Leave other ladies out of this."

"I'll suit myself—blast you too! Wait! I was
wrong. You were not at the bothy all the time. You
were mostly outside, and you fixed my car. You see, I
happened to notice the petrol gauge and speedometer,
and the car had done enough mileage to take your
friends out and get itself back, after—shall we say—
your accomplice had drawn me off. Who was in the
bothy, Steve?"

"No use telling you."

"You don't need to. See! That was left behind, and
there were traces of stag's blood on it."

He had put a hand in his pocket and drawn forth a
short, black-shafted, black-sheathed knife.

"That's a stocking-dirk," he said, "what is called a
sgian dubh. It is worn with the kilt, and you can blood
a stag with it."

"Plenty of these things knocking about in Scotland."

"Take a look at it!"

He handed it across. The black of it was chased with
silver, and there was a yellow stone—a cairngorm—set
in silver at the hilt-end. Stephen drew the short
strong-pointed blade from its sheath. It was serrated
on one side and razor-sharp on the other—a deadly
little weapon.

"Take a look at the crest and motto!" invited Budd.

The polished blade was engraved with a spray of bell-
like flowers above a phrase in Gaelic.

"You got to tell me, Budd," Stephen said.

"Maybe you don't know! Look up the Scottish
Clans in Johnston's book some time. I did. That
flower is the foxglove, and the Gaelic, *Carn na Cuimhne*,
means 'Cairn of Remembrance.' They are the badge

and war-cry of the MacFinlay. I don't need to ask who was in the bothy and who killed the big hart."

"Just as well," said Stephen, putting the sgian in his own pocket.

"Right! Hang it up with the kilt and sporran that will not be worn again." Budd laughed shortly. "Or shall I turn you up and hand it across myself as the missing heirloom?"

"That would be the real show-down. Are you finished?"

"Just about. I was only working up to my leading question. What game do you think you are playing, and what game do you all think you are playing with me? It's up to you, Steve!"

Stephen rubbed a hand in his tousled hair. He was puzzled what to say or not say. This was the show-down, and he wanted to be honest with Budd Hale and with himself.

"I don't blame you, Budd," he said. "You've dug up a whale of an indictment, but I am pleading 'Not guilty' to the main charge. I am playing no game——"

"Aren't you, by heck?"

"Maybe I am at that. Maybe there's a big game at the back of my mind, and the stake still on the board."

"And I'm in on it."

A small flame of anger spiralled up in Stephen.

"That stake is not for coyotes," he said.

"You'll say that in plain language!" Budd drew his knees in.

Stephen controlled his voice carefully.

"An old-fashioned cuss, ain't I? But you should be careful how you play your old game with Marian Finlay while another woman wears your ring."

Budd Hale almost started to his feet, but he controlled himself in time. His voice was dangerous and slow.

"Look here, Wayne! If you accuse me of playing loose with Marian Finlay I'll knock your teeth down your throat."

"Take it easy a little more, Budd," Stephen said patiently. "I'm still asking you. Lady Alice Tromes wears your ring?"

"She does, and much good it will do her." He was only sore now. "I made two mistakes in my time, and I am not going to make a third for even an earl's daughter. That fine lady is playing her own dam' game with me, and with that dude Chester, and with tough little Steve Wayne too. You can have her. I'm finished with the dam' bitch."

"We have struck one bad patch to-day, Buddy," said Stephen quietly.

He lifted to his feet, and Budd looked up at him.

"On your feet, coyote!" Stephen said.

But Budd only laughed at him.

"No, little Stevie! I can take you any time, and you'll not get out of this with a licking."

"Let me induce you," Stephen said, and struck him a full, open-handed blow across the laughter, a blow hard enough to make him blink and dazzle.

He came to his feet quick enough then, blood in his eye and real blood on his mouth.

"I'll take it out of your hide, you blasted little runt!" he cried. "I'll take you right apart."

He didn't, and Stephen was sure that he could. But after the first half-minute Stephen knew that Budd couldn't, not ever, not any more. Stephen had lived hard in open air for ten years; Budd had lived under cover, and his muscle, big as it was, had gone brittle. Stephen should have known. He had seen the thing happen before. A gymnasium boxer will not make the grade in a bare-knuckle rough-and-tumble. An English friend had once explained to him why England in the industrial age lacked tough-bottomed, heavy-weight material. Her big fellows were machine-made and brittle, and the good old days of ploughmen and poachers, blacksmiths and tinkers, bargees and dalesmen were gone for ever—fellows with long, tough, stringy muscle, jaws like paving-stones, and bottom till day-after-tomorrow. England could still match any nation toe-to-toe with anything from one hundred and forty pounds down out of her heavy industries, but industrial districts don't run to poundage. Take the indestructible fighting men of the United States and see where they come out of.

Budd had a useful long left and once knew how to shoot it, as Stephen had found out, but now Stephen saw his shoulder twitch and got inside and under, crossed the right hard, hooked right and left, pounded big fists into the short ribs. He heard the big man gasp as he clinched, tore himself free, shoved him off, took a left on top of the head, crossed the right again, hooked, pounded the soft middle, felt him sag and sink, and pulled the trigger as he came down. That was all. Fast and tigerish while it lasted, but not more than two minutes. Budd sat down hard ten feet back among the stools of cut bracken.

Budd was not out. One doesn't get knocked out that easily with bare knuckles. He was scarcely marked. He just had a soft middle, and had no wind or a bellows in action for half a minute. He held his head between his hands, and his shoulders lifted and sank as he struggled to get his wind back. Being winded only hurts while the diaphragm is paralysed. If he wanted he could try again in half a minute. He didn't. Budd was not yellow, but it would be only plain foolish to keep on trying.

Stephen went over, sat on his heels cowboy fashion, and waited for him.

"No sense in this, Budd," he said, "and maybe you hadn't it coming to you."

"Go to blazes!" said Budd, lifting his head.

"That licking was for Lady Alice Tromes, Budd."

"You can have her."

"Not for me. Pity she was thrown at your head."

Budd started to say something, but stopped himself in time. Stephen flared, and his voice was coldly wicked.

"Keep the lid on it, mister. You might not stand up and take some more, but if you say anything about that lady I shall be pleased to kick your ribs loose from your backbone. And I will, you know."

"Tough, aren't you?"

"Tough as you'll make me."

Budd was breathing easily now, and shook his head to clear the cobwebs off. The only mark he showed was the blaze of Stephen's palm across mouth and chin, though Stephen's middle right-hand knuckle was grazed and his thumb ached. He looked at Stephen, and his eyes were cold and hard.

"Well, here we are again," Budd said. "You've only proved that you can rough-house me, and that changes nothing."

"That was a side-issue. What do you want changed?"

"I want to know where I stand."

"Suppose I don't talk?"

"I can't make you, and that changes nothing either."

"I'll tell you this much. I shot your deer, already dying on its feet. Also I killed that salmon by main strength and ignorance, and they were dished up to you on the laird's table. What of it? The laird didn't know. Marian Finlay was not an accomplice either. You can take that or leave it."

"I'll take it or leave when you explain your presence."

"Why should I? But I will—a little. I own the Croft o' Balmerion over there. I heired it from my grandmother's people and came across from Montana to see it. That explains my presence, doesn't it—same as yours?"

"I suppose it does," Budd agreed, "but it tells me nothing."

"If I tell you one thing, Budd, you'll be right sorry you started this."

Budd sat up straight and looked at Stephen, frowningly intent. He put a quick question.

"Something about Marian Finlay?"

"Something that affects her."

"You can't stop now, damn you!" He was hard touched. "Why should I be sorry?"

"A pretty long story, Budd, and it will do you no good to know it. Just a minute! My turn to talk. I know how you feel. You don't care a cuss about my presence. You are afraid that the girl has been making use of you, and you want to be assured that she has not. She made use of you all right, Budd."

"I'll believe you when you tell me."

"You'll not blame her. Let me see! Her father suffered from loss of memory—you saw that—and needed watching. She did the watching day and night; Ruary Farquhar helped, and I butted right in."

"You would."

"Why not? As you say, I might not if she had a game leg and a squint in one eye. I butted right in, and she was glad of my help after a while. Marian Finlay and I are pretty good friends, Budd."

"Are you putting it mildly?"

"I don't think so. Pretty good friends! She has a better friend. My gawd, Budd! Great gawd, Buddh! If that friend takes a down on you, look out!"

"Farquhar? Why should he?"

Stephen slapped his tight thigh resoundingly.

"You've touched the spot, Budd, and I didn't know where it was until now. Why, dammit! He's just sizing you up to see if he should take a down on you."

"But blast it! Why?"

"Leave it—leave it! We're just jumping about. I started to rub you a little ointment. Where was I? Yes! The MacFinlay needed watching. A fortnight ago we did not watch him well enough. He had the illusion that he was young again and owned everything he could see. He got away to the hills with a rifle—to his old stamping-ground up at Carron. Three of us went searching for him, guessing where he would go. Two of us found the bothy in a state of siege. You were a bigger mark than your flask, Budd. Your deduction was right. MacFinlay was in the bothy."

"Farquhar with him?"

"Am I telling you? Have it all! Farquhar found him there, with your big stag dead behind the house where the laird had killed it. He was entirely sane then, and terribly distressed. He had lost caste. He had done the unforgivable thing of killing a stag on the lands he had sold your father. Ruary Farquhar had to get him away. The girl and I were on the outside. You know how we got him away."

Budd Hale nodded his head heavily.

"Yes, the girl made use of me," he admitted.

"Not as much as you think. Is that all you want to know?"

"You know it isn't. What is this thing that I should be sorry to hear?"

"Damn that tongue of mine!" cursed Stephen. "I should not have mentioned it."

"You can't stop now."

"I suppose not—if you insist."

"What do you think?"

"All right, Budd! You're asking for it. And after all, it is one thing that may make you particularly considerate of Marian Finlay."

"What else have I been, blast you?" he said warmly. "Are you going on?"

"I am. MacFinlay died of blood-poisoning."

Budd Hale's eyes concentrated to pin-points, but he said nothing. Stephen tapped his own breast on the right side.

"A mere graze there above the nipple, but it killed him. He got it in the bothy, Buddy, and it was a bullet-graze."

Budd did not think of doubting Stephen for a moment. The shock showed in his face, but his voice was quiet.

"I threw a shot at the window."

"I saw you, but I did not see the bullet arrive. The laird did not say how he got the wound, and Ruary Farquhar will not talk about it even to me. It was only a scratch, but his blood lacked white corpuscles, and he said nothing about it until too late."

"Does Miss Finlay know?"

"No. She hasn't a notion how he got the wound, and it did not look anything like a bullet-wound when she and the doctor saw it. In fact, Budd, she was not sure her father was in the bothy, and she did not know that I fixed your car. She only made use of you to get you away in case her father was in the bothy and off his head, and when she got home her father was home before her, and she does not know how he got home;

and now she thinks you had only professional poachers trapped. That is the whole case for you, and if you don't let it lay you're several kinds of a blind fool."

"I will please myself about that," Budd said, but without conviction. He sat looking on the hands he had not been able to break on Stephen's head, and had nothing more to say. Stephen had.

"Will you allow me to thank you, Buddy?"

"For what?" Budd looked up quickly and suspiciously.

"For helping me to make up my mind. I like Marian Finlay, and she likes me, and I have just now decided to ask her to marry me."

"That's straight shooting, but how does it affect me?"

"Don't it affect you at all?"

"Not in the least, Stevie. I'll pay any attention I like to Marian Finlay while she is free."

"But not after?"

"You take me for a coyote all right, don't you? Let me tell you that I am in this to marry Marian Finlay."

"Told her so?"

"I will—and I am hiding nothing from her."

"She might not like to know about your divorces?"

"She knows already. I told her."

It was Stephen's turn to be surprised. Budd was assaying some good metal.

"That was square shooting too, Budd," he said. "Pity you insisted on that licking."

"Forget it. We're even, Stephen, in more ways than one— Hush!"

He lifted a warning hand. He was looking up aslant the brae, and Stephen turned head in that direction. Marian Finlay was on the road at the head of the slope, a fair distance away and with trees between, and she had not seen or heard them. She was wearing black, and that colour suited her too. A tall, long-legged, slender—but not thin—figure in black, head downcast, pacing slowly down the road.

She would be going up to Falcon Crag to look again over her mountains and glen, to absorb again the live gentle heat of the evening sun, to begin again to live her life. She had not been out of the house for nearly a week, but she was young and she was turning the corner on grief. Life was again wooing her; all that was in her demanded sympathy and affection; and, these given, the reward would be an out-pouring of affection that would not be niggardly. Stephen knew then that Kirsty Power had been right; and with that knowledge clear in his mind he decided that now or never was the time to put the issue to the test.

He felt in two pockets and drew forth the solitary coin he had on him: a British florin with the royal arms in a cross on one side, and a king's head on the other. He flicked it up high in the air and caught on the back of his left hand under the fingers of the right.

"Call, Budd!" he invited. "Head or tail?"

"What the devil——?"

"And why the devil? Call! It binds you to nothing. Head or tail?"

"Head, you madman!"

Stephen without looking reached forward the coin on the back of his hand.

"Head it is," Budd said.

Stephen jerked the coin, caught it, and threw it down amongst the trees.

"Head let it be. Georgius Rex!"

"What does that mean?"

"King George, fifth or sixth——"

"Hell! I mean——"

"It means that you get a five minutes' start, but don't

you take it, good old Budd. I'll tell you what it means to me. Marian Finlay is going up Falcon Crag. I will sit here for five minutes—I haven't a watch, but I'll guess good measure. In five minutes I shall get on my two round feet and follow her up. She'll be glad to see me, for she likes me, and I like her. Let me wise you up! She is coming out of the doldrums and she is hungry for sympathy and affection. These I have to offer, and I will take what she offers in return, and that may be her hand with her heart in it. If it is, watch your step, Budd."

"Threatening again?"

"Good and hard. Five minutes, Budd! You can please yourself. I'll start counting a few now. Stay in the game, or get out while the going is good. Shut up!"

Budd stared intently, while Stephen counted ten.

"By God! You mean it," he said. "I'm in the game and I'll see you."

He sprang to his feet and went crashing down through an uncut bank of fading fern. Stephen sat down. The backs of his legs were beginning to hurt though he was used to heel-squatting. He stopped counting and went on watching unashamed; and his heart was beating no faster than usual.

Marian heard Budd coming, lifted her head, checked, and half-turned away. He came out on the road in front of her and below. Stephen could see his face but could not see hers. He stood there in front, his hand out, saying nothing, sympathy and appeal in his eyes. She gave him her hand, and her head drooped. They stayed thus moveless for what seemed a long time, and then, whether he drew on her hand or not, Stephen was not sure, it happened all at once. For suddenly she had a hold of the lapels of his jacket and her forehead was boring into his breast. Her shoulders were shaking and she was weeping in sorrow and surcease of sorrow.

Budd Hale knew how to behave. He had one hand gently on her shoulder, and the other was softly patting the dark mass of her hair. He looked up at Stephen amongst the trees, and moved his head forward. Stephen came to his feet and lifted a hand in salute to the victor.

The five minutes were up. He went down to them and forced himself to do the right thing. Marian heard the rustle in the bracken, looked up quickly, drew away with a small startle, drooped her head, but allowed Budd to take and hold her hand. Stephen patted her shoulder.

"Saw it coming a long way off, old girl," he said pleasantly. "I am jealous, but I am happy too."

"Oh Stephen—you dear!" she whispered.

"Course I am. Congratulations, Budd!"

"A good sport, Steve!" Budd said. "I shall remember."

"And keep things under your hat, for God's sake."

Budd nodded, and Stephen, saluting briefly, turned and walked slowly, shoulders back, down towards the river. From the end of the flying-bridge he looked back. The two were going up the slope, and the man's arm was across the woman's shoulder.

CHAPTER XXII

STEPHEN went up to Falcon Crag and sat down, his feet dangling over three hundred empty feet. He did not know whether he was glad or sorry. He did not even know whether he had won or lost. He had a strange emptiness of feeling—except, perhaps, for a small chagrin at himself.

"You don't deserve to win a thin dime, Stephen Wayne," he said aloud.

It was evening now, but the sun was still above the round head of the Muckle Kinmaol, and the valley and the glen were grown sleepy after the long day's heat. Big Ben Shinnoch cast a long shadow on the floor of its own glen, but beyond the shadow the slopes were glowing in the grave beauty of the heather still in bloom. In the bowl of Knockindu he could see the clock-tower above the grey roofs of the peaceful hamlet so secure amongst its own fields, a small place that would endure though cities fell. In the little square fields the corn was nearly ripe and stood out pale and golden among the vivid green fields of aftergrass. Black rooks flew on lazy wings, and blue rock-pigeons flitted here and there on full craws; and the king of the air, a peregrine falcon, soared and slid above the hollow of the valley. A quiet scene, and it slowly got under Stephen's skin. He grew quiet with it.

"Good-bye, Glen Shinnoch!" he said, "and thank you for everything. To-morrow I break camp."

Kenny Alpin was going up the track to the croft.

Sheevaun Power was up there waiting for him, and he was too blame proud and too fond of her to hide her red oriflamme among Glasgow closes.

"You great little spud!" said Stephen aloud. "I have a last job of work to do on you, and it will be done this evening."

It was Kenny Alpin who had induced him to come to Scotland; it was Kenny who had somersaulted him into Marian Finlay's life; it was Kenny who had precipitated this evening's final show-down; and it was with Kenny that Stephen would make a finish. That was about full circle in this brief interregnum. That is what it was, an interregnum, an abeyance in his ordinary life. He had come to Scotland, and done a job of work; and now he was going home to the life he knew, and he need not have any bitter taste in his mouth. But his mood was changing, and he had a bitter taste in his mouth. Now that Marian Finlay was out of his life he had a sudden clear vision of what was wrong with him. He was hit deeper than he knew. He had a bitter taste in his mouth, and a bitter thought in his mind, and a bitter emptiness in his heart; and he knew the cause of the taste and thought and emptiness.

"You poor dam' fool!" He addressed himself aloud. "Playing little-tin-god-out-of-the-machine."

And it was in that mood he heard a light foot rub on the rock behind him. He turned. That was Lady Alice Tromes. She must have been there for some time, for already she was moving away, trying to make her steps noiseless. But one sole had grated over an uneven spot, putting her off balance. She turned her head quickly to see if Stephen had heard, and seeing that he had, turned round full.

"Poor pitiful little tin-god!" she mocked him bitingly, bitterness in her tones.

Out of the knowledge in him he spoke harshly.

"Where are you going? I thought you were gone."

"I am on my way. To-morrow I go for good."

"So do I. What are you doing here?"

"A god must be answered, even a tin one. I came for a last look over all this, so that I should remember."

A tall dark woman of lissome flowing lines, with painted nails and painted mouth, and trained slanted curves of eyebrows over wide dark eyes; but she should have touched her cheeks this evening, for too much pallor came through the powder, or was now coming through. Yet was she vibrant and vivid—and also weary.

"Am I driving you away?" enquired Stephen.

"You are. One should not disturb a god contemning his godhead from his throne on the edge of things."

"Come thou and look over all this and tell me the things I should remember."

"Mock-pearls before no swine," she said, and came slowly to peep carefully over his shoulder. "How can you sit there?" she whispered. "Don't you want to swoop?"

"I do, but I have a prehensile seat to my pants." He patted the warm rock at his side. "Sit you here and tell me what you see."

"I dare not! I would let go all holds."

He lifted his right hand behind his shoulder.

"Come on! I'll take care of you—or swoop with you."

She at once took his hand in a tight grip, and her other hand grasped his shoulder; and so, holding firmly, she sidled down to a seat at his side. Her eyes were tightly closed, her breath held; and a small grimace of desperate resolution wrinkled her nose. Stephen tugged her dress over her silken knees and put an arm through hers, and she put a hand across and gripped his.

"Hold on to me with your old bear's paw," she whispered, "unless you want to launch me over. I don't mind."

"You'll like this in a minute. Open your eyes now and tell me what you see."

She drew in a long breath, gripped tight, and opened her eyes. But she was careful not to look down. Her eyes swung from Knockindu where windows were glinting in the westering sun, to the shadowy solitudes of Glen Shinnoch already brooding in the slow lessening of light, and finally they came back to rest on the Croft of Balmerion smuggled into the breast of the hill.

"I see quietude and beauty and sadness," she said deep-toned, "and behind all I see emptiness—all emptiness."

"Empty as your heart?"

"You do not know how empty my heart is—or how full?"

"It had better be empty," he said grimly. "It had better be empty and swept and garnished."

"For a new tenant? No, Stephen Wayne, I have changed a tenant or two in my time. I am keeping the present one secretly, for a little time."

"More fool you! The game is played and lost."

She gave him a quick side-glance.

"What game is that?"

"The game with one Buddington Hale." He pointed across to the Lodge. "Budd Hale and Marian Finlay went up to that house twenty minutes ago. His arm was possessively on her shoulder, and his kiss is now upon her mouth."

"Oh, Stephen!" she cried in quick commiseration.

"My poor Stephen! My poor little-tin-god-out-of-the-machine!"

"Shut it off!" he growled, giving her arm a shake and making her gasp and clutch. "What about poor, not-so-little Alice Tromes? What a hell of a name, Tromes!"

"I could change it."

"You could, but not here. You are going away to-morrow. Stay away!"

"You are going too. Are you going away from fire?"

"I am going to my own country."

"Thy country is not my country, nor thy people my people," she murmured.

"I know that and be damn'd to you," said Stephen brutally.

"Damn you too, Stephen Wayne!" she gave him back.

They were silent then. Stephen had no more to say. He was finished. And yet he wanted to sit there at her side for a little longer. He had no excuse. Better part with a couple of good curses. He drew his hand quietly from her arm and patted a palm on his grazed knuckles.

"You'll make that knuckle bleed again," she said, and pulled his hand away. "How did you hurt it?"

"In a fight——"

She guessed at once and was flaming angry. She was not afraid of the precipice any longer. She shook his arm fiercely.

"You damn'd little fool! Getting licked by Buddy Hale and losing your girl to him. A fine double crow he has over you. Why did you——?"

"I licked him."

"You licked him?"

"Yep."

"Even so. You lost face. You can't do that; it is not what I would expect of you. I am ashamed for you."

She was really angry at him, and pushed him away.

"Steady! My claws don't hold so good on rock. One or two false impressions have dinted this thing you call your head, blackie. I didn't lick Budd Hale for myself, or for Marian Finlay either."

"Why lick him then?"

"He had it coming to him."

"Oh, Stephen!" Her hand stilled on his arm. "About me?"

"He opened his mouth too wide."

She dropped his arm and turned away from him, her head up and her eyes across the valley.

"Don't be angry, lady," Stephen said. "I got a great kick out of it."

"I should be angry. It was unnecessary."

"Oh, quite! But you're not angry any longer?"

"I should be. I'm just the cave woman after all." She touched her breast. "Blast! In here I'm gloating that one man should go the atavistic bloody savage——"

"There wasn't enough blood so as to notice it."

"Perhaps it wasn't a real licking, Tarzan?"

Stephen grinned at the unmistakable disappointment in her voice.

"All he could take, Boadicea," he assured her. "Have no doubts about that. He hadn't any."

"My chops are fine and bloody," she said, and sighed. "But I am not grateful. Ah, well! All that is over and done with. In your own language, where do I go from here?"

She was looking down at her long, nicely cared-for hands, and Stephen looked down too.

"Not over and done with—not yet," he said. "There's a ring on your finger, painted nails!"

"I could mulct him all right, couldn't I? You wouldn't let me, would you, Stephen?"

"Not if I had the say-so."

"You have." She moved the ring round and gradually slipped it off, holding it in a palm and touching it with one finger. "Nice ring, isn't it? Diamonds and pearls set in platinum — big ones too."

"You could hock it for a hundred?" Stephen suggested.

"Three hundred."

"Bucks—dollars, you mean?"

"No, pounds."

"That's big money. You'll not get a better—even from that guy Chester?"

"Don't be spiteful!" Then she laughed at herself. "When Buddy slipped that ring on my finger I thought he was mine. But the technique was rotten. As you say, I was thrown at his head, and never had a chance. I wonder did I want the chance? Instead of twisting him round my fingers I wanted to scratch him with my painted nails. I tried—with poor old Eddie Chester——"

"And with one Stephen Wayne?"

"Did I try with you too, Stephen?" she enquired curiously.

"You did not," he answered firmly. "With a hobo like me you were one darling girl."

The colour came quick to her face, and her breath fluttered as she drew it in.

"How splendid of you, Stephen!" Then she laughed sadly. "Wait! let me finish this my own dishonest way." She held the flaming and moony ring in the palm of her hand and looked out and up at the falcon that was still soaring, waiting for the right time to pounce.

"Hola! Hola, hawk!" Her voice lifted like a bell. "A bauble for your nestlings to play with!"

Thumb and middle finger flicked, and the ring curved up and out and steeply down. The sun sparkled on it in one shooting gleam, and then it was lost. No sound came up three hundred feet. The falcon slid and dropped a score of feet, and again hung poised, pinion-tips a-flutter.

"Wise old fowl!" Stephen said. "It is not the season for nestlings. Eyas, they are called. A winter flood will wash your bauble down a salmon's gullet to be laid delectably on some poacher's table. Dam' folly all the same."

"Two fools together, aren't we? Thank you for everything, Stephen, and I'm sorry I do not feel more grateful. But you taught me to sit on a high place facing the sun and be sure of my own mind."

"Queen of all you see?"

"With a black hill leaning over me."

"Don't look at it. Keep your face to the sun above that small house across the valley."

"You live there?"

"I own it. And that reminds me, I have one last job of tin-godding to do over there. Will you come across now, and give me a hand? You could laugh at me."

"And spoil the creative touch! Laughter—my sort —is the destroyer. No, Stephen. I am weary."

Stephen sat there gloomily. He did not want to feel as lonely as a god. He did not want her to go away just yet. He got angry with himself and with her.

"Dammit! Why am I lonely? Can't I spend this last evening with one fine woman?"

"You know it all, you little tough," she said. She

changed her mind suddenly. "Very well! Let us spend our last evening together."

Stephen swung his legs and came upright, grasped her under the arms, and—no! he did not launch her—brought her to her feet away from the lip of the drop. The touch of her body sent a tingling shock up his arms, and she relaxed against him as if the strength had suddenly left her legs.

"Come on," he said roughly, and pulled her off the rock.

She came to his side and slipped a quiet hand inside his elbow.

"Let us hurt each other a little longer," she said.

CHAPTER XXIII

THEY walked across to the croft amicably enough. They were in no hurry. She moved with an easy sway that took on with his slouch, and her stride suited his. On the way he told her about Ruary and Kirsty, and Kenny and Sheevaun, and the croft and Lettoch Lodge. She listened and put questions, and at the end she chuckled at him and shook his arm.

"Will you never learn sense?"

"Not never. Why should I?"

"You will go on sticking your head out to get it bloody and unbowed some more."

"Dammit, woman! Ain't this my affair? The croft belongs to me, doesn't it?"

"Be obstinate then. I'll stand away off and catch the pieces."

Coming round the corner of the larches the black-and-white sheep-dog saw them and came down to the garden gate, barking and tail-wagging. The barking brought Kenny to the door. He said a word over his shoulder, and hurried down to meet the visitors. The dog got between his legs half-way down the path, Kenny's complicated stumbling kick was a yard wide, and the dog went streaking for the house-corner. That dog was always getting under Kenny's feet, but no one had ever seen Kenny get a foot to it. There was some understood form of play between them. His fierce dark eyes went from the lady to Stephen.

"I have met this lady," he said. "She is welcome.

I had it in mind that some day you would bring her on a visit, old secret liver. Come away in! Sheevaun is about to cook kidney and bacon for supper."

The lady shook hands with him.

"Could I have some, Mr Alpin? This fellow has abducted me from dinner—and I have heard of your high teas."

"Losh! I'm pleased. Mind you, Sheevaun hasn't her mother's touch, and I'm often thinkin' o' changin' my mind about her." Then he spoke distantly to the house-roof. "Lookin' on I was. A nice two minutes yon, and that half-brick I found was no use to me."

"Only two minutes?" said Alice Tromes. "Had he the other half-brick?"

Kenny looked at the lady with sober scrutiny.

"The sidewinder in the wind-jammer two feet below the belt—did you see that one, Lady Alice?"

"The minute details escaped me," said the lady.

"I'll give them to you at supper," said Kenny. "Come awa' in!"

They went into the living-room, and Sheevaun came out of the back-kitchen. Her sleeves were turned up, and her smooth arms looked like snow and fire: and her hair flowing behind her ears was like warm flame. Stephen heard Lady Alice draw in her breath at the virile loveliness of her, and turned to catch her eyes looking at him in surmise. Sheevaun took no notice of Stephen, but greeted the lady pleasantly and composedly.

"Could I get you some tea, Lady Alice?" she enquired.

"You can, polite damsel," Stephen said, "and some kidney and bacon as well. But pause a while." He turned to Kenny and spoke seriously. "You and I have some business to transact, Kenny, and I have brought this lady as witness. Suppose we get it over with?"

"Whatever you say," Kenny agreed soberly. "Do we sit to it?"

"We do, and I am setting up the show. Lady Alice will sit over here." He shut the back-kitchen door after a peep inside, and placed a chair in front of it. "Be seated, dark one! I will sit over here." He pulled a chair to the doorway leading into the passage, sat down, and tilted back on two legs. "You two can dispose yourselves about." He had the two exactly where he wanted them, but he was wondering dimly if he was not about to make a fool of himself and them.

Kenny leant a shoulder against the mantelpiece, his hands deep in his pockets, his fierce eyes steady on Stephen. Sheevaun, after a startled and perplexed glance about the room, busied herself between table and dresser laying two more places. Alice Tromes looked at Stephen with anxious eyes and bit her lower lip.

"She has no faith in me," was Stephen's thought, "and that little thug will jump on my carcase. Here goes!" He faced Kenny.

"This is serious, Kenny Alpin, and it is between you and me. Ruary and Kirsty, as you know, are taking charge at Lettoch Lodge."

"I am going back to work in three days," said Sheevaun quickly.

"Silence on the left! That means that this croft is on my hands. What about it, Kenny?"

"What about it, Steve?"

"What about it, yourself?"

"I'll tell you." He smiled at Stephen. "There is no man in the world I like better than I like Stephen Wayne, and only one man I like as well, but I will not be his caretaker."

346

"And that goes. Why, if I had a yellow mongrel pup I wouldn't have Kenny Alpin for a caretaker."

"I am sorry about that, Steve. I do love a mangy yellow pup."

"I will be brief," said Stephen, holding himself from dismay. "This croft is for sale—definitely—and I speak as a business man. I am going home, and I will have no dual allegiance. I told you my figure in New York, drunk and sober, and that figure holds. It is a reasonable price. This croft with its sheep out-run, worked in co-operation with the arable acres of Lettoch Lodge, is an economic proposition. With your earnings and your farming you can reach my figure without too much overhead. I'll give you time, but I am doing you no favour as regards capital or interest, for you want to call your soul your own. Now what about it?"

"Is this final, Steve?"

"Here and now, Kenny."

"Here and now, Steve." He struck his hands together, his eyes blazing, and was about to start forward. Steve stopped him.

"Wait, Kenny! There's a snag in it."

"A snag!" Kenny frowned, his mouth half-open.

"The devil's own snag." Stephen dropped an eyelid at him. "I am not keen on selling to a single man. Just a foible of mine. A single man sort of lacks incentive in the daily chores. I'll sell to you, of course, and I know, though you are a cast-iron old bachelor, that you will look round and about your friend's foible. There's no hurry, but I just kind of throw the suggestion in your face."

Kenny solemnly rasped his chin with a palm and looked down at the ground.

"A dam' foolish foible that of yours, Steve," he said gloomily, "but I see your point as a business man ensuring his pound o' flesh. There's no hurry, as you say, but I am prepared to consider the matter in a leisure hour."

He turned his eyes up to the ceiling, whistled tunelessly, and took a careless slouching step towards the table. Sheevaun, with a casual movement, put the table between them. Her face had drained of colour, but now it started to flame. She sniffed.

"Losh! the kidneys and bacon are burning to a cinder. Excuse me, Lady Alice."

Lady Alice, her eyes blazing at Stephen, was on her feet and pulled her chair away; but Kenny was already at her side. Sheevaun, limber as an eel, was beyond the table.

"A traitor in the house!" said Stephen. "The stove is not even lighted."

"What's all the bother?" Kenny wondered. "Sheevaun, my dear——"

Sheevaun looked wildly about her, the wild virgin in her eyes. Stephen could have jumped up and hugged her. But he sat on in his tilted chair, his thumbs in arm-holes, and the situation well in hand.

"Stephen, you devil!" cried Sheevaun.

Next instant his chair went over backwards. He took the worst of the bump on his hunched shoulders, but the back of his head came into contact with the flags of the passage. Hard heels trampled over him and he caught a flash of silk stockings. He was coming up for air when he was set down again. Bump! Kenny Alpin's broad-soled brogues knocked the wind out of him. Faintly there came to his dazed ears the yelp of the black-and-white dog getting out from under. Then he sat up and held his head in his hands.

"That's what a little tin-god gets," said Alice Tromes wickedly. She was standing over him and he

348

could see a slender foot tapping angrily. "She'll kick me in the slats," thought Stephen.

He groaned, dropped his head down, and let his shoulders fall against the wall. At once she was on her knees beside him.

"Damn them! Are you hurt, Stephen?"

"Just a little time," he whispered.

She pulled him from the wall, and he sagged against her. One arm was around his shoulder and her other hand was softly feeling in the tousled hair at the back of his head.

"Ouch!" groaned Stephen.

She pulled his head close, and he got that faint, dark, pleasant perfume. He was not sure whether it was his own heart or hers he heard beating.

"My poor tin-god!" she murmured, and he heard the murmur thrill, and felt it. "You poor tin-god, with feet of clay and head of solid ivory. There is nothing the matter with you."

"There is, woman." His voice was muffled. "There is everything the matter with me."

He turned his head up and looked at her, and saw her moved face and shining anguished eyes.

"Is it that way you feel too, girl?"

She turned his head down and held it, and her heart beat through his head.

"I didn't know what was the matter with me all the time," he said, his voice muffled against her.

Her voice whispered in his ear:

"It is only for a little time, my dear, only for a little time."

"No, by God!" He threw her hands roughly off his head, and faced her on his knees.

"You are the woman for me. Will you take a chance?"

He caught her shoulders and shook her.

349

"Will you take a chance with me?"

"A poor earl's scheming daughter, Stephen?"

"You'll change that rank, damn you. You are coming to Montana with me—and to-morrow."

She caught his hands off her shoulders and forced them down with remarkable strength. She stared into his dominant and intolerant eyes.

"I change my rank only for a higher one," she said. "Mate to a little tin-god with ten Red Indian papooses all my own."

"Tin?"

"No, ten!"

"You take me for more than tin," said Stephen Wayne.

Kenny Alpin and Sheevaun Power came in at the door. Kenny was holding Sheevaun's arm and she held her head up with a great dignity; but when she saw Stephen and Alice on their knees her eyes widened. Kenny said with humble contrition:

"Sorry! We seem to be intruding?"

"Damn you two!" shouted Stephen. "You stove in my skull, you trample on my midriff, and now you won't even give her time to kiss me with her painted mouth."

Alice Tromes caught two handfuls of his tousled hair and pressed her lips hard on his brown cheek. Then she scrubbed his cheek hard with her palm, lifted to her feet, and pulled him to his.

"Had to make sure he was flesh and blood," she said.

Kenny laughed at Sheevaun's astonished face.

"You blind bat!" he cried. "They have been making love to each other for three weeks."

He came and took the lady's hand and kissed it in strange courtly fashion.

"When I saw this lady that first day, I saw her eyes

350

and her smile and I had the second sight," he said. "I knew she was of our company."

Sheevaun was looking at Stephen, and before he could duck—if he wanted to—her arms were around his neck.

"Stephen, you villain—and darling!" She kissed him frankly on the mouth.

"Look at her now!" roared Kenny, his hand to his ear. "Look at her Judas-kissing, and my ear deaf for all time!"

Sheevaun loosed Stephen and turned to Alice Tromes, but Stephen did not see their womanly embrace. Kenny had him in his bear's hug and was dancing him into the living-room.

"Don't you kiss me," warned Stephen, "if you want to keep your nose."

Some time later they had high tea with a good appetite. . . .

But what more is there to tell?